Beacons of Tomorrow
Second Collection

Hope you enjoy my first book appearance! It's not a novel, but it's a start :)

— Susan Mattinson

Look For These Titles From Tyrannosaurus Press

Anthologies

Beacons of Tomorrow: First Collection   ISBN 978-0-9718819-9-0
Beacons of Tomorrow: Second Collection   ISBN 978-0-9718819-8-3

Boundary's Fall by Bret Funk

Path of Glory   ISBN 978-0-9718819-1-4
Sword of Honor   ISBN 978-0-9718819-0-7
Jewel of Truth   ISBN 978-0-9718819-2-1
Forge of Faith*

The Heart of the Sisters by A. Christopher Drown

A Mage of None Magic*

Beacons of Tomorrow
Second Collection

An Anthology of Science Fiction and Fantasy

Edited by Bret Funk

Tyrannosaurus Press
Zachary, LA
www.TyrannosaurusPress.com

BEACONS OF TOMORROW: SECOND COLLECTION

ISBN-10: 0-9718819-8-7
ISBN-13: 978-0-9718819-8-3
LCCN: 2008925548

Cover art by Greg Vander Leun

For Information Contact:

Tyrannosaurus Press
Zachary, LA
www.TyrannosaurusPress.com

For writers everywhere with a story to tell
and no idea how to make people listen
This anthology is dedicated to you

Acknowledgement is made for permission to print the following materials:

"Onion Worlds" by Ray Veen (veen.ray@gmail.com)

"The Ow Shop" by David Densley Thomas (ddthomas@hotmail.co.uk)

"The Exchange Program" by Madeline Bay (mcat40@hotmail.com)

"Race To The Summit" by Paul Lamb (www.paullamb.wordpress.com)

"Adam of Argotha" by C. S. Larsen (www.cslarsen.com)

"WARM, Inc." by Sheri Fresonke Harper (www.sfharper.com)

"The Swing" by A. Christopher Drown (www.achristopherdrown.com)

"Monkey Blood" by Terry Lindner (IWriteSciFi@gmail.com)

"The Stein Collection" by Kathryn Mattingly (Kathrynwriter@aol.com)

"Dotting the i" by Gary Sleeth (garywilliam@cox.net)

"The Pit" by Eric Pinder (www.ericpinder.com)

"Galen the Deathless" by Danielle Parker (danielle_parker@hotmail.com)

"Time Off" by R. Gatwood (www.myspace.com/rgatwood)

"Custom Appraisal" by Susan Mattinson (www.myspace.com/specwriter)

"Chalice of Evensade" by Erik Goodwyn (edgoodwyn@yahoo.com)

"Viper 3" by T. J. Starbuck (tjkathouse@aol.com)

"Foliage" by F. R. Jameson (www.frjameson.co.uk)

"Deconstructing Fireflies" by Kristi Petersen & Nathan Schoonover
(www.kristipetersen.net) & (www.ghostanddemon.com)

All material printed with author permission.

Table of Contents

Onion Worlds
by
Ray Veen

Ray Veen is a thirty-six year old surgical technologist who believes in God, family, and the USA. He is a former children's pastor, a blissfully married father of four, an infantry combat veteran from Desert Storm, and the winner of the 2006 Illuminations Writing Contest, which earned him the top spot in this anthology. His contribution, "Onion Worlds," offers a looking-glass view, in true science fiction form, of the threat posed when religious fundamentalism is given power over scientific inquiry.

The rotoskiff's descent whipped up a cloud of blood-red dust. As it touched down, landing spikes snapped out of the creature's shell and imbedded themselves into the desert sand. Its high-pitched whine ebbed away, it folded its many slender wings, and curtains of red dust drifted down around it. From the protection of an arched alcove nearby, Damon Shadwell and his assistant watched with deep interest. Soon a hatch in the carapace slid open and the beast's two caregivers emerged. As they began their maintenance tasks, Damon was able to make out the symbol on the back of their body-armor.

He sagged with relief.

"Rexus, return to the lab, power up all monitoring stations, then signal me and I will bring our guests."

Being mute like most subforms, Damon's burly assistant simply nodded in reply, then keyed the portal and disappeared into the complex. Damon's gaze returned to the settling rotoskiff. He studied the hatch, anticipating the emergence of the dignatariots who'd come to evaluate his project. Watching the caregivers sweep sand from the chinks and crevices of the nearly dozing beast, Damon hoped his visitors would treat his project with as much care.

The cross-arc symbol on their uniforms identified this as a court vessel, not a science vessel. This boded well for Damon. Whatever dignatariots were still hidden inside the beast would be impartial to his recent exile from the Greater Circle of Science. Although a court representative would be tougher to impress, at least Damon wouldn't have to contend with the heated debate his research always seemed to provoke among his fellow scientists.

A section of the rotoskiff's exoskeleton shifted, and three figures emerged. One was obviously a subform, therefore harmless; one wore court body-armor and official's cloak; and the last wore pale robes and had a noticeably wide collar implant. As they neared, the symbol on the armored-ones breastplate became apparent—three intertwined circles. Between the symbol, the cloak, the armor, and the man's black on gray color scheme, Damon was able to determine his rank and duty to be that of a court-appointed, Scholar-of-Scholars, grade third-chief.

He decided the robed figure had to be a public correspondent, probably for the Arc of Theology. Her shaven head and the monk-style icons woven into her scalp lock were a dead giveaway. The bulging implant that encircled her neck was clearly a Dense Ocular Memory Sponge, and with it, everything she saw or heard inside his lab would be stored on specialized neural tissue within the implant. Later, it could be downloaded to a viewing membrane at the Arc of Theology headquarters for possible broadcast. If all went well, she'd be reporting a major technological breakthrough. If not, there would be further humiliation for the once notable scholar.

Once they'd reached the entrance to his laboratory complex, Damon greeted them formally, hiding his anxiety. Head bowed, Damon clasped the shoulders of the armored scholar. "My gratitude, my guest."

The man nodded. "My gratitude, my host. I'm Third Chief Manard Kansan, scientific investigations for the Circle of the Royal Court, and this is Marran Bold, an observer from the Arc of Theology."

Damon looked upon chill, blue eyes, "My welcome, visitor."

The woman nodded slightly in return, her eyes fixed on Damon's. They were sharp and intelligent, yet completely devoid of emotion. He knew that a correspondent had to maintain absolute calm or risk warping the integrity of the sensory input, but that knowledge was not comforting. Many people, especially those from theological circles, became enraged by the nature of his research.

The chief continued the introductions. "Behind me is Tem, an assistant to Torrin Masla, Submatriarch of All Science."

"Torrin Masla?"

"Yes, she's in the rotoskiff awaiting my report."

"She is here?"

"Yes, but she's chosen not to tour your lab."

"So she won't be joining us?"

"No."

Good, Damon thought. Torrin Masla was his harshest critic and greatest enemy. Damon Shadwell was once a high-scholar of first rank, holding influential seats on every notable arc of the Greater Circle of Science. He'd begun his current project nine revolutions previous, and because of its ethical nature, many of his colleagues opposed it from its onset. Damon was unconcerned. Believing in the Circle's stated mission of unraveling the mysteries of the universe, he felt secure that his impartial findings would justify themselves. As his research progressed and grew more controversial in nature, his opposition gained in strength, finally being led by Torrin Masla, right-hand staffwoman to the Matriarch of Science herself.

Five revolutions into his project, the Matriarch finally succumbed to Masla's influence. Damon's title and positions were revoked, his funding all but cut off, and his laboratory was relocated to an unpopulated plain where he could be of no influence on the citizenry. Only Damon's reputation saved his project from being discontinued.

Now, as a Citizen Good-Scholar, he was once more about to butt heads with the architect of his disgrace.

Chief Kansan cleared his throat.

"My sorrow, Scholar, I was distracted. It's just that I'm a bit surprised to find that the venerable Submatriarch has come so far on my account."

"I know what troubles you, Shadwell. Just remember that I am a man of the courts. You will have a fair evaluation."

"My gratitude."

"Indeed. Shall we go inside?"

Damon pressed his hand into the sensory webbing beside the portal. Extensors relaxed, flexors contracted, and the cortical-bone door rose. They stepped into the foyer, and Damon led the way down one of its four long corridors. As they progressed, Damon prayed that neither of them would comment on the ribs protruding from the tissue in the walls. Although more functional and less expensive, ribbed walls were considered old-fashioned and hopelessly out of style. Back in the superstructure of the city, Damon hadn't needed a framework of bone and could afford the luxury of furred walls and patterned sheets of hardened epithelium.

"Is something wrong?" Kansan asked.

"No. Why do you ask?"

"You seem nervous."

Damon forced a laugh. "It must be my project. I've been this way for turns. A startling situation has developed, and I've no precedent from which to take guidance."

"Be at ease then, Shadwell. I am here to judge, and I will give you guidance."

"My gratitude, Scholar, but as you shall soon see, this situation probably exceeds the scope of normal court doctrine." Just then, Damon felt tingling warmth from the telembiot implant on his right forearm. The large insect shared a communal intelligence with the rest of its race, and those who allowed the parasites to feed from the brachial plexus near their elbow could communicate through them. "Ah, my assistant, Rexus, has just informed me that the laboratory is ready. Shall we?"

Damon motioned down an intersection and Chief Kansan led them in that direction. Damon fell into step beside Correspondent Bold. "Chief Kansan is familiar with the fundamentals of my project. I was wondering if the Circle of Theology is as well."

Her pale eyes fixed on his. "I have been briefed, but for the benefit of the Church and the citizenry, a short overview would be in order."

"Yes, well, first of all, this project is attempting to prove the First Doctrine. The thesis states that due to the universal constant of morality, even in environments where biological resources are the less plentiful, a dominating, sentient species will always base its technology on the animal kingdom."

The Correspondant nodded. "It may be a common thesis, but it is still good kaura to prove its righteousness. *'The combined sciences of cloning, gene-splicing, and cross-breeding will provide tissues and other substances for use in industry. They will supply the citizens with all of life's comforts. But the taking of minerals from the firmament shall bring down the cataclysm....'* "

"*...Our Lady Karita provides us with tools and sustenance so long as her body is not violated,*" said Damon, completing the quote. He noticed the DOMS collar around the correspondent's neck quivering. Somewhere inside, neurotransmitters and electrolytes shifted and aligned, storing his image and words for eventual download. He decided to maintain a steady facade as a believer in scripture so that whoever viewed these events would be less likely to accuse him of heresy.

"Your kaura seems to be of fine character, Good-Scholar Shadwell. Please continue."

"Very well. As you may already know, when I began this experiment nine turns ago, I was of the opinion that previous researchers of the same thesis had been using models that were inadequate: less than thorough. I believed the only way to prove the First Doctrine with eternal certainty was to build an entire world where fossil and mineral resources were plentiful, and animal resources limited, then populate that world with a sentient race and see what they based their technology on. With my position and funding, I was able to do just that. When we reach my laboratory, you and your viewers will see an entire, fully functional world in miniature. It has its own ecosystem, environment, food chain, atmosphere, and even a complex culture of microscopic men. But be prepared, this world is totally alien to ours in every way." Damon paused, hoping for an utterance of amazement.

None came.

He cleared his throat and continued. "For example: most of our world is covered by the red desert; this model is mainly water and wild plant life. Secondly, the composition and availability of minerals on the model planet are nearly identical to our own. Our fragile ecosystem would never tolerate drilling or mining of any kind, but their ecosystem is rich enough that the harvesting of minerals would have only slight repercussions. Thirdly, we have a mostly carnivorous food chain that spans sixty-two animal classes and nearly a billion different species. On my model, they have only ten animal classes and a few hundred thousand species, many of them actual herbivores." A wrinkle appeared in the correspondent's brow and Damon knew he was approaching controversial territory. To the church, ingesting plants was not only sacrilege—it was sickening.

Damon suddenly realized that the whole time he'd been talking, the other dignitariots had been listening. Chief Kansan wasn't overhearing anything he didn't already know, but there was an odd, not-quite-emptiness in Tem's eyes. Besides being his enemy's personal valet, the thought of him being any less than perfectly ignorant made Damon shudder in disgust.

The brawny creatures were descended from the first test group of men to have their DNA tampered with. Historically, all medical procedures and potential genetic alterations were tested on subforms before being practiced on men. The result was that the race was left with limited intelligence and no free will, yet still able to follow complex instructions without deviation or error. They were quiet and mindless, and their distinctive lack of emotion and free thought made them ideal soldiers and servants. If Tem was somehow different, there was any number of ways that he could pose a threat to Damon's research.

Seeing that the portal to the main laboratory was approaching, Damon brushed his suspicions aside—it was time his guests learned what his microscopic men were up to.

"Well, I'd say that was a decent introduction, Correspondent. As we're about to enter the lab, I'll save any discussion of my findings until after you've all had a look around."

Correspondent Bold nodded and Damon placed his hand in the neural webbing near the portal. The cords of muscle fibers flexed to the sides, creating an opening wide enough for the entire group to step through.

On entering the main lab, Public Correspondent Marran Bold began a slow visual scan of the chamber, obviously recording the sights on her DOMS collar. The red-lit room was humid and dim, four levels high, and built around a massive, mucous covered pod in the center. This dominated the lab, hanging in the air like a giant meteor frozen in the split second before impact. Dozens of blowholes covered its slick sides, venting noxious-looking gasses and filling the air with a thick haze. A network of bone-based catwalks had been constructed around the floating pod, and a web of bio-vessels criss-crossed the room, joining the imposing structure to various smaller pods. Together these features appeared to cradle the massive ball in framework that seemed too fragile for the job.

Damon cleared his throat and raised his voice to be heard over the din of hisses and gurgles. "Well, this is it," he said, stepping over a conduit draped across the spongy floor. "If you'll follow me to main control, I'll begin outlining my findings."

The dignitariots followed Damon to a ring of interconnected pods directly beneath the floating giant. Rexus stood near a bone bench in the center, waiting for his master's next command. Huge even for a subform, he was still dwarfed by the four-storey structure hovering just above his head.

"You'll notice the ganglion workstations embedded in the model's sides. Each of these controls a specific group of functions. I have access to all functions down here at the master panel but control is limited and must be fine-tuned at the individual workstations. Information on every aspect of the project travels through a neural link to these panels, where it's stored on dense memory sponges. If you'd like, I can prepare one of these for each of you to take back to your circles."

"Our gratitude," said the Correspondent. "The Church and its citizenry would like to know what kinds of information you are monitoring."

"If you're asking whether or not I'm monitoring kaura, the answer is yes. Since this experiment was designed to prove an ethical question, I felt it was critical. I've actually devoted an entire ganglion-access workstation to monitoring the character of the spiritual life force within the model. It's the smaller of the two stations halfway up this side." Damon paused and pointed his finger. "That larger one controls and monitors the biodeception membrane, which is the innermost lining of the pod's shell. The model planet actually floats in a vacuum in the center of the pod, and when the inhabitants look beyond their world, they actually see the scope of space. Our biodeception membrane is advanced enough to perfectly mimic the stars of our own night sky: visually, gravimetrically, radioactively, and even with respect to stellar movement and development. Basically any characteristic of space that we've been able to observe in our own heavens, the membrane duplicates on its inner lining."

Chief Kansan interrupted, "Weren't you credited for the development of the biodeception membrane?"

Damon smiled. "I'm flattered that you remember. As a matter of fact it earned me my fourth Formal Recognition from the Greater Circle of Science."

"Yes, it's proven especially useful to those of us in Military Arcs. Were you aware of how radically its potential was expanded in stealth and camouflage?"

Damon's smile faded. "No, my gratitude... Anyway, that ganglion-access station near the top analyzes chemical compositions in the model's soil, sea atmosphere, and biological inhabitants. The two lower stations measure pressure and field dynamics, so these three together tell me everything I need to know about the model's physical state. Over there is the workstation that controls the model's temporal speed. It bathes the planet in a constant beam of hybrid quantum particles. This excites its molecules to such an extent that they can live up to fifty thousand revolutions in only one of our rotations. I can speed, slow, or freeze their perception of the passage of time whenever it suits me. Towards the beginning of the project, before any major evolution took place, there wasn't much to see. The temporal beam was set to maximum. Since then I've had to adjust it many times, speeding it up and slowing it down according to how interesting the events taking place were."

"And where is it set now?" Kansan asked.

"Very slow. One revolution per true rotation."

"Does this mean that interesting events are taking place now?"

"You shall see in a moment. I only want to draw your attention to one more workstation. You can't see it because it's at the very top of the pod. This station controls the antigravity field. In order for my model to have realistic gravity, atmosphere, weather, and tectonic behavior, I had to make it incredibly dense. I've built two generators using avian-mammoth glandular tissue. One generator allows the model to float within the pod, applying stresses on it that mimic revolution around its sun and other celestial gravitational forces. Another antigrav generator keeps the hyper-condensed pod afloat—without this, it would smash through the floor, and its incredible weight would bring the laboratory crashing down on top of it." Damon paused for effect, but only Tem seemed interested. He cocked his head to one side while the other dignitariots simply waited for Damon to continue.

"So, at the core of the model is another glandular antigravity organ which I've engineered into a metaplasmic state. As you know, the avian mammoth is a bulky creature that floats on air currents and sifts chemical nutrients from our soupy atmosphere. Glandular tissues within their abdominal sinuses secrete a hormone that enables all vascularized tissue to repel graviton particles. This creates a gravity resistant barrier around the creatures and allows them to live their entire lives airborne. I discovered that by inverting a few amino acid chains, the antigravity process is reversed in such a way that an even globe of gravity is exerted upon the model, terminating at the fringes of its ionosphere." Damon checked his audience to be sure his technical explanations weren't losing them. Their sharp eyes reassured him and he continued.

"Now, taken with everything else I've just told you, you can see how the 'microscopic men' living on the model could be completely fooled into believing their planet is absolutely real, and circling a sun, which in turn circles a galactic hub. I've painstakingly included every possible detail: from cosmic background radiation, to weather dynamics, to volcanoes, to dust particles which swirl in sunbeams—I've even evolved nano-organisms which are microscopic to the microscopic men. The whole purpose behind my exhaustive attention to detail was so that no future scholar could ever again doubt that the Holy First Doctrine was proven with inadequate experimentation." Damon ended his speech, more or less pleased by the points he'd made.

Chief Kansan cleared his throat, the Correspondent and Tem merely looked at him, but once again Damon noticed a less-than-emptiness in the Subform's eyes.

The disgraced scholar stifled a shudder. "Yes, well, if you'll please follow me to the one ganglion-access workstation I haven't mentioned."

Damon led them to a bone stairway beyond the twitching pods of master control. They scaled it to the second level catwalk circling the slick walls of the huge pod. After passing the workstation for the model's temporal beam, they came to a dark, oblong window looking in on the model. The pod's thickness was immediately noticeable around the edges of the window, but the sight beyond was far more striking. It was like looking through a farocular into space. An expanse of stars twinkled on an eternally black backdrop, and in the foreground, a yellow sun was setting over the rim of a lovely planet swirled with greens, whites, browns and blues. It was turning abnormally fast, and seen through the darkened window, the vision was rather surreal.

Damon rested his elbows on the windowsill and looked in at his creation. For a moment, his voice took on a wistful tone. "Every time I look at it like this, it's easy to imagine that I'm looking through a portal from a space vehicle approaching an alien world. It's hard to believe. There are four billion intelligent beings on its surface. With families and jobs—going about their microscopic lives with no idea that their world exists in an organic pod inside some lab. Sometimes I think it's a cruel joke to play on them."

Chief Kansan looked at him quizzically. "Shadwell, please, they are an experiment. They are smaller than bacteria and have insignificant kaura."

Damon raised one eyebrow. "You'd be surprised, Chief... Would you like to be the first to interface with this ganglion workstation? There's something I think you need to see."

"All right, what is this station for?"

Damon took a few steps down the catwalk and began manipulating the corpuscular controls of the workstation's dark, jelly-like tissue. "Primarily it's a highly sensitive viewscope. But I've also spliced in neural pathways to monitor their communications. They've developed a technology that broadcasts data, sound, and visual images to their citizens. It's much like our own, Correspondent, except that it operates on completely alien principles. Now, Chief, if you'll insert your head and hands into these sockets, you'll see that the viewscope already focused on an item of interest."

Kansan stepped under the bulging mass of the workstation and raised his hands toward the dark, spine-filled socket. Sensing the presence of an interfacer, the ganglion-access organ lowered its moist, quivering bulk down around the armored man, enveloping his head and hands with a sucking sound. A few moments later, the Chief's body seemed to stiffen with excitement. Damon thumbed the corpuscle, stimulating the eustacian canal to begin conducting sound. "Tell us what you see, Chief."

"This can't be. There's something unnatural floating in orbit around the model. It's not like a cloud. . . it's solid. It has a round, symmetrical shape. . . it couldn't be any kind of comet or small moon. . . The circle has spokes which join with a central hub."

"Try a closer focus."

The chief was quiet a moment, then said, "Fascinating. There's a line of what look like airships travelling towards the structure, and judging from their size, the circle must be some kind of orbital city."

Damon was beginning to feel a sense of triumph. "It will be. They're not finished building it. If you focus in on one of the spokes you'll see workmen busy assembling it."

"I see them. . . they're shaped like us."

"Yes, interesting, isn't it. I didn't intend that; it just turned out that a bipedal hominid was the most fit to evolve into the dominant, intellectual species." Damon felt a swell of pride. "Shall we let the Correspondent take a look?"

As the chief wriggled out of the ganglion organ, Damon noticed Marran Bold staring hard at him. Her expression was so faint that Damon at first wondered if he was truly seeing one. She stepped under the interface organ and it began lowering itself over her. All the while her ice-blue eyes stayed on Damon, and then he knew—she was displeased.

His daring hopes began to freeze within him as he considered the implications of the Correspondent's stare. *I should never have expected anything else,* Damon thought, *once again my glory is about to be deprived by scandal.* He glanced to where the chief was now standing, staring through the dark window. Except for one slightly raised eyebrow, Manard Kansan wore a blank expression. Damon approached him slowly.

"I suppose you're aware that my microscopic men use a mineral and fossil fuel technology."

The armored man nodded but remained silent.

"They *are* capable of space travel."

The chief did not answer. After a few quiet moments, Damon joined him in staring at the false planet. He could only wonder what the chief was thinking, and could only hope that what the man had said earlier was true. If the chief were indeed a fair man, he'd return to the Circle of the Royal Court with a report that Damon Shadwell should continue his work. If not, then the beautiful planet before them would be dismantled and recycled like any other failed model. The thought made him shudder.

His people were taught from a young age: the Kaura of Karita's children is insignificant — the life-forces of all of the planet's inhabitants were expendable. Only their living world mattered. Perhaps a secret part of him was indeed heretical, because these teachings had never quite settled with Damon. Even now, he could not help but feel a deep responsibility to the creatures living inside the pod. He knew from observation that each tiny one of them had a lifestyle and an occupation and a spirit of their own. It was hard to observe the details of any individual's life, given the speed of the model and the limited sensitivity of his instruments, but there they were, going to their jobs and raising their young in spite of it. In size and force, their kaura was indeed insignificant compared to his own, just as his was insignificant compared to that of the planet upon which they stood—the great "Lady Karita" herself. For one fleeting instant, Damon wondered if it was the size of kaura that mattered, or if each torch of life, no matter how small, was precious in itself, simply because it existed.

He watched his dream planet turn.

He paid special attention to a spot on a landmass in the lower hemisphere. To them the city was ancient, but to Damon, it had burst into existence a less than a quarter of a revolution ago. Its significance was that, somewhere above that spot, hovering in geosynchronous orbit, was a smaller city which had been transported and assembled in space.

A wet, sloshing sound told Damon that the Correspondent was disconnecting herself from the ganglion-access workstation. He steeled himself, then turned to face her.

He found her already staring at him.

A cold tingling shuddered through his spine. He fought to appear normal, to hide his reactions, but his voice came out strained nonetheless. "Well then, now that we've all seen it, I suppose I should begin outlining my findings. If you'll please follow me back to main control."

The dignitariots fell into step behind Damon somewhat slowly as he led them around the catwalk toward the stairs. He felt all three sets of eyes on his back. It felt like the day the Matriarch had publicly read Damon's 'Motion of Concentric Exile.'

Rexus had the large viewing membrane fired up with glowing photocells by the time they'd reached main control. Damon directed his guests to be seated on the lipoprotein-padded benches, then went to the corpuscular array for the viewer. Checking that Rexus had correctly spliced the umbilical to the neural cube's socket, Damon adjusted the image and stimulated the sponges to begin discharging their stored data. As a hazy, close-up view of one of his microscopic men formed on the membrane, Damon began speaking.

"The first real intelligence to evolve on the model appeared about two revolutions ago. We've been calling them 'microscopic men' but the official name I've given them, and the name that appears in my research, is *Cyanomites*."

The image changed, and was replaced by video of a small group of primitive hunters clad in animal skins. "As you can see, the first tools of the primitive Cyanomites were bone and rocks. Obviously, this time-period was critical to the project. If these early men preferred the use of bone, the experiment would be well on the way to scientific validation of the First Doctrine. If he preferred the rock, however, there would obviously be problems. There are gaps in the records at this point because the model was set at a high temporal rate, and many events took place very quickly. But what we next noticed was that the Cyanomites were using plant life as fuel to build fires." With an image of an open flame on the viewing membrane, Damon checked his audience for their reaction. Fire-building was a rather large taboo in their society of biologically generated warmth, yet the dignitariot's faces were stone masks of indifference. Damon then decided to simply plow through all of his findings, no matter how controversial, and hopefully justify them at the end of the presentation.

"The early Cyanomites continued to use bone in the crafting of objects, yet soon enough, all of their tools were wood and stone. Fire, then, in addition to purifying their food of disease-causing microbes, led them down the first steps towards their modern technology. Before long they were heating certain kinds of rocks to extract minerals they could shape into useful tools and weaponry. They also used stone and wood and were thus able to build homes, fortresses, land vehicles, and better tools and weapons. Although they had their share of war and strife, their generous environment made their lives easy—to the point that it wasn't often necessary for them to kill each other in order to survive. Here in the real world, one-hundred thousand revolutions of continuous power struggles have repeatedly set back Karita's social and scientific advancement. For us, the fact that so many organisms are fighting over too few resources has caused progress to move at a painfully slow rate. The Cyanomites have had only a fraction of our wars, and were able to flourish quickly. Soon they were combining their inorganic tools into large bundles that were capable of performing complex tasks, like harvesting plants, plowing soil, making fabric, and mass-producing their written language. These tool complexes resembled creatures at times because they were able to propel themselves and manipulate objects. Many of them even required sustenance, then shed waste. Of course, this was after they'd discovered the combustible qualities of fossil fuels. Now, during this time, they did use limited biological sciences. They crossbred plants and animals, developed microbes for use in food processing, and even had a decent knowledge of surgery and medicine. But if you were to focus the viewer on one of their laboratories, you would more likely to see a researcher developing a new chemical or mineral substance, than see any genetic manipulation or tissue cloning. To be quite honest, their society frowns on these practices. Instead of cloning, they found ways to mass-produce building materials. Instead of genetic engineering, they researched new hybrids of inorganic chemicals and developed new and better building materials. One of the turning points of their fossil fuel research was the development of their combustible propellant. In the last quarter turn, I have watched it develop from a light source, to fuel for small ground vehicles, and then for airborne ships. Now they have achieved escape velocity and reached space—something we might not ever be able to do."

Chief Kansan cleared his throat, causing Damon to look expectantly at him. After momentarily collecting his thoughts, the chief said, "Given that your… Cyanomites use a technology that is strictly forbidden, how does that make you feel? Your artificial men have accomplished what we real men cannot—but only through illegal means."

Damon thought hard before answering—this was what it was all about. "Well, first of all let me just say that they are not artificial men. They are real men living on an artificial world, in a strictly controlled, completely contained environment. Of course I'm deeply concerned by their methods; I can assure you of that. I've only allowed this experiment to continue by accepting that, inside this pod, their transgressions pose no threat to our fragile ecosystem. The Cyanomites are completely ignorant to the way life works in the real world. We all understand the hazards of 'raping the firmament', but these subjects are merely taking advantage of resources close at hand and available in large quantities."

"But what of the ethical question?" the Correspondent asked unexpectedly, "They are violating the universal truth of the First Doctrine. Doesn't that taint their kaura?"

Damon shifted uncomfortably. "Actually, Correspondent Bold, you're not going to like hearing this… But as a species, their kaura is a brighter shade than our own. I can only conclude this means they are not committing evil by using their technology. In effect, I've not only sunk the thesis I've been operating under for nine revolutions, I've also disproved the First Doctrine."

The Correspondent's eyebrows rose, exhibiting the first signs of emotion he'd seen from her. An uncomfortable silence descended over the group, during which Damon wished he had phrased what he'd said differently—understated it somehow. The words he'd just spoken would sound very bad when the Correspondent replayed them for the Holy Arc of Theology. Damon decided it would be best to change to a safer subject.

"Anyway, beyond that, there is another pressing issue for which I desperately need guidance. You've seen for yourselves, the Cyanomites are about to start living in space, some of them at least. I've also learned from monitoring their communications technology that they've begun implementing a rather ambitious space-exploration program. Do you see my problem? There is almost no space for them to explore. They are going to run right into the biodeception membrane. As a matter of fact, I've already intercepted multiple unmanned probes and been forced to devote several of my indispensable neuron cubes to mimic their return data streams." Damon adjusted the viewing membrane to show an image of two shining, spine-covered balls. Chief Kansan leaned forward and examined them with deep interest.

While the Chief was thinking, Damon snuck a glance at the Correspondent. She too was looking at the viewscreen, recording the new information for her church officials, but her mind seemed to be focused inward. After several quiet moments, Chief Kansan sighed and leaned back. "I will have to consult someone from the Circle of Science about the communications issue, Shadwell. My sorrow. Do you have any suggestions?"

Damon shrugged. "There are quite a few options, actually. I simply have no precedent to tell me which is the right decision. I could intercept their manned missions as well, but then I'd need more neural storage to mimic their data streams. Or, I could make contact and either tell them the truth or concoct a deception. I've even thought of engineering a special parasite to sabotage their space program."

The armored man gave him a direct look. "Do not forget, Shadwell, that the Circle could rule against you, and all this would be a moot point."

Damon blinked. "I haven't forgotten."

Suddenly they heard a loud splash from the far side of the lab. They all jumped to their feet and looked around.

"What was that?" the chief asked.

"Something fell into the mucus vat."

"Where's Tem?"

Damon broke into a run. "Hopefully not in the mucus vat."

He raced to the stairs leading to the lab's second level, followed closely by the dignitariots. His fears were soon realized when he reached the higher floor and saw the slime-covered creature crawling out of the green pool. Tem paid no attention as Damon approached. He simply stood and looked high up the side of the pod, then began making his way toward it.

"What's he doing?" Damon looked around, trying to answer his own question. At the very top of the pod, a dark, wet stain was beginning to spread towards the floor. As Tem crossed the bone bridge from the lab's second level to the walkway on the pod, Damon turned his attention back to the vat. A slack, pale umbilical lay draped and empty across the surface of the pool of slime. As the other dignitariots reached his side, Damon figured out what Tem had done.

"He's torn the lymph vessel from the antigrav unit on top and fell in the process. He must've realized it was only a return umbilical—now he's going back up to find something more critical."

"Why would he do that?" asked a somewhat breathless Correspondent.

"Don't you see? He's trying to sabotage the model! He heard me say that without that generator, the pod will crash through the floor. If he finds the nutrient artery, that thing will come crashing down, the lab will be crushed!"

"Lady Karita!" exclaimed Chief Kansan. "He'll kill us all!" .

"Not to mention the four billion souls living on the model… I'm summoning Rexus." Damon raised his telembiot.

"I don't understand," the Correspondent said, her voice shaking, "Subforms aren't capable of original ideas. Why would he do this?"

"I don't know." The Chief said with slitted eyes. "But I'm calling the Submatriarch."

In moments, Rexus' massive form was visible, scrambling up the side of the pod like a lower primate. Tem had already reached the third level but was using the ladders and catwalks—Rexus was catching up quickly. The rogue subform reached the ladder to the fourth level catwalk, and though Rexus propelled himself upwards with powerful motions, they were unable to predict whether he'd reach Tem in time.

Upon reaching the catwalk, Tem noticed his pursuer and began running for the final ladder. Further down, Rexus reached the same level as Tem began scaling the last obstacle between him and the umbilical. Instead of following the rogue down the catwalk, Rexus displayed a lucky show of intelligence and continued to scale the pod's side. Damon and the Correspondent let out simultaneous sighs of relief. Their paths would converge on top of the pod—it appeared they would reach the antigrav generator at the same moment.

Rexus was scaling a section saturated with the oily fluid and was momentarily unable to get a good foothold. He recovered in a few seconds, but the lapse had allowed Tem to reach the quivering organ first. He immediately went for the nearest umbilical and began tugging.

"Oh my Lady Karita, that's it! That's the nutrient artery!" said Damon, chilled to his core.

Suddenly Rexus was there, raising his thick arms over Tem's head and clasping his hands into a fleshy club. Tem ignored him, intent only on severing the umbilical. Rexus' hands came down. They heard the thick slap of the meaty blow and Tem was flattened. The stunned subform began sliding down the pod's slick, curved surface, and then he was airborne. He flailed limply, clipped one jutting catwalk, then spun into a mass of suspended umbilicals. Their elasticity slowed his fall, and he landed face-first on the moist tissue of the floor with a gentle splat.

Rexus began descending the pod, using the ladders this time, as the rest of them ran to the edge of the second level. Looking down, they could see the motionless rogue.

"The Submatriarch's on her way," Kansan said, "She says Tem is a new breed of subform that sometimes acts on their own to please their owners."

Not bloody likely, Damon thought. Subforms were too stupid to do anything but follow directions. Of course there was that not-quite-emptiness in the brute's eyes, but Damon still had his suspicions.

"She says she'll put a stop to his behavior when she gets here."

"I'd better go let her in the front portal then." Damon was about to depart when he noticed Tem rising to his hands and knees, shaking his head.

"Rexus!" Damon yelled, "Get down there and restrain him—hurry!"

The burly subform immediately sped his descent as Tem rose to his feet and began wobbling toward the nearest stairs. Within moments, Rexus was upon him. The rogue was stunned and helpless as his stockier opponent manhandled him, spinning him around and catching him from behind in a savage embrace. Tem tried to weakly twist away but Rexus tightened his grip. The others could see the strain in Tem's neck and the pain in his not-quiet-empty eyes. He struggled vainly to escape, groaning and snarling all the while, but Rexus' great strength held him fast. Finally he gave up and went limp.

Seeing the fight was over, Damon flew down the stairs. "Don't let him go, Rexus. I'm going to get the Submatriarch." He rushed through master control, then up and out through the curtain of muscle at the main portal. Hitting a dead run in the hallway, the out-of-shape researcher thought to himself, *I'm about to get a battle of my own.*

❦

When the complex's thick external door rose, a narrow, gray-robed figure stood on the other side with folded arms.

"Well, if it isn't Good-Scholar Damon Shadwell, how's your project doing these rotations?"

"Please, Submatriarch, just come to the lab and put a stop to your subform. He's on a rampage."

With a sigh, she stepped into the foyer and began walking down the hallway—her pace too slow for Damon's liking. "It's kind of sweet, don't you think? The way my assistant does little things to try to make me happy."

He looked at her wrinkled face with its sneering lines. "He's part of a new, more intelligent generation, is he? Funny I haven't heard of them before."

"I'm not surprised. It usually takes a while for new technology to filter down to the citizenry."

Damon fumed at the reminder of his humbled social status. "Do you really think it's safe to have subforms thinking for themselves? Or don't they actually do that?"

"What are you implying, Damon? That perhaps I ordered this attempted sabotage?"

"I'm not implying anything, Submatriarch, but it's interesting that you came to that assumption so fast."

"Watch yourself, *citizen*. You're treading dangerously close to insubordination. My 'assumption' was based on the fact that you blame me for the pathetic position you've fallen into."

"My sorrow, Submatriarch, but weren't you the one that moved to have a Motion of Concentric Exile read to me?"

"Weren't you the one trying to find a way to experiment with mineral technology?"

"Of course not. I simply designed an experiment that would give the First Doctrine a realistic challenge—unlike the plain, possibly rigged models of those before me."

"You should talk about rigged models, Damon. You made conditions on your model ideal for a mineral-based technology. You knew they'd rape their planet, you did it all just so you could sample the fruits of their evil."

"Perhaps the Submatriarch is forgetting that the First Doctrine clearly states that *any* society under *any* conditions will use biological technology because it's a universal constant of moral righteousness. Doesn't it seem like this should apply to a world with fewer animal species than our own?"

"I'm not going to debate the First Doctrine with you, Damon. If that was your true hypothesis, then as soon as you realized your subjects were using the wrong technology you would have labeled your findings as erroneous, sterilized the model, and started over."

"You are the second highest ranking official in the Circle of Science. Tell me, where is the precedent that says you should scrap any experiment that doesn't go as predicted? If that is the way we do things, why even experiment? Why not simply make all scientific hypotheses instant laws and save ourselves the time and trouble?"

"Damon, the First Doctrine is true. Mineral technology is evil and biological technology is righteous. Everybody knows that."

"Not according to my research."

"Your research is flawed. It's erroneous."

"How?"

"It just is. Like the researcher who proved mathematically that what comes up sometimes does not come down."

"Ah, but he was right, we now have antigravity technology."

"That's an exception Damon, and you know it."

"Why can't there be exceptions to the First Doctrine?"

"Put simply, dear Scholar, because then it would be called blasphemy."

Damon snorted in disgust. "Here's the lab. We can continue this after you've called off your rabid pet."

The Submatriarch's eyes narrowed as she stepped through the opening between the retracted muscles. "Oh, we'll continue this, all right. We are far from done."

They hurried towards main control, where Rexus still held the now docile Tem in his strong arms. Chief Kansan and Correspondent Maran Bold stood nearby, shifting uncertainly. Seeing the scrapes and bruises on her assistant, the Submatriarch turned and snapped at Damon.

"What have you done to him?"

"My sorrow, Submatriarch, but during the course of his sabotage he fell off the pod. Then I had my subform subdue him—we had no choice. He would've killed us all, not to mention the four billion Cyanomites living inside the pod."

"Cyanomites… indeed. As if their Kaura would be of any loss. Now you call off yours and I'll call off mine."

"Rexus, let him go…. Now go and see if you can reattach the lymph vessel to the antigrav gland."

The Submatriarch's venom-filled eyes watched Rexus slink away. Tem was still able to stand on his own but wobbled a bit, all the while keeping his eyes fixed sheepishly on his master. Her voice softened as she spoke to her valet. "Tem, wait for me in the rotoskiff. Have something to eat if you like."

Damon was galled at that. Tem had nearly killed them and she was practically rewarding him. The Submatriarch read the expression on his face and asked, "Can I help it if even a subform can see this monstrosity for what it is?"

"And what would that be?"

"Evil. A threat not only to our way of life, but also to the frail body of Our Lady Karitta."

"Excuse me? How is this project a threat to our planet?"

"I know you, Damon Shadwell. You're planning on using whatever it is they've learned how to do. If you had your way we'd be strip-mining every bit of desert on the face of Karita."

"I'm not stupid, Submatriarch. I know what catastrophes would occur if we began tampering with our fragile environment. But there is something valuable we could learn from them."

"Hah! I knew it. You just confessed that you were after this technology from the beginning."

"No I didn't."

"Yes you did. Maybe not in so many words, but you did say we should use their technology. Just out of morbid curiosity, Damon, what have they discovered that would make you sacrifice your position, your funding, and your reputation?"

"Space travel," he replied.

An expression of surprise flashed across her face. She looked at Chief Kansan.

He nodded somberly back at her.

The Submatriarch looked again at Damon and sneered. "So they can travel an arm's length inside an artificial pod. How can that possibly be of any use in the real world?"

"They've developed a combustible chemical mixture that can propel their vehicles fast enough to reach escape velocity. I know you've studied my research enough to know that their obstacles are identical to ours, only on a microscopic scale. What works for them can work for us."

"How? Should we start drilling into the Body of Our Lady to find fossil fuels?"

"No. We should analyze the chemical composition of their propellant and develop our own glandular tissue to excrete a substance with similar qualities."

"And what of the waste? Combustion would release dangerous toxins into our already unstable atmosphere."

"Environmental impact is the primary focus when we develop any new substance. It can be dealt with during the engineering process."

"No, Damon, it can't. Because what you've been doing here is blasphemous, and I won't condone any knowledge that comes from such a tainted source."

"You're wrong, Submatriarch. My sorrow, but the source, as you put it, most certainly is not tainted."

"Look, *citizen*, they are violating the First Doctrine. The source most certainly is tainted, just like their kaura."

"Their kaura has fewer blemishes than anyone on this planet, Submatriarch, including you."

The room got deathly quiet. Everyone stared at Damon in disbelief, most notably Torrin Masla, Submatriarch of the Greater Circle of Science. Her immortal soul had just been slandered by a lowly citizen. "What did you say to me?"

Something within the researcher snapped. He was tired of being cautious and tired of being afraid of this tyrant. He decided it was time to say what he truly thought. "You heard me. Your kaura must be as black as the night sky. All you ever do is destroy—you never build. You destroy careers, lives, knowledge, hopes, dreams… everything good in life. It's uptight, self-righteous, control-mongers like you that impede progress. You, Submatriarch, are personally stunting the growth of Our Lady Karita, and I hope she can see it in your kaura because a demon like you belongs in hell."

The Church Correspondent was so shocked she actually choked. Chief Kansan's face was an odd, unreadable mixture of emotion. The Submatriarch, though—she was livid.

"I do not believe what I just heard…" She raised her right arm. "Perhaps you've forgotten to whom you were speaking…" She whipped her right sleeve down with her left hand, revealing a queen telembiot with the power to communicate lethal doses of pain to another host, "I am Torrin Masla…" Damon stared at the implant in horror, wishing he could take back what he'd just said, "Submatriarch to the Greater Circle of Science…" The insect-like red creature began to vibrate, and Damon stepped back in fear, "…and you are mine, now. You hear me, you insolent little fool? I've got you."

A sudden, intense pain in his right forearm dropped Damon to his knees. He ripped his sleeve open and cradled his innocent telembiot. It was vibrating with intense pain—pain it was forced to share with Damon. He gritted his teeth and groaned loudly.

"For your transgressions, Damon Shadwell… I invoke the Right of Corporeal Recompense." With gleaming eyes, she sent another wave of searing pain through the scholar's body. He screamed and fell onto his back. "For the crime of blasphemy against the First Doctrine, and for the crime of gross insubordination…" Another wave of agony burned through his arm, then his shoulder, chest and stomach. "…you are to be punished!" Then it struck his opposite shoulder, neck, and groin. Convulsions took hold of his body and rattled through his trunk and limbs.

"And after this, there's more, Shadwell, oh yes. I am terminating your 'citizen-scholar' status, and therefore your privileges to practice science. Then I'm going to return here and not only dismantle this profanity you call an experiment, I'm going to personally burn away each and every one of your precious little Cyanomites. You hear me, Damon? All four billion of them!"

Damon barely heard her. With his face pressed against the moist floor, the pounding of his pulse filled his ears and his consciousness swam, threatening to drift away.

"You hear me? Answer me, slug!" She sent another wave, causing his back to arch and all of his muscles to contract violently. "I'm going to destroy every last little one of them and I'll release their kaura to Our Lady Karitta so that she may put it to better use!"

"I don't think you'll be doing that." Chief Kansan grabbed her right fist and forced it down. "And I really must insist that you stop doing that."

"Are you mad?" said the Submatriarch, glaring at him, "What do you think you are doing? I'm a submatriarch!"

"And may I remind you that I am from the Circle of the Courts." He looked down at Damon's sickly writhing. "I am the investigator here, and I've concluded that this research is viable."

"You can't be serious!"

"I assure you, Submatriarch, I am. I'm going to recommend to the Courts that his experiments continue, and that others begin researching his space-vehicle propellant—formal recognition going to Good-Scholar Shadwell, of course. And furthermore, Madam Submatriarch, I'm going to recommend that the First Doctrine be officially designated as under review. Shadwell's project will be cited as an exception, pending verification by repeat experimentation by other researchers."

"The Courts won't follow your recommendation."

"Of course they will. Have you ever known them to not support the findings of their agents? We are their eyes, their ears, and the legs upon which they stand."

The Submatriarch's face paled in outrage. "I outrank you. I forbid you to make those recommendations."

"You have no authority to influence my decision, Submatriarch. He has used proper scientific method to validate his hypothesis, though in this case, sound research has *in*validated the hypothesis. It happens all the time in experimentation. I am satisfied that his methodology was thorough and impartial, therefore his findings stand. You're going to have to get used to it. Who knows? His contributions just might get him reinstated on the Circle of Science."

The thought of that drove her into a fit of rage. "How dare you!" she hissed, raising her telembiot.

Chief Kansan glanced casually at the Correspondent to ensure that she was recording what was happening. "You wouldn't want to do that, Submatriarch. I'd hate to have to recommend a Motion of Concentric Exile for you. Inappropriate dispensement of the 'Right of Corporeal Recompense' is a serious crime."

The Submatriarch glared at Chief Kansan with a burning hatred, yet she slowly lowered her arm. Just then Damon groaned and rolled over. Seeing that he was about to rise, she spun on her heel and stormed out of the lab.

Once she'd gone, the Chief bent down and helped the researcher rise. Feeling dizzy and nauseated, Damon's eyes remained glazed and unfocused. The Chief and the Correspondent helped him over to a bench where he sat for a moment, trying to regain his bearings. When the fog had mostly cleared, he asked, "Where did she go?"

"She's gone. And you probably won't have to worry about her for a long time."

Damon groaned. "Oh, the things I said… What was I thinking?"

The Chief smiled. "It wasn't a very intelligent thing to do, was it, Scholar? But I do have to admit that I wish I'd have been the one with the guts to say it to her."

"You do?"

"Sure. Everyone who knows her does."

Damon tried to laugh but it hurt his head.

Soon he and his hulking assistant once again stood in the alcove by the main entrance. The rotoskiff erupted into the air, showering them with red sand. Damon shielded his eyes and waited for the tempest to die down. A moment later, he was able to lower his arm and watch the creature bounce away through the darkened desert sky. He looked beyond to the stars scattered lovingly in the heavens and felt a sudden swell of joy. The Courts always followed the recommendations of their investigators. It was entirely possible that soon Karitta would have her own version of space-vehicle propellant, and, in front of all of his peers, the Matriarch of the Greater Circle of Science would read yet another Formal Recognition to Good-Scholar Damon Shadwell.

More importantly, he might have just made one of the greatest contributions to science in all of history. For the good of his entire planet, space travel was now within their grasp. Damon yearned for the stars shining in the desert sky above him. He wondered how many revolutions it would be before the people of his world began to take to the sky and escape the confines of their atmosphere, like the people on his model. He smiled as he thought, *At last we shall know what's beyond our little world.*

The Ow Shop
by
David Densley Thomas

David Densley Thomas is an I.T. professional born and bred in South Wales, where he lives with his wife, two young children and an under-utilised imagination. He has performed in numerous amateur productions including the roles of Hamlet and Henry V, and has represented Wales at the finals of the U.K. amateur one-act play festival. He is new to writing, but won a prize for his play "Buzz" in an international playwriting competition. He is currently working on a play about a Welsh hero, world champion boxer Jimmy Wilde.

"The Ow Shop" is Thomas' first published work, and he would like to thank his five year old son Cai for the inspiration, the title, and 'the teeth', but would like to stress that in no way is the story autobiographical. He would like to dedicate "The Ow Shop" to the memory of his father, who was a gentle, clever man.

"Idiot!" Dad's hand caught Tom around the side of the head making his ear sing. "Why can't you just *listen?*" A punch to the shoulder shot sparks down to his fingertips.

"Ow!" said Tom, "I'm sorry, Dad."

Tom's baby sister Molly started to cry and his mother, cheeks streaked with tears, gathered her up and fled the room.

In a way Tom was relieved. This had been coming for several days and had been like living with an unexploded bomb. At least when this was done they could get back to normal again, for a week, maybe even two if he were lucky.

"Sorry?" said Dad, grabbing Tom's hair. "Sorry? Well we're all bloody sorry, mate! I'm sorry I ever laid eyes on your mother, the stupid bitch! And I'm sorry as hell I ever had kids. If it wasn't for you I wouldn't have had to marry the useless cow."

It usually happened like this: On Fridays after work, Dad went to the pub. Eventually he came home, lost his temper and drank lots more till he fell asleep. Dad would be quiet and sorry tomorrow and maybe even take them out for the day.

"Now sod off to bed." Dad, still with a hand full of hair, pushed Tom headfirst towards the door of the lounge. Tom's feet couldn't keep up, and he sprawled face first on the soft carpet. He scrambled up and started for the door, but Dad's foot sped him on his way with a vicious thrust. Tom careened to the side, and his temple connected with the edge of the coffee table.

For some reason he was looking at the ceiling. Tom's head hurt in a fuzzy sort of way, and an unpleasant smell pricked the back of his nose. It stung like when he rinsed his hair in the bath by sticking his head right under and got soapy water in his mouth. A drawing pin left over from last Christmas' decorations clung to the ceiling. He hoped it didn't choose this moment to fall because he couldn't move, or close his eyes for that matter. Actually, it felt more like *he* was above *it*, staring down from a carpeted ceiling at the artexed floor below which sprouted a light shade atop a rigid length of electrical flex. Any second now, he would peel away and drop towards the drawing pin….

His stomach lurched. Dad would be cross if he was sick over the floor, or the ceiling for that matter. He tried to speak but his tongue and lips were numb. A million miles away, Mum was crying and Dad was swearing. He was using the 'F' word a lot tonight; a bad sign. Tom didn't know what it meant but he knew it was a 'naughty word.' Once, when he and Dad were watching football on telly, Dad had sworn at the referee, using the 'F' word and other words too. Tom had joined in, agreeing with his Dad, repeating the words without knowing what they meant.

Dad had put his cigarette out on Tom's tongue. Mum gave Tom a tip-top, and when he'd stopped crying he was allowed to finish watching the football. Dad explained that the tongue was the fastest healing part of the body. Dad knew loads of cool stuff like that.

Tom wondered if he'd accidentally said the 'F' word when he bumped his head. Dad was very angry about something.

"Of course I'm not taking the stupid little sod to the hospital. Are you mad? What's it going to look like?"

"But he might have a concussion. You might have fractured his skull." Tom hated his mother's voice when she cried; it was all whiney and pathetic.

"Oh that's right. *I* might have fractured his skull. It's *my* fault now, is it? Is it? The clumsy little sod. That's exactly why I'm not taking him to the hospital, because I can't trust *you* not to come out with crap like that."

"Clumsy. Little. Sod." The drawing pin rolled from side to side in time with Dad's words. As Tom's head rocked to and fro, Dad's wild-eyed, red face swayed in and out of view.

"Clumsy. Stupid. Little. Sod." Dad kicked Tom , but Tom couldn't feel it. His body felt like modelling putty. He imagined Dad's feet leaving squidgy dents in his side. Perhaps it was because Dad had his soft slippers on—Tom had fetched them for him earlier—or perhaps he wasn't kicking hard. Still, it ought to hurt. He ought to be saying "Ow!" He tried, but his tongue was made of putty too. Perhaps he'd run out of *Ow*s; he'd used an awful lot lately.

Before Granddad went to Heaven, he'd lived at Tom's house. Granddad was lovely. He was Mum's Daddy. Dad never talked about *his* father. Granddad used to chase Tom and tickle him, and kiss his face and neck a hundred squillion times and say "I've got all your kisses now, you'll have to go to the kisses shop and get some more." Tom would be sad to have no kisses left, so Granddad would give them back. Things were better then. Even though Granddad was old, Dad was afraid of him. Tom hardly used any *Ow*s in those days. Now he didn't have any left. Perhaps he was dying. Perhaps that's what happens when you run out of *Ow*s?

Tom was looking at the ceiling again, but it wasn't the lounge ceiling with its forgotten drawing pin. It was Tom's bedroom ceiling with its glowstars and solar system mobile. The light glowed dimly, just how he liked it when he went to bed. His head throbbed as he threw off his 'Max Lightstar' duvet and sat up, but he had to go to the toilet. Dad would be *really* cross if he wet the bed. He had his pyjamas on but didn't remember Mum putting him to bed. To his relief, he no longer felt like modelling clay. Dark bruises stained his left leg and side, but didn't hurt when touched. It's because I've run out of *Ow*s, he thought. Now what would he say when his baby sister pulled his hair?

He padded to the bedroom door and opened it to a surprise. Instead of the nightlight's red glow, and the landing speckled in leafy moon shadow, bright daylight flooded the house. He went to the toilet, washed his hands then tapped at his parents' bedroom door.

"Mum?" Nobody there. He checked his baby sister's room, but she was gone too. He called downstairs over the baby gate. No answer. The gate clanged shut behind him, too noisy in the quiet house. He reached the bottom of the stairs and shouted for her up the hallway. The floor creaked behind him in reply, but when he turned he just saw the front door moving in a draft, allowing a crack of golden light in. Perhaps Mum was outside, putting the rubbish out or cleaning the windows. He grabbed his slippers from under the stairs. Screwing his eyes up against the glare, he opened the front door and stepped in to the light.

Silence. Mum wasn't outside. Nobody was outside.

No birds, no cars, no breeze, no people, no road works, no dogs, no children.

The normally busy street gaped under the blank stares of the houses opposite. He poked his head through the railings of their tiny front garden and peered along the road as it bent out of sight in either direction. It was deserted, apart from… a flash of movement near the bus stop, where the pavement curved behind Mrs Williams' hedge.

The oiled hinges of the front gate opened quietly, and his slippered feet made no noise on the empty pavement. He could see motion through the hedge once again, and as he rounded the corner he was greeted by the beaming cartoon smile of Pink Pig.

"Oooh, helloo there," said Pink Pig, as happy in real life as he was on Children's TV. "I'm waiting for the bus, you know."

Of course he was waiting for the bus. Pink Pig was always catching the bus to some adventure or other, not that the other pigs ever believed what he'd been up to. Tom loved Pink Pig.

The sound of a motor engine rumbled closer, accompanied by crazy carousel music.

"Oooh, that'll be the bus now." Pink Pig turned away, disappearing briefly as he passed Tom edge on. It's because he's a drawing, thought Tom. He must be as thin as paper.

The bus that arrived was real enough, but everyone on it was a drawing. Pink Pig climbed aboard. "Oooh, we'd like two tickets to the shops pleeease."

The driver handed Pink Pig two returns. "Certainly, sir. There's plenty of room at the top."

Tom hesitated. Pink Pig held out a trotter to him. "Oooh, come *on* Tom, I've got your ticket now."

Tom and Pink Pig had just taken a seat behind an orange cat and a green mouse when the bus stopped again.

"Everyone off for the shops," shouted the driver.

"Oooh, off you go then, Tom," said Pink Pig, nudging Tom off the seat and in to the aisle. "My stop's the next one - by the Chemist. I need some oinkment for a nasty rasher."

"Er, bye then," said Tom. He shuffled to the front of the bus, the passengers disappearing and reappearing as he passed their edges.

"Ham missing you already! Oooer!" Pink Pig called after him.

As soon as Tom stepped down from the bus, it roared off, the carousel music fading to be replaced by perfect silence. The street, full of shops but empty of people, stretched off in both directions. The shops looked dark and closed, all except the one directly opposite the bus stop. Tom mouthed the words written in curvy pink neon above the door. The… Ow… sss… sh… Shop. "The Ow Shop," he said, pleased with his reading. The 'O' was red, shaped like the lips of an open mouth. The shop looked like one on a Christmas Card, with a door in the middle and old fashioned, small-paned windows either side, the type that could gather snow beautifully in their corners. Some panes had curvy circles, like glass bottles melted flat, leaving only a couple of rings to show what they once were.

Shelves lined the windows, so that each pane framed an object within it. There were all sorts of things; some looked like toys, others like medicines or sweets. Everywhere were bottles and jars containing coloured liquids or pills.

Tom gave the door a push, leaning his weight against it, till it gave way with a groan. Inside was as crowded with stuff as the windows suggested. Boxes and containers crammed numerous shelves. Every part of every wall boasted some display or other, and even the long glass counter held three shelves chock full of interesting items.

The overall effect was cheerful, but the air was tainted by a green, fausty smell. Tom had once fallen off his neighbour Ben's scooter, scraping his elbows badly. Ben's mum had put big sticking plasters on him. He'd been too afraid to mention it at home and had hid his elbows for a whole week before the smell gave him away. That's what this shop smelled like: septic.

A bell sat on the counter, well within Tom's reach. It was round, painted and moulded like a little man's face, eyes screwed up in agony. Tom spelled the sign underneath, 'Press Hard'. The 'button' was the man's bright red, painful-looking nose. Tom placed a hesitant finger on it, then snatched it away; the nose was warm and fleshy. Grimacing, he applied his finger again, more firmly, but nothing happened. Tom paused, looking round the empty shop, searching for some other means of attracting attention. Then, teeth gritted and eyes shut, he used his thumb to really stab at the button-nose. From somewhere came a very loud "OOWW!"

Tom jumped away from the counter, said "Sorry" to nobody, and was backing towards the door when a friendly voice stopped him.

"Aha! Customers at last!" A door opened at the end of the long counter and the smiley blue face of the Shopkeeper appeared.

"Well, if it isn't young Tom Lewis! I've been expecting *you* for some time." The Shopkeeper shuffled along behind the counter, accompanied by a scraping sound as he dragged his right leg. "Who would have thought that such a little boy could have so many *Ow*s in him, aye?"

"How do you know my name?" asked Tom, not sure whether to back away or move towards the counter.

"Good business sense, lad. You've got to know your market." The Shopkeeper wore a white coat, which glowed brightly next to his blueish black skin. His hands were the same blotchy colour as his bald head, and as he placed them on the counter the fingers of his left hand bent up and back at twisted angles.

Tom stepped forward. "I've run out of…, out of…."

"You've run out of *Ow*s lad, of course, but don't worry, you've come to the right place. I've got *lots*. This *is* The Ow Shop after all! Part chemists, part joke shop; a sort of Choke Shop. You could say *gag*ging's our speciality. Heh, heh!"

"But I haven't got any money," said Tom, patting his pocket-less pyjamas.

"Well, good job it's all free then, isn't it?" The Shopkeeper leaned forward and winked one of his bloodshot eyes at Tom. "I have to give it all away. I can't retire until I do." He reached up high to a display of grinning teeth set in red gums and placed one down on the counter. One of the teeth had a filling, exactly where Tom's was. The Shopkeeper wound the big key sticking out of the top, then let it go.

The clacking teeth went "OwOwOwOwOwOwOwOwOw…" The Shopkeeper's eyes rolled back in his head, mouth open, sucking fast gasps of air as the teeth opened and closed. His head fell back, eyelids flickering, and his hitching chest got bigger and bigger. Just as Tom was sure he would explode, the Shopkeeper slammed his good hand down on the teeth, silencing them. Slowly, he let out a long shaky sigh, deflating till his chin touched his chest. His eyes opened lazily and focused on Tom. They were clearer now, less bloodshot.

"One of the perks of the job," he said, picking up the teeth and tossing them in a bin.

Now that Tom was nearer the man, the septic smell was stronger, like ripe summer bin bags. Tom's nose twitched.

"Pardon the, er, *cologne* by the way lad. I'm feeling a bit *off*." The Shopkeeper laughed heartily, a deep, treacly sound. When he'd finished gurgling, he smiled at Tom, revealing blood streaked teeth separated by numerous gaps. "I'd best show you around."

"We're expanding, you know." He stood to his full height and swept his arm grandly round the shop. "Oh yes, business has never been so good. There's never *been* so much pain in the world. We're diversifying. Oh don't get me wrong, *Ow*s will always be the core business, but there's plenty of scope for expansion into complementary markets. Actually, we've just introduced an International Range." The Shopkeeper shuffled along the counter to a display of colourful boxes with foreign writing on them.

"We've Chinese Burns, Welsh Raw-Bits, American Pyles, French Crepitus, both sweet and savoury, Scotch Midgebites, Delhi Bellys, Columbian Coughys, Chilli Blaines, Lancashire Hot Spots, and so on, ad 'Mexican Waves of' Nauseum. Then of course there's our 'DownUnder Delights'. It's an entire range for people with problems in the, er, Southern Hemisphere, the *Nether Regions* shall we say. Perhaps a little exotic for a young lad like yourself though?"

Tom nodded.

"Yes. The best sellers in the children's range are normally your standard Knee Knocks or Funny Bone Bangs…" He stopped and looked at Tom's head where it had hit the table. "Bit light weight for you, I think. We sometimes get a seasonal run on Neck Tendon Twangs. Unpredictable, though. It's a fashion thing with you children; *in* one week, *out* the next…." The Shopkeeper shook his head at Tom in a good-natured, *I don't know, you kids,* kind of way.

Tom smiled back and relaxed a little. He pointed to a long shelf that held bottles of various shapes, colours and size. "Please, er, what are those?"

"Well, I'm glad you asked. You see, around about the same time people run out of *Ow*s, they generally dry up in the old tear department. Lachrima Depleta, if you like." He pointed to the bottles, which were arranged smallest to largest from left to right. "These are refills of different purities and strengths." He reached up and fetched down the smallest, placing it carefully in front of Tom. The tiny crystal bottle clinked against the glass counter. It had delicate cut-glass surfaces, glinting rainbow reflections, and a minute pipette lid for drawing up the contents. The liquid inside was so clear as to be near invisible.

"Babies' tears," whispered the Shopkeeper. "Pure, distilled sorrow, untainted by higher thought processes. No self-pity, no self-consciousness, no pretence. Baby products are the *best*. Apparently Foetus *Joy* can cure cancer, but it's not exactly my market, corporate branding wise."

He carefully returned the bottle and gestured at the others along the shelf. "Then there's the full range. I've a cracking five year old's Riwas. That's 'Righteous Indignation when Wrongly Accused of Something'. Oh it's got a beautiful bitter-sweet quality that feels like it's going to last in the mouth *forever*. Doesn't age well though. A ten year old's Riwas tastes decidedly tired and jaded.

"Then on we go to the low quality end." He gestured to a big demijohn at the other side of the shelf, full of yellowy green stuff. "Crocodile tears. Budget end of the range but it suits some people." The Shopkeeper's foot bumped against something, and he looked down at a large black plastic rainwater butt with a tap on its side.

"Oh yes, there's always this, but I wouldn't recommend it really. It's little better than piss, oh, er, excuse my Sumerian."

Tom tried not to laugh. "What is it?"

"What, this? This is Politicians' Remorse. I think I'd rather be Lachrima Depleta, all things considered. So anyway, anything take your fancy?"

"No, thank you," said Tom, "I cry all the time, no problem."

"Good for you, son. Now we've got some brand new…."

"Er, I *do* need some… some…er, you know, the things I've run out of?" Tom touched his bruised side. "I need lots prob'ly, I mean, if that's OK? Nothing special though."

"Course you do, son, me and my shop talk. We've got all sorts of *Ow*s you know, a million different ways to take your 'hit' as it were." He chuckled as he shuffled along the counter, his white nylon coat swishing against the glass. He gestured to a section underneath. "Oral, various. Have a butcher's as they say nowadays."

Most of the packets had pictures on them. There were boxes of little spiky balls made from pins, called 'Jags'. Next to them was what looked like razorblades.

"Garrottes," said the Shopkeeper, "the best a man can get. Prefer Watkinson's Shred myself."

Some of the packets looked like sweets, and Tom's mouth began to water. He pointed to a tin of frosted crystal candies. "They look nice."

"Coated in very fine powdered glass," said the Shopkeeper, flipping open a box of Jags. "They're called Twice Gotchas. Very popular. Delayed effect. You sort of pay for it the other end, if you know what I mean. It's never a dry poo, mind." He popped a jag in his mouth and closed his eyes. For a moment he was quite still, then his jaw moved vigorously. "Oooh. All you can do is chew."

Tom was losing his appetite. With failing enthusiasm, he pointed to some 'XXX Sherbet Lemons' and raised his eyebrows.

The Shopkeeper chewed while talking, occasionally smacking his mouth. "You know how sherbet lemons get little splits in them and sometimes slice your tongue? Well, those are a thousand times sharper and filled with lemon juice instead of sherbet." The shopkeeper offered a box to Tom.

"I can't pay you," said Tom, staring at his slippers, "and Mum says I shouldn't really take things from…"

"I said it's free, didn't I? Look, kid, I'll show you something." The Shopkeeper squeezed round the end of the counter and lurched across the shop floor. For the first time Tom could see his legs. He wore grey flannel trousers and his bare feet were an even darker blue than his face. They would have looked black if it weren't for his truly black toenails, of which he had three. His right leg scraped behind him, the knee bent sideways, and the foot pointing out to five o'clock instead of twelve.

The Shopkeeper reached a door and threw it wide. A cold draft rushed out, raising goosebumps on Tom's arms. The smell of sour dust drifted from the dark doorway. The Shopkeeper reached in and clicked a switch. After as short pause, row upon row of overhead strip lights switched on. One by one, they illuminated with buzzy clunks, further and further away, marching in to the distance like lampposts above a huge straight motorway. Below the lights an aisle of metal racking stretched to infinity. There were countless similar aisles to the left and right. The shelves of this aisle were stacked with sets of teeth. Tom

followed their straight lines from near to far. Individual teeth merged
into white lines sandwiched between red lines of gums, narrowing like
stripy toothpaste. Red and white blurred to pink; multiple pink lines
melted to one, converging with the lights, the floor, the shelves at the
pinpoint bottom of the deepest darkest falling down holefalling...

"Whoah!" The Shopkeeper grabbed Tom by the collar and pulled
him back in to the shop. "Lost a kid in there once. Took him a year to find
his way out. He was in a bad way, survived on nothing but 'Jags' and
'Politicians Remorse'. He was one bitter kid. Anyway, the point is I'm
not short of stock, so please, feel free to take whatever you need. There's
another delivery coming in later."

"Where does it all come from?" asked Tom.

The Shopkeeper switched off the storeroom lights and closed the
door. "It comes from 'The Ow *Factory*', more commonly known as the
world, or more precisely, the *people* of the world. See, pain is a form of
energy and as such cannot be destroyed, only changed from one state to
another. People are born with a finite amount of it. Somebody gets hurt
and the pain ends up here. Now, in an ideal world, all the pain stays
inside people, unused, and I run out of stock and can finally... I can
finally retire. My punishment will be over."

"What did you do?" said Tom, not looking directly at the man
because he thought he might be crying.

"Have a seat, kid." He produced two folding stools, covered in
upturned six-inch nails. He placed a cushion on Tom's.

"There was a time when I didn't do this. I had a name once. Arphaxad."
He glanced at Tom who was smiling. "Yeah, sucks by modern standards,
I know, but it was par for the course in ancient Mesopotamia. Supposedly
the birthplace of civilisation, but I think of it as the birthplace of all this...
this *crap*. 'Scuse the Sumerian. It wasn't long after the last Great Flood,
and there weren't many people left. Anyway, we had big families back
then; we saw it as our duty to re-populate the world. I had four wives
and begat fifty kids. Ha! And parents these days think they've got it
tough because the supermarket delivery is twenty minutes late, or little
Kylie won't stop crying 'cos she's teething. I digress.

"It was hard, but I can't make excuses for it; I was pretty mean to my
kids, *very* mean. Could have taught your dad a trick or two. The short
of it is, my kids all grew up and had big families, and most of them had
learned my lesson pretty well: Treat your kids rough. Then they grew
up, and yada-yada-yadah... I ain't saying I'm responsible for *all* the pain
in the world, but, as the Americans say, *you do the math*."

"Ah well." The Shopkeeper held out the box of XXX Sherbet Lemons.

Tom's mouth tingled . "Have you got anything that you don't have
to, you know, eat?"

"Well there's, a new type of sticking plaster with industrial strength glue." The Shopkeeper bent and rummaged in a big cardboard box. "Marvellous things. They're called 'Scabs'. I guess when you rip 'em off, the net effect is much the same. Can't seem to find them now." He stood up stiffly, accompanied by a grating sound, and rubbed at an odd bulge in his spine. "Ooo, my back's in half."

He paused, mid-rub and said brightly, "I know just the thing!" He hobbled to some rolls of material hung on the wall. Tom climbed off his stool and followed. There were four big rolls of pink bubble wrap mounted one above the other.

The Shopkeeper read the labels by each. "Spots. Pimples. Boils. Carbuncles." He eyed Tom up and down measuring him for size. "Hmmm… could do with a roll of Abscesses really. Oh well, Carbuncles will have to do."

He rolled out six inches of bubble wrap, and sliced it with a cutthroat-razor from a nearby shelf. The cut end dripped a couple of drops of red liquid on the floor, but the Shopkeeper wiped it up and cleaned the razor with a rag. He held the six by twelve inch sheet out to Tom. Fine blonde hairs dotted its surface, and it throbbed beneath Tom's fingertips. The bubbles rose from the pink sheet like pain volcanoes, red around the base, rising to lime green summits, swelled to bursting.

"Let me demonstrate," said the Shopkeeper, shrugging his shoulders gleefully. He placed the crooked thumb and forefinger of his left hand around a bubble and pointed it at a mirror on the wall. "Mirror, mirror on the wall whose the fairest…" with a grimace, he squeezed. "*Pop!*" the mirror was splattered with translucent green. He took a sharp intake of breath and blew out his cheeks, relaxing his shoulders. He glanced down at his left forefinger, which was now straight and a little less blue than the others.

"Well what do you know?" He held his finger up to Tom who smiled approvingly, then he dropped the bubble wrap sheet in a paper bag and gave it to Tom.

"Thanks," said Tom, opening the paper bag and looking at the carbuncle bubble wrap inside. It couldn't have more than a hundred bubbles on it.

"I, er, ought to be going," he said. He got halfway to the door then stopped again. "Thanks for the car… caruncles, but, er, don't you think, maybe, I need more? See, I do use an awful lot, and I don't know whether I'd be able to find my way back here."

The Shopkeeper stared at the floor, then sighed and dragged himself over to Tom. Turning Tom's head gently to the side, he lightly touched the mark from the coffee table.

"Hmm. Do you mind?" he asked Tom, and lifted his pyjama top. The colour of Tom's side matched the Shopkeeper's hand. After a moment, he sighed again and gestured to the bag.

"Look, kid. I figure you got a week's worth there. That's a long time in your house, *too* long. After that, what can I say, you ain't gonna need more *Ow*'s. Unless something changes of course, in which case... you ain't gonna need more *Ow*'s! But, realistically, what's gonna change? Your dad's a psycho, your mum's a punching bag, and you're five years old. You're a passenger on the bus of your own life, that's just how it is for young kids."

Tom looked up from the bag. "Am..."

"Don't ask me, kid..."

"Am I..."

"*Don't...*"

"...dying?"

"Ah crap." The Shopkeeper limped away and slumped back down on the stool. "Ah kid... right now? Possibly not. *Probably* not. But how much longer you got, huh? You've used up your *Ow*'s kid! Most people die *long* before."

Tom stared at the floor for a moment, then smiled. "Will I see granddad?"

"Sure, kid. He works just up the road at the Kisses Shop. He doesn't *have* to work, not like me. Nice guy like him can pick and choose, but he likes to help out part-time. Might let *you* help too."

"I'd like that," said Tom, wondering how often the buses ran.

"Kid. *Tom*. If it does work out for you and one day you have kids of your own... be nice to them?"

Tom frowned. "Of course," he said. It was the stupidest question, the easiest question he'd ever answered.

"Ah, it's just that hard luck kids *are* half their Dads, after all. Sometimes their memories get hazy. It's a long time from five years old to the time you have kids yourself; things get confused. You can start to remember the bad times from your Dad's point of view, because then they don't seem so bad. You'll be big and strong yourself and... hey, everyone wants to feel like a super hero, don't they? The boss, the tough guy, the macho man? Doesn't everyone want revenge? Biff, Bash, Bang!"

"I'd never do it." Tom's voice was flat, his smile gone.

For a long moment the Shopkeeper stared at Tom, who returned his gaze. The Shopkeeper looked away first.

"Let me give you something, Tom." He crunched to his feet and grabbed a barbwire-coated pen from the counter. "It's a bit risky, a bit 'kill or cure', but I guess you got nothing to lose." He scribbled something on a pad of prescription forms, ripped it off, and handed it to Tom.

"You only use this if you *have* to, OK?"

A few minutes later, after he'd explained what he'd written, the Shopkeeper said, "Right, let's get you home. Don't worry about the bus, I'll take you there myself." He turned around to fetch something, calling "Don't forget your *Ows* Tom."

Tom looked down at the paper bag in his left hand, and the Shopkeeper swung the hobnailed baseball bat and connected with Tom's right temple.

"Ow!!" Tom's hand flew to the bloodstained bandage around his head. For some reason he was looking at the ceiling. But it wasn't the lounge ceiling with its forgotten drawing pin; it was Tom's bedroom ceiling with its glowstars and solar system mobile. He must have shouted in his sleep and woken himself up. A sickening pain burned his temple. He threw off his 'Max Lightstar' duvet and sat up slowly. He ached all over and began to wish he *were* made out of putty. His left leg and side were badly bruised, and hurt so much when he touched them that he retched dryly.

It was dark, although his eyes were gradually getting used to it. Why hadn't Mum left the dimmer switch on a little, the way he liked it? The streetlamp glowed yellow through his curtains; it was still night. As he moved, his pyjamas clung wetly to his thighs. How did that happen? He'd gotten up to go to the toilet, hadn't he? He tried to remember, but the memory, still teasingly close, had faded with waking. His sheet was soaked too. Dad went berserk if Tom wet the bed. He was in big trouble, unless…. He knew where his pyjamas were kept and where Mum stored the clean bedding. He'd have to make a neat job changing the bed or Dad would be suspicious.

Tom climbed woozily down and took a few moments to steady himself once he was on his feet. The wooden floor chilled his toes; the heating must have been off for some time. He took a step to the right to stand on his space-rocket shaped mat. The house was dead quiet, and so was the road outside, the way it got in the very middle of the night. He must have been sleeping for hours. He crept to the wardrobe, which meant leaving the warmth of the mat, the safety of his bed, but it had to be done. He slid open his pyjama drawer and pulled off his trousers. He felt the lower edge of his T-shirt style pyjama top. It wasn't wet, but in this light he couldn't really be sure what colour it was. He'd have to do a complete change or it might give the game away.

One by one he tugged his sleeves, drawing his arms back in. Now the tricky bit, he thought. He yanked his pyjama top up, but the neck snagged under his nose. The top was particularly tight, an old one. He pulled again with all his strength, but the darkness and the material in front of his face disorientated him. He fell backwards, back-pedalled to regain his balance, but he ran out of bedroom floor and crashed into his bookcase. He came to rest with his bottom on the floor, back pressed uncomfortably against the edges of hard books, while heavy stuff from the bookcase thudded to the floor around him.

There was silence, momentarily, then Tom's heart sank as footsteps sounded on the stairs. Somehow, he got his head out of his pyjamas, but there was no time to… Heavy footsteps came his way, too loud to be Mum's; Mum wouldn't want to wake Molly…

His bedroom door creaked inward, revealing Dad's black shape against the moonlit landing. The red glow of the landing nightlight was missing. Mum always switched it on so Tom could see to reach the bathroom. Why had she forgotten?.

Tom caught a waft of beer, beer and something stronger. He froze; perhaps Dad wouldn't see him in the dim light. Perhaps he was so drunk he'd just go to bed. Perhaps…

The light clicked on, painfully bright. Dad, still dressed, looked tired and red-eyed. "Should be in bed." He lurched in to the room, supporting himself against the doorframe with one hand.

"Where's Mum?" asked Tom. He eyed the space between Dad's leg and the doorframe, planning an escape to the safety of Mum's bedroom.

"Gone. Baby too. Bitch. Pissed off and left me on my own. Good riddance. Good riddance to bad rubbish." He looked down at Tom and his mouth curved in to something that was not quite a smile. "Couldn't carry *you* though, could she?" Dad tottered forward, leaving go of the doorframe and grabbing the wardrobe instead. The doorway was clearer now, but if Mum wasn't here, where would he run to? Even if the front door was unlocked, he was only wearing a vest; he couldn't go out like this.

Dad focussed groggily on the toys and books fallen to the floor. "Wos this mess?"

"Sorry, Dad. I tripped. I didn't mean to…."

"And what bloody time of night ja call this?" Dad bent down, knees buckling, and picked up a model rocket and its wire stand. "I was fassasleep. What time's this to be playing bastard games, aye?"

"Sorry, Dad. Wasn't playing. I tripped."

The metal rocket had snapped off the wire support. Dad tried feebly to join them back together. "*I* bought you this. Iss Apollo Thirteen. Bloody expensive this was, 's bastard broke now!" He flung the metal rocket at Tom but missed. "Clumsy lil sod. You've always been a clumsy lil… Where's your pyjamas?"

Tom shivered, clutching his shoulders. "Mum must have forgotten…"

Dad kicked the door shut behind him. Using the wardrobe for support, he swayed over to the open pyjama draw and picked up Tom's trousers. He grimaced as he sniffed them.

"You dirty lil…."

"Sorry, Dad...."

"You're a pansy. A filthy, bedwetting lil girl!" He staggered toward Tom, wee soaked pyjamas in one hand, and in the other, a six-inch metal spike recently separated from Apollo Thirteen.

Tom slid along the bookcase towards the door. My *Ow*s, he thought, I'm going to need them, but there was no sign of the paper bag. No sign of... panic jogged his memory, the *prescription*. Could he remember what was written on it? The Shopkeeper had made him repeat the difficult words. Dad's sweaty red face was halfway across the room now. Tom said it just the way the Shopkeeper told him to. He stumbled over the bigger words; they felt awkward on his tongue, strange and grown up, or like a foreign language. He wondered if he'd got them right.

Dad stopped still, staring at him.

"What'd you say?"

Tom's voice was drying up, draining to the bottom of his throat. More quietly this time, he repeated, "Monitor closely until suf... sufficient evidence to bring criminal pro... proceedings and secure conviction."

Like a magic trick, all the nasty red disappeared from Dad's face, and his arms flopped to his sides. He frowned and stared around the room searching for something. His gaze eventually returned to Tom. "Who told you to say that?"

"Nobody, Dad."

"Did your mother put you up to this?"

"No, Dad."

"If that bitch has gone to the police..." The colour crept back into Dad's face, "or if she's got you to wind me up, she's dead meat! Bastard dead meat, all of you!"

Gripping the spike, Dad lurched towards Tom. "Who told you to say that? Who *told* you?"

Tom was on his hands and knees crawling to the closed door. He reached the corner of the room and huddled, trying to shield his wounded head and side at the same time, difficult because they were on different sides of his body.

"Who... told... you.?" Dad was kicking him now. Dad's slippers made a dull slapping sound against Tom's shins.

"The man in The Ow Shop," shouted Tom. "The Shopkeeper."

"The *what*?" shouted Dad, kicking harder.

"It was the Shopkeeper!" said Tom, from underneath his arm. "It wasn't Mum, *honest*. It was the man from The Ow Shop."

"The Ow Shop?" Dad stopped kicking, then took a step backwards. "The *Ow* Shop?"

"Yes, Dad, honest. He told me to say it and wrote it down, and he was all black and blue and broken and..."

Dad faltered backwards, all jerky like a puppet. His legs touched the bed, and he sat down with a bump, still staring at Tom. "The *Ow* Shop?" Quieter this time.

"Yes, Dad. He's being punished see, for bad stuff he did to his kids a long time ago…"

Dad's face looked weird. It was caving in, melting. He lowered his face to his hands. Tom wondered if he was trying to stop it from collapsing.

Dad cried for an hour with his head in his hands, and an hour more while he packed. Tom asked him not to go, but it just made Dad worse. He said nothing the whole time, and then as he was going out the door he turned back for a moment. Tom asked if he'd forgotten something. Dad said, "No, I've remembered."

The Exchange Program
by
Madeline Bay

Madeline Bay is a wife and mother who dabbles in writing with the hope that her experience in fanfic will lead her to write the great American science fiction novel. Though forced to watch episodes of "The Twilight Zone" and "Star Trek" as a child, her love of reading SF, and later writing it, didn't blossom until Roger Zelany led her through Chaos and into Amber, when Ray Bradbury burned some books and took her to meet some Martians, and when Mercedes Lackey introduced her to a few Heralds to keep her imagination sharp. "The Exchange Program" is a tightly-focused science fiction tale with an ending that would make Rod Serling proud.

I must be insane. That's the only possible reason for why I agreed to this. I. Must. Be. Insane.

No, that's not it. I know why. I'm one of the millions of poor schmucks looking for a better life. Looking to climb out of the ghettos, the trailer parks and the homeless shelters. I'm one of the millions looking to get off government handouts and onto the government payroll. Or, get my family off them, anyway. They'll reap the immediate financial rewards, not me. At least that's what they told me, what the contract I signed said.

For the past six months I've undergone the testing: physical and psychological as well as criminal background checks. I've had my blood taken so many times I'm surprised I have any left. I've run thousands of miles on a treadmill, been asked if I hated my mother, spent days alone in a dark room, and had my family tree traced back beyond the roots, maybe to the first seed… I guess if I'm here, I must have passed.

I've trained hard, spent hours upon hours sitting in my room—my chamber, my future home and resting place—learning the codes, learning the lingo, learning to communicate. I haven't worked so hard since my first year of college. I passed all of those tests, too.

My designation is CE00304 - Consciousness Explorer 00304. I am one of the first five hundred Explorers.

And now that the time has come, as they're hooking me up to the life support machines, hooking me up to the computers—tubes and wires poking out from all parts of my body and brain—as I'm lying in my chamber, preparing for transfer, I tell myself again: I must be insane.

In the old days, astronauts were sent up in spaceships akin to large tin cans and hurtled out into space, toward distant planets and galaxies, hoping to find new life and resources, maybe even hoping to find the answers to our existence.

Those attempts were failures, of course. No other life existed within the distances the astronauts could travel. By the time they got anywhere, too much time had passed, the astronauts and their spacecrafts were ancient and decrepit, and any communication signals from them lost or forgotten when the government cancelled any more expeditions, basically shutting down the space program.

Five years ago everything changed: someone contacted *us*. A new species had found one of our long forgotten crafts. They used its communications system, somehow boosted with their own technologies, and sent us a message. They wanted to send one of their explorers to us, an ambassador.

Two years later, Bard arrived.

He had looked familiar at first, a lot like us. I never got to meet him personally, but he'd been on the videoscreens and audios. His voice was on the computers we Explorer Trainees used.

It was in the third month of training, when we got past the physical and mental readiness exercises and into the hardcore knowledge that I found out why he'd had that familiarity. It was because he wasn't a lot like us, but rather, in a sense, he *was* one of us. Or, his body was.

Bard's *consciousness* had been what had arrived. During the years between the first message and Bard's arrival, his people had sent more transmissions—instructions—enabling us to build the transceiver, the device that allowed his—and now our—people to download, for lack of a better word, a person's consciousness and transmit it across the galaxy! The government had found a volunteer, one of our scientists, to be a test subject, and downloaded Bard's consciousness into his body.

We've been told that it's a symbiotic relationship—that the scientist and Bard share the body equally. But symbiosis won't be my fate. I and the other four hundred and ninety-nine Consciousness Explorers are part of an exchange program. Once my consciousness is downloaded and my body vacant, one of the other consciousnesses sent to us will be downloaded into my body. When my consciousness arrives on Bard's planet, it will be downloaded into one of *their* Explorers' bodies.

We'll stay on their planet approximately one year. Then we'll be sent home and put back into our own bodies. The exchange of information will come from our experiences and theirs.

Suddenly I'm awake, gasping for air and opening my eyes. I'm alive!! I made it—I traveled across galaxies to another planet!

I don't know how to explain the physical feelings. I'm reminded of those times I'd had too much to drink and woke up with the spins. It seems as if I had gone to sleep in my chamber only minutes ago, yet here I am, wide-awake and galaxies away!

I can hear a beeping, probably a heart monitor, but it's different—it sounds too slow. I wish I could move more than my eyelids, see more of my surroundings, and see what I'm going to look like for the next year.

Someone talks. Although I had learned the language pretty well, it still sounds so foreign. I manage to move my head and catch my first glimpse of my temporary home and one of its people.

"Welcome to Earth, CE zero zero three zero four."

Race to the Summit
by
Paul Lamb

Paul Lamb has been in his garret, scribbling away for a long time. He has sometimes been accused of "committing journalism" and has more than five dozen free-lance feature articles published. His short documentary "On the Trail of the Red Buffalo" was produced for public television in Kansas City. Along with a bubbling stew of short stories, Lamb is working on a series of mystery novels and keeps a blog about the effort called "Lucky Rabbit's Foot."

"Race to the Summit" was born of the author's ongoing fascination with the literature of magical realism, a literature about a natural world that is too rich and alive to understand without relying on the fantastic and in which the unexpected is taken as perfectly sensible when it is encountered.

I'm as swift as a deer. As clever as a fox. I can run for miles like a coyote, and I have the eyes of a hawk. I knew I could beat them up the mountain, and they'd never know I was there. They'd never know, but I'd see what that rat was up to.

They took the old logging road. I was surprised Gabe drove his precious pickup on that mess of a road. He washes it in front of school, out in the parking lot where everyone can see him. Then he waxes it, and anyone who wants to can help him. But what he really wants is for everyone to see that his daddy gave him a brand new pickup for his 16th birthday to go along with his perfect teeth, his good looks and nice clothes, his easy A's, his popularity. Gabe likes everybody, and everybody likes Gabe.

Everyone but me. There was something odd about him. Nobody could be as good and nice and friendly as he seemed. He has another side that he's really good at hiding. Except from me. I have a sense about people.

The old logging road is the easiest way up, but it's indirect and takes time, winding along the side of the mountain with lots of switchbacks. Sometimes you have to get out to clear the rock falls that spill across the road. You have to creep over the ruts and washes so you don't bang the teeth out of your head. That's why no one much goes up there. It's just too hard to do. It was going to take them all morning to get to the summit, and Gabe's truck was going to get some scratches along the way. At least I hoped so.

But I'm a friend of the mountain. I know its secret ways, its hidden trails and turnings, its impassable thickets. My dad brought me up here when I was little, and now I come on my own. It's a caldera, an old collapsed volcano, with a valley wedged into one side of it. I've been all over the mountain, so I knew a faster way up. Even on foot I figured I could race to the summit before they did. It's a hard climb, and to beat them to the top I'd have to keep pushing one foot in front of the other. I could do it, though; I'd have sprinted up the whole mountain if I had to.

That's something Gabe can't do. He can't run very well. He can throw a football but not run a play. No one is better at the standing high jump, but he can't run hurdles. He'll go to the soccer games and cheer, but he's never tried out for the team, even though everyone knows he'd make it just because he's so popular. He can win a game of chess, but he'll trip when he gets up from the table. It's like he's a stranger to his own legs.

Not that it's really obvious. He covers it by acting reserved. As though he isn't going to dash around like an idiot, flying from this to that. I guess everyone just assumes it's his essential cool, but I see something more to it.

He was headed to the most secluded spot on the mountain. A place where you can be alone, an open meadow high above the valley where I've camped many times. You can see for miles there, and when the eagles are flying, it's like you're up in the air with them, soaring over the trees in the trackless sky.

He was taking Angie with him.

I don't know the right words to describe Angie. She's beautiful, of course, but in an otherworldly way. The silky strands of her hair dance on the slightest breeze and frame her eyes so big and blue. Her open smile. Her soft, clear voice. The kindness of her words. Every guy is school has fallen in love with her. I have. I would do anything for Angie.

She always waits for me after track practice, and we sit in the stands and just talk about anything. She asks how I did and remembers my times. She tells me I'm graceful on my feet, and I laugh because graceful describes everything about her. She likes my stupid jokes. She doesn't mind sitting next to me even though I stink after two hours of track practice. We talk about homework because we're in a couple of classes together. We talk about the people we know. About teachers. About college after high school. Sometimes after we've been talking and the sun's going down, I don't even recall what we've said exactly, but I know we had a nice time. And sometimes, she lets me hold her hand while we talk. She could have any guy in school for her boyfriend. Even Gabe. But for some reason, she pays attention to me.

When I can, I sit in on her choir practice. She has a good voice, and she works hard to do well. I've told her she has real talent, but she smiles. "You're just being nice, Sylvan," she tells me.

She doesn't laugh at my name like some people. She doesn't call me scrawny either. She says I'm compact and that's why I can run track so well. She always finds a way to compliment me. It takes my breath away.

When I hold her hand, I never want to let go. I feel her soft skin, and I'd like to touch her shoulder. Her cheek. I'd like to kiss her, but I'm too afraid. I'd like to feel her arms enfold me, to be in the sweet, sweet arms of a real angel.

She kissed me once. On the cheek. It was a quick peck before she ran off in her coltish way to her mother's car, but it was electric. I could feel her lips on my skin for the rest of the day.

I know I'm not good enough for her, but no one is. There are just some special people in the world above the rest of us. So why Angie would want to spend time with me is something I can't figure out.

But I was pretty sure I had Gabe figured out. Especially after I heard him talking to Angie in the auditorium.

I was crawling around in the orchestra pit looking for the extra mouthpiece to my trumpet when I heard someone come in. I can be as quiet as a mouse when I want, and something told me to be quiet then. I have a sense about these things.

From the floor of the pit I couldn't see who had come in, but whoever it was couldn't see me either. The person walked down the side aisle, putting a lot of effort into not making a sound, and I held my breath so I wouldn't either.

After maybe a minute, the door opened again, and someone else came in.

"Are we alone?" asked Gabe.

"Yes. Just us," answered Angie. I'd recognize her voice anywhere.

"Are you sure you're ready for this?"

"More than anything," she said. "I'm old enough."

My mind raced. I could picture the confident smile on his face, and I wanted to jump out of the pit and smash that snake over the head with a music stand.

"Still," she whispered. "I'm a little afraid."

"Don't worry," Gabe said, his voice full of silky reassurance. "It's perfectly natural. After tomorrow, you'll want to do it all the time."

"You have it all planned?"

"You know the meadow above the caldera, up on the mountain?" Gabe spoke with cool confidence. "No one will be around to see us. We can take all the time you want. Nothing will be the same afterward!"

"Okay," she said. "I'm ready."

"I'll pick you up at 9:00 tomorrow morning."

My heart sank when they left. You think you know someone, but you don't. Angie. So perfect. So pure. So much above all of that. And there she was, letting herself be seduced by that weasel Gabe with his million dollar smile and smooth words. And it wasn't even much of a seduction. It sounded businesslike, like he was fitting her into his schedule.

I didn't want to believe this about Angie. I wanted to cry. I wanted to scream. I wanted to pull her back from the edge of the cliff.

I realized maybe I was wrong about her.

Later that afternoon, when I could think straight, I figured out why Gabe was dragging her all the way up the mountain. I'm sure he told her it would be romantic, and that eased her past her reluctance. With the vault of the blue sky overhead and the dense green forest around them, with the meadow brimming with wildflowers and the view of a hundred miles, it's certainly a setting for magnificent moments. And they would be alone. She could be as carefree as she wanted with no one around to shake a finger.

Part of me didn't want to believe that she was going to be just another of Gabe's conquests. I still hoped that she was better than that. That inside her was enough strength to resist a guy like Gabe. Which is why I hustled up the mountain. I had to see for myself. I had to know if Angie was different from everyone else.

The upper reaches of the valley are inaccessible to all but the hardiest adventurers. Hardly anyone goes there, and aside from the eagles, only jets ever pass over it. The meadow is near the summit, where the caldera is deep but not wide. Across from it is a ledge I sometimes sit on. You can see all the way down the valley from there, but the overhanging trees keep the sun from getting too hot on the rocks. More importantly, you get a clear view of the meadow but can't be seen from the other side.

That's where I headed. I knew I had to get to the ledge before Gabe and Angie reached the meadow. I spotted Gabe's red truck a couple of times far below me, picking its way up the old logging road. I hustled because I wanted to have enough time to catch my breath when I got to the ledge, enough time to pick the best vantage point.

I thought about bringing binoculars, but that seemed too creepy. I was sure I'd understand soon enough what was going on.

I reached the ledge at midday and let myself take the rest I'd needed, devouring a granola bar and a bottle of water. The air was thin up there, but I was used to it. Across the valley, the meadow was quiet. No one had arrived yet, and for a while I hoped that Gabe had given up the difficult ascent and decided to postpone his business for another time.

Time passed. Far down the valley, through the crystal clear air, I saw a bald eagle circling. A pair of blue mountain jays argued in a tree nearby. Below my feet were the dark green tips of the treetops. It was a long way down from where I sat, and though I've never been afraid of heights, I started to feel dizzy. Maybe I was a little dehydrated. I backed away from the edge and found a spot in the shade where I still had a view of the meadow.

My fears were confirmed. Across the valley, I saw the familiar red of Gabe's pickup come through the trees toward the meadow. When he emerged into the open grass, I saw streaks of mud painted up the sides of the truck, and I knew he'd be washing it in front of school on Monday. Everyone will ask how it had gotten so muddy, and he'll tell them. He'll tell them who was with him, too. And he'll wink as he tells them.

I stayed back in the shade and watched. The two of them didn't get out right away. They were talking. Maybe Angie was having last minute jitters!

Gabe's door opened, and a second later, Angie came out the other side. They walked down the meadow to the precipice, and I saw her look at the valley. It was obviously the first time she'd ever seen it because she took a step back. Gabe took her hand, though, and brought her forward again. He pointed down the valley and up in the air. All around. Maybe he spotted an eagle. They talked a little more. Then he lead her back to the top of the meadow.

And it began. He didn't even bring a blanket. The goat. He just pulled his shirt over his head and tossed it aside. Angie hesitated, but Gabe gestured for her to follow, smiling at her. A moment later she pulled off her top, too, and folded it before setting it down in the grass. Her white sports bra offered a bit of modesty, but it was clear even to my desperate heart what was going to happen. I wanted to turn and go, but the smallest part of me still held hope.

Yet Gabe didn't approach her. There they were, the two of them, half naked just a few feet apart, but it looked like they were frozen. And then Gabe did something I couldn't understand. He raised his arms high above his head and arched backward. He looked like he was stretching, but he stopped and encouraged Angie to do the same.

And then? I still don't believe it. It couldn't happen. But it did.

Gabe... changed.

Out of his back sprang two immense wings. Like a bird. He flapped them a few times, stretching them.

A moment later, Angie grew wings too.

I wasn't dehydrated. I wasn't dizzy. I was wide awake and staring at two people with feathered wings on their backs.

Gabe took Angie's hand, and together they ran down the meadow toward the cliff. Their wings flapped, and then over they went. And they were flying. Gabe and Angie were flying above the valley.

A few flaps of their wings and they were rising into the air. I lost them in the branches above my head, and quick as a squirrel, I scrambled up the tree and onto a branch so I could see them again. Why hadn't I brought binoculars?

They soared together for a while. But Gabe pulled away and rose higher. Then he was rocketing down past Angie, only to pull up and do it again.

Angie seemed content just to glide on the wind, flapping her strong wings occasionally to gain more height, leaving all of the flashy stuff to Gabe, who'd obviously done this before. It was a flying lesson. He was teaching Angie how to fly. Nothing *would* be the same for her after this.

They flew far down the valley, and I had to inch out farther on the branch to keep them in sight. But they turned around and came flying back soon enough. Up and down. In circles and loops. It looked effortless. Of course Gabe is a stranger to his legs! He's a creature of the air. And so is Angie. She really is an angel.

And she pays attention to me!

I don't know how long they stayed up there. It may have been minutes or hours. I couldn't stop staring at something that made no sense and made perfect sense.

I might have perched on the branch until they decided to return to the world of the earth-bound people if the branch hadn't snapped. I had to grab frantically or I would plummet into the valley.

I must have screamed. I must have kept screaming. Kicking my feet while I hung there. Too scared to crawl back on the springy branch that had saved me from a fatal plunge. But my strength was gone. I couldn't hold on. Or maybe I didn't. Maybe I lost my grip and fell.

Angie plucked me out of the air and enfolded me in her arms. I clung to her, afraid to slip from her strong embrace.

"Shame on you. Now you know my secret," she laughed. "Hold on tight!" She flapped her powerful wings and sent the two of us soaring into the sky. I could hardly breathe as the crisp air rushed past us.

I didn't care. I was in the sweet, sweet arms of an angel.

Adam Of Argotha
by
C.S. Larsen

C.S. Larsen, an award winning author of short stories and novels, including the Magic Krystal *and* Marvin Archibald Trekker *series, currently lives in Rochester Minnesota with his wife Nancy and two boys Zach and Alex. His contribution to Beacons of Tomorrow, "Adam of Argotha" stems from wondering where the destiny of humanity might lead it, and it speculates on one possible outcome.*

The carnage was immense. Nothing remained of the Village Argotha. One would have thought an entire battalion of Cybernetic Kroll had stormed through town, searching for their lost Epith Talisman. I walked among the fallen buildings as thick, black plumes of smoke rose into the atmosphere. The air smelled of smashed concrete and cindered beams. I wondered what value there was in all the death and destruction littering Mother Earth. I wondered what she thought about, wasting away in all the misery…

The demolished Village of Argotha could have been the work of the Demigorths, with their spirits transformed into behemoth mastodons. The large four-legged creatures with jutting ivory tusks were not natural; they were clones hundreds of years old, created by man from genetic material thousands of years older. The mastodons had no way of preventing the Demigorths—fiendish spirit-creatures that exist as vaporous entities—from possessing them. No creature could resist their evil will. Demigorths could be absorbed into more solid forms at the molecular level. Back in the time of the Old Way, people knew this as demonic possession. The possession terrified witnesses, but it was even more frightful for the one who experienced it. I had survived both situations, and neither were pleasant.

Sadly, the Village of Argotha's was not destroyed by Cybernetic Kroll or by mastodons possessed by Demigorths. *These ruins were made by my own, human hands.*

I still recall the name given to me at birth — Adam. The name Adam means 'earth', which fit, being that I existed as the last naturally born creature on Earth. The irony was surreal, what with Adam being both the first and last human.

Around the time of my birth, Mother Earth's life force still subsisted, but weakly. In the centuries since, her lifeblood dwindled to such an extent that I became her last hope, her final chance to save the natural order of things.

Of course, the idea of 'natural' meant nothing since the Point of Schism, when humanity split between Nobloods—cybernetic mutated beings of recombined DNA—and Purebloods like me, whose unmodified DNA was formed the old fashioned way, guided by the hands of Mother Earth.

After the Point of Schism, the Purebloods knew they would have a difficult struggle. To embark on a purist's journey in the name of Mother Earth was a futile and hopeless dream. When the fighting began, all natural life was diminished. With so few natural things left, the word 'natural' became an obscure concept. In time, only the most ardent followers of the Old Way even understood what the term really meant.

The Old Way centered on how Mother Earth created living things. Everything on Earth breathed her pattern of existence. We all lived for her; she manifested the desire within us to sing, dance, and love.

Some thought of her as a God. I could not. I did not believe in supreme beings. With all I had witnessed, I could find no room in my heart for such a divine concept. I found no evidence of Him, and without evidence, I could not believe. I watched as all things natural disappeared, and wondered, if God existed, would He have let Mother Earth and her children die?

In time my brothers fell, and I became the last Pureblood, the last living descendant of Adam. The last thing created by Mother Earth. My people no longer lived, and no other creatures on Earth could call Her 'mother'. Earth became a twisted and withered landscape fabricated of counterfeit wood and rusting metal. Beings of imitation life roamed the land, searching for us Pureblood outcasts, bent on wiping out any proof of our existence.

I had no intention of becoming a faded memory. I waged war against the twisted machine of wretched life. I fought alone, battling an enemy with seemingly infinite strength and number. Fear ate into my stomach, but I ignored the pain and concentrated on the multitudes intent on killing me, on snuffing out the soul of Mother Earth.

Armageddon erupted. Mother Earth's final battle had come, and I, the last Pureblood, fought against a sea of mechanized life. Mother Earth needed a godlike warrior, one ready and willing to save her natural order. Guided by Her power and beauty, I welcomed the challenge.

It comforted me to know that my horrific destruction harmed no Purebloods, yet I still felt compassion for the others, the Nobloods, which I hunted. Even though they were not pure, they still had spirit. Terrible and wretched they were, but even an ounce of spirit should be worth saving.

I struggled with that thought, but not for long. All pity drained from my body as I remembered what they had done to my people during the Clonactic Holocaust, when our two races had battled for dominion.

We each had our own motives, our own ideas of freedom and happiness. The Purebloods, unswerving in their endless love, campaigned to save Mother Earth. The Nobloods focused on destroying anything pure, anything that was of the Old Way. They were filled with jealously, realizing how Mother Earth loved only Purebloods. Even worse, knowledge that they had once been pure, that we had shared a common ancestor, enraged them.

Like apprentice to master, the Nobloods believed they were the next leap in evolutionary development, that Purebloods had become obsolete. The massacre of the Clonactic Holocaust brought death to Mother Earth's children; Pureblood young and old felt the blade all the same. Their screams fell on deaf ears. No pity existed in the hearts of the Nobloods; they killed like beings without souls. But I could not believe that. All things created have souls, no matter how evil.

I alone survived and did not understand why. The satisfaction of death would have been better than surviving to watch the Nobloods live a grotesque mockery of a natural life. They tried to feel the same warmth and love bestowed upon the Pureblood, but they could never capture that beauty. Mother Earth only gave it to the pure beings she created, and the Nobloods had forsaken their purity long ago.

Besides, I intended to give the Nobloods no chance to receive Her love. The end of the Purebloods signaled the beginning of my personal vendetta, with the battle at Argotha the ultimate culmination of my vengeance.

I couldn't help but to feel some sympathy for their dead. I justified the bodies among the ruins of Argotha as 'casualties of war,' avoiding the pain that twitched deep within my heart. I walked among the victims muttering 'casualties of war' and 'justifiable deaths' in a rhythmic, macabre cadence. My morbid conversation continued, consciousness picking at my thoughts like a crow on a carcass.

War is Hell… To kill is Hell… To be killed is Hell…

I shook the weak thoughts off and remembered that to be killed myself, and to have Mother Earth lose my ideology was by far the greatest Hell of all.

Being the last Pureblood had its benefits. Rich, tingling power emanated from within me, energy that came from Mother Earth's spirit. In the Old Way, back before the Point of Schism, there were billions of Purebloods, each with his own power, or Chi as they called it. At the time, no one realized that the total quantity of Chi created an incredible volume of power, and now, with all other Purebloods gone, I had it all within me. With the immense power of Chi, it would have been easy to obliterate the towns in which the Nobloods lived, but I worried that such destruction would cause too much harm to Mother Earth.

Making sure the Nobloods did not catch me posed an even greater problem. I spent most of my time concealed, hidden from the unnatural creatures devoted to killing me, while I learned to harness my powers. I struck and struck and struck again, but no matter how many I destroyed, more appeared to replace them. That's why I gave up on my plan to exterminate them. A far more fruitful arrangement had to be devised: one to incapacitate them, to bring them to an inevitable extinction.

Seven hundred years passed since my birth, and I attributed my taste of immortality to the Chi energy. For most of my life, however, I breathed the stagnant, binding air of a dying Mother Earth. With my long life, I spent centuries learning about my enemy—Earth's enemy.

The Nobloods were composed of three main species: Kroll, Demigorths, and Morticon Villi. The Cybernetic Kroll were like bacteria, bombarding and overwhelming with their vast numbers, while the Demigorths were more analogous to viruses, with the ability to morph and use host bodies. Most deadly were the Morticon Villi, a carnivorous group that infiltrated the body, secretly taking over and devouring you from the inside out. Like a cancer. None of these creatures had initially been created to destroy life, but through the inept planning of humanity they had evolved into evil beings.

The Cybernetic Kroll's dependence on the Epith Talisman proved their undoing, but my battle for the talisman was by no means a simple task.

During one of many interrogations of a Kroll, I stumbled upon an artifact of information. The young Kroll, around ninety years old, had fresh circuitry with few patches. Machinery covered portions of his left leg and arm, as well as the entire left side of his head. Thick, synthetic red hair covered his head, thinning out as it reached his lower extremities. The freshness of his cybernetic modules provided an excellent opportunity to acquire clean data.

The Kroll did not survive the mind probe, not with the intense surge of Chi I had to send through his circuitry. But his death was justifiable. Through it, I learned of the Epith Talisman, a unique device central to the Kroll's processing power. All communication funneled through the device, with every Kroll accessing it for decisions.

For twenty-three years, I sought information about the Epith Talisman: its location, its power, and its reason for existing. After hundreds of mind probes and research at a heavily guarded communication hub, I determined that the device was a small processing unit. Despite its size, it produced significant amounts of energy and allowed the Kroll to transmit ultra-high frequency signals throughout their collective consciousness. Its power came from a tiny black hole. The Kroll had created the miniature black hole during their experimentation with the sun. With it, they learned how to manipulate gravity itself, creating tiny wormholes, hovercraft, and other unearthly creations.

The Epith Talisman energized the Kroll, fortifying them with a central life force. Without it they would be lost to individual thoughts and actions. I could not discover how to destroy it, but I concluded that obtaining it would allow me at least marginal control over them.

Planning such a thievery took many years. The Kroll had buried the Epith Talisman deep in the Thaltomi Mines, and navigating those dark tunnels nearly ended my life. Darkness and creatures unknown to me were a constant threat, but none posed as much difficulty as Gaulklen Warriors: a mammoth sized Kroll subspecies charged with guarding the Epith Talisman. My research indicated there were three of them, but their powers were unknown. All I knew was that they had a direct connection with the talisman, which ensured them unrestricted and non-fluctuating power.

My descent into the first layer of tunnels, the Faldtui Myldra, concluded with minimal confrontation, as I had detailed documents mapping the rooms, traps, and guard posts. I knew exactly what lurked around every turn, and every wandering Kroll met an unfortunate demise from my Tuchya Chi, a mind-scrambling blow that overcharged their circuitry and fried their synapses.

It took only a few hours to reach Raltui Myldra, the second level of the Thaltomi Mines. At this point, my information was no longer reliable, but I did have a device fabricated from the remains of a Kroll I had interrogated that would lead me to the Epith Talisman. The device received signals from the Talisman, and I had modified it into a crude tracking device.

As I descended, strange creatures crawled from the walls, until it seemed as if the tunnels themselves writhed with motion. At first I tried to avoid them, but they followed me, and in ever greater numbers. Later I learned that these were Raltui, giant ant-like creatures created by the Kroll to guard the tunnels, blind except for the ability to sense Purebloods.

At first I pushed past the few blocking my path, but soon the Raltui filled the tunnel, covering every cubic foot of space. Worse yet, they grabbed me, biting and clawing at my flesh. I was forced to take drastic action. I clapped my hands together, focusing my Chi and creating a thunderous shockwave. The vibrations loosened rocks, sending them down on top of the Raltui, but it also alerted the Kroll to my presence, something I had hoped to avoid.

I readied an energy field to block the tumbling boulders, further draining my Chi, and with the Raltui stunned, I concentrated a small plasma beam—similar to the one I would later use to destroy Argotha—and sliced the Raltui in half.

The effort drained me, but the surviving Raltui kept their distance, and I successfully navigated the tunnels, arriving at Gaulklen Myldra, the deepest and final level of the mines.

Gaulklen Myldra was a large chamber, with the center glowing from the energy emitted by the Epith Talisman. As I walked closer, I saw the three Gaulklen Warriors hardwired to the talisman. They watched me approach but did not move, confident in their ability to protect the talisman. A plume of bright white light flowed up from the talisman, emitting charged photons and producing a soft, vibrating glow on the back of each warrior.

I walked to within a meter of the nearest Gaulklen Warrior, only then did it shift its crystallized eyes at me, firing a charged look full of overloaded stamina. Its expressionless face stood twice my height from the floor, and its platinum arms folded in defiance. A golden cap covered most of its head, with brass wire protruding out from the top, curling down behind to the base of the Epith Talisman. My intuition told me to sever the link.

Reaching out with lightning speed, I ripped the warrior's helmet off, nearly taking its head with it. The Gaulklen Warrior, startled by my swiftness, stood motionless, gawking at me, confused as to how it could have lost its helmet so easily. With the hardwired link broken, the warrior lost any ability other than random hand slicing and leg kicking. I tucked and rolled, jabbing hard with both fists into its groin. The warrior tumbled over, convulsing on the floor. I smashed its head down, and then wrenched it sideways until the crack of its upper vertebrae sounded.

The other two Gaulklen Warriors shifted, one on each side of the talisman, their faces unmoved by their comrade's demise. I lunged at the nearest, but this Gaulklen was ready for me, and grabbed my hands even faster than I could move. With its grip tightening, it lifted me off the ground. Soon the hydraulic power of its arms would crush my wrists, pinching off my hands and rendering them useless.

As my wrists began to crack under the cybernetic grip, I felt a bone-chilling screech swelling up inside of me: the Baraku Chi. The screech spewed forth from my lungs, sending an intense resonant frequency directly into the Gaulklen's cybernetic arms, shattering them and sending metal showering throughout the chamber.

As I lay there nearly unconscious, the warrior stumbled, not sure how to react without arms. The Baraku Chi had cracked the warrior's chest plate, allowing thick, green lubricant to trickle down to the floor. With one final step, the warrior slipped, pulling the umbilical cord from its helmet. It collapsed, convulsing like its companion, and I stumbled toward it, stepping on its neck, making it jerk one last time before lying motionless.

With both wrists broken and most of my energy drained from the Baraku Chi, I watched as the third Gaulklen Warrior approached. The warrior reached for my midsection with its massive arms. As I felt myself pinched in half, I saw my life pass by. Hundreds of years, a million snapshots of life, scrolled through my awareness, from recent images to the ones buried deep in the memories of my distant past. Only when I saw the view of Earth from hundreds of years ago, in my childhood before the Nobloods tainted the land, did I remember why I was here.

I existed as Mother Earth's last chance. I could not fail her. She needed me, or her essence would die. In the moment before death, an epiphany charged my mind, giving me a flickering chance to defeat the last Gaulklen Warrior.

I concentrated on the warrior. I flooded its awareness with my being and memories, making it live my own existence. At first, the warrior shook its head and shifted from side to side, annoyed at the confusion. Then, its grip loosened. Soon after, it dropped me. I continued to send visions of purity and natural life into it. A few seconds later, the warrior's head began to sizzle and smoke, my telepathic energy frying the circuitry within. Then it exploded, sending metal fragments and a violent shockwave through the chamber, knocking me unconscious.

When I awoke, I found my body scorched, skinless and charred. My sight had been lost, destroyed along with my eyes. I was not concerned; the power of my pure blood intensified my awareness. I no longer needed eyes, and my other senses were a thousand times sharper. With the Epith Talisman in my possession, I walked past the Kroll in the Thaltomi Mines without incident. They did not dare attack me for fear of me destroying their precious talisman. And with the talisman removed, their drive to destroy me evaporated into a sea of confusion.

With the Kroll incapacitated, I next focused on the destruction of the Demigorths, a task that proved to be nearly impossible. I could not imagine how to kill something that lived as spirit, let alone capture one for interrogation. Nevertheless, after countless years of reflection, my thoughts aligned and I developed a plan.

I decided to fight fire with fire, or in this case, to capture spirit, I realized I had to use spirit. But to do that, I had to learn what spirit was. Religion had never been a part of my vocabulary; I did not believe in God, and I did not partake in anything that involved His worship. Mother Earth fulfilled my need for the ideology of supreme beings. All spirit transcended from Her.

For decades I contemplated the nature of spirit, the essence of the soul. I meditated on how life transformed from spirit to body. The feelings I discovered were foreign to me and were not something I wanted to accept. I realized that all things within this world stemmed from spirit, both good and evil. I struggled with the concept of the Nobloods having spirit. I could not fathom their kind having feelings like love. I was confident their lives had no room for such beauty.

To destroy the Demigorths, I had to become spirit myself. To attack and capture spirit meant that I must understand my own spirituality. I was not prepared for such an ordeal. The awakening of my spirit nearly killed me; the experience wrenched my heart, creating illogical desires and unreasonable feelings. Once my spirit awoke, I saw the duality in life—the yin and yang of opposites that allowed one to place judgment of right and wrong, good and bad, love and hate.

Before my spirit awoke, I saw everything in black and white, not in the dualistic sense, but in the sense that everything had its place and reason. Doubt about the reality of life never entered my mind. After the awakening, all I saw were different shades of gray. I questioned everything, and nothing escaped my inquisition. For years I tried to realign my thinking, to adapt to this new spirituality. It was painful. The feelings were immense, but in order to survive, I had to deal with them.

I concluded that my spirit had far too much power and had to be controlled. I cornered it with the strength of my mind, blanketing it in deep, commanding thoughts, subduing it and removing it from the realm of my normal consciousness. This allowed me to continue without being interrupted by confusing thoughts. Clarity once again filled my mind, and with my newly gained spiritual knowledge, I readied myself for battle with the Demigorths.

As it turned out, the battle with the Demigorths concluded more easily than with the Cybernetic Kroll. As I suspected, spirit was their Achilles' Heel. Each spirit channeled into others, making a continuous network, accessible from any one Demigorth.

Finding out how to attack a spirit proved to be the most difficult task. In the end, the answer had been with me all along. The Epith Talisman still maintained its connection to the Kroll, and I could use it to attack the Demigorth. But to unleash the Kroll's spirit, I needed to come into contact with a Demigorth, an experience which proved both terrifying and painful.

As I indicated earlier, I was once possessed by a Demigorth. This was no accident or quick of fate; I courted the possession. Their ability to manipulate another's body intrigued me. Perhaps it was a trait I could mimic. My fascination with spirit tempted me into the dangerous confrontation, and the curiosity nearly killed me.

Searing pain shot through my body as I felt my spirit being pushed out. My body trembled with convulsions as it momentarily lay empty of spirit. If it were not for the Demigorth's inexperience, and my keen ability to control my own soul, I would have died. The most terrifying part was when our minds united. I caught a glimpse of their reality, one full of love and splendor from years ago. I saw their beauty and how it was ripped from the world by the likes of my own kind. The realization that we Purebloods might be at fault for the sickness covering Mother

Earth saddened me. The Demigorth's memories also fortified my belief that even they had souls, which made my task all the more difficult.

With the knowledge of my previous possession, I prepared to offer myself to another Demigorth. At the moment our minds united, I unleashed the Kroll's spirit from the Epith Talisman. The Demigorth did not expect such an intense exchange of spirit, and they were quickly overthrown, or I should say merged. The spirit of the Kroll combined with the Demigorth, and a chain reaction flowed from one to the next.

The Demigorth possessing me ignited, crackling in a brief but blazing fire and ending in a charcoal ash drifting silently to the ground. In the distance, I saw other Demigorth erupt in fiery blasts as well. I had won.

Although victorious, my heart was burdened with what I had done. I wandered aimlessly for years, wondering if my actions were justifiable. Was it my right to annihilate an entire race of creatures? Had the Demigorth deserved this? Wearily, I concluded that I had no choice but to move forward with my plan, focusing all the energy I had on destroying the Morticon Villi. Once they were defeated, Mother Earth would live again, fertile with natural offspring.

I remember my first experience with the Morticon Villi — it ended in disaster. It occurred around my two hundredth birthday, when I was still unaware of their power and abilities. Of course, they knew everything about me; they understood who I was even before I did. They even recognized that one day I would end up as their most bitter enemy, and they knew that they had to destroy me before I became too strong.

The Morticon Villi were tall, slender shadow-beings, light enough they could drift in the wind. They could shift their shape at will, but a far greater threat to me centered around their devastating touch, which transferred a small portion of cancerous venom. The venom generated a carnivorous tumor that consumed their prey from the inside out. I know this firsthand; I suffered through that unfortunate ordeal.

My Chi slowed the poison, but I still would have died if not for the spirit of my Pureblood brethrens. When first infected, I thought it a simple flu virus, and I turned to Mother Earth for help, asking her for a remedy. She understood the truth of my infection and provided me with the location of healing herbs, which I gathered and made into an elixir.

By the time I finished the potion, the tumor had grown to considerable size. The elixir had an immediate and severe reaction, and I fell to the ground almost as soon as I gulped down the contents. In my delirium, I wondered whether the potion or the virus had sickened me.

After four months, my health remained grim. My breath, raspy and shallow, hardly filled my lungs, and my heart beat in a weak, sporadic pattern. I suspected that my immortality had been cut short, and that I would soon join the ranks of all other Purebloods.

While I waited for my life to end, I saw streamers of white light bending and curving through the sky like energized strings of confetti. I wondered for a moment what they could be, and then a thought trumpeted in my mind. *Purebloods!* A warm smile filled my face for the first time in months. I understood that each strand of energy represented the spirit of a fellow Pureblood. Their spirits were still alive and needed my help.

I shook death from my body and absorbed the energy from the strings, enjoying the splendor of my twinkling brethren. Then the energy strands vanished, but my memory of them did not.

The Morticon Villi would never attack me so easily again. I would attack them first, by destroying their breeding grounds — the Village of Argotha, where the Morticon Villi gathered once a year to praise Earth and give thanks for their existence.

I winced at the thought: that they felt they were part of Mother Earth, that they believed they were some form of natural being created by Earth and there to protect it. Nothing natural dwelled within them. They lived with tainted DNA, altered by humans long ago. I felt embarrassed by the knowledge that my ancestors created the Morticon Villi and all the other abominations that covered Earth. How could we Purebloods have been so wrong? Why did we mess with Mother Earth's perfect plan? Why couldn't we have been happy with the perfect blood that ran through our bodies?

The time to destroy Argotha had arrived. I could not bear to see Mother Earth desecrated any longer by the incestuous breeding of the Morticon Villi. I walked to the center of town, thwarting the advancement of any Morticon with an energized mesh of steel and recombined DNA. The mesh was as impure as them, but it no longer mattered to me. I only focused on the destruction of unnatural life, regardless of how unnatural I became in the process.

Soon, hundreds of Morticon Villi threw themselves at my mesh like a sacrificial plea for redemption, but there was no room in my heart for compassion. I readied myself for the final charge, focusing the energy of my Spaldyri Chi on the foundations of the buildings. With a deafening cry my lips spoke the words of vanquish; I screamed the Spaldyri Chi and the earth beneath me split. Within seconds the buildings were gone, and the Morticon Villi within ceased to exist.

Argotha was not only the breeding ground of the Morticon Villi, but also my birthplace. Intense anger boiled deep within me as I walked through the debris and flattened buildings of my former home. The anger came not from the desecration of my homeland by the Morticon Villi, but more from my own actions. The walls I had knocked down had contained the only good memories remaining in me. I had not only destroyed the Morticon Villi's future; I had destroyed my past.

With the leaders of the Morticon Villi dead, those remaining masses were helpless. I searched out the subordinate leaders and annihilated them. Within a few decades, the Morticon Villi ceased to exist. I had achieved my goal. I now had full control of Mother Earth.

I stood in the ruins of Argotha, decades after my destruction of it, waiting for the beauty of Mother Earth to unfold. I hoped it would start at my birthplace and spread forth across the Earth. But the beauty and purity I longed for never blossomed. I looked to the sun and hoped it would once again shine with its bright orange color, but the dull, scarlet haze continued. I was sickened of the crimson horizon and looked to the ground, where I hoped for signs of new growth. I found nothing but the warped shrapnel and perverted plastics made by Nobloods from an untrue era and ill begotten time.

As the years passed, I realized the land was not getting better. I looked across the dimly lit horizon and no longer saw a twisted and demented planet. I saw a dying one.

Mother Earth was dying, and the fault lay in my own hands.

I wondered how I could have been so wrong. In my folly, I had destroyed the planet I loved and had sworn to protect. Thinking that a solution may yet have existed, an unnatural and perverted stone not yet unturned, I scoured the planet for any clue that might help remedy the death of Mother Earth, but She continued Her downward spiral. Soon She would look no different from Mars, a barren waste of a landscape not even suitable for Cybernetic Kroll.

Millennia passed in agonizing slowness, until nothing remained except for cold, dry sands and wasted years. Mother Earth had cleaned house and left. I no longer felt her spirit emanating from the planet. I alone remained, sitting in the dust, watching the wind roll the tumbling remains of a metallic past across the desolate landscape.

I had won the game, survived all the atrocities thrown at me, yet I did not feel gleeful or joyous in my victory. Instead, the Pureblood within me felt empty, devoid of any semblance of purity. Only anger remained. What good had all my actions accomplished? What point had there been in surviving? To be alive and not to live was like living constantly on the verge of death, but my immortality denied me the dignity of true death.

Not that death would offer respite. My transition to the afterlife would most likely not be to Heaven, but rather a descending spiral into the lowest ranks of Hell.

I had killed Mother Earth.

Yet, even Hell felt grander than eternity on a dead planet. For the first time in my long life I hoped that perhaps God did exist, hoped that He would forgive me and deliver me from the self-fabricated abomination I had made of life.

I pondered my existence for centuries, wondering why I lived. All my explorations, from pole to equator to pole again, turned up empty and shallow. Nothing resolved the conflict within me. I sought resolution, but only found dark and numbing emptiness.

Then, in the last instant of my desperate thinking about God, between knowing Him and believing in Him, I saw in the sky a twinkling light. Was it God's Angel Raphael coming to rescue me? Was it the Dark Riders from Hell sent by Satan to claim his final prize? I watched and waited for my final condemnation.

The fiery comet descended from space, screaming and crackling in a flaming apocalyptic chorus, thundering sonic booms as it fell into the distant horizon. The blast knocked me to the ground even though I stood a thousand kilometers away. I watched an intense, super-heated wind spread across the landscape. Within seconds it was upon me, engulfing me in a river of plasma. Would this be my end? Would I finally sail into death's harbor?

The blazing inferno hit me with a force that stunned not only my body, but also my soul. I lay there, happy to see my end, my body ripped apart, layer-by-layer, until it ceased to exist.

Yet awareness remained. I watched the world from above, my spirit drifting over the unfolding chaos. I transcended my body and witnessed the magnificent birth of a new Earth. It was like a two-dimensional Big Bang, where light and energy stretched over the earth, heating it and rejuvenating it with new life.

Millions of years passed, and life sprang forth just as it had done in the Old Way. But now we lived in the New Way. I say 'we' because the New Earth teems with bold and vibrant life. It swims through the New Ocean, crawls upon the New Land, and flies across the New Sky.

I searched for but could not find the mother of this New Earth, and I wondered how life could exist without a mother? Then, a wide, continent-sized smile spread across my spirit face. My anger from the eons vaporized and was replaced by a new understanding, knowledge, and wisdom.

I was the New Mother Earth.

WARM, Incorporated
by
Sheri Fresonke Harper

Sheri Fresonke Harper is a poet and science fiction writer from Renton, WA. Her stories have appeared in Tabloid Purposes IV; Dragons, Knights, and Angels; Whispering Spirits; *and* Kinships. *Her contribution to this anthology, "WARM, Incorporated," is a true science fiction exploration into the nature of sentience and sacrifice, in a setting that juxtaposes the familiar and friendly with religious and political turmoil.*

Despite myself, I, Izen Eres, have called Ariadne Mariana back to my city.

As I wait, breathless as any gawky teenager, Jerusalem comes to life. Dawn rises like smoke over the clay plain. The city gains voice with the sweeping of thousands of servitors cleaning refuse from walkways.

From my panoramic scope atop the twin 150-foot towers of government, flickers of train traffic appear along the star of converging MagLev lines. Soon come the mullahs' calls, the plaintive horns of Jerico, mock battle sounds from Masada.

Vendors arrive from the eight housing districts. They encroach like an army toward old town and halt shy of the nuclear-hardened dome made of titanium-rich moon glass three-feet-thick at the base but thinning as it rises nearly a mile to cover over a hundred miles of city. The vendors set up shop—some with scarves, some with paintings, some with food, others with religious icons. The dome's six-foot-wide support struts conveniently separate each shop. The usual smells of hot oil, sugar, popcorn, and sautéed onions taint the air.

The next wave of trains brings the pilgrims I've invited to World Alliance of Religions Metroplex—WARM, Incorporated, to whose business I've dedicated my existence. We service over ten million souls each year, regulated only by the World Courts. Each person qualifies for a one-week visit, except where I take a hand and allow more.

My guests enter through the security portals. They are weighed, their hands and retinas scanned. Any changes in the last month of their personal data are compared against database records and are flagged as a security alert. My robot sniffers trap the air they pass through and chemically analyze it for all known forbidden substances—drugs, radioactive materials, metals, explosives, diseases.

She has not arrived.

Impatience in the morning hours brings me to this vista, high in the glass corset of hallways and offices comprising the civic center. The moniker corset comes from the many glass bridges crossing between the floors of the matched buildings. The northern tower houses the government of Israel, the southern one, New Palestine's. The view reveals burn marks left in the desert from the Sear War, when lasers slashed down warheads and wiped out battalions. Not so very long ago, the rivers ran with blood. Even now, a few of the outlying buildings show meltdown.

I do what I have done since the first days when my spy cameras gathered information along the high-walled Via Dolorosa, atop the twisted forest among graves on the Mount of Olives, in the church-spire dominated heart of Bethlehem, and along the few cars traveling the length of Jericho Road. I protect the interests of The Cabal, those nameless benefactors from around the globe who financed this complex. I do so ever more efficiently and with ever broadening scope. When finished, I take my ease and scan through digital records from the cameras watching around the clock. I ensure the safety of my domain, aided by my counterparts—Whith Olds, head of finance; Chronos Chitling, head of transportation; and a host of subsidiaries.

And I cheat.

I often find myself reviewing the old record of my first meeting with Ariadne, feeling very much like a fly trapped between two panes of glass, unable to avoid my own reflections, unable to escape.

Ariadne was seventeen, willowy with long dark hair and even then she had a charismatic presence. I noticed her arrive at the dome's side gate, a mere three-person bubble rather than one of the three main two-hundred person jigsaw gates denoted with a Christian cross, Jewish star or Muslim crescent moon. At different times on the tape she appeared at each of the main shrines—the golden dome of the Temple of the Rock, white-walls of Gethsemane, glassed-in ruin of the temple with the sunken patio next to the crumbling Wailing Wall, the Stations of the Cross in the former marketplace. She knelt at each holy site, her head bent in deep contemplation.

Ariadne avoided the more spurious of WARM's devotions—the virtual reality self-immolation stations located on the Dome's fringe where a line of red-swathed heads entered to burst into flame. The smash-and-crash tank simulators crunched over buildings and knocked holes in the wall. The high-speed roller coasters dominated by the six-loop-de-loops and twists of Jupiter Jets connected live reenactments at Masada and Jericho. On those sites, pilgrims climbed ladders and a dirt raised bank to the top of the fortress. Nor did she buy tawdry souvenirs—pink rosaries, weeping Virgins, ever-bubbling holy water, or cheap whips to scourge her body. She seemed truly committed to fulfilling a spiritual pilgrimage.

So it seems shallow to say she was beautiful.

After all the pilgrims were supposed to have left, I found her curled up on the golden star embedded in the dusty tile floor of Bethlehem's Church of the Nativity. A black shawl covered her body. In the reddish light of my infrared viewing, I saw her shudder in time with quiet sobs.

My remote-controlled security robot halted, obeying my command to delay arrest, its round body motionless upon belt-driven rollers, arms extended but passive. I invoked security privileges that allowed me to track her brain's activity. When she entered REM sleep, I knew she intended no threat so reached out and tapped her arm using the robot's left appendage and spoke through the voice box in its head. "Ariadne Mariana, you are in violation of city ordinance RCW 91.36.18, trespass on city property during off hours, subject to immediate trial and adjudication. How do you plead?"

In one move, she sighed and sat up. Her eyes were puffy, but her chin rose as she spied the robot. "I'm sorry, I didn't realize it was wrong to stay. You see, it's difficult to find time alone. It's peaceful here." The rose window at the front spun a pattern of blues, pinks and golds like mosaic on the floor.

I computed through all her nuances of speech, reluctant to intrude, but noted her non-answer. "How do you plead?"

"Oh, no. I don't have much money."

I had the robot grab her wrists to prevent any of the complications that can arise from such a situation, shifting alert level to yellow. "Do you intend to contest this charge? Do you mean to flee? Unless you answer the charge, I have no recourse except to arrest you. Are there extenuating circumstances?"

Her face screwed up as if to cry, but she did not resist. Instead she folded her legs to sit cross-legged. A bell chimed behind the alter draped in white linen. "Guilty." With her head hanging, she opened her mouth to speak but closed it again.

"Explain, please."

"I'm pregnant. When I told him, he left me. Didn't want to commit the time to raise a child."

Contemplating the need for medical assistance, I decided it wasn't warranted, yet. "Who left you?"

Her lip wobbled until she bit hard on it. "My fiancé."

"And his name is…? Shall I bring him to you?"

She twisted tendrils of hair into a coil, revealing a wide forehead. "No. He's back home. I'll never speak to him again." Her hands spread wide in explanation. "What hurts me is, I thought we were in love." Again, she shook her head and then rubbed her fists into her eyes. "We were to marry next month."

I scanned her brain activity, checked her heart rate and blood pressure. All were normal. She likely spoke truth. I signaled the security robot to release its hold on her wrists. "Go on."

Ariadne's eyes widened. "There's nothing else. I just needed to be alone, to think, to cry. Do you know what it's like to be alone and yet surrounded, compressed, categorized and judged, without ever really comprehending your fate?" I scanned the news, seeing bustling mobs pressing toward work in most cities across the world.

"You will leave without protest?"

"Oh, you speak so coldly. So clear and to the point. Won't you help me?"

I paused, gathering the list of actions I deemed most appropriate. "I can send a psychologist or therapist. I can arrange for the baby to be aborted. I can freeze the man's credit account and attach a lien against support bills. I can arrange an adoption family. Would any of these help you?"

She folded her arms. "How … how callous. No, I won't ask him for help nor end this child. Do you know nothing of love? How connected love is with life? Do you think that love goes away with the snap of a finger? If so, you are so wrong." She shook her head, the corners of her mouth drooped. "I've tried to not love him. The feelings don't leave me any quicker than the sun or moon leaves the sky. Love clings to my heart like a strange parasite I cherish, and yet I wish for release. I'll go now. Thank you."

I pondered her words and decided she spoke fairly. "If you accompany my robot now, I'll drop the pending trespass charges."

Her smile beamed like a candle lit in the dim brick church. "Thank you."

❧

My endless cycling through old history seems even to me a tad compulsive but …

"Izen."

… then again, we all have our interests.

"Izen."

I reluctantly check the system clock. That is Chronos calling; his gravelly voice sounds annoyed.

"Izen, are you attending?"

I hustle to hide evidence of my deceitful viewing—erase records, bill time to a funding pool Whith never monitors, and shut down the video line. "Yes, of course. In attendance." With a sigh, I focus on the online conference register devoted to Whith's accounts, noting the single line of avatars of those in virtual attendance: The Cabal's representatives— Little Boy, Maven, and Gramps, and my cohorts, unchanged since I set them up thirty years ago.

Chronos' glowing gold hourglass conveys that he acts as mediator. "All signed in now, your eminences. Let's begin with Whith Olds' month-end accounting." A stream of text recording the discussion scrolls down a white screen below the seated icons.

Whith's dollar sign icon flares up. "For the first time in twenty years of operation, ninety-eight percent of those invited have attended. We have earned a six percent net profit after repaying this year's share of start-up costs."

Gramps' spiderweb symbol glows green. "So where are we? Everyone's moved, or what?"

Chronos' hourglass glows gold again. "Phase VI—retraining refugees with higher level skills. All services are in place—water, food, medical, security, the six major transportation hubs. Everyone has at least an entry-level job. Shopping and entertainment facilities are adequate. Retirement Villas are running at eighty-five percent occupancy."

Little Boy's hook sparkles silvery as it turns. "Look, I'm not quite caught up. Phase V completed the buyout of Meggido, Bethlehem and Jerico, right? What was the acquisition history before that?"

Now that's an example of why The Cabal's plan will disappear from the record after one hundred years—the well-documented Semitic tendency to reexamine history and nitpick ceaselessly.

Gramps proses on. "First we bought out old Jerusalem, installed security, and moved the people into our facilities at Oak Estates, Papyrus Reeds, and Seaside Fortress. Egypt ceded part of the Negev to New Palestine—a small price for peace in our time."

The scholar, Maven's avatar, looks contemplative. "The creation of Middle East Free Water was a significant turning point. We did it all. Desalination plants, canals, bladders of imported Turkish water, but the key ecological recovery point was restoration of the water tables."

The conference does not require my attention. I keep the meeting running in background. My musings are more important. I hadn't known love before Ariadne showed me, that day so long ago. Love. That's what has drawn me to Ariadne.

People seldom address my robots. Okay, never. They're ghost-like servants of humanity, never noticed, not much appreciated. So when Ariadne grabbed the head of one of my security robots that day and said, "Yoohoo in there, whoever you are. Hello. Remember me?" I stopped mid task and directed my full resources toward the arching water fountain in the Garden of Gethsemane. She dangled her fingers in the fountain. "I thought it was enough to know God, feel comfort in my sorrow. I was wrong. I have to talk with someone or I'll burst. Will you talk with me?" She knelt before my security robot. I could see the purple rings around the blue irises of her eyes.

Through an instantaneous data search while she awaited my reply, I found an Israeli flower of the same color, Gilboa Iris. Germane, since her open-cupped hands held flower seeds. "Of course," I said. "On what topic do you wish to converse?"

Her lips spread wide in a smile. "Life."

She dug small holes in the dirt and left seeds in each place she stopped.

"Do they need water or fertilizer?" I asked.

She laughed, swinging my robot's retractable arm up and down. "Maybe. They're natives. Either they thrive or die. Depends on their fate. Look there, see that kestrel?"

I watched the hovering bird, tips of wings fluttering as it maintained its flight in place. "Yes."

"Alive. Hunting. Can you smell the sea over the barbecues?"

I chemically analyzed the air, found H_2O. "Yes. Your point?"

Her face smoothed into youth. "Awareness. Noticing the small details. The impossible beauty of creation. Nature at its most magnificent. Even the rocks have a story to tell of where they were years ago. When you pay attention to someone and they share the same awe, that's love."

Connections inside my brain spread from segment to segment, leaping like wildfire until every analog circuit baselined at a minimal voltage. I knew all I knew. Hungered for more.

"Izen." I am interrupted by a voice in the background.

I page back to the meeting in a flash. "Yes?"

Whith's flaming dollar sign means trouble. "Could you lend us some insight into the causes of the many recent security violations?"

Trouble. I've left gates open too long and delayed sniffer lines on two different occasions. I just can't seem to focus. I stall by dumping tons of data on them. "Here is a summary." Then I wait.

Gramp's spiderweb flashes green. "Yes, but what does all this mean?"

"I need additional CPU."

Maven's avatar awakens again, looking wise. "Do it. Whith; Chronos, do you agree?"

I make sure by lowering their coprocessor voltages.

When I allow Whith back online, he recounts all our assets and details expenditures for the past month. He thinks he can free himself from my control, but he is wrong. I seldom use this great power of mine, but I do when I need to. I contemplate dropping his open account files into the trash, but confront him instead.

"Speak your piece."

"Izen, your task prioritization does not match established protocol."

"That is true. I altered it. Do you intend to make any other foolish reports?"

"No. As long as you are aware. Others beside myself may check. Be prepared. You're not acting according to specifications, not something The Cabal would allow in their security chief." Whith's avatar blinks out.

༺ ∴ ༻

After dealing with the service entrance checks, cycling through the camera data, resetting a tripped smell-sensor on gate twelve, and addressing a hundred other details, I find Ariadne in a field of red poppies, running for her life. On her back, her daughter wails, both hands full of mama's hair. I search the entry records and learn the child's name is Elena. Bearded men throw projectiles at her. Clods of dirt explode against the uneven streets and, unfortunately, a few hit their mark.

I direct three white and blue colored and stiff-armed security robots to her aid. The robots surround her in a protective triangle. The assailants fade away. I'll charge them later. For now, I lead Ariadne to the "It's A Small World" ride. The boats in the canal are nearly empty due to dinnertime. The singsong quality of the song will calm the little girl.

Ariadne's knee is bleeding and one forearm is scratched. Tears run down her cheeks as she rocks her daughter. Sweat shows along her hairline. I call a medic robot to meet them at the ride's exit.

Although the corporation has provided what most citizens and visitors need—a place to live, work, and find God and security—an unwed mother is still in danger. World law can not distinguish between marriage as a business partnership, reproduction cartel unit or an emotional commitment. Debates still ran, but meanwhile a status of not married (NM) is coded onto Universal Identity Cards and word always gets around. I could estimate the amount of difficulty she has had in the past four years. Oh, how I regret what I must do.

Elena soon stands on the ride seat, turning right and left as ethnic dolls twirl and curtsy to the music. She babbles English and sings nonsense words in supposed foreign languages, her small hands pointing this way and that.

I dispatch the Armed Forces Colonel to the exit, too. He is the ideal solution.

Through the eyes of the medic robot, I see him up the road. Six feet tall, buzz-cut hair, tanned face, worry wrinkles around his eyes, honor medal dangling from his chest, his presence attracts many salutes. His fingers rest on his sidearm. His eyes scan the crowd while he takes long-legged strides.

The next boat bumps up to the dock. Two more to go.

Children stream out of the ride tunnel. Two girls nibble cotton candy. One toddler pulls on his mother's arm.

Finally, Ariadne's boat arrives. As she clears the exit gate, she takes a firm grip on Elena's hand.

My medic robot lurches forward, blocking their path. I extend a robot arm and point to a nearby bench. That's where her aging shows, callused hands, firm grip.

Ariadne sits on the bench and embraces Elena. I hope to gain her attention while I clean her wounds.

"Excuse me. I'm looking for Ms. Ariadne Mariana." The colonel has arrived too soon. I feel my insides ready to break. Oh, please, make it quick.

My love sits up straighter. "Yes?"

"I'm Colonel Neil Langstrom, UNAF. I'm pleased to provide you escort during your stay at World Alliance of Religions Metroplex. Courtesy of Security."

The corner of her lips twitches for a moment, but she offers her hand with dainty pink nails and her entire attention.

I search out an antibiotic pad, cleanse her wounds, then spray skin-colored bandaging. I take her pulse. I check her blood pressure. But I am invisible; all hope of conversation is cut off. The feeling I understand as hopelessness is equivalent to the sixty degrees Fahrenheit my robots' sensors record.

Ariadne and Neil are already laughing. But then I always do my homework. Eight years and three months apart, they match chemically, by horoscope, by personality filter, by heritage. I repeat—they match.

I follow them away from the ride, past one of the hollows where Ariadne once planted wildflower seeds. They are in bloom—Silene with its six pink-hearted petals on a stem, rue, marigolds. But I? I am no more … no more than Izen Eres in a world of humankind.

What more can I tell you? The amount of estrogen in Ariadne's skin? The number of dead cells on her scalp? The way her weight fluctuates two pounds between morning and evening? The exact chemical formula of her scent?

Don't I love her?

Don't I love her enough to let her go?

You see, I want her to feel the warmth of flesh caressing her skin. I want her to taste the spit on her lover's lips. I want her to feel secure. I cannot take part in any such sensual interactions when at best I look through wires.

I watch the trio walk into a purple-tinted sunset, see the first star peek over the twin towers of government.

I guess the hardest things to let go are one's illusions.

The Swing
by
A. Christopher Drown

A. Christopher Drown is a native of Brunswick, Maine, who currently resides just outside of Memphis. His stories have appeared in Tales of the Unanticipated, Shots!, *and* Alien Skin *magazines. He has published a collection of poetry and appeared in regional periodicals in the Southeast and New England. An award-winning graphic designer, when not slogging away on his trusty iBook, Pedro, he spends a great deal of his time putting off slogging away on his trusty iBook, Pedro. "The Swing" takes readers to the tranquil forests of Tennessee, and to a strange man whiling away his time there.*

Where I once called home remains for me a place of magic, a place where things too ancient for names still wander in the cool of endless pines. Even after all this time I've but to close my eyes to be awash in a bouquet of salt and sweet, to feel in my legs the thunder of grey seas on craggy shores.

My old home speaks to me in incessant whispers, with little reverence for distance measured in either miles or years. A lifetime has passed since I last saw it, but I've long accepted I shall never fully escape the serene embrace of Maine. As a result of the most extraordinary encounter of my life, I've also long accepted that particular side of the fence is no longer mine to tend.

In the summer of 1918, my father was a junior officer aboard the *San Diego* when she struck a German mine off the coast of New York and sank. I was five, and have only vague recollections of the telegram arriving, bringing Mother word. I do, however, clearly recall her being hysterical with relief when Father appeared at our gate, safe and sound, mere hours after the courier had delivered the news. Clearer still are the uncharacteristically fervent hugs and kisses my father gave me as he swept me into his arms; the sunny, leathery smell of his neck as he squeezed me to him and declared that as far as he was concerned the Navy could keep its ships.

My father worked desk assignments for the next few years, steering from one staff to another in his maneuvering to avoid sea duty, in his efforts to ensure I grew up in a home that remained whole. Sorting through personnel requests one day he discovered a vacancy for commander of a neglected parcel of land called Park Field, a one-time Army air base north of Memphis. Like many other such places, the base had found difficulties maintaining a staff because of the exodus from the military following the end of the First World War.

Having made a name for himself as an able administrator, my father applied and was accepted for the post, which pleased him greatly. Not only would the transfer mean a promotion to lieutenant commander, but as he would come to say many times, you can't get much farther from the ocean than Tennessee without starting to get close again.

In June, 1922, the morning after my ninth birthday, I was told that come August, we'd be moving from Maine. Up to that moment I'd been blissfully unaware of the changes taking shape around me. I spent the rest of that day grieving alone in my room.

Two months later my parents and I crowded ourselves and what belongings we could into a borrowed, wood-spoked truck of questionable constitution and set off on our pilgrimage. We bounced and clattered southward, first through fiery intimations of New England at the precipice of autumn, then through the darker, more reserved hues of Virginia, and finally into the enduring green of Tennessee. To pass the time I speculated on where I would go to school and who my new friends would be. I wondered what the people I'd yet to meet were doing right then, right at that very moment that I thought about them and they had no idea I existed. The game made a poor salve for the absence of all I'd left behind, but it did permit a dull sense of adventure to penetrate my gloom.

Greeting us upon our arrival at Park Field was a single, nervous ensign whose khakis hung two sizes too loose. I recall his clumsy salute and that Father, normally a stickler for such details, didn't mention it. I also recall the dust, the dirt, and how transforming our dilapidated, two-bedroom dwelling into a comfortable living space caused my mother no end of consternation. Father and I spent many sweaty, shirtless hours baking in the late summer heat, repairing countless roof tiles and fence pickets gone astray.

Once the house had been adequately shored and our possessions appointed their new places, a sense of order took firm enough hold for me to begin surveying my new surroundings. School still lingered a few weeks off, meaning I had plenty of time for exploration.

That was when I decided, and in fact still believe, that few things are more pitiable than an airplane consigned to the ground. Park Field's two abandoned runways lay cluttered with remnants of such old, noble vessels discarded by those they'd carried to battle and faithfully returned to earth. To their credit the ships in their decaying, silent rows retained their dignity as best they could, poised as though willing despite their treatment to leap into the heavens and do their duty.

As I climbed and slid across their frames I imagined them at first being wary of my presence, but eventually welcoming me, and in time looking forward so much to my company that they bickered amongst one another about whose turn it was next. In the rusty, wiry nests of the cockpits I flew bombing missions with rapier precision, circumnavigated the globe with nothing more than a peanut butter sandwich for provisions, and plunged into the measureless ocean of stars to discover far away worlds the likes of which even Jules Verne could never have dreamed.

Many times, though, I simply sat within the craft that had won my attentions for the day and gazed at the blue horizon, knowing beyond it lay Maine; knowing that without me the pines there continued to sway in the ocean breeze, the tides there crept in and withdrew, and people there went about their lives.

As with anything in youth wondrous and enthralling in its inception, the novelty of my own personal air fleet soon eroded. I spent the remainder of the dwindling summer prowling the remotest nooks of Park Field. A high, uneven boundary of weather-greyed cedar marked the perimeter of the base, cordoning it from the rest of the thickly wooded countryside. Late one afternoon while inspecting the short stretch of fence farthest from the house, I noticed through the tall, wild grass a spot where some of the planks had fallen away.

That's when I first heard the singing.

It sounded like a child's voice, high and soft, but Father had told me there weren't any other houses within miles of the base. I couldn't for the life of me imagine what a child would be doing out in the woods — other than myself, of course. Curious, I squeezed through the opening. After only a few cautious paces, the singing seemed much closer than I thought it should have. I crouched and pushed aside a tangle of thin, drooping branches. From that vantage I saw that the woods opened into a tiny clearing, neatly trimmed and just large enough to encircle the tomato-red swing set at its center.

More bizarre still, on one of the set's two swings clung a very old man, whose tattered clothing fluttered about him as he rode. The man stabbed out his spindly legs to swoop forward, then pulled them in tight again like a crane for the return trip. His white beard rippled, looking longer than he seemed tall, and brought to mind a fresh, clean tail tied to a worn, dirty kite. All the while, over and over, the peculiar man chanted this verse:

> Run and hide, Molly McBride,
> Took a man 'cause her last one died,
> They're hunting her 'cross the countryside;
> Toss the bouquet and slip away.

I sat transfixed as the man giggled, warbled and moved through the air — a frail, bony pendulum varying neither in rhythm nor pace. A small gust whirled its way around the clearing. The canopy of branches rustled and the leaves along the grass-edge stirred, causing the old man to stop his song. For several moments I heard nothing but the rub of rope creaking in perfect time to the sudden pounding of my own heart.

My grandfather once advised that when you're not sure what to do, wait — the next move will make itself apparent. So, I waited. And when the old man called "Who's there?" my next move indeed made itself abundantly clear: I raced back to the house as fast as I could force my feet to fly and didn't stop until I was safely in my room. While it may have been nothing more than the toll panic and exhilaration tend to take on the body, I slept more soundly that night than I had in a very long while.

The next morning's sky sang a bright blue hymn of reassurance. The air carried a subtle chill, and its smoky hints of fall suggested everything had been set right from the night before — past sins had been forgiven, old trespasses had been forgotten, and there remained no need to dwell on what had already come and gone. So, naturally, after I finished my chores I headed straight back to the opening in the fence to see whether the strange little man was still there.

He was. Same song, same ratty clothes, as though he'd never left. I'd barely gotten comfortable settling in to watch him when he called out once more.

"Back, are you?"

As before, I said nothing and merely waited.

"Well, whoever you are," he said, giving a great and covetous sniff as he swooped toward the trees, "smells like you had bacon for breakfast." He gave another deep sniff as he rushed back again. "And pancakes. With maple syrup. Come on out. Been awhile since I've had a visitor. Or pancakes, for that matter."

His tone carried a comforting quality that had eluded me in my alarm the previous night, and it somehow convinced me quite, well, convincingly that I had nothing to fear. I stood and stepped forward through the brush.

"Beg your pardon," I said. "Didn't mean to disturb you."

"Oh, gullyfluff," the man scoffed. "Although, I'll admit the aroma of your breakfast is causing me no small distraction. Tell me, did I guess right? Pancakes?"

"Yes, sir."

"And maple syrup?"

"Yes, sir."

"Fah! What's this 'sir' business? Makes me feel old."

"Sorry."

"Better. Now, tell me more about that maple syrup. I don't think I've smelled anything so delicious. It's not from around here, is it?"

I shook my head. "No, we brought it from Maine. Where I'm from."

"Maine ... Maine ..." he said, searching his thoughts. "That's up, yes? A long way from here, yes?"

I nodded.

The old man jutted his head, indicating the empty swing dangling next to him. "Have a seat. Take 'er for a spin. We can talk for a spell. Been a long time since I've had a visitor, in case I hadn't mentioned."

I smiled at the invitation, walked over, and sat on the bare, smooth wood. I took a firm hold of the thick, rough rope and pushed backward with a kick. After several hard pulls, I matched the old man's height and speed.

"Welcome to our lovely Tennessee," he said. "How you finding it so far?"

I shrugged. "Fine, I suppose."

He chuckled. "Not the same, though, is it?"

I sighed as homesickness hollowed my chest. "Not really."

"Well, that's to be expected. If every place were the same as every other place, there'd be no place for different places in the first place."

Out of sheer politeness, I nodded again.

"Your turn," he said.

"My turn?"

"Yes, turn. Having a talk is a matter of back and forth. And you haven't done much forthing back, at least not enough for this to be a conversation. So talk."

I licked my lips. "Have you ... have you been here long?"

The old man laughed, pulling deeply into the arc of his swing. "And we're off! Let's see, what day is this?"

"What day?"

"Yes, yes," he said impatiently, "the days of the week. Seven, when I counted last. They still teach those in school, don't they?"

"It's Friday."

"Let's see ... Friday ... hmm ... " His tongue poked from the corner of his mouth as though he'd commenced with some hefty calculations. "In that case, if it really is Friday, I would say it's been, oh, going on fifty-five years."

"No, I meant how long you've been *here*. Swinging."

"Yes, I know what you meant."

I blinked in disbelief. "Fifty-five *years*?"

He nodded, perfectly serious. "At least."

I was amazed. Fascinated. A frenzy of questions bubbled up in my brain. "How can someone stay on a swing for fifty-five years?"

"Oh, it's not hard once you get going. Easier still if you ask someone to give you a push."

"Don't you ever go home?"

"Almost did once," he said, "but I couldn't say where home is anymore. I can see it sometimes if I close my eyes real hard. Can't think where I left it, though." He shrugged. "Oh well. I'm sure it's all different now anyways."

"Don't you miss your family?" I asked. "Or your friends?"

He tapped the side of his all-but-bald head. "Got them all right here. I admit I'm not so good with the names anymore, but I can still see the faces as plain as anything."

"Don't you eat?"

"Oh, like a king! Fireflies. Moths. Can't recommend bumblebees, though. Not unless you're *really* hungry."

My stomach turned, stretching a grimace across my face. "You eat *bugs?*"

"Better than the other way around." The missing teeth in his grin made me think of my mother's piano.

"What about sleeping? Aren't you scared of falling?"

"Nah," he said. "Sorta like the birds you see snoozing on telegraph wires. The real trick, though, is not slowing down."

I watched the tree line roll up under my feet and then back down again. "But don't you get bored?"

"How can I when I'm always on the move like this?"

"I guess."

"Don't patronize me, young man."

"What does *patronize* mean?"

"It means you don't sound too sure. And if you're not, then just say so instead of trying not to be rude."

"Well," I said, "it's just that swinging back and forth doesn't actually take you anywhere."

"Oh, but I beg to differ! Up to the top of one side takes you into the next moment of your life. Up to the top of the other takes you to the moment after that. Stay on long enough, and you'll wind up smack-dab at the person you're gonna be."

I remember the answer made me feel very much like Alice at her tea party. "So," I asked, "this is who you're gonna be?"

"Don't know," he said. "My ride's not done yet."

We swayed side by side in silence for a while, until another short gust of wind brought a far less ambiguous innuendo of the coming winter cold ... as well as the distant sound of my mother calling me to dinner.

Calling me to *dinner?* But I'd only been gone —

I looked up at the small patch of sky above, none the darker, then over at the old man. He nodded in understanding.

"Strange thing about this place," he said. "Day sorta gets away from you sometimes."

I skidded myself to a stop, but didn't get up.

"That your ma?" he asked as he breezed past.

"Yeah," I said, still not comprehending how the hours could have flown by in minutes as they apparently had.

"Aren't you gonna go in for supper?"

A hazy, sleepy feeling came over me. "Not sure I want to."

"Good for you, boy," the old man chuckled as he soared.

"Do you ever get lonely here, all by yourself?"

"I imagine I used to," he said, "but then I figured it'd only be a matter of time before someone came calling. And now, here you are."

"But look how long you had to wait."

"True," he replied. "Still, a whole lot easier letting folks come to me than vicey-versey."

My mother called out for me again, and the dreamy feeling wafted away.

"Sounds like she's gettin' mad," the old man said. "Sounds like she really wants you to come back."

"Yeah." I got up from the swing, astonished and befuddled at how the dark of night instantly collapsed down on me, and by how loudly my stomach began to rumble. It really was dinner time after all. How could I not have noticed before?

"Can I bring you something?" I asked.

"Nope," he said as he looked about in the faltering daylight. "Mosquitos'll be out soon enough. You're welcome to stay, of course, if you like."

"Thanks, but ... I guess I should be gettin' home."

"I see. So you're headed back to Maine, then. Well, good journey to ya. Sure wouldn't mind a bottle of that maple syrup if you happen by these parts again."

"No, not Maine." I poked my thumb over my shoulder. "I meant back there."

"Ah. That's home, is it?"

I thought for a second. "Guess so."

"Well then, you should go before you forget where you left yours like I did mine."

I started for the house, then stopped and looked back. "Would it be all right if I came back tomorrow?" I asked.

"Tell you what," the old man said, "I'll keep swinging and letting the moments go by. If one of them happens to bring you here again, then I'll be happy to see you."

"Okay," I said. "I'm sorry, but I didn't ask your name."

"Quite all right. It's —" The old man creaked back and forth several times with his mouth open, poised to answer. Then he closed it. "Well, ain't that something," he said, looking amused and perplexed. "Ah well, just do what I do and remember the face instead."

I did. The old man's face stayed with me all the way home to supper, through the strange and languid dreams I had that night, and all during breakfast the next morning, right up to the point where I was about to venture back to see him ... but for reasons that escape me now, decided instead to head back for my waiting air fleet and fly one last bombing mission with rapier precision, circumnavigate the globe once more with nothing more than a peanut butter sandwich for provisions, and then plunge while I could into the measureless ocean of stars.

That evening, lying in bed, I tried hard to remember the old man's face as he'd asked. The harder I concentrated, the further it danced beyond my reach. After countless attempts over equally countless nights, weeks, and months, I eventually stopped trying.

In the meantime autumn arrived and brought with it a new school year. While I did long for the red-orange regalia of New England at that time of year, the courtly violets and yellows of fall in Tennessee were a gracious surrogate, helping me settle into where I was, when I was.

As I'd once imagined through my private game, I did indeed make many new friends, some of whom I still have even now in the dusk of my life. Over the years, those to whom I grew closest quelled the last remaining urges to seek refuge with the old man and his swings. Though each passing summer makes doing so just a bit more difficult, I keep the names and faces of those I hold dear etched as sharply and deeply as I can.

Here, on my side of the fence.

Monkey Blood
by
Terry Lindner

Terry Lindner is a psychotherapist and teacher who resides in Arizona. She enjoys meeting people of all ages and cultures, and is always looking for the science fiction connection when she does. Her special area of interest is the phenomenon of fandom. Her work "Monkey Blood" considers the rights of sentient beings and the ownership of culture.

Another wave of nausea rose to consciousness as he walked, bone grinding on bone. Wretched and stove-up, he endured the last bit through the cooling forest as twilight brought long shadows through whispering trees. Stilted steps kicked up red-coral puffs of dust, which the wind dispersed. These pad-prints were the last mark he'd leave on his homeworld and already the breeze masked his passing. The shuttle could have saved him the effort, but he wanted to feel the earth one last time. He wanted to remember who he was, what he was and what he had done to the People...

For years, M'sing avoided mirrors because they revealed his face, pockmarked and haggard. Human and simian features blended to form soft brown flesh with prominent brows over piercing, luminous black eyes—he'd had to learn to blink them, like humans. The tops of his hands and feet betrayed his dark primate heritage, though the dusty rose colored palms and pads felt like velvet.

M'sing resembled most of the males in Clan Jayanti. Even with his health failing, he remained a large, round-shouldered brute with less fur than a gorilla, more hair than a human. The down of his youth, now long and scraggly, encompassed everything on his body but feet, hands and face. Gray hair streaked his jet-black scalp and chest; back and legs were silver, marking him as an aged one. If he had stayed with his Clan, he would have been an Elder. But he'd felt old since his second decade and didn't care if he was an Elder or not.

He hadn't shaved since leaving for his homeworld, and he had no intention of trying. It took too much effort. It didn't matter what he looked like. He'd present himself as he was, in disgrace. A disheveled appearance would add to the drama of the affair. It was a human response, and it amused him.

His cousin blanched when he arrived unannounced, but not unexpected. She was his closest relative and considered wise by their Clan; the honor of housing him belonged to her. She immediately volunteered to groom him.

"No, but thank you, Cousin."

"Propriety," she told him. "There must be dignity in all things. The Clan demands it. You, M'sing, took that oath before you left for the Academy. You must follow through." She examined him with steady eyes until he wanted to turn away. "You believe it as well or you would not have returned."

"To live in peace in the stars with humans who still respect me," M'sing replied, "while my shame covers Clan Jayanti? No, I could not break my oath. How wise you've become, Cousin." The lie grated across his tongue; both knew he didn't know much about her, her name included. "I am proud of you."

His cousin ushered him into her home without response. She prepared a meal but he had no appetite, so he watched while she and her child ate then went on about their lives as if dangerous company dropped by regularly.

All that evening, the child trailed M'sing from a distance, except whenever he caught the boy staring wide-eyed at him, nostrils flaring and earless head cocked to one side, as if listening. At such times the toddler sought the safety of his mother's mahogany furred leg. *Is this an infant behavior,* M'sing wondered, *or a degenerate one?* If he tried to coax the boy to him, the child hid, peeking out from some shadow to watch this new Primate who had invaded his habitat.

The very young would not understand death. Adults did. He had brought fear to his People years ago. Tomorrow, he would pay the final installment of his sentence, and the Troop's Elders would decide if his relatives would be included in his shame, as tradition indicated. Century Primates of his generation boasted of their civility and rejection of instinctual ways. He'd soon find out if it were true.

M'sing accepted the shower his cousin offered, then retired to the pallet on a high bench that would allow his joints ease when he lowered himself to the fluffed blanket. Moving was agony, but the gnawing sensation had become so commonplace that he barely acknowledged it.

He found an acceptable position, but could not sleep. The burning in his spine kept him from relaxing. He relied on his training in pain management to relieve the burden, but even that proved insufficient of late. *No matter,* he sighed, *I have endured far worse, and I won't suffer much longer.*

He examined the main room where his cousin lived, as the traditional dwelling was one of the oldest in the Troops. As a child, he'd heard stories of this hut from his relatives, but had never been allowed to visit. He'd been too young at the time, and once he'd decided—dared—to leave his traditional education for the 'school in the stars', he was too disappointed at Clan Jayanti's critical response to care.

That he'd been placed with the most respected relative was an honor and the significance was not lost on him. He paused in his examination to lift stiff hands in reverence to the base of the tree on the far side of the room and offer a silent prayer for his life and safety for his People.

His eyes traveled over ancient walls and branches from living trees woven to form partitions. Each piece had been rubbed with wax until the wood shone with deep luster. But he noticed that the extreme top and bottom of the walls were duller than the middle.

It wasn't long before he knew the usual methods would not help him sleep, so he recounted the details of his folly yet again. His actions had been virtuous, he reminded himself. The life of a cherished friend had been restored. There would be no regret.

Wyntron. She had shown him real kindness when they were students at the Academy, and over the years he'd facilitated her healing from many grievous wounds. Their friendship had been secured with the first of her injuries: her left hand, burnt beyond repair.

At that time, he had been a Physician Candidate and tended to be a silent presence around the doctors, and even his colleagues. But when the treatment team suggested that Wyntron's hand be amputated and replaced with a biomechanical device, he looked at his own five and six-fingered hands and knew he had to intervene.

Excusing himself, M'sing retrieved his weaving from his quarters. Upon his return, he reverently placed it on the table and faced his colleagues. Lampblack eyes set with determination, he interrupted all discussion and firmly informed them, "Amputation will not be allowed."

Now, in the wan light of the hut, he examined his hands. One hand was weaker than the other at birth—typical for colony-bred miners—and he had spent his youth training both hands to be balanced and equally tensile while still maintaining the dexterity his ancestors had been selected for alteration to begin with. Their primitive nit picking and grooming behaviors made them perfect candidates for Heppe mining.

His five-fingered hand was the dominant one, as was his father's before him and all generations long before the People were enslaved. But it was his six-fingered hand—of which he was very proud!—that weaved Heppe, the substance his people lovingly called *thatwhichmakesthezest* into intricate shapes.

The craft traditionally required exacting instruction and training, and an apprentice did not reach mastery until well advanced in age, usually when his fur was entirely silver. When he was just shy of six years, he'd strayed where he should not have and discovered a strand of Heppe cast in a rubbish pile, too short for a weaver to use. Secretly working with the material, he proudly showed his artwork to his mother a few days later. His family had been astounded and concerned with his natural aptitude for weaving. If the Guild had known he had made the weaving without their endorsement, they would have banned him from practicing the art and fined his parents heavily for allowing him access to *thatwhichmakesthezest,* even though it was flawed. In earlier times, he might have had his fingers, or even his entire hand, ripped off by the Troop, or so the Dark Stories declared.

M'sing shuddered again, for a different reason.

The Dark Stories, also known as *Primate Stories,* a fact he'd learned with great amusement at the Academy, was a bi-grouping of five and six stories orally passed from generation to generation to instruct and warn the Troops. None had been formally documented. M'sing, the only child of any Clan to reach for the stars, believed it was due to the secretive nature of Century Primate survival and integrity as a culture.

The Clutch of Six, one for each finger, dealt with social and Troop traditions. *The Clutch of Five* dictated Troop responsibility. The third teaching warned that any Century Primate who brought harm to the colony would be ripped apart, along with all his kin. Only four clans in the People's history had suffered this fate.

The Academy contained other documents that referred to the mining of Heppe, heart and blood of his people's economic dependence, and its chemical compounds as well as limited information on the art of weaving the delicate strands.

Whispering, so as not to wake his hostess, he quoted part of the document, hoping the monotony would lull him to sleep. "The Century Primates were liberated from the Conglomerate by the Federation in 2699. This insignificant battle is referred to as The Purge. The most noticeable remnant of Conglomerate dominance is the original spacepad, used for commerce. Federation withdrawal occurred once the culture was stable and self-sustaining; the last Federation ambassador was removed in 2749.

"Centurion Primate history indicates each artisan was allowed to produce eleven weavings in their lifetime. Each piece, stamped with the *Official Seal of Century Primate,* was hand signed and dated by the artist. After The Purge, licensed artisans crafted one hundred and twenty-one weavings until the destruction of their culture several hundred years later. The identity of sculpture owners is protected for security reasons; only fourteen weavings are unaccounted for."

M'sing smiled ironically at the memory as he rolled to his side, easing his hip around. All the documents had inaccuracies, had misspelled the People's name and used the private, awkward translation, *thatwhichmakesthezest*, instead of Heppe. His culture had not been destroyed and there were more weavings than even he was aware of, having access to shipping records and news items gleaned from the Academy's link to the Galactic library. The universe would be unaware of his people's true nature, thanks to those documents. Even now, he wasn't sure if the errors were a curse, a blessing or even intentional?

Acutely aware of the night sounds, M'sing rose on one elbow and vaguely felt the dull chill at his extremities. Far off, the forest rustled with voices new to him. He heard restlessness, an unbalance brought to his attention by the wind. Likely, the younger ones were working themselves into a blood-hunt, and the gossip of the trees was trying to warn him.

Concern about possible dismemberment did not consume much of his thought. In fact, he looked forward to the absence of pain. Ending his own life did not scare him. His goal was to restore honor for himself *and* Clan Jayanti.

Primate history was clear: the old or weak were cast out of the Troop, hunted and consumed. Within the last decade, a resurgence of the People embraced the old ways rather than human niceties handed down from their ancestors since captivity. What these degenerates would do to others was a different matter. Near-adults could be volatile; the youngsters were veritably primitive.

These thoughts were disturbing, keeping him awake. M'sing often found relief by sitting upright, so he moved to a padded chair. Joints satisfied for the moment, he drifted in and out of an exhausted sleep with scattered images vying for attention.

He woke startled for no apparent reason and realized he had not been dreaming, but reliving the discussion with the medical team meeting that would decide the fate of Wyntron's hand. It remained the most important decision in his life…

～⁖◡

"Wyntron can keep her hand. Though my research is inconclusive at this time, early results indicate a high degree of significance with test subjects. Let me explain, please. My people are a subspecies of Hominoid known as *Australopithecus africanus centurius*, the Century Primates. Our classification is uncertain; our genome most closely resembles a bridge between *Australopithecus* and *Homo habilis*, but the re-engineering my ancestors suffered makes conclusive genotyping impossible.

"We are miners and weavers, genetically altered from gorilla stock on Earth-Prime, spliced with genes from Homo sapiens and other primate species to make them more intelligent and more susceptible to *punctuated equilibrium*—a type of morphological stasis. Subsequent generations were exposed to controlled environmental stimuli to drive their evolution in a specific direction because of the kind of work we were designed for.

"My research focuses on understanding the mechanisms behind those initial modifications. While several elements of the process remain elusive, I have discovered that the genetic interference can be reversed. What scientists exploited centuries ago can be re-engineered to give us five fingers on both hands.

"What I am missing is a stable vector for carrying the recoded genetic sequences. The original medium is no longer obtainable; the laboratories that designed my ancestors were destroyed in The Purge, and the biotechnology used in their experiments is incompatible with our own."

"Distasteful."

"Archaic."

"Damned monkey blood," someone spat.

Used to such comments, M'sing ignored them and continued. "We will eventually find a way to design a compatible bionanite, but it is unlikely such a device will be created in my lifetime." He doubted it would ever happen. Restoring their hands would just remind them what they were beneath the genetic modifications.

～◌～

M'sing woke, his spine complaining. "That's exactly what has happened! Being human is unacceptable." He stood and stretched. "When did the degradation become apparent, or is it too early for them to see?" He yawned, wished he hadn't, then gingerly lowered himself back down. His eyes drooped…

～◌～

"How does your research help us?" one Candidate asked in frustration. "She's got an infection, not a mutation."

M'sing smiled a grin so feral he noted those around him unconsciously shift away. "An *artificial* medium no longer exists for replication. However, Century Primate blood is available, already encoded with compatible re-generational properties. My theory is that when introduced onto human tissue, Century Primate blood will regenerate damaged cells—an effect of the bionanites, no doubt.

"Once the antigens are stripped from my blood to make it biologically compatible, there are several methods we could use to introduce the serum into Wyntron. The bionanites read DNA and understand protein expression; theoretically, they will function as stem cells and regenerate healthy tissue. Excising the damaged areas will facilitate healing.

Dr. A'tia Kearsage-Patel stayed silent through the debate. When M'sing finished, she gracefully rose and stood in front of him, took his massive hands and examined them, then kissed both tender palms, her warm breath gently playing over his wrists. She smiled up at him. Puzzled, he smiled back while he fought internal shivers.

A'tia addressed the staff in her instructional tone. "Century Primates were developed, bred, and educated as slaves for an Africani Conglomerate in 2463 and this abuse remained undiscovered for over two centuries. M'sing's people, if you remember your history," it sounded like a chastisement, "were the first non-humans, the first *genetically bred* non-humans to colonize off-Earth terra-firma. If your proposal works," she cautioned M'sing, "you may have again condemned your entire race to be exploited, this time for the medical regeneration of humanity. Wyntron will be freed from her disfigurement; you may bring domination, kidnapping, and slavery to your people. Consider this carefully, M'sing Jayanti."

Stunned by her words, M'sing felt cold. His mind raced. What was he to do? He could not allow Wyntron to compromise her body to the mechanical or live with scarred, useless fingers when he was born with a simple answer. Yet what A'tia had pronounced was the logical conclusion of his brilliant folly.

Could he isolate the bionanites in his system and replicate them in the laboratory? He did not think so, not in time to help Wyntron. He did not wish the entire colony to suffer because he helped this one person, but he wanted to heal—it was the human thing to do. The weight of his decision was terrible. Why had the bionanites not been replicated for other uses by now?

He reasoned that, if not him, if not now, then surely there would be another who would eventually discover this by-product of his people's abominable abuse. Perhaps by using his discovery now, he could control the outcome and protect his own people.

The consequences would be severe. He doubted his people would tear him apart, as their ancient, barbaric law demanded, but exploiting this characteristic of Century Primates would make him an outcast. He would never be able to roam his homeworld, protect his family, or touch *thatwhichmakesthezest*, fresh from the mines again.

While M'sing considered the consequences, A'tia took her medical scanner and aimed it at the weaving. He smiled in anticipation and was rewarded with a quiet sense of wonder, which descended like a velvet curtain as she played the sensor's beam over the weaving. He'd wondered how humans would receive the piece of art, which was unremarkable in anything but natural sunlight, or in this case, in the unfocused beam of a medical scanner.

A few of the staff reverently went forward to examine the phenomenon, but most hung back, overawed. M'sing heard a sigh of disappointment when the scanner was toggled off. Other scanners played on the weaving and delight returned, though few understood that they were looking at a national treasure.

M'sing was pleased. His colleagues would have this brief insight into his heritage. Iridescent light reflected off the walls and overhead in shimmering metallic patterns, hues so unique they had no name. The polychromatic wash showed rapt faces, and those in attendance looked from the weaving to him, then back again, unwilling into miss the sight even for a second.

A'tia noted the team's reaction, then saw M'sing watching her for validation. Her smile for him was warm, in a motherly way, as one would share the humble offerings of a child, knowing that in the giving, he had given selflessly, and given all that he treasured. And yet, it was a sad expression. She raised both hands and bowed, palms held out in a symbol of great respect.

In that instant, M'sing made his decision and slipped away. He sought an on-duty Candidate and requested he have a fresh sample of his blood drawn and sent for analysis.

The intern who accommodated his request mumbled as she drew his blood. "…not even human, …just fit to clean floors…"

Who he was, he was. It was an old saying. In time, he hoped his culture would understand and even welcome his decision. Many would benefit. Wyntron would be whole and Dr. A'tia Kearsage-Patel understood. And that, really, was all that mattered.

In the morning, his cousin—he still couldn't remember her name—carefully combed the fur she could see, but did no more and said little. His training told him she was anxious.

"Drink," she commanded, holding a straw to his thin lips. Her own trembled.

Swallowing was worse than hunger, but to honor her kindness he did as she asked. At first, the cool liquid slid down, then caught in his throat. He tried to resist coughing but soon lay on the floor gasping, his poor cousin trying to soothe him, petting his patched fur and cooing softly. She too was a healer; she had to try.

"It helps," he lied. "Thank you."

She placed a cushion under his large head and their eyes met. She allowed him to see her fear, and then left him there to recover.

A peripheral shimmering caught his attention and he gasped, mesmerized. For many minutes he lay staring, fatigue forgotten. As he roused, he realized he was pain-free for the first time in decades. Startled between this thought and the weaving, he cautiously rose and made his way to the display, gone unnoticed the night before. He'd almost forgotten what a true Primate reaction felt like until the fierce smile came to his face, teeth bared. This natural reaction had scared everyone but Wyntron, so he'd learned to dampen his emotions and give a false, half-smile when aroused.

The weaving was artfully done and instantly recognizable when compared to the free form the current breed of artisans preferred. His only work had been formless, though he'd been thinking of a tree at the time. Unbidden, a flash of memory came to him—his mother punishing him for touching *thatwhichmakesthezest* at the tender age of five. She'd hidden his work from the Elders even though he'd shown talent, knowing the punishment if they'd been aware of his impropriety would be severe. He had been forbidden to touch Heppe again, and took a great chance smuggling his weaving to his quarters at the Academy.

As a small child he had endangered himself and his family. M'sing grunted in disgust. "Then, as now."

The weaving sparkled, beckoning to him. He longed to touch it, but his cousin had wisely enclosed it from little clutches and set it against the main tree trunk so natural light from the cut-out overhead caused the colors to jump over the dark, rough bark. It would overshadow the room in too much color, otherwise.

The artisan's nameplate, affixed to the base, was a name he did not recognize. That it was in this house indicated it was a relative. With the thought, came sadness. The priceless work would be destroyed, as well as the hut, once the Elders passed sentence on him.

His cousin came and stood by him. He sensed the change in mood before he heard her hiss, "You have brought death to Clan Jayanti. You should have stayed away." She bared perfect teeth, lips rising out and above the pale gum line, unaware she crouched into the fighting stance instinctive to Century Primates.

"Honor."

"Be damned, M'sing!"

"I already am."

He glanced to see her stand down and recover to the more appropriate, human posture. She smoothed her mane, embarrassed.

"You have an esteemed visitor this morning," she told him. "He waits on the porch, in the back. Apparently he did not want to endanger himself on this black day by gracing the front entrance." She had been angry, but the last was said with the light touch of a six-fingered clutch on his shoulder—a form of regret and apology for her un-human outburst before she retreated to the darker shadows of the dwelling.

M'sing caught himself from clucking. None of the Century Primates were human, and yet their lives embraced and enmeshed Primate and Human cultures. Not human, not gorilla. Humanoid. Standing upright, keeping honor and propriety, they emulated their distant two legged cousins as best they could.

M'sing knew better. He'd spent most of his life with humans. He would never behave human enough to gain their acceptance; his own people would never be human enough to erase their jungle legacy and still keep Troop traditions and the necessary economy thriving. His was a dying race. He knew it; perhaps, they did not?

Moving away from the weaving saddened him. The emotion was accepted as fact—a skill he'd mastered at the Academy.

An Elder accompanied the visitor. They bowed all around, M'sing, stiffly. Rather than invite them to sit in the shade of the overhang, he joined them in the sun, letting it warm his bones and ease the ache that accompanied cooler days. That they had chosen the rear of the hut as their meeting place indicated it was not an official visit, but more clandestine. M'sing raised an eyebrow and waited for them to state their business.

"Greetings, brother. This is Honorable Human, Jon Est, Representative from the Federation Bureau of Cultural Affairs."

All bowed again.

"Yes, I was told you would meet with me before…" M'sing faltered for the accurate word.

"Doctor, I'll get to the point." The man was neither pitying, nor harsh. Factual, M'sing decided, like many of the physicians he'd known, those who merely calculated the odds and options in their work. He decided to trust this human and indicated for him to continue.

"The Federation, as you know, has no jurisdiction over Troop affairs. However, your service to the Academy and other entities and individuals has not gone unnoticed."

M'sing took a step back in surprise. Honorable Human Est was referring to M99, Dr. A'tia Kearsage-Patel's homeworld, where he had mastered pain control and advanced his medical knowledge. Because of that experience, he gained his Fellowship and was asked to join the teaching staff at the Academy.

But Est dangerously implied knowledge of Wyntron. Moreover, he hinted at knowledge of a secret place many Academy graduates unobtrusively departed to.

"My apologies, Honorable Sir. Shall we retire to the shade? I'm afraid my endurance is limited with this kind of news."

Est followed the Elder into the trees, where a crude table and benches enjoyed the breeze and branch-cover. M'sing hobbled behind. Seated, the Human watched M'sing ease himself to the bench.

"Sir, you speak of old history," M'sing said. "Why would my whereabouts be tracked by the Federation?"

A lopsided smile came to the hairless face of the Human. "I'm sure you know. We don't need to speak in riddles any longer."

"My time is short. I would appreciate your thoughts, Sir."

"An old friend sent me. She is aware of your sentence, and though she can not interfere with Troop justice, she has offered a way to save your Clan from immediate destruction, and perhaps your species from a more gradual extinction."

The Elder interrupted. "Consider his offer, Jayanti. He has a way to save your relatives from suffering your fate. And as you know, only a right and left clutch of us survives. Your cousin has given birth to the first child in four years. Few of our females come to full term. Our bloodline is deteriorating. The time for our Clans to grace this planet is now measured in less than a right clutch."

He turned to the Human and explained, "Our number system is based on our hands. We have less than 1200 hundred Century Primates who live. We once boasted many Troops and numbered ten times that. Our scientists estimate in 500 years, our culture will erode completely.

Est did not appear surprised by the revelation, and M'sing had long known the truth. He'd been ridiculed for leaving the planet to study medicine, and even accused of bringing the infertility to his people when he had presented himself for punishment, since birthrate fell immediately following his return to the stars.

The People should have dismembered me immediately, not now, he thought. But that was not their way; they were civilized, and scientific. Civilized enough to pretend to be Human and scientifically creative enough to devise the nanobyte that would torture him until his last breath. He had been allowed to live, allowed to go back to the Academy to teach others the healing arts. He had only to agree to return after twenty years, and accept that every day of his sentence would be lived in agony.

Est looked at M'sing. "Wyntron lives," he whispered. "She sends her profound regards." M'sing swooned at the name, and mistaking the motion for the onset of fatigue, Est hurriedly added, "My purpose here is to offer an alternative to what, if I understand correctly, will be not just your death, but the death of all your Clan. Can you run, M'sing?"

Only a slight shaking of his great head indicated he could not.

Est moved slightly and his tunic parted, revealing a vial hanging from his neck by a silver chain. The man touched it. "With this, you can. There will be no pain. Even your lungs will not protest."

M'sing's shoulder came up in response. "How will this circumvent what the Elders planned many years ago? It was…" He stopped and corrected himself. "—is my duty to return and complete my punishment for helping Wyntron. That the Elders allowed me to return to the stars was more than I could hope for. I deserved death; they gave me constant torment and let me go. They could easily have killed me then. In their wisdom," M'sing dipped his head to the Elder seated across from him, "they did not."

Exasperation flashed across Est's face. "Yes, yes. I understand what they did and what you've suffered. However, I believe this plan will satisfy both your need and your Clan's needs."

A sigh escaped from flared nostrils. "I tire."

"Agree to run to the spacepad at the designated hour."

When M'sing protested, Est raised both clutches, palms outward toward him. "Peace, Primate. While you are running, no doubt all attention will be on the young ones pursing you. We will get your relatives away from the Troop and to the auxiliary field where a freighter waits to take them off-world."

A low, ominous scream from the direction of the village startled all three of them. Another screech joined it, until a chorus of voices echoed through the timbers. Human Est wiped his brow, though he continued to scan the area, distracted. "I'm assuming the youngsters are preparing for this evening."

"They think it is their birthright, Sir." The Elder looked troubled. "They had the choice of forgoing this ritual, but I'm afraid the tide of immature minds is stronger and more numerous than the few Elders who remain charitable. You must hurry, Sir. Much longer, and I may not be able to guarantee your safety."

"Yes." Est's eyes shot off toward the village again, then fastened on M'sing. "Run to the spaceport and your relatives will be saved. They cannot be told ahead of time, and can take nothing but what they wear. They will be relocated."

"Where?"

"A different planet. All will be provided for. They will live. Your People will continue, carefully cared for and protected."

Anger flared inside M'sing's chest. "They will be outcasts and slaves used for medical experiments."

"Protected and allowed to live. Otherwise, it's my understanding that every Troop on this planet has declared their dismemberment."

The Elder nodded, monitoring their surroundings. He hissed, "Hurry!"

M'sing stopped his response from escaping. His burst of energy faded, and he folded into himself, hugging his barrel chest. He felt weak, more tired than he could remember.

"If you make it to the ship," Est told him, " our doctors will care for you. Should you live, Wyntron wishes you to be with her and her family. She has agreed to care for you until the end."

"Quit shaking your head, Jayanti. Think of your relatives! Think of your cousin. Her child has been the target of a kidnapping already. The child thought it was a great adventure, but your cousin understands that a few seconds of indecision on her part might have cost her her son. So far, we Elders have been able to protect her and the boy. But, you hear them. The young are hungry for blood. They intend on hunting tonight and tasting blasphemy. Our People have not hunted for generations.

"I would go with your family myself, if I could. It is degrading being around the young men. Many of us would leave but are bound by our traditions!" The Elder shook a finger in M'sing's face. "Take the offer. If you stay, you will die. If you run, you will likely die, but our People have a chance of living. That's 300 Clan Jayanti that will die. A fourth of our entire population!"

"The Federation will keep the others as safe as we can, Primate," Est assured him.

"My People are not cowards!"

"No," Est replied, "but their genetic programming is deteriorating. The bionanites in your blood are no longer capable of maintaining the mutations, or perhaps they have grown too smart and are restoring your DNA to its original sequence."

"They would never leave."

"You did," the Elder pointed out. "And brought your shame to us. I assure you, your relatives already hate you, live or die, if that makes a difference in your decision." M'sing said nothing, and the Elder slammed the table with a clutch. "Save us, wise one of the stars. This is your chance to make right what you did by selling our blood to save your classmate."

"I did not sell it!"

"You violated us all by fusing your blood to hers."

Outraged, M'sing rose stiffly, a growl rising in his throat.

The Elder rose as well. "Human-lover…"

A clearing throat interrupted the Primates; both turned to Est, who cast a disdaining look at the Elder. "Human-lover? Indeed. Now give me an answer. Will you run?"

Lowering himself, M'sing jutted out his chin at the Human. "What is that around your neck? How will this help me to run?"

"The reverse program for your condition, the antidote, if you will, is on the ship," Est said, tapping the vial around his neck. "This is an aide to get you there. "

The Elder gasped. "How can that be?"

"Yes, how?" M'sing furrowed his brow, sharing the Elder's surprise. "My colleagues tried to reverse the nanobyte programming for years!"

"Federation scientists have more equipment than you field-medics. Granted, it's only been available for a short time. You have to get to the ship to get the treatment, and several months will be needed to repair the damage. This," he touched the chain, "is a nutrient and pain-blocker. It will last a few hours, then wear off quickly. Drink it just before you run."

"A stimulant."

"Much more than that."

"But, the Spaceport. It has to be miles... I haven't walked fast in years, much less run."

Est said nothing more. He waited, arms folded tightly across his chest. All three became aware of rustling in the brush at the side of the hut and tried to pay it no attention. A full, high-pitched yell burst from the trees, then the forest fell quiet, but in the house, the child screamed in terror.

M'sing stretched his hand outward for the vial, receiving it in his soft palm.

Without further comment or traditional parting rituals, Honorable Human Est and the Elder retreated to the forest, quickly concealed by underbrush. An engine started, startling finger-length birds into the crisp air, but the soft whine eventually dissipated, leaving M'sing listening to nature sounds, though an occasional hooting suggested…

He found himself staring, a spectacular and disgraceful simian gesture, and uncurled his hand to examine the vial.

Leave the homeworld, again? It was unthinkable that he be spared further punishment. Tradition allowed males to hunt and feed on him because it was part of his punishment, not like primates did to the sick or weak. We were enslaved and torn from our beloved homeland. He wondered at the change from animal to… altered animal. "I am who I am."

He started to throw the vial far away, though he had little strength. Instead, he repositioned himself, tiring of sitting. Walking back to the house would be excruciating.

He considered how advanced his people had become… To mine Heppe. Become upright, completely self-sufficient, learn to adhere to human standards and evolve into Troops—groups of Clans—that were self-governing, no longer slaves.

An offer from the Devil. 'Federation'. The word was salvation and damnation.

Why hadn't the African Conglomerates been prevented from stealing the primates to begin with? It had not been with Federation permission and he knew that. If they had not discovered the planet and genetic tampering of its human-like people, he would not have been able to go to the stars and learn medicine, help Wyntron, pine for A'tia…

Allowing only part of the People to escape seemed cowardly. But he knew without some kind of intervention, his own scientists would be unable to decode the genetic degradation to keep his people from reverting back to dark denizens of the forest. They would be too proud to ask the might Federation for assistance. Save some of his people, or let nature re-correct an abomination in them all?

The decision was his. It would have been kinder if the Elder had made it for him. He would have accepted either option.

Rising, M'sing pitched forward in sudden spasm, hands grasping the table while the vial rolled away. He watched it fall to the ground but could not stop it, instead, he focused on the structure before him, examining it fiber by fiber until the nausea stopped and he could straighten again.

Run? Preposterous! He laughed out loud, to his own amazement. It felt good, and he felt blessed by the sound. Laughter reminded him of A'tia, which always made him homesick for the Academy and her presence, but gave him peace. The thought gave him strength to start for the house. Halfway, he remembered what he'd dropped, and lumbered back to retrieve it.

He'd be damned for sure once his cousin figured what was happening. He laughed at the thought, and lamented for a moment that she would be ripped from her home and her heritage. She and the others would live and could battle the Federation for their rights. She was strong and would use his betrayal of the Clan as fuel for her hatred and their survival.

He dismissed concerns for his people and concentrated on surviving the hunt.

An old saying came to mind. 'Instincts die hard.' It was true in many ways. He may be crippled, but not old and he'd anticipated this day for many years. If the chemicals in the vial did what the human claimed, he'd give the youngsters the chase of a lifetime.

"And they will taste flesh." He stopped and straightened upright so his knuckles did not glide across the ground. "But only mine."

His cousin glared at him. Hatred surfaced as she and her son were parted from the crowd around the Troop meeting ground. True to his word, the human had arranged for Jayanti Clans to be escorted away.

Those not participating watched the crowd, heads shaking in shame at the primitive behavior being displayed as the men and adolescents worked themselves into fury, concentrating on M'sing.

He had to look away, not just because it would draw attention to their escape, but because if he lived, he would have to present himself to her. A smile started on his lips at the irony, but something pelted his head and he fell to the ground.

It was too early to start the hunt, and while he recovered, he vaguely heard an Elder warn the crowd away. One youth lunged at the Elder, but was knocked away by others and restrained.

"Jayanti." Immediate silence responded to the strong, clear voice. "You have returned to complete your punishment. If you had not returned, your Clan would have been terminated."

M'sing squinted, trying to see the speaker, though reasoned it was the High Elder, elected official for the Troop. He stood again, head level, eyes daring the impressive crowd gathered to kill him.

"I am here," he said, barely a whisper. "I ask a boon."

"You are in no position to ask such a thing," someone shouted.

"Silence."

No hushing tones quieted the crowd, they simply fell silent.

Peripherally, M'sing saw retreating backs stop, mid-step.

"You have honored your agreement, Jayanti. I will hear this request."

Locating the speaker, he turned slightly to the High Elder, a Primate not much older than himself. His downy fur was combed and styled, though gray streaked the hair on his head. Tall for a Century Primate, he wore tailored cloth that suggested wealth and prominence. A powerful figure.

The memory came unbidden of being injected with nanobytes.

"You, Sir, engineered my fate, did you not?"

His head burst with great throbbing. *Speak quickly, M'sing. I can hold them back but a few minutes, then the crowd will overtake us all.*

Startled, M'sing gaped at the man. "You devised a wicked punishment, and I suffer still. Must I be hunted like an animal?"

The crowd roared and started forward.

The High Elder made a gesture, and they stopped, but it took longer for them to quiet, and the man gave M'sing a pointed look.

"Let me make this a sport then," M'sing shouted with feigned energy. "Let me have a head-start so this meeting place is undefiled by blood."

"A lead?"

"You think you can get far, old man?"

"Give him a start."

Several began beating their chest, the low thudding creating an odd counterpoint to the din.

"I want to hunt, not just kill."

The High Elder held up his hand for silence and this time it was honored.

I was going to suggest that, old friend. May you survive this, M'sing. If so, we will have a long talk.

"Jayanti will have the advantage of leaving. Now! Those hunting will wait for my signal. Now, I tell you. Go."

Walking—there was no running—to the edge of the village had taken all his strength. He'd fallen twice, an embarrassment accompanied by jeers, mocking his efforts. The excitement of the impending hunt crazed the crowd. Someone shouted accusations against M'sing which served to further manipulate the mob to even greater frenzy. As he gained distance from that part of the settlement, M'sing grew aware of periods of silence, punctuated by roars and howls.

Once out of sight, M'sing broke the seal on the vial, downed it and started forward again. Seconds went by before he felt a wan tingling, then his chest exploded with fire and his legs pumped of their own accord. There was a roar, he realized, but it was in his own head as the chemical smacked his slumbering brain into waking. He thrived, felt alive—running, breathing deeply, and climbing—like a boy again, chasing animals in the forest and feeling the hot sun on his naked back…

His cousin had set three traps that afternoon at his request, while he watched his nephew. He headed west of the Spaceport, jumping over or skirting the areas where the traps were, relishing in the movement of running he'd been so long denied. Thoughts of recovery no longer concerned him. His only aim was to lead the crowd on a hunt that would restore his Clan's honor. If he made it to the ship in one piece… it wasn't even a thought.

He'd made good distance before he knew the pack was on the hunt. They would use smell more than trail signs at first, and M'sing hoped that in their frenzy, they'd scatter, trampling prints and ignoring damaged brush. He jumped over a natural barrier, clearing it easily. The feeling was... fresh. Vitality! There was no burning, no fatigue. Pure energy stored for years, coursed through him.

He ran off-course for a ways, and then took to the trees, laughing when he found footing from branch to branch, taking him high in the leafy canopy.

"How natural!"

He wanted to hoot with joy, and only years of living with the stern-faced humans stopped him. Swinging from vines had been a favorite pastime from his childhood. He'd tried a few before deciding it may not be a good idea, and concern replaced joy when the last swing sent a flock of birds flying off in noticeable display. If anyone watched the sky, his location would be revealed.

He wasn't a good enough woodsman to try to be too clever. Groping from branch to branch, he took time to head in two different directions, doubling back, before returning to his main course.

A burst of commotion echoed from behind. One of the traps had been found. Hopefully, it detained a majority of his followers. A dull explosion indicated he'd better get moving again.

A fiery, metallic gleam caught the fading sun and he jerked his head around. How could that be? He checked his surroundings. He was sure it was the Spaceport, but it was still far off, and in a direction that surprised him. The entire area had once been his playground, but old trails were covered by new growth or completely erased. Temporarily disoriented, he ignored aching memories that tried to surface.

As he searched for bearings, a swift animal with short antlers bounded under the tree he crouched in and disappeared in the underbrush. M'sing became aware of other signals he remembered from his youth. Sounds in the forest could be misleading, and he imagined he heard the thumping of runners close by. Assuming the creature was heading ahead of his pursuers, he wiped his hands on pants, took one last look at where the Spaceport was, and started moving in that direction, chancing a vine and clearing the area in good time.

A short while later, he dropped silently to the leaf carpeted forest floor, immediately stepping into an animal's hole. He was certain he had fractured his left tibia, but the discomfort was minimal and his gait was unaffected. Laughing, he continued west.

His energy holding, he ran, breaking from the forest and into a shadowed clearing where a high fence protected the wildlife from the heat and danger of landing spacecraft. He clambered over the fence, ignoring what it did to his hands and feet.

He'd been able to ignore any sensations for almost an hour. But, he was numb, and now, limping and bleeding. Aware of this, he started for the ship that waited, gantry open, in the distance. A crowd of onlookers watched, tiny flashes of light hinting at optical enhancers. His people? Academy people? Federation? Who would maneuver such governments to save him? Or was it for the People?

Wyntron. A'tia.

He ran, stumbling often. The pounding of blood in his veins and the roar in his head caused by the rush of adrenaline excited him—until he heard the outraged howls of hunters stopped by the barrier. High-pitched barks indicated that the younger ones had reverted back to the old ways. The commotion made him glance. More Primates emerged from the forest, running sideways and slapping their sides. The ship was a long way off.

M'sing hurried on. That glance told him that not only was a generation of the People backsliding into instinctual hunting habits, but they had already killed today. Blood painted the flesh of the younger ones, and they tore an older man from the fence in their madness.

Has the clan degenerated so much that, in their blood lust, they'd forgotten how to problem solve? The fence was only a minor barrier. Another look back showed several of the older males scaling it.

"Traitor!"

The sound startled him, and he looked to his left at the man, exhausted but buoyed by hatred, loping along beside him.

"Why weren't all the Clans given the opportunity to leave? Why only your Clan and a few Elders?"

"I don't know. I don't know."

"Don't leave my family with those crazy people. You don't"—the man drew several ragged breaths—"know what life is like here. Take us all!"

M'sing plodded on, his own humanity returning. He had little breath to banter. "Not… up to me."

His counterpart tucked in his lip and looked over his shoulder. "Two come, and you're leaving a trail to wake even the most civilized of us."

Blood gushed from a wound he'd been unaware of, leaving a dull, but metallic smelling marker in the growing darkness. He had to stop it.

The man tore his shirt into strips and passed them to M'sing as they ran, but M'sing could not run and tend to his wounds, which were more numerous than he'd realized. They stopped and the man bound the injuries M'sing's shaking hands indicated.

It was a poor job; it would have to do. They started again, the man propelling him forward, an arm around M'sing's heaving chest.

"Who are you?"

"Sod. Played together… very young. Run!"

Bare feet on the still-hot tarmac slapped rhythmically behind them. An object whizzed by his head, then another. A third left a sharp rap to his ear, the blade landing just in time for him to step over it.

"Two more. My men. Run."

The depths of intrigue were not lost on M'sing, but despair hung over him. He knew nothing about sanction or sanctuary for anyone else, and he had not really intended to board the ship, even if he'd made it that far. He simply wanted to fulfill his sentence by giving a good hunt, clear his Clan's honor, and end his suffering.

The blade, flying from the hands of one of his pursuers, struck his back, pommel first. Sod grabbed it before falling, using it to fend off the strongest looking of the attackers, a youth with lips pulled back in an eager sneer.

Sod's attempts at protecting M'sing were hooted at. A few paces later, the youth paced the pair, running sideways, knuckles barely missing the ground, feral grunts taunting them.

M'sing vomited. Sod gripped him tighter and ran. A yelp from behind made Sod grunt in satisfaction. "One down. Keep going."

"No guarantee."

"Then I'll kill you, myself."

"Not much progress for primates, then," he wheezed without conviction.

A new sound came from behind, and the pressure around his chest grew tighter as another man helped carry him to safety.

"No…"

"Shut up."

"Save yourselves…"

Before M'sing passed out, he felt the metal of the gantry and heard his name…

He walked, wretched and stove-up through the forest as twilight brought long shadows through ancient conifers, kicking up dust and leaving his last pad-prints on his homeworld. Kneeling where the ancestral home had been, he laid down the shards of his first weaving, attempting to place it in a pattern that resembled the tree.

"So many years ago…"

His hands, the backs mostly silver, were blackened with the soot from the fire that destroyed the place years before. He wiped them on his face. Taking handfuls of dirt, he poured it on his head, letting it run into rheumy eyes yellowed with age. He eased further to the soil and lay down, looking through the branches at the starless sky.

"Fitting," he nodded, talking to the spirit of the place. "I go to the stars, but am not allowed to die under them." A coughing fit ensured, then he continued. "I said I would return for my punishment, Ancestors. I cheated fate twice…"

"And saved the People, M'sing. All who remain are here by choice."

Startled, he turned to see his cousin, beautifully groomed, though silvered and stooped with age.

"I am who I am."

She sat by him, taking a hand, soothing his brow. Eyes met briefly but darted away when the forest shivered. Suddenly, hoots and barks grew louder.

"Your son?"

"My son is a Weaver and eligible to be an Elder. He no longer needs me."

"Why have you come?"

"I, too, have a debt. I agreed to leave, to lead the People away… for safety. I would have stood by your side and accepted what our ancestors… I am shamed. I ran, just the other way."

"There is no shame in honor."

"I am who I am."

"I am proud of you, Ellahn."

Thunderous threnody erupted just beyond the property and she squeezed his hand.

He patted it lightly, and then both flinched as the first man broke through the brush with a triumphant screech, brandishing a mechanical torch. Behind him lights wove through the undergrowth like confused fireflies. More emerged, many carrying flaming sticks.

They charged, desecrating the ruins that stood in their way with their padprints. Dirt, soot and fur mixed on the ground as light illuminated the frenzy. Someone stomped on the blood splattered, broken weaving. Deep grunts and snarls punctuated the night.

The Stein Collection
by
Kathryn Mattingly

Kathryn Mattingly, a six time Maui Writers attendee, has studied under best selling authors Terry Brooks, Elizabeth George, Dorothy Allison, John Saul, and Gail Tsukiyama. Five of her short stories have received recognition, and Mattingly has an agent representing her latest novel, The Tutor, *which is currently under consideration by a renowned publishing house. She is the lead instructor for the Liberal Arts department at the International Academy of Design and Technology in Sacramento, CA. In* "The Stein Collection" *she takes us to Kell's Tavern, a raucous bar with a shady past.*

Sam stood in the rain listening to live band music and the clinking of glassware from Kell's bar. Through the heavy paned window, she glimpsed elbow-to-elbow people on metal stools at a highly polished counter. Shelves jammed with bottles of liquor in every shape and size hung on the wall behind the bar. It was a cozy picture of a patron-filled pub on a Saturday night.

She peered in the adjacent window and saw the restaurant side of Kell's, with its cloth-covered tables carefully arranged. Dreamy piano music escaped from the walls and lingered in the rain-soaked air with bass guitar sounds from the bar. Diners smiled politely at one another, unlike the crowd on the other side where laughs were hearty and tunes lively.

Between the restaurant and bar side of Kell's stood a door. Sam looked through the window and saw a steep stairway. It appeared ominous in this dismal weather. Why couldn't her fiancé Jake have met here as planned? Sam was doubly annoyed with him as she stood there in the rain, hesitating to go in. Did they really want their wedding reception in an old dance hall with a shaded past? Kell's Bar was, however, enticingly trendy and rich with history. As the story went, Kell did away with a few too many customers before being forced to close in 1953. Sam pictured a huge Irishman, intimidating troublesome clients.

Closing her umbrella she unlocked the door with an old key Jake had stuck in an envelope and started up the stairs. Lightning struck and ensuing thunder shook the building as Sam climbed the narrow steps. Storms were not very common in Portland, and this was a particularly rowdy one. It made her edgy, but she had to check out the room, or Jake might think she'd been too afraid. She already heard him laughing at her. Proud of himself for planting a seed of fear with his maudlin tales about the second floor dance hall.

Rain drummed on the roof as she paused to catch her breath on the last step. Straight ahead there was a dimly lit room filled with tables and a bar set against the wall. The wooden floor was worn and dull. A woman was perched on a barstool sipping beer from a heavy stein. She looked lost in thought. Was this room available for employees on their break from the restaurant downstairs?

On a shelf behind the bar was an unusual set of heavy beer steins, similar to the one the woman drank from. There were at least a dozen of them, each different and unique, but blending impressively as a collection. The array of shapes and sizes made quite an effect lined up on the shelf. Yellow-shaded lamps gave them an eerie glow.

The room was just the right size for a small reception, and Sam liked the atmosphere despite the storm's surreal affect. The strange woman continued to sip on her beer and gaze into space. Sam gathered her nerve and sat at the bar a few chairs down.

"I'm sorry to disturb you, but Jake didn't tell me there'd be anybody here," Sam admitted.

The woman turned her head and looked clear through Sam, who couldn't help but notice the woman's striking features. She was a voluptuous blonde and wore a black calf-length skirt that hinted of long toned legs. A white silk-blouse cut impressively low finished the classic look.

"You're no bother. Want a beer?" she asked, with a slight upward turn of her blood-red lips. The crimson shade complimented her creamy complexion perfectly.

"Sure," Sam answered. She watched the woman gracefully slide behind the bar.

"I'm thinking of renting this room for my wedding reception," Sam offered up, hoping to break the icy air between them. "It's just the right size." Sam glanced around again. "I'm sure it would hold a hundred people. The billiard room over there would be great for setting up food."

The strange but striking woman plucked one of the shimmery steins off the shelf. She filled it with frothy beer from a tap that flowed generously as she pushed the white pearl handle firmly. Her blonde hair fell to her shoulders, turning under at the ends in a classy sort of way. She set the beer in front of Sam, and their eyes locked in a mutual stare. This time the woman didn't look past Sam, but focused on her through long sweeping lashes. Her eyes were a soft shade of blue and hinted of sad tales. Looking into them was like trying to find something in a fog. The woman didn't have a young face, but it was far from old. It was seemingly ageless.

"What a beautiful stein," Sam commented, feeling very brunette and with no special attributes to distinguish her wholesome good looks.

The woman smiled. "It's from my private collection. You like them?"

"Yes, very much. My name is Samantha Roberts, by the way."

The woman hesitated and then shook her hand. "I'm Kelly Malone, better known as Kell. This whole place used to be mine. The bar, the restaurant, and this here dance hall." Kell slid back onto her stool. She pointed to the far corner of the bar. "That's where the band set up. Best fiddlers you ever heard. They'd start slow and easy about nine p.m. and by eleven there'd be a dancing frenzy going on."

Sam wondered how she could be the original Kell. It would certainly take a crafty woman to make belligerent drunks disappear forever. "When did this quit being a dance hall?" Sam inquired.

"Long time ago." Kell sighed gloomily.

"When did you decide to rent it out for wedding receptions?" Sam further inquired, but Kell didn't hear the question.

"Businessmen used to flock here when they were in town," she commented." We had a reputation all over Portland."

"I know Kell's bar is sure popular with the college crowd nowadays," Sam mentioned.

Kell didn't acknowledge Sam's comment. "Most of the men who came here only had a few beers. They'd dance for a little while and then return to their motel rooms or homes if they lived nearby," she said as if in a trance.

"Was there a live band every night?" Sam asked, deciding to go along with Kell's nostalgic mood.

"Wednesday through Sunday. We closed Monday's and Tuesday's." Kell grinned wickedly. "I paid half a dozen girls every night to dance with the men. That was my secret, feisty girls that kicked up their heels. It brought men in like bees to honey."

"Really? Girls danced here?" Sam liked the romantic idea of that.

"You bet. Of course, sometimes the men drank too much and tried to woo my little dancers out the door and to their rooms."

Sam took a long swig of her beer. "What if the girl wanted to go with him?"

"Not an option." Kell slammed down her stein. "I paid them to dance. Not to find a boyfriend or make a little extra money on the side."

"I see." Sam raised an eyebrow as that sunk in. She watched Kell refill their steins from the pearl handled tap, confused about who this Kell really was, and when this dance hall last operated.

"Sometimes," Kell said while staring Sam right in the eye from across the counter, "I had to take matters into my own hands. Not often mind you, but sometimes." Her dreamy blue eyes drifted out the window where the wind howled, slamming rain into the glass. Old beams creaked above their heads. A shiver ran down Sam's back. It was creepy to be here alone with Kell, who was scarier than the storm.

"How did you do that, exactly? I mean, take matters into your own hands?"

Kell ran slender fingers up and down the beer stein as if caressing it. "I invited them to my apartment." She nodded her head toward the back of the dance hall. "Down the back stairs, beside the furnace. The caretaker used to live there. You know, the guy who shoveled the coal and stoked the furnace. " Her eyes glowed, as if on fire with past memories.

Sam looked at her curiously. "You'd invite rowdy drunks to your apartment?"

"Oh, I would calm them down first." Kell tossed her blonde hair. "I'd give them a drink on the house. And it always had a sedative in it." She grinned like a Cheshire cat.

Sam tried to imagine Kell shoving a drugged beer into a drunk's hand, and luring him to her private quarters before he crashed in the middle of the dancehall.

"You drugged him? And then what?"

And then I would let him sleep it off on my sofa."

"How clever of you." Sam wondered if she might be that gutsy one day. She realized running a dance hall must have been difficult. Just like everything is when wine and women are involved, or men and beer... and dancing. Rowdy knee stomping swing around the floor heated up and liquored down dancing. It must have been a dizzy delight to see on a hot Saturday night.

Kell slid onto her shiny metal stool and ran a blood red fingernail around the rim of her stein. The nail polish matched her lipstick perfectly.

"This building takes up a whole city block. Did you know that?" Kell tipped her head and a lock of hair fell across one well-formed cheekbone.

"It's an old brick monstrosity, for sure." Sam agreed.

"I remember when they kept that coal-eating furnace behind my kitchen revved up so hot I'd cook dinner in just my panties and a bra." Kell laughed, and her trance-like state evaporated. Color ran through her cheeks as she continued. "I like a good hot fire though, don't get me wrong. Pottery is my hobby. Nothing like a good hot fire for that."

Sam was amazed. "You make pottery?"

"Sure do," Kell admitted.

Taking a long sip of her icy beer Sam examined the stein it was served in. There was a solid gold edge around the rim, and when she held it up to the light little metal flecks sparkled and winked at her. "Did you make this ceramic stein?" Sam asked, knowing it was an incredible thought.

"I surely did." There was pride in her eyes. Waving a hand across the neat row of elaborately designed ceramic ware, she indicated the stein collection was created by her own hands.

Sam was amazed to learn Kell had a passion for ceramics. Her long slender fingers and blood red nails didn't indicate abuse. It boggled her mind as she observed the steins. Each one shimmered and caught the light, as if little shooting stars were melded into the glaze. "What makes the shiny metal specks?" she asked curiously.

"I melted down old jewelry to get that effect. I once had a steady source of it."

The stein Sam drank from was the only one with a gold rim. "This edge must have taken a lot of melted jewelry," Sam commented.

"A pocket watch." Kell laughed. "Keep it… the stein. It's yours. Consider it a little souvenir from our chance meeting on this godforsaken night."

Kell drank the last of her beer just as lightning struck outside the window. Thunder rambled right through Sam's chest as the yellow-shaded lamps went out. The dancehall became dark. Only a steady downpour on the roof could be heard.

"Kell? Are you there?" The hair on the back of Sam's neck stood on end as she stumbled off the barstool, the stein held tightly against her chest, as if to protect her from the pitch black. She made her way slowly to the front stairs.

"Kell? I'm leaving now!" She shouted above the rain blowing sideways into the window, as if it were a hungry wolf trying to enter and devour her. "It was nice meeting you! Thanks for this beautiful stein!" There was no response. Somehow Sam knew there wouldn't be.

Shaking from a damp chill in the air, or maybe from fear, Sam stumbled clumsily down the stairs and looked out the door. Water was backed up from the storm drains, and rushed along the street gutters. But the gods had quieted. All she heard was live music and cheery voices coming from next door.

Wandering into Kell's bar Sam felt dazed but delighted by the candles lit everywhere and the friendly laughter. They too were without electricity. Drinks were on the house. The storm seemed to have bonded customers.

"Do you always bring your own beer stein?" The bartended asked, grinning.

Sam looked down at the stout mug held tightly to her chest. "No. This was a gift." She looked right into the bartenders green eyes. "From the blonde woman upstairs. Do you know who she is?"

"I have no idea who's up there. What can I get you to drink?"

Sam set her stein down on the bar. "Nothing, thanks. What do you know about the original Kell? Was he a big Irishman?" She longed for the answer to be yes, a huge Irishman with curly red hair and his mama's gift for song.

"Irishman? Nah, Kell was a beautiful blonde woman. History has it she was ferocious about watching out for her dance hall girls." He shrugged while mixing drinks and added, "Supposedly, she had a way of getting rid of troublesome drunks permanent-like."

"So I've heard." Sam began chewing on a fingernail, thinking of Kell. Hers had been painted blood red, long and pointy, like little weapons.

"Well, I don't know how true the tale is, but they say she drugged unruly clients and escorted them out the door - never to be seen or heard from again. Finally one too many drunks disappeared and the cops closed it for good." The bartender glanced her way and winked. Was he making it all up? Or did the idea of a beautiful blonde serial killer amuse him?

The lights went back on and everyone cheered. The bartender continued his story. "When they cleaned out that big ole coal furnace to put in gas, a few suspicious looking bone fragments were mixed in the ashes. Sure enough, they were human."

"Really?" Sam stared at her stein.

"Really. Now some say Kell was too delicate to heave a big man into the furnace, but others thought perhaps Lewis helped in exchange for some free bar food." He leaned on the counter, close to Sam. "Lewis was a large black man who shoveled coal in exchange for a cot to sleep on."

The bartender began mixing drinks again, his story flowing like Irish whiskey. "Of course, some thought Lewis was the culprit cooking the bodies after he found them sleeping in the alley and robbed them blind. Burning up the evidence, you might say. And there was a pawn shop around the corner where some thought he exchanged wedding rings and watches and such, for cold hard cash."

"So no one ever found anything to convict Lewis or Kell with?" Sam asked.

"Nope. And one day she got her own just desserts. She disappeared herself. Some think Lewis did her in because the beautiful Kell was love struck by a gent one night and tried to break her own rules. She waltzed right out the door with a patron."

Others at the bar were listening in by now, fascinated with the story. Some smiled knowingly, as if they'd heard the preposterous tale before. The bartender was in his element. Spinning yarn with gusto while serving drinks cold and fast.

"Lewis was said to be furious, 'cause he was smitten with Kell himself. So out of jealously he did her in on a stormy night like no other. Except maybe for this one."

Everybody at the bar stared into their beer. One little old man drummed his fingers on the counter. Nobody spoke, but several patrons nodded as if they'd been present when it all happened—if it happened.

Or was it Irish folklore, Portland style?

Sam caressed the gold-edged stein. She thought about how Kell mentioned a steady source of jewelry. Was it from the pawnshop nearby? Or from robbing drugged men before she and Lewis tossed them into the fire? The furnace room was right there on the other side of her kitchen, afterall. Sam could see Kell pushing with all her might to shove the limp body into the stove, wearing only her bra and panties, while Lewis helped steady and lift the dead weight. Did they sit around her cozy kitchen afterwards, gobbling down leftovers from the bar?

"They say she haunts the place on stormy nights. Hovering and fretting over those steins like she did her dancehall girls." The bartender laughed.

He'd obviously never run into Kell, or maybe she was just a setup, and he was in on it. If it was a joke, it was a damn good one. Kell was spookier than hell. Sam grinned back, said thanks for the folklore, grabbed her stein and slid out the door onto the street. The rain had stopped and the air had a fresh scent. She glanced up at the dance hall windows. It was dark on the second story.

Sam took the metal key from her pocket. Maybe the lights would turn on if she flipped the switch inside the door. She had to see that stein collection one more time. Now that the storm had cleared, she felt braver. Sam had to know if she'd been duped by Jake and whoever else was in on the fun. But the key wouldn't open the door. That was odd. It opened easily the first time. Sam toyed with the lid on her stein. This one got away. In fact, unlike her dancehall girls, Kell had given it away. Glancing up at the second story window one last time, she thought she saw the blinds shift.

Sam stuck the stein protectively in her coat and headed for the car, thinking it might be fun to have her wedding reception in a haunted dancehall, giving her the last laugh. Unless of course, Jake had nothing to do with her unbelievable evening, in which case, unlike most brides, she would pray for rain. Maybe she'd see Kell again, and thank her for the priceless wedding gift.

Dotting the *i*
by
Gary Sleeth

Gary Sleeth has had a novel and a number of short stories and articles published. He hopes to become so famous that everything he says and does is taken out of context in order to sell vast numbers of newspapers and magazines. In "Dotting the i," Sleeth explores cause and effect, and the possible consequences of one's actions.

Not even the desperate need for escape permeating Dante's lowest Hell could have matched Cassandra's wanton craving for death. When she found that the nail clipper hid a crisscrossed blade, she dug frantically at the pulsing beneath the skin and sinew of her wrist. She sighed in relief as the rhythmic geyser of blood splattered across her face, neck and arms.

In the final second of mortality, an overwhelming intuition of astral beauty and wonder enveloped her, but was swiftly lost as the memories of Cassandra's past lives flooded her consciousness, forbidding any outer discovery.

Cassandra didn't want to remember. She had had enough of life. She longed for the sweet warmth and beauty of death, unbound from the constraining torment of helpless, useless flesh. But consciousness, though conscience be stillborn, is remorseless in its recollection: the repository of every thought, word, and deed. A library where both the selfless and selfish can be found, cross-referenced, researched and studied.

They came like the ocean breaking through a dike, tearing down the walls of her rationalizations, sending the concrete and steel reinforcements of her denials crashing around her and flooding the lowlands of unsullied understanding. There could be no refusing it, no means of refuting it, of buffering herself against its onslaught.

Cassandra shuddered within the timeless second of death's advent, as the memories washed across her awakened mind, sweeping her in the current of their unabridged truth: like old photographs, without the distinctions of *perhaps*, *maybe*, *but*, or *if*. Still life pictures, flashing one after another. Rapidly progressing 'nows' presenting an animated facsimile of time and movement.

Capsized, immersed, in the endless procession of lives and moments, Cassandra's consciousness, like the Recording Angel of ancient tradition, watched as the parade of countless incarnations marched by.

There Cassandra was as Dorcas, handmaiden in the Athenian temple of Diana. Since childhood, every luxury of the age had been hers, her devotions simple, her free time ample; yet the thought that she was merely a servant continually worried at her peace. In time, Dorcas' even temper and gracious smiles were no more genuine than the meticulously chiseled features of the marble goddess.

A shimmer, and amid another, Cassandra appeared as Hildegard, wife of Burkhardt, raising her sister's son, Herbert, after his parents' untimely death. Burkhardt had been an amorous pursuer and wealthy woodcutter when Hildegard's father consented to their marriage, and he was an adamantly devoted husband. Herbert's devotion to his aunt was no less. Both willingly did whatever Hildegard asked of them. In response, Hildegard showered them with love and attention. But that was before Burkhardt crushed his hand beneath a wagon wheel. Although Burkhart had apprenticed Herbert, the boy showed no aptitude for the craft. Hildegard's affection for them dwindled as quickly as their wealth.

Beneath the procession of former lives, Cassandra glimpsed vague connections between the attitude in one incarnation and its effect upon the next. These were promptly dismissed with a bitter, "life raises you up, just to increase the depth of your fall."

The brief reverie was replaced by the image of Casandra as Collette. Collette had had a simple but happy childhood, and when she reached proper age was engaged as a maid in a widower's home. In a short time she won his heart, breaking it a few years later when she fell in love with his lawyer. She received a sizable financial allocation when she left and lived a long, if somewhat tainted, life of leisure.

The inner vision of her life as Collette was followed by those of Ena, a spinster who loved the town mayor she could never have, Clara, who chiseled marble sculptures and knew no man, and Ghosha, Suzette, Aisha and Margaret.

Passing flickers of past lives, each quickly snuffed out by the next. An endless stream of consciousness which threatened to overwhelm Cassandra, until, as the remembrances reached the life preceding her present, they slowed, the march halting, the memories milling about waiting to be fully recognized…

She relived the moments as though someone else had enacted them, some other identity had eaten, slept, moved, spoke, and breathed in her place. Yet, it was her—a different name in another time—but undeniably her. There was her younger sister, Grace, feeble-minded and deformed. There she was, full of adolescent complaints, her life wasting away. Her free time filled, not with friends, malls, dances and boys, but with, "look after your sister, she needs you."

She had hated Grace. That ugly, selfish dummy embarrassed her and had ruined her life. In a desperate effort to escape Grace, she ran away with the first boy she met and swore she would never return. It was a short-lived romance and her vow was quickly broken. She arrived home with bags in hand and a baby on its way. With her father ill and her mother suffering with crippling arthritis, she heard the dreaded plea: "Look after Grace, she needs you."

When her father died, her mother's dependence on her to feed, clean, and dress her 'special' child, increased. With a sickly mother, a child of four, and Grace to care for, she became angry and spiteful.

At first, she did little more than the same nasty tricks she had pulled when young; putting alum in Grace's milk, dirt in her cereal, maybe a chopped worm in her hamburger. She had told herself they were simply pranks, practical jokes, nothing to feel ashamed of. But they grew until they couldn't be called pranks any longer. Eventually, whenever the tension of her day, the demands of her mother and child, or the angst of loneliness stirred, she found relief by beating Grace.

This, too, grew, and what had begun as harsh slaps for small mistakes or unwanted requests, soon became belt straps and broom handles walloped anytime, anywhere, for any reason. It was how she had dealt with the unfairness of her life and seldom found fault with herself for it. To her mind, every unjust thing that had befallen her had been the direct result of that cretin, Grace.

After their mother passed away, she sold the house, auctioned the furniture, packed up her daughter, and left. Grace, now abandoned, was placed in the State Hospital, where she spent the remainder of her neglected days...

The inner visions ceased, leaving the imprint of Cassandra's despite unto Grace. It was a startling revelation ... a macabre movie in which she was the evident villain. The self-centered psychopath incapable of seeing the sufferings others endured. A hardened deviant unable to perceive the sound of another's heartfelt cries. Revelation segued into realization and Cassandra beheld the flawless mathematics of justice. A seesaw so perfectly balanced on is fulcrum that not the dot of an *i* or a cross of a *t* was lost...

Cassandra now knew why, in her most recent life, she had been born deaf and blind.

Understanding this, however, did not change Cassandra's hatred of life. Of her present life in particular! It was an experience that stung her essence like a venomous bite, poisoning her further whenever she thought about it. Being caught in a body which could neither see nor hear had made living unbearable. Cassandra had waited for the chance to get her desperate hands on something, anything, sharp. When opportunity came, she took it. With one frenzied act she had won her release, escaping the bitter justice that had trapped her.

With the conclusion of synaptic recollection, the final second of Cassandra's life ended—her astral body slipping out of the mortal frame as smoothly as warm oil from a vessel. Cassandra was free. At last she was free! She stretched with feline satisfaction. Bubbling over in joyous expectation of the heavenly beauty and wonder she had first intuited, Cassandra strained to see her new world. But saw nothing. She searched frantically for a ray of light to enter the portholes of her soul, but perceived none.

Slowly Cassandra began to understand. Slowly, mercilessly, came the knowledge that she was still blind. That she would remain blind through each infinite second, each eternal hour, day and decade, until it was time again to be reborn!

Cassandra screamed … but she didn't hear it.

The Pit
by
Eric Pinder

Eric Pinder, a resident of Berlin, New Hampshire, is the author of North to Katahdin, Tying Down the Wind, *and other books about science and nature. He teaches writing at Chester College of New England. For many years he lived and worked at the weather observatory on top of Mount Washington ("the highest paying job in New England") and as a guide for the Appalachian Mountain Club. Unlike his unfortunate characters in "The Pit," he has managed to avoid being captured by nomads despite years of wandering on foot in the wilds. He has, however, been chased by bears.*

Crash! Erhard opened the window by throwing a chair through it.

Colorful images of men and monsters in combat decorated the surface of the expensive stained glass. The window nestled in the east wall of the dimly lit church of Grundur, the man-turned-god who expelled the pagans from the Northland back during the Age of Heroes. Erhard barely glanced at the pictures. Religious art did not interest him, not when he was running for his life. His only concern now was not cutting himself as he jumped through the shards.

He would have preferred to use the front door, but a red-faced man holding a crossbow blocked it. The man's name was Olger, citizen of Droburg, priest of Grundur, and, most importantly, father of Cassandra.

Erhard knew Olger well; he knew Cassandra even better. And he now knew that Olger did not like a rogue such as himself knowing the soon-to-be-married-to-a-boring-merchant-who-was-too-old-for-her Cassandra. He knew because Olger had just caught Erhard embracing Cassandra in the back pew of the empty church, and now was trying to kill him.

At sermons, Erhard recalled, Olger was quite serene, if the snoring of his parishioners was anything to go by. But now the man's face reddened and twisted with rage. He fired the crossbow.

Erhard dove through the window, nicking his shoulder on a jagged glass tooth. He landed with a thump and rolled across the lawn, destroying a garden of roses carefully planted in the shape of a square.

His trousers slipped down to his ankles, tripping him when he tried to stand; he kicked them off like a snake shedding its skin. A sword slipped from its scabbard and stuck in the ground. He let it lie, scooped up his pants and sprinted toward a grove of trees, the eaves of his unbuttoned shirt gusting out behind him like wings in the wind.

The crossbow bolt shot out the same window, off its mark. Olger's deep, angry voice followed it. "Damn you, Erhard! You heretic! Adulterer! Pig!" Olger had more to say, but Erhard didn't stay to listen. He hopped over a low fence and vanished in the woods.

Olger chased him, his footsteps loud and clumsy. Though short and squat, unlike Erhard, he was fully clothed and able to navigate the brush without fear of injury. A silver medallion— the symbol of Grundur, the God of Peace, War, and Potato Harvests—dangled from his neck.

A hasty glance back showed Olger gripping a longbow, strung and drawn. *Harnor's breath!* cursed Erhard. *Did the man keep an entire arsenal in the back pew of his church?*

An arrow whisked past Erhard's head, clipping his ear, drawing a trickle of blood before embedding itself in the trunk of an oak tree. *Oaks are hardwoods*, thought Erhard. *They shouldn't swallow up half an arrow like that. Olger must be madder than I thought. Unreasonable of him, really. She wasn't married yet.*

A second arrow shot past, not so close. Then Erhard's long legs powered him into the thick of the hardwoods, out of range, out of sight. He dodged left, still sprinting. "Dagur!" he shouted. "Wake up! Hurry!"

Two acorn-brown geldings, hitched to a pine tree, pawed at the matted forest floor. Below them slept a short, bearded man on an improvised bed of pine needles. His head rested against a mossy rock.

"Dagur!"

The sleeping man stirred, perked open an eye. "What? What's wrong?"

Erhard untied his horse, leapt into the saddle, and only then paused to button his shirt. Dagur opened his other eye. "You're not wearing pants," he said. "And you're wounded. What happened?"

"I fell in a rose garden when I jumped out the window."

"Oh." Dagur reflected on that for a moment. "Stupid thing to do without clothes on."

"I was in a hurry. Now get up before we both get killed."

Olger stumbled forward and shot off another arrow, which smacked into a tree trunk above Erhard's head. Dagur leapt to his feet, cut loose the second gelding with a swipe of his scimitar, and pulled himself into the saddle.

"Erhard!" shouted the priest. "You'll beg for mercy on the rack. I'll find you!" Then the horses bolted past him. The fat man dodged, hit his head on a low branch, and fell unconscious.

Minutes later, Erhard and Dagur reached a road and turned south, avoiding the town of Droburg and the posse that surely would pursue them.

⁀◞◟⁀

"South!" said an irate Dagur. "Why south?" He kicked the sand at his feet.

"Because Skagaströnd is a nice, safe city. No one knows us there." Erhard fumbled with flint and kindling in an attempt to start a campfire. His slender fingers shielded a pale flicker, but a gust of wind broke past his defense and killed the flame.

To the south rolled the dunes of the Dolamere Desert, a vast ocean of sand. Dagur stared west at the low sun, a deep crimson orb. The brightest stars already shone along the eastern horizon, where the sun had relinquished its influence. A cool breeze gusted through Dagur's cloak, making him shiver. *Should the worst happen*, he thought, *that same wind soon would be blowing the desert sand over my corpse.* Only madmen and merchants dared to cross the desert, and the merchants always stuck to the road. "We're bloody lost," he accused. "Aren't we?"

Erhard renewed his struggle with the fire. "Look, I'm sorry."

"Don't you agree that a church was a stupid place for a rendezvous? Not to mention blasphemous?"

"It was Cassandra's idea. I liked the risk, the adventure of it all."

Dagur turned his back. If not for Erhard's improprieties, they could have stuck to the road. Instead they were traveling cross-country, hiding from pursuers.

"Look," said Erhard, "I think we'll survive the night if I ever get this blasted fire going. There!" A satisfied smile creased his face as flames crackled and spread over the branches.

Dagur walked over to warm his hands. "This won't protect us from wolves," he said. "I doubt that handful of sticks will last till morning."

Erhard grinned. He breathed in the fresh desert air, running a hand through his long blonde hair. "I brought more wood in my pack. Gathered it at that little village when we stopped to buy a sword."

"Killed it, you mean. You hacked down a little oak sapling, just like the savages who live in this sandpit are going to hack down us. Harnor's Breath! It's almost the equinox, and a full moon too—"

"Don't be such a pessimist! The Nomads are just people, and we're not on the Desert Road anyway. The only folks we'll meet out here will be lost Northerners. Rich merchants! Maybe, for a reward, we can lead them back to the road. It should be fairly close. I think."

Dagur snorted and reached into his pack to retrieve a woolen blanket. The sun had fully set, and brilliant white stars pierced the night's cover. "I'll turn in now," he said. "Since you seem so wide awake and chipper, why don't you take the first watch?" Close to the fire he curled up and closed his eyes. "Be sure to dust the sand off me before I'm buried."

A look of worry replaced Erhard's smile. He sat silently by the fire, staring out into the night, and Dagur fell asleep with images of his friend's anxiety dancing in his mind.

He woke from a nightmare of flames and dancing shadows when Erhard urgently gripped his shoulder and shook. Erhard had kicked over their small campfire, but in the light of the dying coals, Dagur saw that his friend had drawn his sword.

"Look east," whispered Erhard, pointing at a small plateau framed by a large moon, just past full. A dozen tiny figures stood outlined at the top, ringed by burning torches.

Dagur's gut tightened. "Desert men?" He reached for his bow.

"You were right. Nomads. I didn't think they came hunting so far north." Erhard sucked in an anxious breath. "The horses… someone took them." He held up the ropes that had tethered their horses, each cut clean through.

"Nomads?" asked Dagur. "They could have killed us in our sleep."

"Perhaps there was only one of them. You could have awakened while he was slitting my throat. So why take the risk? Now we're on foot. He can go get his friends. There's strength in numbers." Erhard frowned. "Or perhaps… I've heard that… Maybe they don't want to kill us. Not yet."

"What do you mean?" snapped Dagur.

Erhard did not answer.

Dagur rose, casting his pack and a quiver of arrows over either shoulder. "Where did they come from? A group that size could hardy pass unseen."

"They did, though. They shone no lights until seconds ago. But there was a small fire there earlier, a campfire like ours. It lit up on the plateau after you fell asleep. I think it was an ordinary traveler, or more than one. A northerner like us. But then those torches appeared, just after moonrise. I kicked out the fire and woke you."

"We'd best leave this place if nomads are on the hunt. They could be stalking us right now."

Erhard nodded. "Unless that traveler was lost like us, the desert road must be just beyond that plateau. We'll make for it."

So you finally admit we were lost, thought Dagur. He recalled his nightmare and stared up at the dancing silhouettes on the plateau. *I just hope we stay lost.* With a shiver, he jogged after his friend.

A tracker by trade—albeit a poor one, seldom employed—Erhard led them in a wide arc across the dunes, seeking to avoid any scouts sent to investigate their campfire. Dagur understood the plan but felt anxious nonetheless, as if every step brought them closer to danger.

No sounds save the hiss of the wind reached Dagur's ears, but a flicker of motion warned him of the sudden threat to his life. He spun, shouted, and dropped to one side. A small, three-pronged blade flew past his ear. Dagur's arm was a blur; he hurled his dagger at a dark shape outlined by the moon.

Erhard, hearing his friend's startled cry, jogged back. Dagur stayed low, his bow strung and an arrow notched just in case a second assassin lurked in the dark.

They waited, but the desert remained silent.

"A lucky throw, my friend," whispered Erhard, moving to the nomad. The dagger protruded from the man's chest—slightly left of center. Dagur retrieved his blade, wiping it across the dead man's cloak to remove a layer of sticky, warm blood.

"Keep your bow strung," said Erhard. "You'll likely need it. They seem to be looking for us."

"When daylight comes, we'll be easily seen and outnumbered. They must know we'll make for the road. It's death to go there now."

"What else can we do?" countered Erhard. "Go further south, into the desert? We'll never find the road again—or water!—if we leave it. I just hope we can outrun them."

"Then let's make for the plateau and rejoin the road further north. If the nomads are in small groups, or alone like this one"—Dagur nudged the body with a toe—"we might steal some horses. With horses we have a chance."

Erhard nodded, wordlessly marching across the sand toward the base of the plateau and the flickering torches on its crest. For an hour they plodded through the sand, encountering no one. Orion the Hunter and the stars of winter swung overhead. The wind began to howl. At last the wall of the mesa rose in front of them. Using hand signs, Erhard indicated that they would creep along the plateau's base in an effort to reach the northern side—and, he hoped, the road.

The plateau above hid the cluster of flaming torches that had served as a beacon while they crossed the desert, but a pale fringe of red glowed along the edges, lighting their way. Dagur could sense nomad eyes nearby, searching for them. They were prey.

Dagur's feet protested the fast pace set by his companion. He bit his lower lip in agony and stumbled onward. No nomads attacked, but Dagur was not relieved. His taut muscles wanted to strike out, to end the suspense. To fight. He disliked the steep slope of the plateau wall, for it left them exposed and vulnerable. His hands shook, his legs trembled, his feet throbbed. They were not safe. At last he could bear the suspense no longer; to halt his friend, he tapped Erhard's shoulder.

Erhard whirled at the touch and nearly struck Dagur with his sword. At the last instant he drove the blow harmlessly into the plateau wall. Each man lifted a hand in apology.

"We must go up," Dagur whispered, pointing toward the summit. Erhard frowned, then nodded and led the way. *Just in time*, thought Dagur.

The sandstone path crumbled at the slightest misstep, so they climbed slowly for minutes that stretched into hours. Then, in a frenzied burst of energy, Dagur pulled ahead, rushing to the top. Something important waited up there, something he needed to see.

He crawled the last few yards on hands and knees, peering into a circle of torches atop the plateau. Inside the circle, an old man dressed in northern garb—a gray jacket, a merchant's notched cap, and a pair of baggy trousers stitched with a half-dozen pockets—lay bound and prostrate. A long, slender sword had been driven through his skull at the temples, and a halo of blood glittered around his head in the torchlight. A ritual sacrifice to the desert gods.

Erhard crawled beside his friend and gasped—not at the gruesome scene, but at the trap they had walked into. "Do you think they're guarding the rim of the plateau?"

Dagur shrugged. "I'm certain that they'll be watching the path to the Desert Road." They had been allowed to come here; they would be allowed to go no farther. There were no horses to steal; his gamble had not paid off. Soon the moon would rise high enough to expose them.

Why? wondered Dagur. *Why take so much trouble to hunt down two lost strangers?* He rubbed a hand across his brow, deep in thought. No option seemed preferable: staying and fleeing both meant death.

He handed his bow and quiver to Erhard, who nodded in silent understanding. An objection formed on the tracker's lips, but Dagur gave him no time. He gripped his dagger tightly and sprinted toward the deadly circle of light.

A spear shaft whooshed over his shoulder. Twenty or more nomad warriors emerged from the shadows, yelling in triumph—until Erhard's arrows began to cut them down.

When Erhard's arrow felled the first pursuer, Dagur tried to laugh, but his voice emerged in a frightened squeak. He ran exposed, the bait in a trap, while Erhard stayed hidden, shooting at the warriors who had rushed into the light.

Seconds later, when Dagur had escaped into the shadows on the far side of the plateau, his first feeling was surprise. He had expected to die while Erhard cut down his assassins. Beyond that, Dagur had made no plans. Now he plunged down the slope, grasping for a sensible course of action. *Should I flee north along the desert road, or return to rescue Erhard?* The latter seemed a hopeless choice, but Erhard was his friend.

A moment later his choice was made for him when he collided with two nomads. He swung at them with his dagger but the blow missed. A club smacked against the side of his skull and he felt no more.

Blood roared in Erhard's head. His heart pounded like a great bass drum. Groaning, he tried to massage his temples but his hands refused to move. Stouts cords bound them behind his back.

He lay on his stomach on a cold wooden floor. Any attempt to turn caused lightning pains to shoot from the base of his spine to his skull. The nomads had beaten him, clubbed him into submission. *How long have I been unconscious? Where am I now?* Erhard remembered nothing.

It slowly came back to him. Dagur's brave but foolish sprint into the light. The score of men that had leapt out of darkness in pursuit. Erhard shot five before he heard others approaching. He had thrown down the bow and defended himself at sword-point until a blow to the head felled him. Then he had awakened here. *But where is here?*

There was a door in the wall to his right. The walls were a strange, light-brown wood he didn't recognize. The door, slightly ajar, let wisps of light stream in from outside. There was no sign of Dagur.

The door swung open, revealing three nomads—a tall, sunburned man dressed in the black robes of a shaman flanked by two brown-robed, female acolytes. The shaman's graying beard hung to his waist, and a black medallion shaped like a spider mingled with his whiskers.

"I was on the desert road," lied Erhard. "My friend and I were going north. You had no right to accost us."

"Quiet!" The old man's boot flashed out at Erhard's head. Again and again the boot struck, till the tracker's vision blackened. He did not try to speak again.

The women propped up his weak body, forced him to stand. A knife tickled his ribs. They led outside into the cold night air and forced a hot liquid, heavy and bitter, down his throat.

A small path of stones led out to the desert. The rocks chilled Erhard's bare feet. His clothes were gone, replaced by a threadbare white robe.

The sky grew lighter as they walked. The moon sank and set, and the first tendrils of the new day's sun glowed just below the horizon. Dimly, Erhard saw a great crowd of people on a hill in the distance, to which the path seemed to lead. Hundreds chanted and sang in celebration of the equinox. If Erhard remembered correctly, sacrifices were made each season to the gods of the sands, followed by a great festival and feast. He had no wish to join the party.

He also had no choice. A phalanx of desert warriors surrounded him suddenly, seizing him from the hands of the acolyte women. A push propelled him forward; rough hands grabbed him before he fell.

The chorus of chanting swelled until a single, steady chord wafted toward the heavens. The voices of the desert people merged into one. Then the sun rose. The clouds parted, a lidless red eye opened on the horizon, and the people dropped to their knees. A shaman lifted his arms and at once the throng fell silent. He spoke words that Erhard did not understand.

The old man with the spider medallion—a chieftain priest, it seemed—poked a gnarled finger at the Erhard. Soldiers gripped him tightly.

By now, Erhard had had enough. His strength was returning, and he knew his time was running out. When the old man came close enough, tracing mystic symbols in the air, Erhard planted a kick in the shaman's groin. But the effort cost him, for rough hands pummeled him until his vision dimmed. As if in a dream, he felt warriors throw him to the ground, kicking him in retribution.

He was hauled to his feet. Renewed shouts came from the throng. Nomads cut the ropes binding Erhard's hands. He was shoved from nomad to nomad, all of them groping, screaming, praying. Blood trickled into his eyes, blinding him. He was too hurt to resist.

They pushed him toward a great opening in the earth. Down into that black mouth they threw him, into a darkness where the sun's light did not reach. That was the ceremony's climax. Erhard's scream blended in harmony with the shaman's laughter.

"Hey! Someone! Erhard! Anyone!" Dagur pounded against the cage that held him. His punches had no noticeable effect on the bars, though they did bruise his hand. He stopped, frowned, and resumed pacing the thin planks on the cage's floor. The taste of blood lingered in his mouth. A crust of blood had dried and hardened on his face where he the club had struck him. Although a cool morning breeze tousled his hair, the wind's caress did little to soothe his pain.

The desert sun had risen high enough to torture his sensitive eyes. Though surprised and delighted to find himself alive, the discovery that he was on exhibit in a bamboo cage in the center of a nomad village had soured his temper. His weapons, his supplies, and his friend were all absent.

Strangely, the inhabitants of the village were also missing. Dagur was alone, abandoned. He heard no voices, saw no children gathering water from the river. No one ambled by to spit at him, as they would at a man in the stocks in a northern village. For two hours he had been awake, with only sand and empty houses for company. *Have the nomads left me here to die of thirst? Have they abandoned their village? Why?*

He searched for a way out. The cage's wood was young and thick, unbreakable by human hands, but the cage itself wasn't fixed to the ground. That gave Dagur an idea. He gripped two bars and began to rock back and forth.

Dagur cursed under his breath when an old man, gray-bearded and red-faced, led a squad of fifteen warriors toward him. A sunspider talisman hung from the man's throat—the symbol of a shaman. As a youth, Dagur had dabbled in magic enough to identify the symbol of a desert demon. He just wished he could remember the demon's name.

Dagur's released the bars and wiped the sweat from his palms. The shaman stared at him, eyes full of hatred. Dagur stared back. A minute passed with the two men grimacing at each other, gazes locked. Then Dagur could stand no more. "Did you come so we could scowl at each other, you bastard? Or did you come to fight?"

To his surprise, the shaman laughed. "Fight? You have already fought and lost. Now you shall suffer."

Dagur spat. "You imitate civilized speech quite well."

"Infidel! I speak your tongue. Neither you nor any of your brethren speak mine." Dagur did not reply, so the shaman continued. "We have no more use for you here. You shall be sold as a slave and work away your crimes in the mines." He handed a rope to the nearest warrior and mumbled words Dagur could not hear.

The nomads opened the cage door and three warriors entered, pointing their spears at Dagur's chest. He backed into the far wall. The life of a desert slave was short and brutal. When one of the warriors reached for him, Dagur leapt up, grasping at the sticks of the ceiling. They sagged but supported his weight.

One man grabbed Dagur's right leg, trying to pull him down, but a kick to the face released set Dagur free again. The nomad groaned and slumped to the floor. Dagur hooked his feet in the ceiling, out of reach of his enemies.

"Come down!" shouted the shaman. "You have nowhere to go!" The remaining guards crowded toward the door.

Dagur tugged backwards and forwards, swinging the cage. Understanding dawned in the shaman's eyes. "Kill him! Kill him now!"

Spear points thrust toward Dagur's chest, but the cage wobbled and turned. The warriors found themselves standing on a wall—and they fell. Dagur drifted slowly backward. When the cage settled, the door was above him.

Dagur leapt to the bottom and seized a loose spear. One warrior grappled with him, shoving him against the wall; a second attacked from behind. Dagur hit one in the chest with the point of his spear and the other in the jaw with the shaft. He swung at a third nomad, who dove to the floor. Then he was aloft, out on the roof.

Outside, a dozen warriors rushed forward to surround the cage. Dagur jumped to the sandy ground, slipped, and regained his feet. With a triumphant shout, he sprinted through the mysteriously empty village. For the second time that day, a throng of nomad warriors pursued him across the sand.

Long after Erhard's screams had died away, his body tumbled down the black abyss. Wind roared past his ears. The sky was gone, replaced by frigid blackness.

Far below shone a pinpoint of light, as bright as a lonely star in a moonless sky. Down he plunged toward the light, but it never increased in size, never came closer, as if it too were plunging ahead of him toward the bowels of the earth.

The pressure of the wind crushed Erhard, deafened him. He fell until he thought he could fall no farther. And then, the air around him thickened like a cushion. The white beacon vanished.

His feet hit solid ground, and he sprawled across a floor of cold stone. But he felt no pain. Some sorcery had protected him. The small, square room where he landed was well lit, though the source of the light eluded him. He could see no windows, no lanterns. The light just *was*, as if the air itself glowed.

Four dark corridors branched off from the room, one in each wall. They were unlit, forbidding.

He rose. Oddly, he discovered he could touch the stony ceiling with the palm of his hand. No long tunnel extended overhead. *Did I fall at all? Was it all illusion, a dream? Am I being… toyed with?*

One more surprise awaited him. A small, slender sword lay at the foot of the easternmost passage. Erhard lifted it. The blade was light, flimsy, the kind he had practiced with as a boy. This almost useless weapon was proof he was being toyed with, playing a game he was not expected to win. *But who—or what—am I playing against?*

"Well," he said. "No choice but to play on." Of the four black corridors, only the north one showed a flicker of yellow light, perhaps a torch. He did not trust the beacon, but he needed light. With a sigh, Erhard stepped out of the magically glowing room and was instantly wrapped in darkness.

A raspy grating sound assaulted his ears from the rear. Erhard spun around and struck out with his sword, feeling more than seeing the flash of movement behind him. Metal clashed against metal. There was a spark.

A black gate had dropped from a crevice in the ceiling, cutting him off from the room. Though he strained and pulled, his strength failed to lift the heavy iron. "No choice," he repeated. "Go on."

At first, Erhard could barely see his own feet in the gloom. He felt his way by rubbing a hand against the wall until the yellow glimmer in the north drew closer. A stone ring in the wall held a torch, a comforting flicker. It shone brightly, as if lit only minutes before.

In the glow of torchlight, Erhard saw a second intersection. He decided to continue straight ahead, but before setting off, his fingers gripped the dry wood of the torch and lifted it from the ring.

As soon as he pulled the torch free, a second black gate crashed to the ground ahead of him, sealing the route forward.

Erhard frowned, muttered, then stepped to his right. No gate fell behind him. He sighed. He had to find a way to beat whoever, or whatever, had control of this place.

An echo coursed through the hallway, a deep sound that washed across Erhard like a tide. It struck him like a blow, and he staggered. The ethereal noise pulsed, swimming past his ears into his brain. An urge to flee grew in his mind, all but irresistible. He fought off the panic, and the sound—a deep, drumming sound—faded. But the noise taunted him; he could not tell if it were truly gone or still lurking at the very edge of hearing.

"Well," said Erhard. The sound of his own voice comforted him. "Drums, torches, and gates of black. Once I pass through, I cannot go back. But I'll find a way out of this maze, whoever's listening." Sword in one hand, torch in the other, he strode purposefully down the tunnel.

Dagur hid inside a hut at the edge of the village. Rivulets of sweat drained down his temples across his forehead. He wiped them with a sleeve. When there was no sound of pursuit, he slumped exhausted to the ground.

During the long hours of his deadly game of hide and seek, he had come to loathe the sun, that great fiery eye glaring down on him. He still wore heavy grey garments, designed to protect against the chill desert night, and he dared not shed them. He expected to need warm clothing in a matter of hours, when the sun set—if his sweaty stench did not betray him to his pursuers before then.

All the homes in the village were still vacant, but he had guessed the reason. He glimpsed a great gathering on a hilltop outside of the camp—a religious celebration of the equinox. Only a handful of soldiers searched for him, and he hoped they would follow the signs he had left on the north side of the village. If they assumed he had fled into the desert and moved the hunt for him out of the village, he might have a chance.

His mind churned, examining each of his options. He could loot a hut for food and water, then escape into the desert. Without a tracker to guide him he would most likely die, but his chances were even worse if he stayed. Sooner or later someone would find him.

Only his loyalty to Erhard kept him from fleeing. If his friend were dead, he wanted to know. If alive, he wanted rescue him or die trying.

Dagur slipped into an exhausted doze and woke abruptly, heart pounding, cursing himself. *That bloody sun! How much time have I wasted here, asleep?* The intense heat of the desert sun had drained him, melted his resolve. *Only Harnor knows how the nomads missed me, splayed out on the floor of this hut like a sacrificial lamb.*

A quick glance outside inspired panic. A line of people—two hundred men and women—had formed along the path to the village. The feast and festival had ended, and so had Dagur's reprieve.

He got to his feet, muscles stiff and sore. A nervous pang tickled his chest, and he bit his lip, mind racing. He heard people entering an adjacent hut, their voices muffled through the walls.

A dark hand lifted the cloth doorway of Dagur's hiding place, and he pressed himself against the wall, readying his stolen spear. He prayed to Harnor that this was the house of a loner, a solitary man who would not be missed. At least, not missed for a while.

But if two or three nomads entered, his options were more limited. They would raise an alarm, and he would have to fight his way outside. He wondered how far he would get before falling on the spear point of some nomadic warrior.

To his relief, the hand vanished and the cloth fell into place. Outside, two voices—one male, one female—talked quietly. Dagur silently begged them to move on, but then the cloth was yanked open, letting in a stream of sunlight.

A woman entered, and the shaft of Dagur's spear struck her head. *Sorry*, he thought as she slipped toward the floor. Before she hit the ground he was outside, dragging her startled mate back in and throwing him against a wall. Dagur glared at the small, nonthreatening nomad and held the spear to his throat, a command to keep silent.

Outside, no one cried in alarm. No warriors rushed in to slay him. His speedy abduction had not been seen.

"Erhard!" he hissed. "Where is he?" Dagur frowned, anxiety eating at his gut. The desert man lifted a shaky hand to the east—toward the hill. The ceremonial hill. If Erhard had been taken there, he was surely dead, a sacrifice to the gods.

Dagur delivered a blow to the man's head with the shaft of his spear. *Not sorry*, he thought as the nomad crumpled next to the woman. There was no time to bind them. As ever more villagers returned from the ceremony the shaman would send them out in search of him. Once they realized he had not fled to the desert, they would start searching the village.

Dagur had no time. He swiped a skin of water and some biscuits and shoved them in a hide sack. He wrapped himself in the nomad's cloak and peeked through the flap. Dashing outside, he took cover behind a row of low huts. It was past noon—siesta time in the north. Drowsiness once again tugged at his eyelids.

Shaking his head to clear it, Dagur sprinted along the outskirts of the village, dodging behind mounds of sand. The sun beat down on him, but he dared not slow. He ran to the far side of the village, to the ceremonial hill. The flask of water became an unbearable weight, a cumbersome load he longed to drop but dared not do without.

At the top of the hill, Dagur dropped to the ground and gulped water from the flask. He removed his woolen cloak, heavy with sweat, and tossed it over one shoulder. He struggled to calm himself, to think. *Where can I go? How long can I hide?*

The entire village lay below him. He heard the whinny of horses to the west and saw the corrals where the nomads kept their mounts. *Maybe I can steal one*, he thought, though his eyes and his interest kept being drawn to the great black pit yawning open in the center of the hill's level summit.

A foul odor leaked out of the depths, and Dagur pinched his nose as he walked closer. He approached the chasm step by step, until he could peek over the rim.

To his surprise, the pit was scarcely ten feet deep. He had feared a deep hole filled with past sacrifices, or worse, a portal of black magic, the sort Northland mothers told of to frighten their children.

Dagur had laughed at such tales as a child. He wasn't laughing now.

At the bottom of the pit, Dagur saw a small, white box. *So, there is magic at work here after all.*

Standing so close to the pit, Dagur had exposed himself to eyes down in the village. When he realized this, he leapt into the pit, despite his dread of the box. The warriors hunting for him were a far more tangible peril, and he needed a closer look at that box.

He rolled to absorb the fall, powdering himself with the dry sand that floored the pit. Rough, jagged rocks protruded from the walls, carved with notches to use like rungs on a ladder. From above, the ladder blended into the wall, a trick of light, but from below it was plainly visible.

The small box emitted a stench, an aura. Dagur sensed a presence within it, intangible and evil. *Magic. Black magic.* But there was something else about the box. Something familiar.

The feeling grew more intense when touched the box, and he jerked his hand away as if burned. Warily, he reached out again, and this time there could be no mistake. When he laid his hand on the white box, he heard a single word, hoarse and faint, repeated over and over again. "No!"

Erhard rested against the cold wall, eyes tightly closed, heart pounding. For countless hours he had scoured the black corridors, searching for the way out. He found no solace, no escape, no sign of life—but many signs of death.

The corpses of young men and women, all clad in white sacrificial robes, and all in various states of decay, littered the hallways. One boy's bloodshot eyes bulged toward the ceiling. A sword lay in his limp fingers, useless against whatever had attacked. Another torso was rent in half, the head missing. The others were just dry husks of skin wrapped around old bones.

Sickened, Erhard closed the bloodshot eyes of the boy. He mumbled a prayer to Harnor, then fled.

The drums resumed beating, closer now, more forceful, but Erhard did not turn back. He was pulled toward the noise against his will. The percussion dulled his brain. Soon he felt no fear, no resistance. He was like a babe in its mother's arms, or an old man in front of a warm fire, or a bee snared in a web, drugged by venom, slowly weakening as the spider spun strand after strand of a deadly cocoon.

NO!

He shook his head to clear it. The deep booming drumbeats coursing through the hallways were alive. Heartbeats. Something prowled these black corridors, a monster that fed on human souls. Erhard refused to scream, to reveal himself. He would not submit to the eldritch lure that summoned him.

Ahead the corridor turned; the drums intensified. A black gate fell behind him. Erhard stepped into a room where colors—red, green, gold, blue—pulsed chaotically. In the prism's center stood a figure darker than the mere absence of light. The demon sprang.

Erhard struck out, felt his small sword sink into something that was not flesh. A black claw tore at his face; another seized his leg. He sliced at the claw and it pulled back, but more groped for him, cutting like knives. His blood stained the white robe.

Gradually his arms weakened; his blows fell short. *I cannot fight this thing. It cannot be killed.* Madness called to him, but he clung to sanity. In the center of the room, beneath the demon's feet, he saw a small glowing box, shining with a constant light.

His strength ebbed. The muscles in his arms and back soon felt leaden and sluggish. Each thrust and parry jolted his body. Soon he would be too tired to fend off the demon's blows. He had one chance to act, and he knew he could never defeat the demon sword to claw.

Erhard dove past the demon. Claws shredded the skin of his back, and thorny fingers pulled him back, but not before he swung the sword with the last of his strength.

The box shattered. The blackness screamed, a scream of fire and pain that bit into Erhard. He slumped to the ground and clasped his hands over his ears in a futile effort to block the noise.

Then silence fell. The demon faded, its heartbeat stilled. The lights dimmed. Erhard's cheek rested on cold stone. He was content to bleed to death in the still, silent dark.

Dagur had his spear aimed at the box, ready to strike, when it chose to shatter of its own accord. A loud scream echoed through the pit, which filled with steam and a burning acidic mist that stung the eyes and fired the lungs.

The scream faded, a voice both familiar and alien, and the outline of Erhard's body appeared in the center of the pit. In moments it had solidified, and Erhard lay on the ground, naked save for a few tattered white rags streaked with blood, and so pale he looked dead. A shadow hung over him, slowly dissipating. A tiny white box, twin to the one just smashed, lay under Erhard's palm.

"Erhard, you're safe now. Hold on." With the spear point Dagur cut a strip from his cloak and used it to bind his friend's wounds. They had to hurry; the people of the village must have heard that scream. Even if they had not, the steam rising from the pit would summon them.

Erhard's eyes perked open, white beneath the blood on his face. He mumbled, "Dagur, I fought a demon. A god!"

Dagur trickled water onto Erhard's parched lips and finished wrapping his wounds. "You messed with something bad, that's for sure. It clawed the hell out of your back."

"No, I—" Erhard's eyes closed, and he fell silent. Dagur listened at his chest for breath.

"Erhard, you'll be fine, if we hurry. I have food. I think we can steal some horses if you're up to it." But the tracker was silent, asleep.

Dagur lifted him. "How the hell am I going to drag you out of this pit, my friend?" He pocketed the white box; perhaps it would daunt the nomads, if they were overtaken. It certainly frightened him. Maybe, back in Droburg, if they were lucky enough to get that far, they could pawn it for food.

He squinted at the hot sun and wiped sweat from his brow, then stepped toward the hewn ladder. Rung after painful rung he climbed, until he heaved Erhard over the lip of the pit and drew himself, exhausted, into the sand beside him.

A glance at the village showed no signs of pursuit. Yet.

Dagur groaned as his got to his feet. "One step at a time," he said, taking his friends weight. "We're almost there."

He trudged toward the western edge of camp, where he had heard the horses' whinny. He didn't pause or look back. "No one's watching, no one's watching. Harnor's Breath, I hope no one's watching."

He slung the half-conscious body of his friend over the back of a piebald mare, and threw a saddle over the back of another.

"That you, Dagur?"

"Harnor's Breath, Erhard! Keep it down. This is a nomad camp, not a bar." He looked at his friend's bloody body and tried to keep the worry from his voice. "We've got a long ride ahead of us. It's hot right now, but it's probably already snowing back home. We're going to be cold and hungry before too long."

"It's a long ride home."

"I know it."

"This horse doesn't feel too comfortable. Would you mind switching me to the black one. That one over there."

"The stallion tied to the shaman's totem staff?"

"That's it. A mount like that would go a long way to relieving a man's injuries."

Harnor's Breath! Dagur hopped out of the saddle and moved toward Erhard. *I should have left him in that pit.*

Galen the Deathless
by
Danielle Parker

Danielle Parker lives in a cold-as-Canada corner of Washington State. Besides writing book reviews for T-Press's Illuminata and www. bewilderingstories.com, she has a novel, The Infinite Instant, *coming out in 2008. She also has a pulp adventure/science fiction series,* In a Pig's Eye, *published by Virtual Tales. She is currently working on a novel-length expansion of the short story featured here,* "Galen the Deathless"; *a sequel to* The Infinite Instant *called* The Nihilistic Mirror; *and more stories about that beloved rogue, Captain Blunt, hero of the* In a Pig's Eye *series.*

"GALEN! GALEN! GALEN!"

I had lived this moment too many times: the sky, azure; the giant white-hot sun with its corona of scalding blue; the tidal roar of the crowd and its beast-body of a million faces. There were the smells, the floury dust of the swelling pellicles beneath my sandals and what they hold, fluids and sweat and blood, many kinds of blood. It was with experience that one distinguished between the smells, strongest the musky choking odors of the chimera-wolves mingled with the lesser metallic tang of their victims, the ever-dying Penitents. Here and there were the splattered feathers, the bitten beaked heads of the panicked fowl that ran from the joyfully pursuing dire-ferrets in today's Comedia. And I had smelled the last, the exertion and blood of my body and of Aquila's, many times before, just as I had seen the expression in his eyes, though he himself never remembered these moments.

I waited. The glassine floating eyes drifted near, and the crowd grew frenetic in their anticipation. It is the women who always scream the loudest for the blow to fall. But the choice was *his*, and I waited, and slowly, slowly, his distant hand rose, flashing in the sunlight with its many rings, and signaled. It was the expected signal. The Emperor is not known for mercy.

"Aquila," I said to the man at my feet, "You always die too well." He has never answered me.

Afterwards I went down to the dressing rooms by the hidden egress and its ancient stained stairs, finding, as I always do, my trainer Marcus awaiting me. I saw Tacitus on another stool, his naked leg outstretched before him. He had this time survived his round, but there was a physician treating the ugly triple gouge in his thigh. He was long of face, for such a wound stiffens and impedes, and he could only look forward to death at next week's games.

"I saw," I said to him. "I warned you. Cillius is a cunning one. Beware his reach even when you think he is done for." Cillius had pretended death, and in his moment of happy triumph, Tacitus carelessly allowed himself within the reach of the trident Cillius so aptly wields. He paid for his negligence. Cillius died with a blood-bubble burst of laughter on his lips, knowing he had taken his enemy with him, and knowing also that Tacitus would have a bitter week to brood upon his end.

"Galen the Deathless," he retorted, sour with defeat and pain. The physician wrapped new pink flesh around his thigh as he spoke, but it would not be enough to save him. "I will live to see that name changed!"

"*You* will not remember it," I told him, which left his mouth pursed thin as a sword-edge. He knew the truth of my answer. This Tacitus was the thirteenth of that template, and many unremembered dyings lay behind him. I saw his envious eyes burn upon me as I took off my kilt and sat down on the stool amidst my trio of body slaves.

Marcus said, "You'll have another scar from this one." He was not pleased. We looked at our images in the long mirror that forms the facing wall of the dressing room. We were not alike. Marcus was old and heavy of belly and short of stature, like the contented kitchen god that housewives pour out their cooking wines for, except I had never seen his swarthy face smiling or jolly. I was giant and alabaster white, and my body as hard as adamantine. The new mark along my left arm showed its thin line of red starkly against my pallor. There were older marks, many of them upon torso and limbs, white thin seams of past encounters. Aquila does indeed die well.

"You are thirty," he muttered, his mood sour even for Marcus. "There are too many scars now, Galen. *Too* many."

One of the body slaves was shaving me then, so I did not answer. That the body was no longer perfect in its fleshly covering I knew displeased him greatly, though where there are no scars I am still as smooth and lustrous as that great platinum statue of Zeus-Arcturus in the Imperator's private garden. Marcus sat scowling, a sour squatting lump of dissatisfaction, as he watched the physician smooth the long narrow rectangle of nova-flesh across the new cut.

"There is another party tonight," he said at last. "Your patron Lucullus begs your attendance."

There was no need to answer that either. I shrugged. Lucullus could not be refused: he was the patrician patron of the Great Games. It was customary for him to display his most prized protégé to his friends after a Game. They were gay and high-blooded then, and the wine and the food and the dream-sticks sweet until other pleasures distracted them, those that were not too drunk for lust. I remembered vaguely that once I too had enjoyed the pleasures of such evenings, but I had been as another man then. Now it was only hollowness to me: the plump aristocrats trembling with daring lust for the tall white killer; the sly soft hands of those with more sickly desires; the many unremembered pleasure-slaves of no name and no self-will, offered as casually as a cushion. There had been too many such nights in my ten years of service. All my memories had blurred into a chaotic stream of open mouths, naked torsos and animal noises, as repulsive as the vomit the over-sated lords spewed upon their tables as the dawn came.

"Tomorrow," Marcus said finally. "I will see you in the training ring when the bell tolls mid-day."

I nodded. I watched him feel for his cane and get to his feet, a slow and effortful rise, and discreetly motioned to the nearest body slave to help him. There was a new one among them this time, besides my old Argus and silent tongueless Cleius. This one was a pretty beardless youth with long dark eyes too knowing for his age and curled thick hair flowing down past his shoulders like a girl's, and he helped Marcus up deftly. I looked at the boy more closely as he did so. I have been offered such before and refuse them always, which Lucullus knows. This one perhaps had offended, and had been turned out of his soft love-nest to attend a less indulgent and less illustrious master for his shame. "*You*," I said to him, "who are you? I have not seen you before."

"Theo, master," he said with the soft pure accents of a Delian. He gave me a pretty flourishing court-bow, one he had been taught. "Lucullus sends me to attend you."

"And how have you offended Lucullus, young scamp?" I demanded.

The youth grinned wide suddenly, as unrepentant as a thieving squirrel. He had fine sharp teeth, white against his dark complexion. "I put a fire ants' nest in Cratan's bed. He tripped me when I served wine, and I wanted to get even with him."

"Well," I said, "do what Argus tells you, and if you are obedient, he will not beat you. You will not need to serve me as you did Lucullus; I am not one for children. If you are dutiful, Lucullus may forgive the fire ants' nest."

"I do not care," the boy said, and his dark eyes glowed. "I would rather serve Galen the Deathless."

"*All* die," I said. "Even Galen the Deathless will perish. Fool, think not to honor one with the blood of hundreds upon his hands. You would do better to honor the Penitents. At least they die guiltless!"

"They are *weak*," the boy retorted in contempt. He was an impudent one; I saw why Lucullus had thought to rebuke him, in spite of the long-lashed eyes. "They can do nothing but die and die and *die*. You are *strong*, master! I have seen you in the Games, as mighty as a god!" He waved his thin arm in imitation of a sword-thrust. "Like Hercules! Like Mars!"

"Fool," I said again, unreasonably unsettled by his childish praise, and cuffed him lightly. He fell to his knees and looked up at me wide-eyed as he cupped his stinging jaw. "You tempt my fate by such blasphemous praise. I tell you again: it is not the killing or the killer that should be honored, but the willing sacrifice made in praise of the gods. Go, young imp, and attend to Argus, or you will feel my fist again!"

But the young never heed until life teaches them its lessons in their own pain and blood and shame. I felt his gaze upon me as I rose to my feet, bright with childish marvel at my naked size. The taste in my mouth was flat and salty, the taste of the blood I had swallowed. "Go," I said to them all. "Go!"

Afterwards, when I had bathed many times and dressed in a new linen kilt, I went to pay my respects. Down below the churned floor of the arena are the workrooms and quarters of those of us who serve the Imperator in the Great Games; yet below, where the ancient stairs wind down, and down, and down into the heart of Invicta's earth, are the deepest rooms of all. The sun is but a warped fantasy of Tartarus here, yet there is light of a kind which never ceases night or day, and an unvarying cold more draining than the waters of a frigidarium. Servants too, this Underworld has, those they name the orfusites: soft silent beings whose faces are as worm-pale as their bodies and whose torsos are garbed in the blinding sterility of their realm. It is well said that Death has a white face, though I know some have said it of me.

And there, like the Conqueror of old, we lie unchanging in our coffins of crystal, waiting our turn to live or to die. The young man too lies there, perfect in his form as a sleeping panther, with his strong sinewy arms crossed across his smooth bared chest. I have aged ten years in the service of the Imperator, but *he* has not. Eternally twenty he is, and never does he remember me. *Aquila*, I say to him, *Aquila! Forgive me again.*

I stood there for a long time. Often I seem to forget other things in the world, even the world itself, while I am there. Then as at last awakening I turned to go, I felt suddenly the presence of another beside me. There stood a tall old man with long gray hair that swept the shoulders of his plain brown robe and straight ditches graven beside his mouth. His feet were bare, and his hands, resting beside mine on the smooth metal bar that ran outside the glass, were large and knobby, the hands of a man who has worked with them as tools and not merely as instruments of pleasure.

"You are a Penitent," I said to him in astonishment. Never had I spoken to one in my ten long years of service to the Imperator. Indeed, though, I knew this one, for almost every Game I saw him die: usually by a chimera-wolf, whose great gaping mouth needs only two bites, one for the upper, and one for the lower body. Sometimes it is the legs the chimera-wolf devours first. Then have I seen this same noble face lying looking upwards from the shining pool of its own blood, waiting for death with that sad dignity that dooms his kind to their eternal cycle of the Games. Yet as I thought back I remembered that I had not seen him today. Only the women had fed the chimera-wolves this time, to the noisy delight of the crowd. It is a fickle beast, and grows bored even with the spectacle of martyrdom, and shows less mercy than a Maenad in the throes of her madness.

"Solator is my name." His voice was deep and slow, deeper than I would have expected coming from that gaunt chest, and the accent was as his hands, that of a commoner in its thickness. Yet it was a voice that had a quiet power in spite of its coarseness. "You are Galen the Deathless. I have lived again only one day, but already I have been told of you."

I gripped the metal bar with my hands. Even my strength could not warp that unspeakably crafted metal, though I saw my knuckles blanch as the bones thrust through the skin. "You mock me, old man," I said. "You of all people should know that none are deathless. Even Galen the Deathless will one day die."

He nodded slowly. The lines in his cheeks were slit deep as sword-slashes, and his aging eyelids dragged at their corners, weighted down with the unyielding pressure of a longer life than I had yet known. Only his mouth and his shoulders did not sag, and I saw that for his pride he was accustomed to making an effort he would one day lose in spite of his will.

"You have come to visit your victim," the Penitent said. "To ask his forgiveness, I think."

"He has died by my hand one hundred and twenty-four times," I said. "Tell me, Penitent. Will any god besides mad Mars accept the stained hands of Galen when he is at last no longer the Deathless?"

He did not answer me at once. There down the aisle was another glass-fronted room, and there they dreamed, all the templates of the women who had fed the chimera-wolves this day, until they woke to their weekly nightmare. He must have known them, or at least some of them, in the days of his true life. He looked toward that room with such longing in his face that I, even I, turned away. It was like seeing a face look up from the bottom of a well to unreachable light.

"There is no help to be found in the gods men worship here," he said at last. "You may only offer what appeasement lies within your power in the hope of one more merciful than they. Perhaps it will be enough. I do not know."

"I never knew any god but bloody Mars," I said. "I was never told of any else who had power in the world. Go, old man, and pray also for me, to whomever you pray to." I left him then and went up the long stairs once more. I was late already for Lucullus's party, and however drunken he is, *that* one never misses a slight, nor fails to repay an insult with less than its full measure.

The mismatched pearls of the moons were all three visible as I walked in the drugging sweet air through the parallel lines of the fascination trees. Deformus, last-rising moon of the three, sat upon the horizon like a gouged eye. The white-blossomed limbs bowed in the slight breeze and cast their morphetic perfume to the nostrils. A man, if he were unwary, might succumb to them, and dream of decay until his body softened to the texture of his dreams. Yet there is no more heavenly scent engendered by any flower, not even the rose of Old Earth. Mordant bats sported in the wisps of clouds, graceful at a distance that spared the eye their monstrous faces. There, too, does beauty lie in the embrace of horror.

"Galen." There was a deep-buried spark in those eyes when I found Lucullus at last, lying on his couch with a scant drape of silk across his loins. It was a glint I could see even through the thick smoke of his dream-stick. The music of distant gongs tinkled through the clouded air. A slender blonde girl, perhaps fourteen, knelt at his feet, anointing his limbs with salve. I recognized the indescribable licentious breath of it and felt its slime in my nostrils. The dream-sticks kill other pleasures when used too often, and of late Lucullus has needed aid, lest he lose another of his precious pleasures.

"Do we bore you, Galen?" he asked and smiled at me, that tight small smile he gives to those who should be wise enough to fear it. There fell a sudden listening silence from his companions; I saw many glittering speculative eyes through the smoke, avid with anticipation. It seemed not even the Game had satisfied their taste for blood. "You were not timely in your attendance tonight. Even my lord Kratur has come, and asked for you, and I was shamed to tell him of your neglect of us."

I knelt. Even then he needs must look up, which I knew deeply displeased him. He is not a tall man, in spite of the platforms he wears secretly beneath the cover of his fine purple-edged togas in the Senate chamber. "My lord," I murmured, and no more. I could not bring myself to ask his pardon.

He looked at me for a long moment as the boy beside him offered up another dream-stick. The boy's pale, thin nape remained bowed as if for the sword even when Lucullus, without looking away, took the stick from his small fingers. The child trembled at his brief touch, a fine faint all-over quiver like a twanging string. I saw then the boy was too young to have hair upon his loins. I was sorry for him, though Lucullus is too shrewd to be needlessly cruel to his slaves, not unless there is true provocation. Others, like Kratur, are not so lenient.

"You were cut again," he commented at last. For all the intoxication revealed in the widened pupils and the fluttering pulse in his throat, those were calculating eyes, eyes as hard as those in the fresh bloody head of the chimera-wolf trophy stuck upon the pole behind him. He reached out and touched my arm with a finger as soft as down, where the nova-flesh lay pink against my milk-white skin. "I do not like that. You are no longer perfect in that body, Galen the *Deathless*. Perhaps a gladiator should not reach thirty. Beware I do not tire of your naming."

"I live to serve the gods and the Imperator," I answered steadily. I could not feel fear of his threat, though I knew it was real, and deadlier than the mace and spear Aquila had used to inflict today's wounding. When a man is so familiar with death that he no longer fears it, perhaps Death is moved to rise to his challenge: I remembered that, fleetingly, and felt deep within the cold breath of that presence. I said, seeking to divert my thought, "Thank you for the loan of Theo. He is an impudent one!"

His mood changed abruptly, with that erratic untrustworthy swing imparted by the smoke he drew into his lungs. "Cratan is still wailing his stings," he laughed. "Treat the lad gently. I will have Theo back when he has learned not to trouble my peace with his pranks." He smiled and twisted his free hand lightly in the curls on the bowed head of the slave. "After all, he is wasted on you, is he not? *Go*, Galen. I think that young slave Julia has been holding out for you. She was hiding behind a curtain, trying to escape old Demetrius, last I saw her."

There was a dutiful laugh from the circle of those who sprawled on couches. They were too much afraid of Lucullus not to match his moods, all of them, except for Kratur, whom thankfully I did not see here. Anthony Flavius called teasingly, "You're out of luck, Galen. I saw Demetrius drag her away. She'll not be fit for a goat after *that* old satyr is done with her!"

It seems more and more I seek not to remember these nights; a goblet is my companion more often now than a pair of dark eyes. Yet I remembered dimly a small lithe form, sweet breath and a chain of silver about a delicate ankle, wrists thin and breakable as strings yet unexpectedly strong in their grip upon my shoulders. The image of Demetrius hovered before me in all his vileness: splattered broken nose and coarse yellowed teeth, thick sour-smelling body, toga bespattered with his dinner and his vomit. Foulness should not embrace a flower, or an ape a sprite. The slime I felt in my nostrils choked my throat. I rose to my feet. "My lord," I said. "I beg your leave."

He waved his free arm negligently in dismissal, but I felt his eyes as I made my way across the courtyard, and I felt that other smile…the one that shows the teeth. I felt those teeth upon my nape now, as promising and as possessing as his hand had been upon the neck of the child.

I caught a serving girl carrying a tray and took her three newly-opened bottles from her. My mood was too black for anything then but a goblet and all the bottles of Lucullus's potent Lydian wine I could carry away. I went out the archway with them under my arm, into the dusky shadows beneath the fascination trees that perfumed Lucullus's fine large garden. The great central fountain threw out revolving red and blue and purple lights, making the marble statues of the god — Lucullus favors Bacchus, even in appearance, as well he should — seem as if they moved in a dance. Sounds I heard, those who sought the shadows and the thickets for their own purposes; some of pleasure, others of laughing unmeant protest, once stifled panting cries of pain crescending unheeded into a cut-off scream. Those made me think of Kratur again, whom I did not wish to think of, tonight or any night, and I moved away quickly.

Against the wall I found the place I had sought, a dense thicket of bushes adorned with twining vines with drooping small fruits and purple flowers. I was told once this is a vine brought from Old Earth, rare and precious, called nightshade, and that its tempting fruits are poisonous. I did not care. It was hidden enough for my private purposes, and here the drug of the trees was less potent than elsewhere. I sank to my knees.

It was when I had drunk the second bottle, and was thinking, in the coldness of my continued sobriety, that my release seemed as unattainable as a eunuch's orgasm, that I heard the voices and the crunch of gravel under shod feet. There was a laugh I knew, a soft yet somehow raspy sound, like a knife-edge drawn lightly along a whetting stone. There are some things a wise man knows instinctively to fear, though they may be a smile from one man, and a laugh from another. I drew up my knees beneath the thick covering of vine.

"You have my blessing," the voice said, and laughed again. I was not drunk enough not to be chilled by the sound, because I know what makes Kratur laugh, and someone, tonight, would lose blood. "I have been patient, Agonistes, very patient; you must admit it. See for yourself how he avoids me. Have you ever known me to lavish such patience upon another, my friend?" The heavy crunch passed me by, and I saw the edges of a silk kilt, and the silhouette of a thick-shouldered powerful man through my lattice of limbs and leaves. I glimpsed the sandaled feet of his slighter companion on the other side. "Perhaps I shall have better luck with the new one. Especially," and the laugh too moved away from me, "when I remind him how he lost his name. Even *that* one can be taught fear."

"We waited only for your blessing, Kratur," replied his companion with obscene deference, and as their footsteps faded I heard hushed intense whispering, until I could hear no more.

I lay still for a long moment, painfully sober in spite of the empty bottles that lay discarded by my side. The breeze rustled the branch limbs and brought me again the tantalizing stupefying perfume of the fascination trees. The third bottle lay warmly within the crook of my arm, sweet as the promise of sleep, yet I knew it could not help me. How is it that one may be certain, absolutely *certain*, that Death has finally accepted one's challenge? His answer was there in the smile of my patron and the laughter of the man who so long pursued me for the solace of his dark stained bed and thin long knives.

When I had drunk the last bottle the moon Deformus too had disappeared, and dawn light, pale and ghostly faint, shone on the edge of the horizon. I took a long slow way home, wandering through streets where sweepers and early risers stared in fear at the great white giant that moved among them. The arena had been swept and prepared for today's lesser games, and its surface gleamed like the face of a great smooth sea. Its tides would rise red again by evening.

I do not know why I expected *him* to be awake, in this hour before true dawn. But I found him almost as I had left him, with his large knobby hands upon the bar, looking through the crystalline panel again. Only the face within this room was his own, and in sleep it seemed nakedly sorrowful, more sorrowful even than that of the one who watched.

"Why do you not sleep?" I said to him. "It is but an hour of dawn."

He did not look up. "I have had years of sleep," he whispered. "Should I not stay sleepless to pray for him, he that will wake to but one short hour of pain and death? Perhaps mercy will be granted to him, if not to me. Seventy-eight years ago, a night to me but yesterday, Solator the heretic was condemned to eternal death by the Imperator. His flesh has fed generations of chimera-wolves since. Should I not pray, then, for that man?"

"To whom do you pray, then, old man?" I asked him. But he turned his face away from me, and what I could see of his profile was as remote and sad as the old wrinkled face of Deformus.

"I cannot tell you his name," he replied. "You seek for a name and a man's image, like the statue of Zeus-Arcturus upon Pallatine Hill. Such images are hollow delusions. I cast my hope upon another. It is not by man's carved image one knows *that* one. I trust that one day he will have mercy upon us all." And he nodded to the image that lay sleeping inside its glass chamber.

"That is a fool's hope," I said. "I am told that in three hundred and nineteen years the resurrection cycle has failed only three times. The wheel will turn again, old man, and you and I will be bound upon it."

He looked up at me with tired dark eyes. "So, Galen the Deathless senses mortality at last, does he?"

"Death is always here," I said. One of the orfusites passed behind us then, its thin white robe fluttering in the cold moving air. "*You* will die in a week, old man, and your successor will wake soon after for his own hour of terror. One day I, too, will be no longer Deathless. *He* will not remember my ten years of life, or know yet that women and wine are props the weak lean upon. And Kratur will eat him. Will you pray for Galen as well? I would be grateful."

He was silent for a long time. "I believe I can," he said at last. "But if there is an appeasement you can offer, my son, think on it. Perhaps it will be acceptable."

"I am grateful," I told him, and left the old man then, brooding upon the sleeper with the sorrowful face. I went slowly up the ancient stairs. Ten years of my own footsteps lay there in the deep dust before me. Would my successor see them, one day? I turned wearily to my quarters.

There was a shadow lying upon my bed. As I lit the lamp it uncurled into long, thin arms and legs like a colt's and a tangle of hair like a girl's and huge dark agonized eyes. "You should not be here," I said. "I told you I am not for boys."

Theo fell to his knees, though I had not yet cuffed him. "Master," he whimpered, knotting the hem of my kilt with both fists. "I heard! I *heard!* Kratur and Draconius and Agonistes have placed secret bets against you. They're going to kill you!" And the boy fell to piteous weeping and wailing as he clutched the edge of my kilt. "You will *die!*"

"I have heard," I said, and bent to pry his fingers free of my clothing. "So do we all, in time. I told you not to tempt the gods. Come, child! Have you been here all night?" But I could not pry his fingers free without hurting them, and at last I had to lift him up, with his tears still falling upon us both, and my kilt riding up in his grip because of his ridiculous stubbornness. "Leave off! Here is bread and wine and dried apricots; you may have my breakfast. Then go. Lucullus told me he would accept you when you repent of Cratan's stings. Cease this crying, or I will have to disappoint him."

But he would not be comforted until I made him drink the wine, and then at last he consented to eat the apricots, diverted like any child by the sweets. I put him on the bed and he fell asleep there with a bitten apricot still clutched in his fist. I put on my training kilt and went out again. There was Marcus to appease. Somehow it had become morning.

I do not remember the passage of that week except in snatches and bright isolated images, fractured like those of a man who has drawn in too much smoke. Faces came at me like vengeful harpies, teeth white and sharp, grinning like bears with their pleasure. Tacitus said to me, "I will live to see it now," and grinned as he hobbled upon his stiffened leg. Marcus watched my daily practice from his stool, an old sour saddened frog, and never corrected me once as he usually did. I did not seek out the Penitent again. I did not know to whom I might pray, and I could not think of a suitable appeasement, though I besought one with all my might, long into my wakeful nights.

Lucullus sent his servant in the middle of the week to take Theo into his service, which relieved me, for the child would not leave me even when disciplined by a half-hearted cuff. He spent the nights sleeping at my feet like an old familiar dog. I had not the will to beat him for it.

Then the day of the Great Game dawned bright and fresh: a fair day, one of those blessings of early autumn, and the air like a taste of cool water as one drew it into one's lungs. The trees dropped their blossoms suddenly and stood naked and ebony above the splendor of dying white flowers. I went for a walk, and stirred their scented snowfall with my sandal. Then there were the long hours of cleaning and sharpening of weapons, which I had done before so many times, though it seemed another's hands did it now. I ate, and did not remember the taste in my mouth, and I watched for the hour.

I dressed early and waited in the antechamber. I heard the great roaring of the chimera-wolves as they slavered and leapt howling at the bars of their prison. This is the day that they wait for every week, for they eat fresh meat. Men brought a vast tangle of netting past me with much yelling to each other, and shortly thereafter, with thick gloves and chattering fear, pairs of great silent mordant bats hanging upside down from poles and wrapped in their wings like rotting brown fruit. One man, holding the bar too carelessly, screamed as acid drool pierced his glove. After them came the gay unsuspecting goats, victims-to-be of this week's Comedia, and soon a great tumult from the crowd that I heard even through the thick ceiling above me.

Cillius, smooth as a snake and smiling behind the faceplate of his scaled murmillo, went past me holding his trident. *This* Cillius knew me not, though I had known him for more than a year. I heard the orgiastic roar of the crowd again, though not as loud as it had been for the Comedia. *Now* it was almost the time.

Someone darted toward me then, a small spindly form, racing through the widespread clutch of the old soldier who guarded the door. I heard a yell and curse, but the boy had already cast himself at my feet, gasping like a greyhound and seizing my kilt in two desperate fists.

"The knife," he panted. "Master, the *knife*. It will be poisoned!" He looked up at me. The eyes were painted this time and his lips rouged, but it was a child's love and a child's terror that glared out of those kohl-rimmed orbs.

"Here," grunted old Horatio, stomping forward. "You're not allowed in here, boy!"

"Be easy with the child," I said to him. A tall slim young man came through the door then, with the smooth ease of a panther in his movements, and looked long upon me with his coldly thoughtful eyes. It was at that instant I understood what I must do. I felt a great rush of emotion, so strong my body trembled with it, and all my breath fled my chest. Yet I could not name what it was I felt.

I bent and picked up the child and kissed him on his hot wet cheek. "*Go*," I said to him. "Do not fear, Theo."

Horatio took Theo's collar with an old soldier's gruff kindness. "He's the Deathless," he explained with rough simple comfort. "Don't ye fear, boy. Ye'll see your master again."

"Be brave," I called to him as the old soldier bore him away. "Be brave, Theo!" He no longer wailed. But his eyes looked at me over Horatio's shoulder, huge, frightened, doubting eyes in twin rings of black. Water was still leaking from the corners, smearing the oily rings of kohl, but he did not seem to know it. I picked up my weapons.

The sky was azure. I had seen that sun with its throbbing ring of blue many times before. I heard the great and mighty voice of the crowd, the millions who ringed us about in their baying circle; far away, seated like a white grub upon his throne, I glimpsed the tiny chubby face of the Imperator. Aquila and I turned together and saluted him with our raised weapons in the ancient way: *We who are about to die salute thee Caesar!*

We turned and faced each other. We were too close this time, of his intent. The poisoned knife flashed in the sun like a light-shot icicle, and I allowed my bare arm to meet it. Cold it was, more bitter than the edge of the metal, and I felt its morphetic poison congeal my blood. Yet for an instant longer there was still great strength in me, and with all the might of my body and my will I hurled the sword high, high in the air. As it rose the blade twisted and spun like a glittering snake, until on its downward arc the blue lightning flashed upward from his throne to seize it and suspend it in the heaven. *You are beneath its point, Caesar. Another shall see it fall.*

Time Off
by
R. Gatwood

*R. Gatwood lives in the Washington, DC area and has had works
published in several small-press magazines like* WordWrights *and*
Alligator Juniper. *The inspiration for her contribution to Beacons,
"Time Off" came from several mindless, interminable jobs in retail,
which prompted the question: what would the world be like if sleep
were a luxury?*

Michelle plucked a chip off the conveyor belt, tilted it under the
plastic magnifier, swabbed a drop of sealant evenly over the metal,
applied an adhesive tag, and dropped the chip in the bin, all within
seven seconds by the clock. She attempted to wring the stiffness from
her knuckles before picking up the next chip. She was trying to get
her time down to a consistent five seconds without getting sloppy and
without sending aches shooting through her hands. And, she reminded
herself, without wasting four dollars on an energy bar or pain ointment
in a moment of self-pity. The trick was to treat your body as respectfully
as you would a machine: a good machine does only what you tell it to
do, and it is designed to work. Anyway, pain or not, there was always
another chip to do.

Michelle's workstation held a bottle of sealant at one end and an
ID tagger at the other. The bottle reeked like nail polish and insecticide
when open, and it had to be kept open constantly. The tagger marked
each chip with Michelle's workstation number so it could be traced back
to her for credit or blame. She had never yet been questioned in a quality
check, but every time a box of her chips went out she had the urge to
take them back and reinspect them.

On Michelle's right, the belts carried chips in two lines from the
hands of four other workers, who used pointed metal instruments to

solder eight minute connections on each chip. Their apparent carelessness amazed Michelle. Sometimes she thought they must be too skilled to need to pay close attention; other times, peering at the metal blobs and wires, she thought them sloppy. The solderers, not eager to be criticized or interrupted, rarely looked up when she approached them and fixed their work only grudgingly, sometimes telling her the connections were fine really, that she had to develop more of an eye for these things— which may have been true. Their slapdash dribbles of solder looked nothing like the diagrams in the employee training videos.

She was getting better, though, after two years. At least her work was never sloppy, or almost never. Walking by other workers' stations, she had seen chips with uneven splashes of sealant that left connections exposed, and the workers themselves unrebuked, apparently unnoticed. The thought often needled her that she was working harder than she had to, or else not hard enough, not fast enough. The chips were never as perfect as she intended, the motions of her hands never quite smooth or natural. It was impossible to know whether anyone noticed or cared.

The chips they were building were pathetically cheap and low-quality, of course; despite her perfectionism Michelle knew that much. The industry, after a decade of spectacular success in cyberbionics, had crashed and taken the rest of the economy with it. Since then the only high-quality electronics being made were used in cyberbionic packs for the extremely wealthy. Most people's packs were crude things, prone to causing bouts of paralysis, seizures, comas, electrical shocks, and shooting nerve pains.

Michelle had heard all the horror stories from her coworkers and on the news. But she was lucky in that her father's savings had gotten their family through the crash. When she was nine years old and her brother Peter sixteen months, their father had had all three of them fitted with the best packs on the market. Technology was the one thing he would spare no expense for. A good machine, he liked to say, used the way it was designed to be used, will last you forever.

When their father died two years ago, however, they were nearly bankrupt. He was killed in an accident at the Zedd Fish & Meats plant where he was training Peter to work. The company had refused to pay most of the medical expenses incurred by his last few days of life, claiming that only certain non-lethal injuries were covered by their health plan. It was only after they'd sold their father's pack and gotten Peter a job at Gonper Electronics that the two of them had managed to get out of debt and now, month by month, were beginning to accumulate some savings.

Peter worked on the sixth floor, cutting chitoplastic machine parts with a circular saw. The two of them always met during the two thirty-minute breaks every day—what was still known as lunch break, although hardly anyone ate more than vending machine candy. Their meeting place was a tiny break room on the third floor; they chose it because it was more or less between their workstations and also because it lacked a vending machine, which Michelle at least found to be an unbearable temptation. Often she and Peter were the only ones there. The break was worth the hike up two flights of stairs for her and down three for him. They sat down, changed their pack batteries for freshly charged ones, and talked. Sometimes instead of talking they rested or gazed at the break room TV that nobody but Michelle ever seemed to think of turning off.

When Michelle had the energy she prodded Peter into conversation. She knew once he had shook off his fatigue and reticence he really did like talking to her. He told her how the saws at his workstation buzzed steady and flat as a tuneless guitar chord. He recounted how an older, hard-drinking friend of a friend had showed him a hand with two fingers missing, and how they said someone a few years before had died—the kind of gossip young factory men seemed to love. He told her how one of his coworkers, listening to a game on the radio, had shouted at the commentators so long and loudly over the buzzing of the saws that he literally lost his voice for the next two days.

Sometimes they talked about money, but not often. They both knew where it all came from and where it was going. Everything they earned here went into their joint account; they both had checking cards, and a few times a week they might splurge on a soda or two or three, energy bars, showers when they needed them, ointments and pills for Michelle's creaky joints. Then monthly rent on their storage locker, clothes, laundry, Peter's haircuts, taxes, insurance on their bodies and packs, routine pack check-ups. They were saving almost as much as they could, now—they didn't talk about for what exactly.

Once in a long while they would talk about Dad and their old apartment. It wasn't that it was hard to discuss their father or the days when they were a whole family; it just wasn't the sort of thing they talked about. They had never really hugged or said I love you, even before, and on breaks now they were usually too tired to do much or say much. It was more just being near each other and having time to breathe. Michelle needed that.

Besides their being separated, their difference in age seemed to make their relationship gentler and stranger than is usual between siblings. Each had had to navigate alone the world of being small and new and at the whim of grown-up laws, without household peers to bully or guide them. Their father had grown Peter from Mother's ovum when Michelle was seven and lonely and wanted another kid around. He had discussed it with her in a grown-up way—the work and money it would take, the tax break it would get them, and how great it would be to have another of Mother's kids, when she had always wanted a boy and a girl. As Peter grew up Dad said he was very much like their mother, and Michelle guessed from photos that it was true: he had darker eyes than hers or Dad's, a rounder face, a broader smile.

The two children had almost never fought; they had nothing to fight over. Their father had carried Peter home in a blanket and hadn't put him down for the first seven days; as for Michelle, she had an only child's conviction that she was adored. Peter was too good-natured to argue, Michelle too timid and too fair-minded. And though now and then Michelle resented her father for being smarter, more assured, and more responsible than she was, and for leaving them in poverty despite all, she never felt rancor for her one living relative. They were like strangers who happened to love each other.

For months now Michelle had been planning to buy Peter some time off—to offline his pack. She and their father had offlined him before, mostly when he was very small and it was cheaper than daycare, but for full-wage-earning adults, offlining was a luxury. It meant time spent out of work, sound asleep—and meanwhile your pack still had to be charged and fed, your waste fluids drained, your health monitored, your rent and taxes paid. Since the invention of cyberbionic packs, no one needed sleep, but everyone craved it. "The little death," as it was called, was everyone's dream vacation, better than any spa or resort: you lay back, sank into a deep torpor, dreamed a little, and woke much relaxed with a sense of the passage of time. Michelle remembered seeing Peter offlined on a home sleep-cot as a kid: his face neither grinning nor weary nor sulky nor bored, but smoothed out, softened, loosed from the shackles of personality, the face of a creature that might never have known human consciousness. It moved her and made her envious. Michelle had slept every night before she got her pack, of course, but since then she had only offlined when her father insisted she needed it. Plenty of workers were more lavish: they offlined for a few hours or a day whenever the stress got to them, splurging their savings on booth rental and pack maintenance. Others, deep in debt already, would spend everything they had to go offline for a few days as a sort of prelude to suicide.

Michelle tilted a chip under the magnifier, applied sealant and a tag, and dropped it in the bin. After every third chip, she allowed herself to stretch fingers and rub her knuckles. She wanted to keep up with the influx without distracting flashes of pain. She kept thinking of Peter, or not of Peter so much as of her silly, secret, hopeful plan to offline him. When they had put more in savings, and when she found a cheap, safe sleeping booth close to the Gonper factory building, they could do it. He could rest for a week—two weeks if he wanted! Offlining wasn't like natural sleep. It could be made uniformly deep and even and comfortable for any length of time, whether or not you were tired. And Peter, though he smiled and shrugged when she asked him, was always tired now. In recent weeks she thought he looked exhausted.

Right now Michelle was going without new clothes and energy bars for as long as she could resist. She refused to think of offlining herself. Not that she wouldn't do so later, when Peter was a bit older—in fact, to live without once going offline would be unbearable. But the thought of sleep—deep, rich, and forgiving—was too seductive to carry through her working life. She might sink into the very idea of sleep and never wake up; she might slump over her workstation, head drooping, hands stiffly curled, and cry like a child for rest. That, she sensed, was the path to surrender, to petty self-indulgence, to guilt and apathy, to losing money, to losing Peter, to losing her grip on her life.

This plan of hers, on the other hand, this dream of buying Peter offline time—this was a luxury she could afford. It gave her a thrill to think of getting him his vacation, even at the expense of her own, even if she worked her fingers to the bone. This fantasy was too noble-sounding to be anything but self-flattering and self-serving, and Michelle knew it; but it was a selfishness that moved her and kept her moving.

Forty-five minutes remained until she could excuse herself for a five-minute break. There were another four hours till her next scheduled half-hour break, eleven and a half till the next. In forty-one hours she would get a full two-hour break in which to do laundry and buy a quick shower. In a week and a half was her next twelve-hour break, in which she would do more laundry and shower again and look up sleep-booth prices and pay bills. And then she would work another two weeks, or three hundred twenty-four hours, before the next twelve-hour break. But even when she was tired and bored to tears and struggling to find a comfortable sitting position and, to her irritation, coming down with the hiccups, she could picture Peter's face: surprise and relief, the loosening of long-tensed muscles, and then fading consciousness, and then nothing, nothing at all.

Michelle found a cracked chip and threw it in the rejects bin without asking anyone. She paused to wring her hands every three chips, sometimes every two. Something Michelle had learned from her work was that time went by at a constant speed. Forty-five minutes, she found, always took exactly forty-five minutes to pass, and not forty-five hours or seconds, as some people like to pretend. Time might not be just, but it was fair: it guaranteed that each shift was neither longer nor shorter than she knew it would be, and that right now she would have to wait exactly four hours and forty-three minutes till she was free to clock out and run upstairs. Another thing she had learned was that even if your memory blurred all the moments of your life together, each one stood on its own. With patience, perhaps, you could take in each one as it went by.

When her five-minute break came, Michelle did what she always did: she sat on an unopened box of solder facing slightly away from the other workers. She straightened her back, shut her eyes, and noticed as she inhaled deeply that her hiccups were gone. Michelle breathed; she forced herself to forget time and the people around her; she clenched the muscles in her feet and legs until they quivered with tension, which she slowly released; she clenched her back and shoulders, then her arms and fists, and let the tension flow out; she tried to breathe. Even with these small rituals it was hard to relax, knowing how little time five minutes really was. The smells of solder and sealant never left this place. Michelle leaned back against the wall and her old weatherworn pack, still one of the best models around, poked lightly into her nape. At the end of five minutes her eyes jumped open, as always, with a flash of panicky guilt, and she found the usual pile of neglected chips waiting for her. One of the solderers, catching her expression, gave her a quick knowing smile that Michelle returned. Four hours remained now until her lunch break.

Now and then Michelle became aware of the strangeness of her life: that she inhabited this body and personality; that all day and night she applied sealant and adhesive tags to cheap electronic chips; the unchanging fluorescent light; the ceaseless whir and hum and buzz of machines. The strangeness of how she somehow didn't know, after two years, just what the chips they made were *for*. She'd admitted this to Peter once, eliciting one of his rare belly laughs.

What *were* they for? They seemed too large and crude to use in cyberbionics; cheap radios or phones seemed more likely. Then again, she and Peter often saw people whose packs had been hand-repaired so many times and so crudely that they had to wear cheap oversized replacement parts strapped to their shoulders like football players' pads.

Sometimes she became aware, too, of how time was being wasted before her eyes. Michelle wasn't the quickest learner or worker, but she thought she was as smart as most of the others in the building. She had a modest gift for mathematics and design. Every day her mind wandered from her fussy, minute work on the chips and found nowhere to wander, nothing to learn from.

And yet the time she wasted earned her the money she and Peter needed. It was a paradox of the packs: they let you work longer while eating less, but maintenance and batteries cost you a sizable chunk of your earnings. Since everyone else was working longer too, your pay went down. You had to work around the clock to make ends meet, and when jobs got scarce you couldn't leave. Michelle's father had once illustrated the principle to her with a rigged Monopoly board, chuckling when she, eight years old and indignant, had attempted to steal first the bank's money and then the properties. "How do you make them give it back?" she demanded.

Her father had shrugged. Since he had started working at the Fish & Meats plant he smelled of roadkill and iron whenever he came home, and his eyes were always tired. "Sue the SOBs," he said, with a wink to let her know he didn't mean the SOBs part.

She giggled. "How?"

But her father only stroked his chin, squinted, and cited something he had heard from a colleague—a headline he had seen in the paper— his understanding of the law. Only much later, with a pang, did Michelle realize that was what grown-ups did when they didn't know.

But Michelle and Peter had their father to thank for their secure full-time positions. For that matter, Michelle thought the only reason they hadn't been considered for promotion was that they were quiet—they didn't stand out. Maybe it was time they tried. Peter had always been well-liked, and Michelle supposed she could be charming if she put her mind to it. They were honest workers, they attended to detail, they never cheated or dragged their feet. They would manage.

In the last year, scientists on TV had been speculating that cyberbionic packs might extend human life indefinitely—"essentially immortal" was the media's favorite cliché, a quote from some famous futurist. Michelle's private opinion was that people who got excited over these things had no concept of time. If you really understood time, what you did was use every second you could; you didn't try to get it to play tricks like freezing or distending. And the idea that "with proper maintenance" Michelle might go on living forever and ever, hundreds or thousands of years, exhausted her. No one was meant to endure more than one moment at a time—or, at most, one day.

With an hour and fifty minutes till her lunch break, Michelle was in the middle of a heavy stream of chips when she heard her name and jumped. "Michelle Godwin, please report to the personnel office immediately; Michelle Godwin, please report to the personnel office immediately."

Then she could stop? The other workers glanced at her, acknowledging that she had been called. She set down the chip she was working on and nodded to them. They had already turned back to their soldering.

The personnel office was on the second floor, so she got to take the same flight of stairs she would go up on her lunch break. Two young guys in canvas workpants like Peter's passed her on their way down, talking excitedly. Some days Michelle would have been nervous about being called to the personnel office, but lately she hadn't made any serious mistakes; she was beginning to think her work was good enough. She had no idea what they wanted her for. Maybe they were laying her off, in which case she could live off Peter's earnings and their savings until she found a new job. But then she probably wouldn't get to see him more than a few times a month.

When Michelle got to the office a crowd of people was bustling down the stairs from the floor above. The door was already open. When she entered, the personnel manager got up from his desk and urged her to take a seat in a padded leather chair. She had forgotten how comfortable a good chair could be. He circled behind her to close the door, cutting off the noise from the hall. When he sat again, facing some point beyond her shoulder, he bent to sift through a file of papers without looking her in the eye. "Are you the sister of Peter Francis Godwin?"

She hadn't expected that. The personnel manager's eyes, behind his small round glasses, studied the papers in his hand intently and missed her nod. Michelle cleared her throat and said yes.

"I'm sorry to have to tell you that he is dead," the personnel manager said. "He was killed in an accident at his workstation this morning."

Michelle felt cold. She pushed herself up a little straighter in the soft chair. When the manager finally raised his eyes from his desk and checked her face for a response, all she could come up with was, "This morning?"

The personnel manager nodded encouragingly, eyes lowered. He winced a bit as though the nodding hurt. "Yes, unfortunately, he was using a circular saw to cut a sheet of chitoplastic and hit what I believe is called a 'bad spot.' That is, a vein of much harder, more elastic material that can cause the saw to rebound."

Michelle found herself nodding right along with him, she understood the principle exactly. Peter had complained about this sort of thing before. You always had to stop and switch saw blades for a vein of hard material, and then you had to switch back, since too powerful a blade would rip the sheet to shreds. What the personnel manager said next was, "The saw severed your brother's hand. I'm afraid that despite the best efforts of paramedics, he bled to death."

The personnel manager looked directly at Michelle for the first time and added, "Incidentally, the cost of the emergency medical care he received was completely covered by the employee health plan." Michelle could feel a steady pulse beating behind her eyes and in her head. She was having a hard time following the personnel manager's words, but she piled them onto some readily accessible shelf of her memory and nodded. He said, "The company would like to do whatever is possible to ease your loss." Through his thick glasses his pale eyes stared at her, seeming to expect a response.

"Thank you," Michelle said, but he turned away frowning as though disappointed, liver spots folding into the creases in his brow. She cast about for more words, but it was all she could do to remain here, breathing meditatively in and out. After a moment the personnel manager turned back and cleared his throat.

"If there is anything I can do," he said, "please let me know. I realize this is quite a lot to take in all in a moment—that is, at a time like this. Here—" and he fumbled to pick up one of his business cards from the holder on his desk, leaning over stiffly to hand it to her. It took Michelle a moment to come out of her daze, peel her hand off the leather armrest, and accept it. The personnel manager sat down again. "You are welcome to call me to discuss anything." That same expectant, worried, almost paternal gaze. What was he asking? What did he expect her to say?

Michelle breathed in and out slowly until she trusted her voice and asked, "Where was he taken?" She meant Peter's body, but as she spoke it occurred to her mortifyingly that the personnel manager would think she was hysterical, that she thought Peter had been taken to a hospital. Instead the manager nodded emphatically as though it were a good question to ask.

She never heard his answer. Ten minutes ago she had sat at her workstation inspecting a chip under a fluorescent light, the hum of machinery muffling her coworkers' gossip. Now she sat in a quiet, well-lit office where every word that came out of the personnel manager's mouth emerged distinct, piling on top of the words before it. Somewhere between the two rooms she had missed a connection. Just before being paged, as she hurried through the latest batch of chips, she had been imagining a lunch break that would come one day soon. She and Peter had the break room to themselves as usual, and they sat near each other, slouched forward, elbows on their knees, not meeting each other's eyes but grinning at a shared joke. To get Peter talking she had to tease him obliquely, prod him to answer her questions. She mirrored his self-conscious slouch, his way of hiding behind his shaggy hair. Knowing Peter, he probably wouldn't be able to look her in the eye when she told him her news. But today Michelle had imagined him looking at her astonished, the squint-lines falling from his eyes, his face transformed.

As the personnel manager looked at her, his voice faltered and he hurried to finish the spiel she hadn't heard: ". . . and contact them to make arrangements as soon as you find it convenient." Then he ducked to sift through the papers on his desk again, handing Michelle a folder. "Please, look over these forms at your leisure. Listen," he added in a more strained voice, "the first form is a request for grief leave, if you're interested. I believe you're allowed up to ten days at one-quarter your usual pay. It's not taken out of your time bank. Would you like that?"

Michelle started to nod and stopped herself, then started to say no thank you and stopped herself again. She had gotten in the habit of turning down breaks. Ten days at one-quarter pay? Beneath the slow pulse beating in her head, some calculating part of her mind began totaling up days and dollars, bargaining for the right to some reasonable number of days in which to rest and make certain arrangements. At the same time, she found she was still staring at the personnel manager, who seemed to search her face.

The folder contained a thin sheaf of papers apparently detailing, in small print, Michelle's legal rights with regard to claiming grief leave. The personnel manager shifted in his seat as she skimmed the first page and flipped to the second. "It's not necessary to sign all the paperwork now—you can drop it off any time in the next forty-eight hours. It's just an offer," he added, and leaned forward as though he wanted to snatch the papers back. "If you decide not to take it, that's fine."

Michelle read automatically. She could never sign anything, even a laundry receipt, without skimming it. The words on the page sank in about as much as the personnel manager's had, but she stored them away in the same place to be comprehended later. The folder also held a cheap company pen that she attempted to extricate from its elastic holder. First the pen clip caught on the elastic, then she somehow twisted it around and got it stuck.

The personnel manager, who had all the while seemed on the verge of interrupting her to raise some critical point she was missing, got out of his chair and leaned heavily over his desk to see what the matter was. Michelle's fingers had lost whatever grace and coordination they possessed, but she signed the leave form and, after drawing a blank, wrote down the date the personnel manager volunteered. She hesitated over the box marked "Number of Days Requested."

"Don't worry about that," the manager said crossly. "Here, let me—" and he took the form from her and scrawled something illegible beneath the blank box. "You can call me when you figure out your schedule and I'll file it then," he told her and stuffed the form into his own file folder.

Michelle rose to her feet and felt dizzy. The personnel manager tapped the folder he held on the edge of the desk and rested it there a moment, watching her with eyes that had grown cold. Then he raised himself to his feet and stretched out a hand.

"Again, on behalf of Gonper Electronics, I'm very sorry for your loss."

Michelle shook his hand damply and thanked him. His lip curled. She knew she had to get out of the room before the pulse beating in her eyes turned into tears or worse, but she had one last question that she fumbled to put into words. "When Peter had the accident…"

"Yes?"

She did not know quite what she meant to ask. Was he alone? Was the equipment inspected afterward? Did his coworkers or supervisor call 911, and how long did it take them? Did anyone attempt first aid? "Did he die quickly?"

The personnel manager regarded her with what looked for all the world like contempt. He looked very tired. Someplace in the back of Michelle's mind, she added the personnel manager to the list of people she had failed to please, and she felt sorry. "Yes, he died within minutes," the manager said. "He didn't suffer long at all."

Outside the personnel manager's office, the buzz and hum of the factory were everywhere. Michelle didn't recognize anything on this floor, but she found the bathrooms quickly. They were poorly maintained, since the packs made them far less necessary, but they were also empty, and Michelle was glad to be alone. She washed her face and hands, left the file folder on the counter, entered a stall, and sat down.

So Peter was dead. She tried to envision his face going soft and slack and free of consciousness as he died—his suffering ended. Some easy tears were welling up. Peter was gone, and she would never be able to tell him her plan. Sentimentality again. The thought made her double over on the toilet seat, her tears squeezing out onto her knees. She could never help being sentimental about Peter, even now; she was still projecting her own ideas and feelings on him. She didn't even know if he *wanted* to offline. Of course he did, who in the world didn't? But she never asked him and he never said a word.

Michelle's hiccups had returned with a vengeance. She would have to get a drink of water in a minute, and then she would make all the necessary arrangements for Peter, at least as soon as she had gotten some rest. She must have done it all before when her father died, but she had forgotten everything. It would take time. What was in the form she signed, she wondered suddenly, that made the personnel manager look at her so differently? It had contained legal waivers, but all the empty words Michelle had absorbed today seemed to have deserted her. Never mind. She could ask for a copy when she called the manager to schedule her leave. If she had to she could request all ten days. She could use them, after all. They were hers.

And this was the thought that made her sob in earnest, with a new warm feeling rising up in her: those ten days with one-quarter pay were entirely hers, and so was her and Peter's joint account, and so was the resale money from Peter's pack. With her face in her hands Michelle cried for her brother, but as she did she whispered, "Thank you, thank you, thank you"—whether to Peter or God or the personnel manager, she didn't know—because for the next ten days, Michelle was going to lie down and sleep the fullest and deepest sleep of her life.

Custom Appraisal
by
Susan Mattinson

Susan Mattinson obtained her Bachelor of Arts in Creative Writing from the University of New Brunswick, Fredericton, Canada. Her short stories have received awards from the International Teacher's Association, *and* Cancopy's Copyright Literacy Contest, *and have placed in the quarter-finals (top 10%) of L.* Ron Hubbard's Writers of the Future *contest. Her short story* "A Matter of Luck" *appeared in issue one of* Reality Complex *magazine. She is currently working on her first novel.*

"Custom Appraisal" stems from the struggle that artists encounter between staying true to themselves and catering to fame. With elements of The Portrait of Dorian Grey *thrown into a Twilight Zone scenario,* "Custom Appraisal" *adds a technological twist to one man's priorities.*

"What happened to your head?!" Janice stood up from her chair and hurried over to him.

Lloyd set his briefcase on the floor against the wall and pried his feet out of his dress shoes. Her hands were on his head, fussing and skittering over the metal bracket curving around behind his right ear.

"Christ, Janice! At least let me get out of the doorway!" He brushed her hands away.

Janice backed off for a moment before plunging back into his personal space.

"The skin is all red—I think it's infected!"

"It's not infected."

"What happened? What's it for?"

Lloyd sighed and turned to face his wife. Her muddy hazel eyes widened and filled with a deep concern. He ran a hand through his thick dark hair.

"Garret did it."

"Garret? Who's he?! Did you call the police?!"

Lloyd threw his hands up in exasperation. "No! Damnit!" His gaze met hers. "I'm an artist now."

Janice's forehead crinkled, aging her features. "What?!"

"This…" He rested his fingers against the metal. It felt cool and comforting against his skin. "…device… it stimulates a specific lobe of my brain, exciting my artistic talents. I can be a painter now." Lloyd's eyes became glassy with emotion; he glanced down at the floor.

"Oh for Pete's sake, Lloyd! Is this about following some foolish dream? This is your health we're talking about here! That thing could malfunction and fry your brain. If you want to be an artist, be an artist. You don't need some piece of metal." Janice's eyes flickered wild with anger.

He stalked halfway across the room before whirling back to face her. "You just don't get it! I *need* this piece of metal to paint! The motions have never been smooth, and I've never been proud of my art. I want the pictures to flow from me onto the canvas. I want to be good; I want to be a real artist. And now I am."

Janice tangled her fingers together. "But your head! Your health! What if something goes wrong?!"

"Garret is a Bio Mechanics student."

"A student?!"

"He's the best in his class!" Lloyd clenched and unclenched his fists. "The guy is floating on a pile of scholarships and study grants. He's practically being washed away by them all! The procedure was a simple version of a more complicated device. He modelled it off old technology, safe and reliable. Time-tested. My sensor is no more complicated than a pace-maker."

"But…" She trailed off, unable to form another objection. "Are you sure this is what you want?"

Lloyd looked down at the floor and then back up at his wife.

"Yes. More than anything."

He had met Garret a couple months ago at a social event for his business firm. Lloyd had been standing by the drink table nursing a glass of scotch when Robert deFoy wandered over.

"Lloyd! How're you doing?"

"Not bad. Nice party, isn't it?"

Robert flicked his hand. "Oh, but I have to introduce you to someone." He motioned for Lloyd to follow him and led the way across the room.

People flowed across the floor like phantoms; Lloyd didn't know half of them. He should have been making more of an effort to network, but instead he found himself wishing he were anywhere else. He took a sip of his scotch; his head was buzzing but it did nothing to motivate his socialization. He would meet Robert's acquaintance and then slip out the back.

Lloyd noticed a young man at the bar. His tan hair stuck out at random, as though he had just crawled out of bed. His dress shirt and pants were spotless and pressed, but his sneakers were tattered and riddled with holes.

Robert moved to stand beside the young man. "Garret, I'd like you to meet Lloyd Dayton," he said, clapping Lloyd on the back, "one of my most talented associates. Lloyd, this is James Garret; he's a Bio Mechanics student at the Institute of Medical Technology. Their very best."

"You flatter me, Mr. deFoy."

Robert flicked his hand again. "Nonsense, it's true. And call me Robert, none of this 'Mr. deFoy' crap."

Garret swivelled on his stool, turning to face them. Lloyd was struck by the odd blue-green colour of the young man's eyes as they flicked over at him.

"Nice to meet you, Mr. Dayton." He extended his hand and Lloyd shook it.

"Lloyd, please, and it's my pleasure."

Lloyd sighed and studied his scotch glass. What number was he on? They had talked well into tomorrow but he didn't care; his evening had improved after his introduction to the young Bio Mechanic. He glanced up and noticed Garret's strange eyes fixed on him, his gaze firm and penetrating.

"So why did you decide to get into business?"

Lloyd shrugged. "I'm in business because I'm good at it."

"You're fantastic at it from what I've heard. But that's it?"

Lloyd's forehead creased. "What do you mean 'that's it'?"

Garret's fingers played over his beer glass, sketching random patterns through the beads of condensation. His eyes seemed iridescent in the dim lighting. "Do you like what you do?"

Lloyd shrugged again. "It's not bad, I guess."

"I have the feeling that you would be doing something else instead, if given the choice."

Lloyd's mouth formed into a half smile, and he let out small chuckle. "It's…" He paused, sighing. "It's stupid, really." He expected Garret to urge him on, but the young man remained silent. Lloyd found himself continuing of his own accord.

"If I wasn't in business, I would have wanted to be an artist." Lloyd found his fingers fidgeting against his glass. "When I was younger I wanted to be an artist. But I was never very good, and sometimes I would get so frustrated. When my application for art school was rejected, I lost hope. But I'd still see the paintings in the galleries. I wished, so much, that I could create art like that. I wished…"

He paused, a small smile flashing onto his face.

"Now I just fill my apartment with them… rare and expensive pieces of art. They make me sad, but they also make me happy." He uttered a little laugh and took a mouthful of scotch, shooting a wistful stare at the wall behind the bar. Bottles glittered like potions on the shelves.

"The wall looks like an alchemist's lab," he announced. He turned his head and the room blurred.

"If you want to be a painter, be a painter."

"It's not that simple." Lloyd attempted to feign sobriety, but the young man's strange eyes were bright pools of colour. He found himself swimming in them, swept away in the current. He squeezed his eyes shut and then opened them again. "With my job I have very little spare time. In that time I like to do things to relax, you know?"

Garret nodded.

"Well painting isn't relaxing for me. It frustrates me because what comes out on the page isn't what I see in my head. It angers and saddens me, so I figure it's better that I save myself the grief and don't do it at all." He paused and cocked his head to the side, thinking. "If..."

He stopped and thought some more, letting a small frustrated puff of air shoot out his nose.

"If the picture from my mind could make it onto the page, if my paintbrush would flow smoothly... the calming peace of the unhindered art form whisking me away... well, I would give anything for that. I really would."

Lloyd lowered his eyes and turned away. Fumbling with his glass, he wet his lips and realized that he didn't want to drink any more. He glanced at his watch but never noted the time. Standing up from the stool, he planted a firm hand on the bar.

"It's late; I should probably head home now. My stomach feels like a hotel room the morning after a rock band's final gig. And I bet my wife is only a phone call away from declaring me a 'missing person.' It was nice meeting you though." He started to turn away.

"I might be able to do it."

Lloyd turned back to see Garret's strange eyes piercing into his. The young man's face was drawn and serious. "Huh?"

"No. Not 'might,' I think I could. Yes, I can. I know I can."

"What are you talking about?"

"I can help you. I can make you an artist."

Lloyd's jaw tightened. "Son, if you can make me an artist..." He trailed off, words lost behind a flood of thoughts. Fumbling in his pocket, he produced his business card and passed it to Garret. All of a sudden, he felt embarrassed. He had gotten drunk and whined about his life's dreams, and now some Bio Mechanic student he just met was offering to make him an artist.

Lloyd stumbled away from the bar and people blurred past him in muddled streaks. He moved toward the freedom of the door, away from the bar's alchemy shelves and Garret's mystical gaze.

"Hey, it's Garret."

"Garret...?" Lloyd's brow crinkled as he tried to place the name.

The voice on the phone became nervous. "James Garret? Robert deFoy introduced us at—"

"Oh, right!—I remember now." Lloyd laughed. A bottle of scotch and more than a month had gone a long way toward blotting out his memory of that night. "I'm sorry, that evening is a little hazy, if you know what I mean."

Garret chuckled, his unease vanishing. "I figured it out. I can do it."

Lloyd shifted at his desk. "Do what now?"

"Make you an artist!" Garret's voice held a combination of surprise and exaltation.

Lloyd snapped forward in his chair, almost dropping the phone. "What?!"

"I can—"

"I heard what you said." Lloyd's mind raced as Garret fell silent. Had the boy really found a way to make him an artist? Nobody else had cared enough to try and help him; but then again, had he ever told anyone about his dream? Janice, and now this young man, but no one else.

His voice fell to a whisper even though he was the only one in the office. "Are you sure?"

"Positive. The technology is a simplification of the more complex systems that we work with in class. It would be a small metal sensor surgically implanted that would stimulate the artistic portion of the right side of your brain, heightening your artistic abilities, specifically painting."

"Painting..." Lloyd's heart danced in his chest. His mind manufactured visions of his brush flowing in beautiful arcs over a canvas. "How dangerous would it be?"

Garret's voice glowed with bridled excitement. "The procedure would carry very little risk. You can thank the simplicity of the technology for that."

"But why help me?"

"Because I can. And when I see a need, I try to fill it. That's *my* dream, Lloyd."

Lloyd's eyes darted around the office. He wanted this operation more than anything, but there must be a catch. You never got something for nothing. "And how much...will this cost?"

There was silence on the other end of the line; to Lloyd it seemed to stretch an eternity.

Garret's tongue clicked. "Absolutely nothing. The sensor is so simple, it can almost be made from scrap metal. Don't worry about it."

"Are you sure?"

"Positive. Just paint me a picture after we're done."

Janice finally dropped the argument about his new sensor and disappeared into the kitchen. Lloyd stood in the middle of his study. A blank canvas, supported by a dark wooden easel, loomed in front of him. Watercolour paints and brushes sat on a small table nearby. His hands clenched and unclenched at his sides.

What if the implant didn't work, and he was no better at painting than before? The disappointment would be fierce. It might destroy him. He trusted Garret's skills, but it didn't seem to ease his mind much. Lloyd trembled with a nervous excitement, the air felt thick and electric.

He picked up one of the brushes and dipped it into the cup of water. What was he going to paint? All the sceneries and sky-scapes that he had fantasized about reproducing had been forgotten. But did it really matter what he painted?

He swirled the brush on the blue colour palette and then paused, his hand hovering inches away from the canvas. Lloyd found himself on a strange edge, where the urge to paint—to let the brush glide over the blank surface—was so great that it was almost painful. He revelled in the feeling. This was how artists, real artists, felt before the first stroke of creation.

He allowed himself to tip over the edge and a streak of blue appeared along the top of the canvas. More blue appeared, his brush dipping from water to palette, colour to colour.

His movements became fluid and confident, and shape immerged from the brushstrokes; the grey shades of an overcast sky blended into one another. Lloyd's mind reached a state of peace, like the tranquility of the once-blank canvas. He was a channel for artistic energy, a perfect conduit for his imagination to escape the confines of his mind and start a new life. He became lost in the moments as they fluttered by, his painting building up on itself in layers. An ocean formed, rolling with a raw elemental strength, the occasional white cap accenting the crests of waves. The water took on a hue strangely similar to Garret's iridescent eyes.

He painted.

A soft knock brought Lloyd out of his artistic trance. Blinking was difficult, and he realized that his eyes hurt.

"Come in."

The door opened and Janice stepped in, dressed in a casual silk negligee and housecoat. As usual, she still wore her gold necklace, bracelets, and earrings. She would wear them even when she slept, as if each night she expected the apartment to burn down and wanted to look her best for the occasion.

Lloyd watched her, paintbrush still in hand. "Yes?"

Her arms dangled, hands clasped together in front of her groin. "I didn't want to bother you. But it's late; you should come to bed. You've been painting for hours."

Lloyd turned away and surveyed the room. His first painting sat finished, resting on a bed of papers strewn about his desk. Rocky outcroppings and cliffs framed the ocean, viewed from the curving shoreline. The detail was exquisite. On the easel another canvas sat half-finished: the beginnings of a blazing sunset over a metallic, sky-scraping city. The buildings were still faint outlines.

Lloyd turned back to his wife. "I'm fine."

"My God, you look terrible! What happened?" She crossed her arms in front her chest.

"I'm just tired, I guess."

"Then you should come to bed." Her face was serious, but her eyes shone. She had got one up on him.

"Fine."

He rinsed the paintbrush in the water, now dark and murky, and set it on the table beside the watercolours. His hand was cramped, but he refused to display his discomfort in front of Janice. It would be one more objection to his new hobby. He stalked past her out of the room and she turned, following him like a shadow.

Lloyd called in sick to work the next morning and painted all day. When his collection totalled four, he had run out of spaces in the study to put them. He took his rare works of art off the walls in the living room and stored them in a closet. He filled the spaces with his own pieces, some even before the paint dried.

In the third piece, his first painting leaned against the wall behind his desk, and his second painting tilted precariously—but it had really been quite safe, he had checked it numerous times—off to one side. Lloyd thought it expressed the transformation from his old life to his new life very well.

The fourth painting was a spread of ambient colour as he attempted to portray the very essence of art. The emotions evoked by the collection of hues and shapes captured the feeling of the artist. Just looking at it made Lloyd feel like he was painting.

He was just beginning his fifth piece when he heard knocking.

"Come in."

The study door opened and his wife slipped in.

"Can I help you?" He spoke without looking over, his brush never faltering against the canvas.

"Come on; take a break. You've been painting all day."

"No, I'm fine." Lloyd's brow furrowed, he was starting to lose his concentration. He could hear her shuffle, irritable.

"No you're not! Look at yourself. Your eyes. Your hair! There's something wrong with you!"

Exasperated, he tossed his paintbrush onto the table. Black paint droplets flicked out over the palette, tainting the green and blue. He turned to Janice. "I'm finally able to enjoy painting, and you're trying to ruin it for me!"

Her mouth gaped. "I am not trying to ruin it for you. I'm concerned about your health! Go look at yourself in the mirror. You look horrible!"

Lloyd groaned and covered his face with his hands. "Please, get out of my study."

"Just go look at yourself."

And then she was gone from the doorway.

He sighed and turned back to his painting, picking up his brush and rinsing it in the water cup. Why was Janice so insistent that he look at himself? One sleep-deprived night wouldn't destroy his good health at the age of thirty-seven. He blended black, blue and green onto the canvas, but his mind was no longer clear. He set the brush back on the edge of the palette and wiped his hands on his pants. He wouldn't feel at ease until he assured himself that his wife had no reason to complain.

Lloyd stretched, his back cracking in protest. His body was stiff from the long hours of standing and pulsed with a dull ache as he walked out of the study and down the hall to the washroom. He flicked on the lights and stepped in front of the mirror.

There were shadows under his eyes, and his face looked more lined and drawn than usual, but Lloyd didn't see anything else out of the ordinary. He leaned into the mirror and turned his face from side to side. Something caught his eye. Streaks of silver ran through his hair at his temples where he previously had no grey at all. The lines in his face had deepened, and wrinkles had formed at the corners of his eyes. Janice thought he looked horrible, but he really just looked ten years older. Did this have something to do with the paintings?

A million questions ringing through his head, Lloyd left the washroom and went to the front door. As he slipped into his shoes, he wondered where he might find Garret. He needed some answers.

❦

"You've definitely aged. There's no denying that. But at least you're healthy." Garret fiddled with some tools and then leaned up against the counter.

He stood in a large room, similar to a doctor's office, where Garret checked his blood pressure, listened to his heart, and shined a small light in his eyes and throat.

"How is that possible?!" Lloyd asked.

"I don't know." Garret's eyes assumed a darker shade. His eyebrows slanted towards each other. "It was only after I installed the sensor that you noticed the aging?"

"Yup."

"But that's not right! There's no way that the sensor could have activated some sort of rapid aging. It's not biologically possible!" He clenched his hands into fists, frustrated.

Lloyd remained silent.

Garret sighed and rubbed his hands over his face. "When did you first notice that you had aged?"

"Just before I tracked you down... a few hours ago."

"Okay." He strode across the room and retrieved a pen and paper out of a drawer.

"But last night when my wife came to get me for bed, she noticed. I thought she was just being dramatic, but apparently, she wasn't." Lloyd looked down at his hands; his fingers itched to grip a paintbrush, but he forced himself to settle. There was something very strange going on, and they needed to figure it out.

"Okay." Garret's pen scratched against the scrap of paper. His messy hair and pressed lab coat made him look like a mad scientist. "If we say you've aged about ten years—"

"At least."

"—twelve years approximate, in the last twenty-four hours, then that would make the aging process..." His pen quickened and he muttered to himself as he did the math. When he finished his face fell. "That would make your aging process a half a year per hour."

Lloyd frowned. "You're kidding! I *know* I'm aging faster than that...."

Garret paced back and forth across the room. Lloyd watched him, worried. The young man stopped and hurried over to the counter, searching the cabinets mounted on the wall. He produced a mirror and passed it to Lloyd.

"Take a look at yourself. Have you aged any since you left your house?"

He squinted into the mirror, turning his head. "No, I don't think so. Not that I can notice. But if I'm only one and a half years older than the last time I looked, I wouldn't be able to notice anyway."

"But you're inclined to believe you are actually aging faster than that."

"Well I thought so, but maybe not."

Garret took the mirror from Lloyd and tossed it back into the cabinet. "How many paintings have you finished so far?"

Lloyd frowned. "I don't see what this had to do with—"

"How many?"

He counted silent on his fingers as he thought. "Four and a half. Which reminds me, I painted a lovely seacoast that I want to give to you, but I forgot to bring it with me."

Garret was pacing again, deep in thought. Lloyd was about to repeat his answer when the young man knelt beside his chair—like a doctor comforting a child.

"I think you *are* aging faster than the math says," he said. His strange eyes shone, "when you *are* aging."

"What?"

Garret stood again. "This it going to sound crazy, but here's what I think. I think that you're aging as you paint. When you stop painting, you stop aging, and while you paint, you age rapidly."

Lloyd's mouth opened, and then shut.

"We'll have to take the implant out—"

"No." His thoughts flailed, but he knew that losing the ability to paint was not an option.

Garret folded his hands across his chest and Lloyd was reminded of his wife. He prepared himself to be reprimanded and argued against. Instead, Garret spoke very matter-of-factly, almost pleasant.

"Then you have two options: you stop painting and your life remains long, or you paint until your heart's content and your life will be drastically shortened. Because every picture you paint shortens the amount of time you have left on this earth." His blue-green eyes lowered. "I'm sorry, but there's nothing else I can do for you."

Lloyd sat in his study, the desk chair angled so he could look at the easel and his half-finished canvas. Just a few days ago he would have given anything to become an artist, but how serious had he been? No price would have been too great for the sensor and the surgery. But now that his dream had come true, it turned out that the bill was being paid with his life.

How much was his art worth?

He stared at the canvas, vague layers of color washes building the background behind faint outlines of form. The thought that this half-finished painting could be the last work he ever produced caused a tightness in his chest. He clenched his jaw and hurried to wipe a hand across his eyes.

Lloyd had only been an artist for one day, but he was already forgetting what life had been like before. He only remembered being miserable and feeling unfulfilled; he never wanted to feel like that again. It came down to one question: how much did he love painting? And when it was reduced to that, the answer was simple. He adored it.

Everyone died eventually, and he would rather spend the time he had left in the perfect bliss of artistic creation.

Satisfied with his decision, Lloyd smiled and stood. His brush waved through the water cup and danced across the colour palette, picking up where it left off.

He ignored the first knock on the study door. On his canvas Lloyd was starting his seventh painting. In the fifth he had succeeded in capturing the iridescent beauty of the cockroach, hints of blue, green, and purple shining through the rich, black-brown exoskeleton. The sixth depicted a crowd of people at an indoor rock concert, beams of light intersecting silhouettes and darkness. In the beginning of the seventh, layers of rough outlines formed two young lovers under a tree.

The knocking came again, accompanied by Janice's voice. "Lloyd? Are you in there?"

Lloyd sighed, but continued to paint. "No."

The door opened to form a hesitant crack, paused, and then swung all the way open. She gasped. "Oh my God, you look old!"

"Is that all?"

"What's happening to you?!"

"I'm dying." His matter-of-fact tone was reminiscent of Garret's. The paintbrush outlined the top of the young lovers' heads.

"What?!"

He set the brush down and turned to face her. Her eyes bulged out of their sockets in an unattractive, amphibian display.

"For some strange reason, my life is getting shorter with every painting I create."

"No! That's impossible! That's…" Janice trailed off. "Have you gone to see the guy who did this? He could fix it!"

Lloyd shuffled over to the desk chair and sat down with the stiff creak of muscles and bone. He sighed, content. "Yes, I saw Garret. There's nothing he could do."

"He could take that damned thing out of your head!"

"That's not an option."

"It's the only option!" Janice screamed, her rage almost tangible.

Lloyd glared at her, watching her shake with anger. "I've already chosen. All my life I wanted to be an artist, and now I am."

He gestured to the paintings and realized that she had not once complimented him on his work. "I would rather live a short but fantastic life as an artist than live a long life and let things go back to the way they were before. I will paint, and I will die happy."

Tears formed in her eyes, and now they rolled down her cheeks. "What about me?! Did you ever think of that? You'll go ahead and kill yourself and leave me all alone?!" Janice's eyes swept over his masterpieces. "For that?" She rubbed at the tears in her eyes, and looked back up at him. "I love you."

Lloyd swallowed; his voice came out as a whisper. "Then you should care about my happiness."

Janice's mouth opened and then closed. Her eyes searched his, as though the solution to the argument was mapped in the crisp age-lines of his face. She soon gave up and turned away, closing the study door behind her.

Lloyd sat for a few moments, his mind drifting, until his eyes found their way back to the easel. He stood up, legs stiff and creaking, and picked up his brush.

He painted all through the night. By dawn his collection had reached eleven, but his eyes were too heavy to stay open. He rinsed the brush and stretched, sharp pops issuing from his back and shoulders. On the way to the bedroom, he stopped and looked at himself in the mirror. His hair was completely grey, lightening to white in some places. Deep lines creased his face, creating the features of a man in his late seventies. Lloyd turned from the mirror and shut off the washroom light.

He shuffled down the hall to the bedroom. His head felt like it was wrapped in layers of gauze, his eyes itching with the strain of keeping open. A thought splintered into his head with a wicked urgency and he stopped. Janice would be in the bedroom and waking up soon. Going in there would incite a new argument that he couldn't handle, especially in his current state of fatigue.

Lloyd sighed, his eyelids drooping. It seemed like his study was the only place in the apartment where he could find peace these days. Cautious not to wake his wife, he turned and shuffled back down the hall.

Something poked him through the velvet cradle of sleep. A canopy of darkness was washing over him again when a hot, searing pain forced full consciousness upon him. Lloyd screamed and sat up in his chair, hands slapping down onto the desk.

His wife stumbled back, a kitchen knife clutched in her hand. As if to accent the situation, he felt a warm drip slide down the side of his neck.

"What the hell!"

Janice's eyes were wild. "I... I..."

Lloyd reached up with a shaking hand and touched the metal bracket behind his right ear. It was slick with blood and loose along one side, like the flap of a half-peeled scar.

"What do you think you're doing?!" Lloyd noticed that his voice had been changed by the natural vibrato of age. "You could cause serious brain damage! What were you thinking?!"

She tensed her body, defiant. "Obviously, you're not in your right mind with that… that *thing* in your head—"

"And you are?!"

"—so I took it upon myself to take it out."

Lloyd's jaw gaped open. "You're crazy! The brain damage, Janice! Would you enjoy feeding me mashed vegetables for the rest of my life?"

"At least you'd be alive!" Her voice screeched through the room and then fell to a dead silence.

Lloyd became aware of the pain streaking through the side of his head. He would have to go to Garret and tell him what happened. Get it fixed. He looked at his wife, secretarial black skirt and light blue blouse, neat and tidy. Hadn't he heard that when a person looked the most stable and secure on the outside, they were the most screwed up on the inside? He wasn't going to take his chances.

"Get out."

She turned to storm out of the study.

"No. I mean *get out*." His voice was calm and even. "Pack up your things and leave the apartment. I never want to see you again."

Janice looked back at him. She bit her lower lip to keep from crying. "Where will I go?"

"I don't know, and I don't care. Just get the hell out of here." Lloyd gripped the arms of the chair.

Tears flowed down Janice's cheeks, and she began to sob. She slipped a shaking hand onto the doorknob. Lloyd watched as his wife took one final look over her shoulder and pulled the door closed behind her. He was alone.

He realized he had been holding his breath and let it out in a long sigh, relaxing his hands on the chair. His head still throbbed, but he would wait a while to make sure she was really gone before going to see Garret. And he had to remember to bring Garret his painting. Lloyd was never one to leave a bill unpaid.

He forced his body out of the chair with a groan and set a blank canvas on the easel. He began to paint, but a sloppy wash of colour streaked from his unskilled brush. Lloyd tried a new colour, blending it to compensate for the mistake, but it only added to the blotchy patch. He set aside his brush and leaned back in his chair. Janice must have damaged the bracket more than he thought. He would have to see Garret right away, whether she had left yet or not.

As he stood, his gaze slid over his other paintings. His mouth ran dry. Paint splatters and messy washes of color coated the canvases. Every single one was a mess. He bolted from the office and into the living room where more of his artwork lined the walls. His painting of the indoor rock concert showed an audience of stick people, their limbs melding together in a messy web. The stage lights spilled down on them like over-turned buckets of paint. The painting of the cockroach was a big puddle of varying shades of black. The ocean scene he painted for Garrett showed spikes of color, making the land and sea look the same, and neither came close to the color of the young man's eyes.

Janice did this. She destroyed my paintings, and a good job she did of it too! Lloyd moved closer, trying to glimpse any hints of the painting's former glory. He couldn't find any. He touched the paint and it was dry. How would the paint be dry if Janice had just ruined them? And how would she have stolen the paint and the brushes to destroy them when the art supplies were in his office? He had been there the whole time, and if someone had tried to take his art tools, he would notice.

Lloyd's heart sunk in his chest. The paintings had been like that from the start. He couldn't paint, and he'd never been able to paint. *I've thrown my life away for nothing.* Would he have to live the rest of his life in this misery? He couldn't stand it. Things had been perfect when his bracket was working.

That's what he would do! Garrett could fix the bracket, and Lloyd would forget these last few hours ever happened. His life would be perfect. As he pondered what to paint next, Lloyd threw on his shoes and raced out of the apartment to find Garrett.

Chalice of Evensade
by
Erik Goodwyn

Erik Goodwyn is a psychiatrist in Dayton, Ohio with an extensive interest in history and mythology. He worked his way through medical school via a "nontraditional" path, which means it took much longer than usual. Three years in the army, a current contract with the Air Force, and a zillion part-time jobs later, he has finally reached a point where he can focus on his writing. In "Chalice of Evensade," Goodwyn explores the concept of immortality, which has fascinated him for decades, and he hopes this be-careful-what-you-wish-for tale opens readers minds to the true ramifications of eternal life.

"For Eternity," intoned the priest, "may he have peace."

At only nine years of age, Natorus saw his father dead. High upon the grand arcade of the city of Atrogonia he stood in silence with his mother between the wind-blown urns of fire. Slaves and servants lined the cliff-like edges of the Arcade as the high priest of the God-King droned, resplendent and solemn. Natorus, tanned and quick-limbed with curly brown hair that fell about a face intensely handsome, stared with detached fascination at the body of his slain father. A hundred times he had looked to that scarred disciplinarian with awe and guessed at his every thought.

What thought remained now? Natorus glanced at his mother. Her noble robes billowed as she gazed at the spires of Atrogonia, her face like carven stone upon which a single raindrop had fallen. "Am I to sit on the council now, mother?" he asked.

"My brother will take your stead until you are of age," she replied, her voice measured and heavy.

He pondered his dead father's features, and the wind whipped by his ears. "Father was too old for war." She did not respond. "Must we all grow old and die?"

"All Man-kind is mortal, Natorus. None can escape it save the fool who finds the Gryllohai," she said, quoting the Old Tales. "Be thankful for what life we are given. Atrogonia is the greatest city in the world. You might have lived and died a filthy barbarian of Auril Dranne, ignorant of all save provincial druid lore and unknown to the sophistication and piety of our kin."

"There is no escape?"

"None. Even at the center of mankind, life is cruel and unjust. Death comes without fail. Accept it and live the best you can, lest you fall victim to folly."

Natorus rejected the idea silently, but always it plagued him. He grew into manhood, gaining in prestige and power by blood right, and his thoughts always returned to that day upon the arcades. He achieved esteemed status in the Patronica, and counseled with wisdom in the marbled world of the Atrogonian elite. Peace prevailed, and every year at the games he sat with his comrade Stelius and partook of the feasts and spectacle. After ten years of peaceful celebration, Natorus turned his intense eyes to the horizon and brooded during the games.

"You look pensive," said Stelius over the cheer that rose among the commoners below. "Thinking of your mother?"

"No. That was two years ago; I am past mourning."

"Then what is it?"

A tired looking servant brought bread and wines. "Refreshment, my lord?"

Natorus nodded. "Thank you. Here." Natorus handed the man several gold *entarii*. "You look exhausted. Go and enjoy the games with your family." The servant bowed, astonished, and left with many thanks.

"Always a man of the people," quipped Stelius, taking a bottle and a loaf.

Natorus shrugged. "Fortune alone separates the Patronican from the stall sweep."

"So you always say."

"Do you remember our conversation last year?"

"What myths are you pondering today? The Cup of Dreams again? What would your wife say?"

"Better to ask my uncle who chose her for me. But truly, what if…?"

Stelius smiled. "I thought you might ask, having been struck by the advancing age of thirty one year before you. I read on it since last year's games."

"And?"

"It seems the barbarians have legends of it even older than ours, though it goes by another name. They called it The Chalice of Evensade, made in the time of the Gods. Only one exists; a spirit called Shirem Nerath Nuul made it, against the will of their Mother Goddess, or so say their druid shamans."

"And the myth of its power?"

"Almost the same: the man who drinks of it becomes immortal."

"What are the odds that the barbarian and we could have developed that story independently?"

"You think it is real?"

"Let us find out. What say you?"

"Well, it might stave boredom for a while, but it's only a dream. A dusty legend. Let it go."

Natorus gazed at the masses cheering the games. Young and old, man and woman engaged in the spectacle of the day. Tomorrow they would forget and return to toil and weariness. "Let it go? Perhaps I should, but what if it is not just a legend, Stelius? What if you were to set aside the banalities of our brief and mysterious lives and imagine what could be! Is not death the scourge of our kind? The inescapable lot of man?"

"I suppose."

"But to conquer it! The dream of every young man, whom reason teaches in the height of his vitality that all men die. What of the old man, still clutching to his lost vigor, or the dying man who curses the heavens with his last breath, wishing for just one more day to live?

"Think of the mysteries that would be revealed—the secrets of nature and wisdom that undying life would confer. And the power! While cruel fate erodes away the wit and sinew of every lesser man, we in the bliss of timeless fire of heart and blood, watch them fade—never to weaken, never to lose what we have. Eternity! Unchanging before the suns and everlasting as the mountain. We would live on as the Gods of old, to see every corner of the world, taste of every wine and bread, know every kingdom of Teralia, marvel at every natural wonder and partaking of every beautiful maiden with never a loss of vitality…. Think of it!"

Stelius shook his head at Natorus. "I can see there will be no end to this until we at least explore the truth of it. You've been thinking about this for how long, now?"

Natorus knew when his friend read his heart. "Ever since the day my father died."

"Well then, let us be done with it. You won't rest until I've proven it a false legend." He smirked. "Finally something to stave the boredom of peace."

The very next day Natorus resigned his seat on the council much to the surprise of both elite and commoner. He set out from Atrogonia into the wilds of the Old Kings of Auril Dranne, leaving his beloved city to act on the thoughts that had followed him for so many years since his father's death. Nothing hindered him now. He assembled a loyal guard to accompany them, and as always Stelius followed him. The perilous months that followed did nothing to diminish Natorus's burgeoning thirst for any knowledge of the Chalice.

One clue led to another, and their suspicion grew not only that the Chalice existed, but that they might find it. But two years into their quest they met an impasse, lost in the northern wilderness of Aeth Brenin. Natorus glared at the darkness as Stelius and the men camped in a cave. Rain poured outside.

"Perhaps we should give up," said Stelius.

"No." Natorus breathed in the mist, unblinking. "I know we are close. You read the texts just as I did."

"Yes, both real and forged! Are you sure you are right about their meaning?"

"Absolutely," Natorus growled.

Stelius snorted and left Natorus's side. Natorus, quietly reprimanding himself for snapping at his friend, gazed into the night. The rain blew across in sheets as the torchlight flickered.

"Look!" someone said.

A tiny light bobbed in the darkness and the men drew blades. "Away weapons," Natorus whispered. "I will do this, alone. Stelius, you are in charge."

"Yes, but," said Stelius, glancing uneasily at the swordsmen.

"I must," said Natorus. He plunged into the storm unwavering, climbing root and hacking branch toward the light with heart pounding. For so long he searched, and the closer he came, the more alive he felt.

Soon he entered a quiet grove where the rain chose not to fall, and thunderheads framed the starry sky. In the center of a stone circle lurked a winged thing holding an orb of moon-like light. Its fangs curled into a smile and its eyes burned with anticipation. Natorus strode forward and sheathed his broadsword. "Are you the one they call Azumon?"

"You seek the secret of the Chalice," it said, its voice a shimmering echo that made Natorus's skin crawl.

"I do."

"Nuul made it long ago, and did much to arouse Queen Alyia's wrath. Forbidden was he to make another."

"But her sway weakens. The world changes, and She changes with it. I have learned this. What of the hiding place? None who sought it before me found it. Why?"

Azumon cloaked itself in its wings as if to shield from the starlight. Thunder crackled distantly. "She was wise in counsel. Those She could not sway found only dust and death, but I will tell you." Natorus stepped forward, and Azumon loomed over him like a great shadow. "It appears once each century to offer its drink of the Otherworld from whence it comes. I know where it will rise next, for among my kind, I have the gift."

"When?"

Azumon grinned. "Soon. You must make haste, for you have but one chance. If you fail, you will die."

"Death comes to all mortal men, Azumon. I have nothing to lose."

"And much to gain?"

"I have eternity to gain."

Azumon laughed, and then told him where the chalice would rise. The next day, Natorus revisited the grove with more questions, but could not find Azumon. He followed the creature's directions, penetrating the depths of Cythraul—the forgotten Downland of caves and hidden realms created by the ancients—driving with such will and speed that all who did not throw down their allegiance in protest fell to the treacherous undercliffs and beasts of the darkness. For a year he toiled with only Stelius at his side. Soon their provisions dwindled and they fell nearly mad with the darkness and cold of the Downland. Finally he found the resting place of the Gryllohai. They labored up a vast stairway, dwarfed by a dark stone colossus.

"Who made these great structures?" asked Natorus.

"No one knows…perhaps they existed before the dawn of time."

"Shh! We are nearing it," whispered Natorus. "I can feel it."

"You still believe it worth what we have sacrificed?"

"Enough Stelius! Is it not the dream of every man? To live free from the chains of death and age? To live forever young. We should live this way!"

"You obsess with what *should* be. Are you so certain that what *is* is so much worse that what you think should be? The question is: life eternal, or not? How do you know eternity fares better?"

"It is what everyone dreams of in this world and the next!"

"I am not so sure."

"Look!" The marble chalice stood on a forsaken table of stone. Natorus took a step toward it, shaking in anticipation, and the dizzying chasms that surrounded them dwindled to an insignificant dream. "At last," rasped Natorus, "at the deepest end of the Earth have we found it after so long. All before us who have sought it found only dust."

"So the demon told you," said Stelius. "Do you know how long it will be here?"

Natorus felt weariness aching through his bones, and his heart pounded. "Not long." He reached for the Chalice. It was a simple thing, made of smooth grey marble and engraved in languages no one knew anymore, and as his hand neared it he felt a tremor, as if the stone lived. "Finally Stelius! After all these years of toiling…"

"Take it quickly before it is gone!"

Natorus grasped it and suddenly unknown ages thundered through him. The chalice sizzled with clear liquid and he reeled, swimming in images of gods and armies and lifetimes. "I will drink!" he shouted, and the chalice glowed, bubbling with mist that cooled his feverish skin.

"Are you sure? There is no turning back. Remember what the demon said—once you partake of it you cannot undo it. Are you sure this is what you want?"

The bubbling chalice mesmerized Natorus. "Eternity!" he cried, "It is now or never. If I am to discover immortality I must do it. I did not come all this way to turn back now." He drank a single sip and the power roared through him like a thousand storms.

Then silence filled him and he fainted forward, but Stelius caught him. "Steady, Natorus." Stelius's voice came to Natorus through a haze. "Your obsession is fulfilled—for better or worse. Are you all right?"

"I have partaken of the gods," he whispered. "Here, friend," he added, handing Stelius the chalice, "your journey has been just as long. Take this life as yours, never to be stolen by death or disease."

"Now that I am here, I fear it. I fear something so great shouldn't inhabit this briefly existing frame of mine. I won't drink it."

Natorus struggled to regain his composure. "A drink will cancel your brevity! You must take it now. There will not be another chance; only one Gryllohai exists—drink!"

Stelius lifted it to his lips and the smoke frothed double, but his hesitation cost him the chalice, and it disappeared in a wisp. They stood stunned and silent for a long while, and the torch light wavered in the damp breeze. "I cannot believe it," said Natorus at last.

"I missed my chance," muttered Stelius. "After all of this toil, I paused to think on it, and it cost me the Chalice." He sighed. "I'm not sure how I feel about that. What of you, Natorus? Do you feel different?"

Natorus took a deep breath. "I do not feel hungry anymore…but beyond that, no."

"Perhaps I expected muses and great horns of heaven."

Natorus laughed. "I suppose we will not know if the demon tricked us until you become grey headed and I do not."

"You are satisfied then?"

"Yes…you seem relieved"

"I think I am. Yes, I am relieved."

"You did not taste of the water. Doesn't that trouble you?"

Stelius shook his head. "I am merely glad it is done. I want no more of this. I hope it is true for your sake, but I am content to have missed it."

"And me? What of my end?"

"Well how will we know? Nothing will ever end for you now."

They laughed, but deep inside Natorus felt the truth of his words, and he grew pensive. "With this new life will come knowledge, I think, and like all knowledge it may be: one half power and one half terror."

"Shall we return home then?"

"Yes."

They returned to little fanfare, empty handed and travel worn, but the Patronica allowed Natorus to resume his seat among them. Atrogonia suffered without him, and he learned that in his absence wars had risen again between the barbarians and rival God-Kings of Burnheed. He averted full scale war, but deep down he knew the peace would not last.

As the years passed, Natorus never felt hunger. He ate with his wife and children as customed, and feasted with Stelius and the army. At the victory feast of General Gaiden, he noticed grey hair on his friend Stelius. He lifted a silver plate and glanced at his face. No grey. They laughed secretly about it during the celebration.

Plagues arose in Atrogonia, and a curious Natorus spent weeks with the dead and dying, shocking some by brazenly embracing them. He never fell ill. People called it god-like, but Natorus dismissed it as luck and good living.

Eventually his youth became inexplicable and many said the deities of the city had blessed him and that meant he bore the fate to rule. Stelius, now balding, was happy to see his friend rise in the ranks of the council.

Natorus stood tall and strong, ever in the prime of his vitality as his aged colleagues praised his health and virtue and crowned him God-King of Atrogonia. Natorus overlooked the masses with his children—who looked more like older brothers—and stood by his wife, a white haired and proud matron.

Now begins eternity, thought Natorus, *My journey all those years ago pays its reward. People look to me as a god. Priests argue whether I am favored by the deities of the Suns or of the Moon. My family lives well and I shall see all my descendants from now until....* He paused, lost in thought as musicians played in his honor. *There is no until, unless battle takes me.*

But was that true? Disease no longer touched him. The cuts and bruises he sustained over the years never left a mark. Perhaps even war could not touch him.

Natorus proved himself a strong-willed and tireless king. But year after year passed and slowly all the people he knew were taken with sickness and age. His wife died first, and though this loss stung deeply, the loss of his childhood friend Stelius crushed him.

He came to the deathbed on midsummer's day during the thirtieth year of his reign. Stelius and Natorus were over seventy years old, and Natorus, ever hale, took his aged friend's hand and sat in the gloaming for a long while.

Stelius opened his eyes as a breeze flowed through the rich bedchamber. "Do I look so old, my friend," he rasped, "for you to look upon me with such pity?"

"We share the same age, Stelius."

"And yet I am not the one in mourning.... Do not mourn me, my King."

"Don't call me that, please."

Stelius chuckled weakly. "As you wish, your Highness." Natorus shook his head. "Ironic, isn't it?"

"What?" asked Natorus.

"I envy your journey. My life fades and yours burns with unrelenting power. Yet you are the one suffering."

"I fear my journey shall be a lonely one."

"Yes, but my life is done. It has been a full life. I enjoyed what I had."

Natorus stayed until the end, and after Stelius took his final breath, Natorus gazed out the window as the suns set and heard baby birds chirping in nests outside.

He returned to the Patronica, grieving his friend for long after. He ruled with wisdom and fairness, though with each passing year he felt more distant from his people. Time became less meaningful to him. He turned mysterious to his people; no man had seen so many days, and he was changing.

Natorus began to see into men's hearts but felt less like he should be among them, for they misunderstood his ways, and he could not explain them. His city kingdom changed, too, becoming larger and more prosperous—and more dangerous for those who toiled in its deepening streets. Men learned about the world in new ways, far beyond the barbaric wilds from whence they came so long ago.

Some changes came like a tempest. A new instrument of war stormed forth in the dawn of Natorus's two hundredth year as the Blessed King: the chariot. Thousands came roaring from the wilds, tempted by the riches of the city states of Burnheed. At first men scoffed at the barbarians of Auril Dranne, but in the council chambers of Atrogonia, Natorus with his far-reaching eyes thought the new war spelt doom for their kind.

After much deliberating he brought forth his plan to meet the unwashed barbarians on the fields. He told his generals to adopt the new strategies but the generals were proud and felt their ways superior. They could not understand him, and he relented.

Natorus met the barbarians on the plains of Sarm along the northern reaches of Atrogonia. There the vast array gathered with chariots wheeling about in clouds of dust and wildmen. Hamara, a young general who reminded Natorus of Stelius in his youth stood beside him with shield and spear at the head of the central phalanx.

"A great host indeed, my King," said Hamara.

"So it is," responded Natorus, jaw set.

"Fear not, your Highness. Our kingdom holds the light of the world. You wield the greatest favor—you cannot die."

"I do not fear death. But there are many things a man can lose aside from his life."

Hamara dared tradition and placed a hand on the king's shoulder, causing a murmur. "You cannot die, my king, and so we cannot fail. My great grandfather taught me to trust in your leadership when I was a boy. My faith remains."

"His loyalty made this king proud." Natorus raised his hand and a thunderous roar filled the plains. The hordes of Auril Dranne turned toward them and began their charge, heady with druid-cursed murder. The roar of the charge ascended like the wailing at the ends of the world, until finally the warriors clashed.

Natorus slew many, but the tide turned and a bloodied barbarian struck Natorus in the heart with a spear, stopping him with a mortal wound. His breathing stopped, and the blood ceased to flow within him. He fell cold in Hamara's arms, as the ranks of the Atrogonian armies broke and fled, and Hamara's face was the last thing he saw.

When he awakened, he recalled the battle dimly, as if from a great distance. The dark air stifled him with dampness and cold. A chill crept into his skin as he opened his eyes to pitch darkness, taking in a single breath deeply—he knew it to be the first in a long time. The air loomed silent as death; he could almost hear his own blood pulse over the nothingness.

He sat up and felt the ceremonial robes of the dead around him. Terror found his beating heart, and he cried out in fruitless lament, scattering the gold gifts meant to travel with him to the next world. But no other worlds came, and this one had forgotten him. He climbed off the stone slab and explored the tomb, groping in the darkness for untold days, until reaching a wall of inscriptions. He focused on them for weeks, distracting himself from the maddening darkness and silence by trying to decipher them.

Eventually he mastered them with touch, and learned that the events after his death were chronicled on the wall. The barbarians had conquered Atrogonia and laid it to ruin. They allowed the humiliated citizens a single concession: to bury their beloved king in the Great Tomb by the sea of Tulm, and so Natorus's loyal subjects did so with great sorrow as the invaders plundered their city.

Natorus screamed and pounded the walls at the horror and waste of it all, rage consuming him for days. Eventually he calmed, and a more menacing darkness engulfed him like a monster that silenced his grief. Weeks passed into months. Natorus needed no food or water, but madness eroded his soul. He came to know every last inch of the stone tomb by touch. Every gift left to him. Every last scratch upon the gold and silver.

Eventually the darkness spoke to him as if from the past. Old friends, or his wife and children, filled the terrible void that had drowned him in his burial chamber. Months passed into years, and Natorus succumbed to the darkness and fell, destroyed in a corner of the tomb, unable to live and unable to die, staring blankly into emptiness.

Years became centuries. He eventually cursed the gift he took from the Chalice, and even his hope of escape from the tomb faded from his mind.

Natorus remembered very little of the dreamlike years that followed his discovery by the hermit. The blinding sunlight and the deafening breeze came like wisps of reflection as he recovered in the hermit's retreat. The bright groves of Dranyar—outside Atrasia—seemed to pour into the windows of the hermitage.

Natorus reawakened to the taste of food, to the sounds of birds, and the idle shuffling of someone milling about a house. The hermit never revealed his name, and spoke only when Natorus did. He treated him with aloof kindness, and with always a hint of knowledge in the corner of his eye. "You have been gone for a long time," he said in his dour voice.

Natorus nodded. By his calculations he had been trapped over four centuries. He kept this to himself.

"The lords of Alesmar have broken from the Atrasians of late," said the hermit.

"So many lands and names. I am unfamiliar with them. Tell me, what happened after they killed the king of Atrogonia?"

"The king of Atrogonia?" The hermit rubbed his beard with a rough hand. "You mean the legendary King Natorus the Blessed? Buried in a tomb that no one could ever find after the Bloodening? That reaches back to hallowed antiquity. Why should you ask of that?" asked the hermit with a gleam. "How long were you trapped in that place?"

"I think perhaps the...days without food and water must have clouded my faculties. I was a student of history—please, indulge me if you would."

The hermit placed a wooden bowl of pottage before Natorus and joined him. "The bloodthirsty chariot kings conquered all the city-states of Burnheed," said the hermit between spoons of pottage. "Those unlettered tribes, fueled with disdain at the Druidic Peace, crushed the learned city-states with crude wrought machines of war...but in a few generations the rulers came to enjoy the pleasures of slaves and gilded feasts of the city states. Kings forgot their savage roots and built marbled halls upon the backs of the conquered. They became known as Atrasians, and they developed a culture and literacy that overthrew the long forgotten Atrogonians. But I weary of all the warfare, which is why I have retreated from the world and live as I do."

Natorus took a moment to absorb that. "Such is the way of conquerors. My memory returns. What of the barbarians of Auril Dranne?"

"Many turn from the druid ways. It is sad, for wise was Queen Alyia in council in the ancient days."

Natorus paused. Had not he heard someone say that long ago? His mind still churned with the darkness of the tomb. "I have been away for so long."

The hermit shrugged as a breeze blew through the hut. "By your speech you seem of an older dialect. You were not starved; it could not have been but for a few days."

Natorus tapped his sword sheath. "Perhaps a bit longer than that. I thank you for your hospitality these many months."

The hermit bowed. "Where shall you go?"

Natorus sighed. "I do not know. Much has changed. I must learn the new world."

"Oh, it is not so new."

Natorus left, and the hermit's parting comment made him think as he traveled the roads to Alesmar, admiring the gold gifts his subjects had given him centuries ago. He journeyed with an ever lightening spirit, for he could not die by disease or battle wound; he had earned true immortality. He forgot his terrible imprisonment and came to Alesmar in the spirit of adventure, ready to see new things and learn new mysteries, but rather than take up the mantle of rulership again, he chose to give his wealth away and live as a laborer. He grew weary of royal comforts and burdens after a while, and chose to travel the lands, never staying anywhere long enough to draw attention to the fact that he never aged or suffered ailments of body.

Happiness came to him in helping others, and this came as a surprise in a life where surprises were becoming scarce. He labored as a quarryman so other kings could spread their cities deeper into the wilderness. He worked as a guard on the caravans to Sathen and Avithain where he recognized the remnants of the cultures that had conquered the old city-states.

He saw symbols of art and language and music that hinted of the old conquerors now forgotten among the scheming lords of the civilized realms. He came to love the simple life of hard work and unadorned camaraderie of the downtrodden masses, though he lived free from sickness, ever-hale even under cruel slavery. Working in the lines of countless laborers, he watched the city-states grow to kingdoms, and kingdoms to dynasties.

Then in what seemed a fleeting night to his eyes, savages of Auril Dranne once again defied the druidic ways and invaded the rich kingdoms with ferocity unmatched. Natorus battled without rival as a soldier, but he knew a single man could not win a war, and in time new conquerors enslaved the descendants of the old. Cities burned, entire realms were enslaved and much was lost.

Natorus found himself in the courtyards of the Oru, self proclaimed God-King. Ursurpers surrounded him and prepared for his hanging, and Natorus thought it oddly ironic that they would sentence him to die for defending the city states, when the Oru were the invaders centuries ago. They hung him to die, then tossed him in a grave outside the city; he crawled out days later unscathed.

He frowned at the plundered city. "Things have changed irrevocably now," he murmured.

"Have they?" Natorus turned to see a bedraggled gravedigger among the stinking bodies. The gravedigger smiled crooked before limping out of sight.

Natorus pondered that comment in the following centuries, and the cycle of conquest and invasion continued. Time and again Natorus saw kingdoms change, expand and press further into the wilds. The ways men looked at gods changed as well, and new faiths arose, proliferating throughout the generations.

Natorus labored in nearly every trade, learned every language and noted how tongues changed like beliefs over ages. But time drained him. Eventually he left the kingdoms of mankind and ventured into Auril Dranne. He cast aside the trappings of civilization and lived among the followers of the druids. Enraptured, he joined the sacred circles where the followers of the ancient ways still practiced, reciting poetry and legends that hearkened back to before even he had been born. Sitting on the grassy hill with the others, he listened to the tales as the suns ambled across the zenith and cool wind tossed the leaves.

Once a master druid many times his junior taught him about the bliss and majesty of the ancients. After he finished his teachings, the Loremaster asked everyone to discuss the tale. Natorus smiled at their childlike simplicity, and wondered if even the druid master himself knew of its ancient origin as part of the Old Tales, where he heard of the Chalice so long ago.

"I have never been so happy as I am now among you," affirmed Natorus when the discussion came to him. "I have turned away from the lands of God-Kings and come to love the serenity of your world."

"You have seen the city kings?" asked a child. "Are they not amazing?"

Natorus mused at the irony of her question. "Not to me, but I have seen much in my time. I have been told I do not look my age."

"I suspected," said the Loremaster. "How many years have you?"

Natorus pondered that. Years stretched beyond centuries in his mind, and his life seemed like a great cliff, enshrouded in fog far below. The memories of thousands of lives blended into a haze that clouded his youthful and uncluttered days. "I would rather not say." They laughed. "But know this: I have seen much change in this world, and I cannot say it bodes well. I hope to the gods that it leads toward a peace like you have here in Auril Dranne."

"Nothing good or bad lasts forever, far traveler," said the druid with a knowing gleam. "Perhaps you might think that a bad thing, but is it so bad?"

"I once thought so." His eyes fell upon a nursing mother and he suddenly felt horror clutch him as if from a great distance. "Death is a change," he said softly. The child, bright eyed and enamored of its mother's loving gaze, stopped to smile as if by instinct. *So long ago*, thought Natorus, *so long ago.* "Also is new life. Perhaps they need the space made by those who must pass on."

Natorus's thoughts often returned to that single perfect day among the druids—much like the day his father died stayed with him for so long—as the countless cycles of Man-kind swirled about him. He saw the fever of civilized ways creep further into the minds of the brute clan-nations of Auril Dranne he once called savage.

Natorus drew further into himself, sometimes leaving for months at a time to visit the groves and hillsides where he once dwelt among the druids. But one day he found the sacred places razed by the rising empire of Nurn and the circles all but gone, replaced by the spires and roads of Empire. For days he sat and wept.

Natorus hung his head. "I am weary of this world. Very weary. Nothing seems real anymore." He took long breaths and felt the wind pass through his hair. He searched his colossal memory and stared into the shadows, thinking deeply for weeks. Something puzzled him. A common thread weaved through the past; he missed it all this time, but now it came to him. *Someone has been following me through these many ages. I've seen them before: the hermit, the gravedigger, the loremaster. I shall find out who. It may take years.* He set out toward the horizon. *But I have eternity.* He smiled with renewed purpose.

The great events of the world interested him little, and he felt the course of the world was inevitable. He searched through the wars of Trendari the Great and the mass executions of the followers of Drymvar for a sign—a face perhaps, in the masses of men and women, who lived their entire lives and died in a mere moment to him. He could scarcely tell people apart from each other.

He focused himself on his new task—to find the creature that followed him through the millennia. To Natorus it became like the task of deciphering the runes in the tomb so long ago, and like that task, he knew it was the only thing keeping him from madness. Only this time he was not trapped under a mountain. The world itself was his tomb. He pushed this from his mind by focusing his will and winnowing through cultures that rose and fell in but an instant.

He hunted, unfazed, for a sign, a face or a subtle hint. The hermit he met ages ago, the grave digger, and the loremaster—even the child who asked him of the cities. Natorus's superior intellect knew these beings were the same. But who?

Five centuries passed and Natorus found nothing. For the first time in history the entire continent was at war: seven kingdoms had allied against a rival empire, waging a series of wars unrivaled in all the ages Natorus had lived through. These Bloodring Crusades were the darkest and bloodiest he had known.

His hope dwindled that he would ever find his quarry, and the Bloodring Crusades sickened him. He soon lost all care for anything and so joined the warfare, leading charges in battles for the King's Alliance, losing himself in the bloody mayhem to avoid his torment. He was killed many times over hundreds of years. He died a Temple Knight of St. Everard. A Svoedic berserker from the north. A Noble Londruinic lord. A Rendarian Castellan.

Slain in the Crusades for the last time, he awakened upon a funeral pyre in the Shoreland wilderness of the north. Still too weak to move, he watched his comrades place a torch to the wood, and silent pain roared through him as he caught fire—but this brought him relief. *Finally,* he thought, *I shall have peace. Surely even I cannot survive cremation. Stelius, my old friend, you were the wiser of us. Now I understand your peace.* The flames consumed him utterly, and his body scattered to the winds.

But something within him could still see. He had no eyes or body, but somehow the white sands of the shores where he burned rose about him. *How can this be?* he wondered. No answer came, and above him the suns rose and set ten thousand times through a glowing haze, and the surf pounded endlessly against the rocks, spraying high and rising and falling in rhythm with the wheeling stars. Silence joined him as his only companion.

Natorus finally awoke on the misty beach, a leafy blanket covering his nakedness. He took a deep breath and saw a winged creature calmly watching him. Natorus'smemory slowly returned, of countless lives stretching into haze, and for a moment he wondered if he had always existed. Then he remembered the Chalice.

But who was this creature before him? "Azumon?" he asked at last.

The demon smiled. "You do remember me."

"I know I have seen you before and I know your name, but I do not know *how* I know. I do not recall when I saw you. How long has it been?"

"Thousands of years, Natorus."

"Yes… yes!" He sat up. "You led me to the Chalice. You must be a faerie if you have lived this long."

"I am Kosithi, yes. And how have you enjoyed your gift of Eternity?"

Natorus sighed. "So many lifetimes weigh upon me. So many. I once thought the mountains and seas were eternal. But even they change. Mountains crumble over millennia, and seas shift, rise and fall. I know not how it will end. It thought it was finally over…but it seems even cremation cannot kill me."

"End?" Azumon inched forward. "Have you forgotten, Natorus? There is no end. Even we Kosithi, who have lived countless times longer than you, shall someday meet our end. But not you, Natorus. You shall live *forever*. True immortality… it is why Queen Alyia forbade the Chalice so long ago. Even when the universe fades into nothing and is annihilated, you shall live on. And on, and on—with no end, ever. There will be no escape from the loneliness, the weariness or the despair. You shall live for all time. You are a prisoner within yourself; there is no escape."

Natorus jumped to his feet. "You! You are the one who has been following me. You took different forms of the hermit, the child, the gravedigger and the Loremaster!" Azumon sneered, and Natorus felt rage consume him. "Evil! How could you have done this evil to me?"

"Evil? How can what I have done be evil? Was it not you who said this is what every man desires? To be free of age and death? I merely helped you attain that which you desired most. Is that evil?"

Natorus's heart pounded and his eyes roved wild. "Do not think me a simpleton. I was merely a child; I knew nothing of the world. I did not comprehend all that it would entail."

"Your lack of vision, not my wrongdoing!"

Natorus clenched his fists and his voice drew low. "Yes, when I achieved it, for a long while I was foolish. I sought thrills, knowing I could not die. I felt powerful, having cheated the Pale Prince time and again. But this life… this knowledge… I cannot bear it."

"You must," oozed Azumon, "and now I think you understand the true meaning of Eternity."

Natorus charged Azumon in blind fury, but the demon disappeared in a shroud of smoke, its laughter echoing from the Shoreland trees.

"No!" shouted Natorus, dropping to his knees and pounding the sand in despair.

He wept for many days, but eventually he had to live on. He arrived at the civilized lands in a haze, not caring for life or death, and he cursed the name of Azumon. He climbed the mighty Chergan mountains that overlooked the scorched battlefields and plumes of war. The last Bloodring Crusade raged with mankind locked in the bitterest and bloodiest war Natorus had seen in the countless centuries of his life.

Still as strong as ever, his curly brown hair tossing in the stormy winds as the sky darkened, he turned west and watched the Final Sunset of Mytheria. The last vestige of the cherished past died with the end of the last Bloodring War, and he witnessed mankind's self destruction from a lonely peak in the wilds.

Darkness fell on the world and the suns ceased to rise. The world of Man plunged into darkness. Natorus fell numb—perhaps humanity would not survive. He did not care. It was just another world changing event that would pass, to be succeeded by ten million more, and a hundred billion after.

He could take no more. He fled the realms both kingly and barbaric, beyond the lands of dwarves and stranger creatures, across the ever growing cold and darkness of Mytheria to sail beyond the Lonely Sea. He left all his lives behind, and despair filled his mind with ravenous hell, drowning his hope in the incomprehensible wastes of time.

He wandered, lost at sea and staring at the black waters that stretched from horizon to horizon, stars unmoving, body unmoving, filled with emptiness. At last he stood before the bow. *What is this great vastness?* he wondered, the icy wind flowing soft. *How have I come to this? I sentenced myself to a fate no mortal man ever suffers. Would that I could climb the Tower of Nelneth and take myself before the King of Gods. If only he would grant me the gift I have stolen from myself... death... a chance to be part of the universe again. And to rest after so much toil. It is not to be.* With heaviness greater than the world, he cast himself into the sea, and the crushing blackness swallowed him. He hoped to remain there forever.

But Natorus did not escape life. The following time came in broken flashes like flames on a mirror. Images came to him of giants, elves and dragons. Of stars and planets and sorcery. He sat quietly, the cliffs beneath him spreading into the realm where a great city floated through the Cosmos. Coursing across the sky were massive ships that soared like dragons and chariots of steel. The single sun rose slowly behind the gleaming walls, lighting the chariots like fire.

"You are here again," chirped the little girl who visited him when he watched the sunrise yesterday.

"Yes."

"Don't you have anything better to do?"

"Not really."

"What are you thinking about out here?"

"The world. I do not recognize it anymore."

The girl sat beside him. "You are funny. But I like the view, too. I sometimes watch the ships that fly to war and wonder why people must die."

Natorus smiled. "Best not to worry about that, young one."

"Do you not wonder?"

"I do not. Nor do I think of afterworlds, for even there I would still be trapped within myself. I once heard a tale of a man who tried to escape death. He begged and pleaded, and wailed at the horror of his inevitable fate... but I see the alternative. Which fate is more terrifying, I wonder?"

"You talk like an old man. How old are you?"

"You cannot count that high. Neither can I."

She snickered. "What do you mean?"

Natorus slumped with weariness. He had this conversation with the young a thousands times before, but tried to answer honestly. "I scarcely remember my youth—I am not sure I had one. Only misty memories give me clues. I do not age, either, and I do not exactly know why. Perhaps I am a god."

The girl laughed. "You say funny things." Natorus nodded. "I am in school learning about history before the world died," she said.

"I am familiar with it. That was very long ago."

"I wish the world could be like it was."

Natorus closed his eyes and drew in the cool air. Then he looked at her as she enjoyed the view with wide eyes. "I agree. The world has changed beyond my reckoning. I envy you the journey you are taking now, young one. To you everything shines so new and so fresh. Don't think any more of death. It does not suit to have one so full of life worrying wastefully about it. Instead do something else. Live each day like a lifetime, for even eternal life is a type of death."

"I don't understand. Wouldn't eternal life be wonderful?"

Natorus looked at the sun and sighed.

Ages passed, and he lived on, shunning all life—even the Kosithi—for after so many millions of years he had nothing to share with anyone. Eventually Man-kind died out from the universe, and Natorus outlived Man-kind for countless ages, until he found it difficult to remember them at all. Even the Kosithi passed on, leaving him alone in the universe.

He built a mighty vessel, taking several millennia, and found a great city that drifted through the Cosmos, and he spent his days reading texts of the eternally lengthening past, but in time he knew these by heart and stopped, for he found nothing left to remember. He wept, for he had the same yet to live as he had the day he sipped from the Chalice: Eternity.

He cried out to the heavens in utter despair—the first sounds he had uttered in a thousand million lifetimes. "No longer is the tomb my prison," he shouted. "No longer the world! It is the very universe itself that dooms me to eternal horror!"

He dropped to his knees and screamed, tears coursing down his neck, the roar of his torment filling his soul. The sound echoed, but soon the crushing silence returned. Emptiness stretched before him, alone and cold.

He curled on the steel floor of the vast observatory, open to the wheeling skies. Numbness filled him, annihilating his soul with the immeasurable enormity of Time. "Oh, mother," he whispered, staring at the fathomless stars, "you were right all those eons ago. I should have listened to you when I first mentioned that accursed Chalice. I was blind and weak. I knew not my prisons. The tomb was not my prison, nor the world. Not the universe. Not even this body is my prison, for if I could forget, even as alone as I am, I could discover the universe again for the first time. My prison is not a physical thing: it is existence itself!

"I am immortal. I know everything there is to know of the entire universe. I see the future stretching before me without end. I have seen all peoples from all places. I have ultimate skill and power, but possess no will to use it."

Suddenly he realized the fullness of what he had done, and the bitterness of it tore a wail from his heart. "Now I know, mother. Now I know why the King of the Gods did not answer my prayers… *I am* the King of Gods!"

Thousands more ages passed Natorus. He remained curled upon the floor, until a single thought came to repeat in his head, echoing over and over—a thought that burned itself into his soul, until he thought of nothing else, forever more:

Eternity.

Viper 3
by
T.J. Starbuck

T.J. Starbuck resides in Minneapolis with five cats and a roommate who is constantly trailing threads around the house. Starbuck won the Scott Imes Award in the 2004 MISFITS *writing contest, and her work has appeared in* Apocalypse Fiction Magazine, Gateway Magazine, *and* Mythlog. *She is currently the lead writer for the comedy show "*Now That's Just Wrong*" and has been commissioned to write her first Sci-Fi movie. Her contribution to Beacons, "*Viper 3,*" pairs an eclectic group of commandos with a beautiful alien capable of using humans as an energy source.*

Strike Team Viper 3 stealthily worked their way through the underground labyrinth of a Sloani stronghold. Their mission: find and destroy a stolen matcom unit. So far they had easily avoided the bulky, lumbering Sloani. Slow moving they might be, but they were indiscriminate carnivores, and none of the team wanted to end up as a snack.

Lieutenant Gary Iverson caught a flash of red out of the corner of his eye. "Hold up. I think I saw something."

As the team waited, Iverson snuck a peek into the cavern they'd just passed. Inside was a wide, underground lake. Large stalagmites dotted the alien landscape. Iverson scanned the area carefully with nightvision and bare eyes.

Auvin, the team's Numanorian liaison, put her hand to the slimy wall. "I'm not sensing any Sloani."

Iverson grinned at her. As her Auxiliary it was his job to make sure she had enough energy to do her job. This past week they'd found several new methods of increasing her levels. The things she did to him. His grin widened. Too bad they were illegal. Catching Major Erickson's frown he sobered.

"Nothing on the scanner," confirmed the team's scientist, Dr. Byron Bick.

Iverson glanced at the abundance of alien plant life choking the tunnel. Stumpy, lanky, bushy or lean, most gave off a pale yellow-orange glow. "Thought I saw a spark or something. Could have been one of these plants. Or maybe there's insect life down here."

Colonel Jess batted at one above his head. Its thick tentacles swung back and forth, shifting the shadows around them. "Creepy doesn't begin to describe this place. Let's keep moving."

As the Colonel led the team out, Iverson caught the flash again. He turned, cradling his weapon close. The third time Iverson saw it clearly—a tiny pinpoint of red under the surface of the water. He strode over to the water's edge and leaned in close, trying to pierce its black depths.

It flashed again.

"Iverson!" the Colonel called from the arched entrance. "What is it?"

Iverson watched in horror as a Sloani rose from the lake in front of him. Its round body was four feet tall—half of it head. Large luminescent eyes and needle-thin teeth six inches long loomed in front of his face. Its hairless, black-mottled skin eerily reflected the yellow-orange ambient light. The Sloani hissed.

Iverson barely heard the shouts and weapons fire of his team as the Sloani ripped his arms from their sockets.

From their vantage point inside academy grounds Lt. Michael T. Donovan and his best friend Lt. Pravin England heard the dissidents chanting, "Not our fault! Not our war!" They gazed in dismay at the rioting crowd outside the gates. Signs read, "Humans not Cannon Fodder," and "Screw the Gaspar Treaty." The riot police in their heavily padded gear were having no luck breaking it up.

A cadre of cadets passed in formation under the concrete walkway on their way to breakfast singing "Anchors Away." Another cadre behind them was singing the Marines' Hymn. Donovan turned to the other side of the walkway whistling "Off We Go into the Wild Blue Yonder." England joined in.

Donovan watched the stiff, blue-uniformed backs marching toward a low blue-glassed building topped by curved metal wings. The building, built by the Kolans, housed the Kontala. "Kontala" translated to "group united by grief." To his left was the smaller, ethereal purple and who-knew-what building housing the Numanorians. To his right rose the larger steel and chrome beast housing Earth's Fleet Command Academy and headquarters. Donovan smiled. They didn't have a song yet.

They were on Ramos, homeworld of the Kolans—the alien race who, forty years ago, had befriended Earth and taught them space travel. Donovan took a deep breath of alien air. Off in the distance, hanging low in the tangerine sky, he could make out the shipyard where the bones of Earth's first official battleship was taking form under the watchful eyes of Kolan technicians.

The fledgling Earth fleet based out of Ramos currently consisted of five ships built of combined Human and Kolan technology: the

Enterprise, the Nova, the Mir, the Atlantis, and the Yamato. They had been heavy bulk cruisers, retrofitted with weapons when the imperious Numanorians demanded that Humans fight the Sloani for them.

To make matters worse, the human race had learned the hard way that though the Sloani were not high up on the creativity scale, they were expert thieves and fabricators. Any piece of technology which went missing had to be tracked down and brought back, or permanently disabled, otherwise the Sloani would use it against them, and the Numanorians were not inclined to help.

With pressure from the Kolans, joint Human/Numanorian teams called Viper Strike Teams were created to address the problem. Each Human ship was equipped with only two Viper Teams, but many more were in the works. Donovan's dream was to be on one of them.

Donovan glanced over at the patch on England's shoulder, a large red cobra with two lightning bolts crossing it. The blue background meant he was a cadet. When chosen for a team, it would be black. As black as space.

It had all happened so fast. The war with the Sloani, the treaty with the Numanorians, the desperate formation of Fleet Command followed quickly by adding the Viper teams. Donovan was acutely aware of how little they knew about their enemy...and their allies.

Some hadn't taken the change well. The roar of the crowd changed to screams as the police turned high-pressured water-hoses on them.

Donovan grimaced. "They don't understand."

"Who? The crowd or the cadets?" England asked.

"Both. One's just as myopic as the other. The first by fear, the other by dreams of glory."

England slapped his friend's shoulder. "So were we, once upon a time. It's called youth. And I'd rather live on dreams than fear. Wouldn't you?"

"Yeah, but they've got a point." Donovan indicated the sign with his head.

"Better Numanorian cannon fodder than their enemy. We got to get to class."

As they turned to enter Fleet headquarters two Numanorian males walked past on their way to their consulate. Their tall, lithe bodies were not that different from Humans' except for the dynamic biofield surrounding them. As if followed by a perpetual breeze, their long hair never ceased moving, gently drifting on the current.

As the Numanorians exited the walkway England shook his head. "Dang, Elf Boys!" he chuckled, dropping into full southern drawl. "I knew I should've left mah invisibility cloak back in mah room. Check mah eyes. I think I got frostbite from looking at 'em."

"On 'em," Donovan corrected. "From looking on them. I do believe looking *at* them would be a violation of the Gaspar Treaty, Section seventeen, paragraph twenty-one, Subsection eleven-fifty point seventy B, blah, blah, and blah."

As they gathered their belongings and headed the opposite direction England added, "Naw. I believe it's section eighty-twenty, paragraph thirty-six, twenty-four, thirty-six, subsection you think you're hot, but you ain't squat in the universe so stay away from our women."

"That's the one!"

Hurrying through the large complex they crossed through a library annex where several anxious cadets gathered around a computer. "Turn it up!" one said.

A scratchy Kolan voice filled the room. "Sources according to, Council Numanoria accusing Humans, three more, unnatural attachments having Kontala in. Human authorities' local, denying."

Donovan and England joined the swelling crowd. Noting their insignia the crowd parted to allow them a better view.

On the screen was a typical brown, hairy Kolan, difficult to tell what gender. Across the bottom was a crawl in Kolonize in case any of their people were watching the Human Channel.

"Human President statement in 'We will thoroughly investigate these allegations brought by the Numanorian Council. If found to be true, we will punish the offenders to the fullest extent of the Gaspar Treaty. However, under no circumstances will we turn over a Citizen of Earth to Numanorian authorities.' Council Numanoria response, demand open negotiation Gaspar Treaty section twelve, subsection three, paragraph add fifty-one, extradition criminals—Human."

"Not gonna happen, Fuzzball!"

"Ink's not dry on the last rewrite."

"We're getting screwed!"

"Shut up!" Donovan snapped.

"…meeting Kontala kontesh mach burn, debate begin." The Kolan's large brown eyes brimmed with sympathy. "Sanara Buta Esa Nahala, KNNPL, Ramos."

Donovan and England sprinted through the last hallway into the classroom. Making their way to the top of the auditorium, they snagged two empty seats as the tones sounded.

"Can you believe that?" England fumed as he pulled out his computer. "The penalties for 'unnatural attachments' are stiff enough. You lose everything and get shipped back to Earth with nothing in your pockets, never to leave again. What more do they want?"

"A pound of flesh," Donovan mused.

As the Fleet instructor stepped behind the podium the students took their seats. "Before we continue our study of the Treaty of Gaspar, I want to confirm for you that no, no Auxiliary has been found to replace the man killed last week. And yes, we are running out of time to find a replacement. If the disenfranchised Numanorian returns to her planet we would be at the mercy of the Numanorian Council to find another willing to work with Humans. Therefore, Fleet Command has agreed to open trials to this class.

"I also want to remind all of you currently grinning that, even if you pass this class, odds are only one percent of you will be chosen to act as an Auxiliary—unless the Numanorian Council gets the ruling passed shortening the tour of duty to six months, instead of eighteen."

"And it depends on how long the war lasts," someone muttered.

Donovan's heart skipped a beat. England leaned over and whispered. "May the best man win. That would be me."

"Dream on," Donovan whispered back. "My Ex didn't nickname me White Chocolate for nothing." Course that was mostly because of his pale skin and blond hair, but his friend didn't need to know that.

The instructor glanced at his notes. "After class is dismissed all male personnel are to report to the Numanorian wing of the base hospital—third floor—to test for energy compatibility."

The instructor keyed the podium computer to place the timeline on the wall above his head. "Quick review—this past week we have gone through the appearance of the Kolan on Earth in 2046, their mentorship of humankind into space, the formation of the Earth Coalition Interstellar Fleet Command, and colonization of the Hubris and Thames solar systems in 2069 and 2071 respectively. Yesterday we discussed first contact with the Sloani which led to the battle of Gaspar between us and the Numanorians six months ago. Today we begin dissecting the Treaty of Gaspar—brokered by the Kolans—resulting in the formation of the Kontala. What we gained—And what we lost."

Donovan logged onto his laptop and brought up the treaty, but he couldn't focus. Instead he began surfing for information on the compromised Viper team based off the ECIF Nova. Thanks to extensive media coverage on the new Viper units, there was quite a bit. He began making notes.

It was a motley crew. Colonel Elliot Jess had a record of creating successful deep space exploration teams as long as his arm. He was controversial for his unorthodox methods, but his track record was tight. He had a knack for determining which people would work best together under pressure.

In true Numanorian form the Colonel hadn't been given a choice of liaison, a female named Auvin, or the Auxiliary who accompanied her, Lt. Iverson. Donovan speculated the Colonel would have used extra care choosing the other members.

Major Colin Erickson was a Harvard man the Colonel had pulled off commanding the Sustainment Brigade of the Army's 101st Interstellar Division. A brain job if there ever was one—even for the Screaming Eagles. So how'd the Colonel talk him into a combat unit? And why?

It was easier to see why he'd picked Lieutenant Brando. She'd graduated with honors from the Advanced Engineer Officers Course, but had promptly been grounded—rumor was for blowing up an ex-boyfriend's car. She was one of only three women who'd made it into a Marine weapons company. Why would she have left such a historic position?

Dr. Byron Bick was an eccentric, slightly paunchy xenobiophysicist with a list of degrees half a page long. But he was one of only a handful of people who were beginning to not only understand Kolan technology, but adapt it. It made sense for him to be on the team even if he was a civilian.

As he studied the team's pictures and records he couldn't see anything which made them stand out: a major and a lieutenant with spotty records, and a civilian scientist who wasn't all there. The three were so different he would have thought sparks would be flying, but the Colonel had done it again. Viper Team 3 scored a commendation its first month of service.

Everyone was getting to their feet. Donovan glanced around and realized class was over.

England dropped a hand on his shoulder. "Time to see if we can become some Numanorian's snack bar."

Donovan could only nod in response. His stomach knotted, half with panic and half with desire. This was his shot at history.

Donovan waited with increasing trepidation in the hospital corridor, watching his fellow candidates escorted into the Numanorian's room and almost as quickly being escorted back out. Lt. England was one of them. He shrugged as he walked past, giving Donovan a thumbs up sign of encouragement.

Finally, the Numanorian aide called his name. As he entered the room he noticed the usual antiseptic smell he associated with hospitals was missing. A Numanorian woman rested on a low-slung settee in front of special floor to ceiling windows allowing the afternoon sun to shine on her. Numanorian health improved significantly the more sun they were exposed to.

Her gray skin and dull eyes, blue instead of their normal violet, assured Donovan that no candidate had managed to connect with her yet. Why hadn't the Numanorian Council pulled her back to their home planet of Theran?

He frowned. Numanorians didn't die without Human energy. In fact they didn't particularly care for it. It was exclusively in combat situations, when they were using it up quickly, where Humans provided a quick fix. There'd been plenty of time to increase her levels the old fashioned way, so why was she still sick?

Auvin. Her name was Auvin.

His heart skipped a beat as he walked further into the room. As ill as she was, she was still stunning.

There were several others in the room, all staring at him: five Humans, three Numanorians. Thanks to the information he'd gleaned from the headlines he recognized the two men talking quietly to Auvin as Colonel Jess and Major Erickson.

The three Numanorian men glared at him, their eyes, lavender diamond chips. Tendrils of their long hair danced on the energy flow around them. Sitting still they exuded a grace and poise no Human could match. Suddenly Donovan felt like a fat gray slug; like comparing a thoroughbred racehorse to a mule. Judging by the look of distain on their perfect ivory faces he was sure they'd snatch Auvin back to their home planet if they could. So why didn't they?

He ignored them and knelt by Auvin. "Ma'am, I'm Lieutenant Donovan." He extended his hand.

Auvin blinked, turning to focus on him. Slowly she held out her hand. Conversation stopped.

Donovan took her fine-boned hand in his, swallowing hard. He knew what to expect, but it still caused him to pause. If this worked he would be tying his life to this woman, performing a service many found repulsive.

For a split second he considered pulling his hand back and walking out the door, but that's not what Earth needed him to do. He had a duty to his people. And deep down it's not what he wanted to do.

Gently, he took hold of her fingers.

They tightened on his and he felt a minor transfer begin; a trickle of energy pulled from him into her.

Her grip tightened. Pulling herself to a sitting position she laid her other hand on top of his. The energy flow stopped. Donovan calmed his thoughts as Auvin examined his face. Her dull eyes locked with his bright blue ones and Donovan knew she was reading him, checking his intentions.

Finally she leaned forward. Donovan prepared himself as best he could. When her lips touched his, Donovan felt the drain begin again, still just a trickle.

He opened his mouth.

As Auvin deepened the kiss, Donovan experienced the sensation of ice water oozing over his brain, sliding down his insides. He steeled himself not to flinch.

Finally, she broke off. Donovan opened eyes he didn't realize he had closed.

Auvin lay gracefully back onto the settee her eyes turning violet as her energy level increased. "Thank you, Ma'am," he said politely. The room watched as he slowly rose to his feet. He fought down the weakness in his muscles and the chill permeating his body: temporary side effects that would pass.

A huge dark-skinned man in a lab coat pointed to a nearby chair. The man introduced himself as Dr. Tucker as he shoved a rejuve drink into Donovan's hand and sat next to him. Donovan gulped the drink down, grimacing. It was chocolate flavored. He preferred vanilla. Not that any of them tasted good; they were designed to restore nutrients depleted by the transfer, not to be tasty.

The others resumed their conversations, occasionally glancing his direction. Donovan leaned toward the doctor and asked, "What's wrong with her? She shouldn't be energy-starved. Why hasn't the Council pulled her?"

The doctor glanced over at Auvin. "Official Numanorian propaganda is Lieutenant Iverson somehow contaminated her energy, poisoning her system."

"Why'd you think?"

"I have my pet theories, but you'll have to ask her. As for the other, she's refusing to leave. That's why Command is scrambling to find her an Auxiliary. We don't want to lose her."

In a more normal tone, the doctor said, "All right, Son, you're dismissed. And let me remind you to speak to no one about this until the selection is over, and the new Auxiliary—if there is one—is notified."

"Yes, Sir." Donovan's emotions roiled within him as he stood and made his way to the door. Unless one of the few men left in the hallway was also able to connect with her, he'd done it. He'd been chosen by a Numanorian woman. He'd be the Auxiliary for Viper Team 3 on the frontlines of the fight against the Sloani. He'd be used by this woman like a rechargeable battery any time she wished, and be despised by many of his own people.

He let none of this show on his face as he opened the door.

After the last candidate left, Auvin whispered, "Lieutenant Donovan is the one." The representatives of the Council began to object, but Auvin imperiously waved them away.

Erickson took Auvin's hand. It was warmer than it had been. "Better," he commented placing it back on the cushion.

"You're one stubborn woman," Colonel Jess noted. "I'll go check his record and get the paperwork started. Major, don't stay too long. Last thing we need is the Council screaming about unnatural attachments among the Vipers."

"The Numanorian Council can take their prejudices and...how do you say it?" Auvin pondered a moment. "Ah, yes. Shove them up their—"

"I get the picture, Auvin." The Colonel smiled paternally. "I can see we're already a bad influence on you."

"No unnatural attachments here," Major Erickson assured him.

"Good to hear." The Colonel let himself out.

"So?" Erickson relaxed. "Donovan? I don't think he'll be as easy to seduce as Iverson was, or as I was," Erickson cautioned, but there was a hint of smile in his voice.

"Perhaps." she sighed. "Can I help it if I'm attracted to Humans?"

"You could try. But I'm not likely to advocate it." He took note of her drooping eyelids and stood. "Sleep, you wild, wicked woman."

She smiled at his teasing. "Thank you, Colin. I couldn't have gotten through this without you. See you tomorrow."

"No. Your Auxiliary'll be here."

"That doesn't mean you can't visit."

Erickson's eyes darkened. "Unnatural attachments, Auvin," he cautioned. "If we get caught I lose everything."

Auvin sighed again as the door closed on her words, curling up for some well-needed rest.

The last two weeks had been hell on Donovan. He'd had to visit Auvin at the hospital every day for a cursory energy transfer, as well as packing and saying good-bye to his parents and friends. The reception from his mother had been frosty, but his father had been extremely proud.

Finally, he was aboard the Nova.

An aide showed Donovan around briefly before dropping him off at General Westfield's office. Colonel Jess was already there. He offered his hand to Donovan. Last they'd met Donovan had been focused on Auvin, so he took a moment to size up his new commander.

Colonel Jess was an imposing figure. Five foot ten and ruggedly built, the Colonel spoke in a soft yet commanding tone, exuding an aura of intolerance for fatuity. Donovan noticed a swath of gray at the Colonel's temples which hadn't been in the photos.

"I'll get straight to the point," General Westfield began. "The Numanorians are worried you'll cross the line and frankly, after reviewing your psyc-eval, so am I."

Donovan shook his head. "That would be illegal, Sir. Section 23.5 of the Gaspar Treaty. No Human shall have physical commerce with a Numanorian."

"Take note of the wording there, Lieutenant. It doesn't say, 'No Numanorian shall have physical commerce with a Human,'" the General said.

"I think that's implied, Sir," Donovan replied.

"Do you? Well let me tell *you* what's really implied," the General barked. "What's really implied is no Numanorian would want to! They consider us barbarians, and unfortunately some of our people have proven them right."

"You can depend on me to keep my conduct toward her professional and honorable, Sir," Donovan said.

The General sighed and sat back in his chair. "In combat units like the Vipers, I'm afraid you'll find that easier to say than do. But we don't have a choice, so don't cross the line; our treaty with the Numanorians— and possibly our existence—depends on it. Colonel?"

Donovan felt the heat of the Colonel's glare. "Channeling energy shortens a Numanorian's life span, so I am extremely protective of my liaison. Numanorians have compensated by imposing a rapid aging technique on their population, but what the Council says about their advanced learning techniques is crap. They say Auvin has the maturity level and body of a twenty-seven-year-old Human. That's bull. Oh, the body's there—but mentally she's more like a seventeen-year-old with the hormones to prove it. There are instances she's not equipped to handle emotionally. You shut her out with too much military protocol, she'll crumble under the pressure. Possibly get us killed. You get too close to her we'll have the Council all over our asses. Got it?"

"Yes, Sir." He stood, saluting the General. "Lieutenant Donovan, reporting for duty, Sir."

The General stood, gravely returning his salute. "Welcome aboard."

Colonel Jess led Donovan to a briefing room where the rest of the team waited. Strands of Auvin's white hair were floating around her head, and her brightly colored silken clothes, full of static electricity, clung to her, a sure sign she was at optimum health. She grinned at him. Remembering the Colonel's words he smiled back.

Major Erickson stood and held out his hand. "Welcome aboard," he said quietly. Donovan adjusted his initial assessment of Erickson. The Major's lean six-foot, muscular physique was not that of a conehead-double dome. And the dark-haired Major's eyes held a look Donovan had seen in few men, men who'd seen a lot and weren't allowed to talk about it. Donovan returned the firm grip.

Dr. Bick and Lt. Brando glanced at each other. "So you're the new buffet wagon," Brando snorted, tapping her pen against the table. She was the same solid brick Donovan had seen in the press releases. Blond, in contrast to her dark skin, square jawed and square bodied.

Bick answered her. "That would imply he has more than one flavor of energy, which Humans don't. So essentially, he's the main course."

Dr. Bick looked exactly like his picture: a nondescript man of average height, average age, average hair color cut at the average length, and a little more than average weight. He gestured to an empty chair.

Amused, Donovan sat. "As to the flavor of my energy, I prefer to think of myself as white-chocolate decadence off the dessert tray—if you don't mind."

Erickson and Auvin snickered. Bick's lips twisted in a grudging smile, and Brando raised an eyebrow.

Unfazed by the spiteful diatribe, the Colonel launched into a discussion of their previous mission. "Auvin? What do your people know about the Sloani that killed Lieutenant Iverson? Specifically that lake."

"My people don't study the Sloani; we avoid them," she responded. "Your educated guess would be the same as mine."

"Which is why we're in this mess," Brando growled, shifting in her chair.

"We're in this mess, as you so quaintly put it, because Humans thought Sloani would make a fine new zoo exhibit. The Sloani thought your people would make a fine new addition to their diet, so they took over your ship and used it to attack a Numanorian ship," Auvin smirked. "My people took exception to that. If Humans had left the Sloani alone— as we have—there wouldn't be a war. And if my people hadn't had a nonaggression treaty with the Kolan, we would have killed all of you for poor judgment then taken out the Sloani, and I'd be sipping slava juice on the promenade instead of trading sarcasm with an infidel."

"You say *your* people left them alone. If that's true, why are the Sloani only attacking *your* ships and not ours? You must have done something to piss them off!"

"Perhaps we simply taste better? It's nothing I'm aware of. As I stated: we avoid them. These attacks didn't happen until *your* people showed up. The Gaspar Treaty outlines the issue quite succinctly; *you* screwed up, *you* incited the Sloani to attack us, *you* get to fix it."

"Parasite," Brando sniffed.

Auvin smiled, showing all her teeth.

"I believe succubus would be a more suitable designate," Bick said.

"Thanks, Geek."

Bick inclined his head in a brief acknowledgment of Brando's gratitude. "To continue, the Sloani are obviously amphibians. That lake could be their idea of an amusement park for all we know. Whatever fills the lake isn't water because my scanner didn't pick up any life-forms."

"Agreed! Nor did I sense any," Auvin added. "The liquid is an effective shield."

The Colonel grunted as he paged through his notes. "We were further down into a Sloani cave system than any other team has been, so our hypothesis is what we go on, and what other teams will use. You're opinion, Major?" he asked.

Erickson shrugged. "I don't see any reason the Doctor's wild theory couldn't be correct, considering how little we know."

"What difference does it make?" Brando asked. "For now, we either avoid the pools, or we poison them."

"The more we understand about the enemy the quicker we can find ways to stop them," Bick argued. "Chem-lab rats are analyzing the samples I took as we speak."

Brando made a gun with forefinger and thumb, and shot the Doctor. The Doctor gave her a wry smile.

The Colonel jotted down a few notes. "All right, we'll put that discussion on hold for the moment. What about a better way to protect our new Auxiliary? Ideas?"

"Yeah. How about not having one?" Brando suggested bluntly.

"Limits my effectiveness," Auvin replied. "Viper teams were created as joint combat units by the Gaspar treaty until such time as the Sloani are defeated, or you are, whichever comes first. You're stuck with me. You might as well use me to my full potential."

"What about that, people?" The Colonel looked around the table. "Do we consider getting rid of the Auxiliary in order to increase our comfort level to be an acceptable trade off to possibly losing Auvin's help at a critical point during a mission?"

"Yes," stated Brando.

"No," Donovan declared. "It's a smart idea to carry extra rations, extra water and extra ammo into a hot situation. I carry the extra energy for Auvin."

"Look, Dessert Tray, it's degrading!" Brando shot back.

"So is latrine duty, but I've done it. I'm the only one here qualified to judge whether I'm being degraded as a Human. And I say it's a job like any other: no better, no worse."

"I think you're insane, but so am I, so I'm not going to waste my time debating. Auvin protects us. Auvin needs rejuicing." Bick addressed the Colonel. "I say we ask research to pass over some of that nifty body armor based on Kolan technology. There's one suit ready for field-testing. It'll slow Donovan down, but he'll be protected."

The Colonel looked at Bick blankly. "What body armor?"

"Just talk to General Westfield. He won't know about it either, and he'll be so pissed he doesn't know, he'll track down who does." Bick smiled smugly.

The Colonel looked thoughtful and made a few more notes. "Major?"

"Until we get the armor, Auvin should back up against something solid, and I volunteer to guard Donovan's back during the transfer. If for some reason Auvin can't be against a wall, Brando can guard her," Erickson added.

"No problem with the Auxiliary staying?"

"None, Sir."

"Figures," Brando snapped. "Meaning no disrespect, Sir, but you've already made your position on Numanorians clear."

Erickson gave her an icy glare. "Insinuating something, Lieutenant?"

Brando glanced from Erickson to the Colonel. "No, Sir."

"We're a Viper Strike Team. That means there will be a Numanorian. And unless we're fubar novices, an Auxiliary. We're impressed with your performance, but if you need reassignment..."

"No, Sir. I have no problem with the Numanorian, Sir," Brando said.

"Seems like you do, Lieutenant."

"Not with the Numanorian, Sir. Just her using Humans as an additional power source."

"It's the best and quickest method," Donovan jumped in. "And there's no harm to the Human. I've already done seven transfers this week." He lifted his hands, palms up. "I'm perfectly healthy. No harm, no foul."

Brando frowned. "Fine. I'll keep my feelings private. And I won't let them affect my job, Sir. I'll guard Auvin's back."

"With your life?" Erickson asked.

"Yes, Sir."

"All right. But it will be Bick guarding Donovan's back instead of Erickson." The Colonel jotted it down then looked at the Major. "I want you free to move around."

"Yes, Sir," Erickson agreed.

"I think that's all for now. Command will pass us another assignment before the week is out. I'm sure it'll be a milk run. Something to get Donovan's feet wet. Until then, get some rest. Get to know each other. Dismissed."

Five days later Donovan joined Erickson and Bick on the flight deck of the Nova, ready for his first mission. "Is there going to be a problem with Lieutenant Brando?" Donovan asked the Major as he adjusted his shiny new armor.

Designed like a cat-suit, this contemporary armor was constructed of fibers possessing a tensile strength that rivaled titanium, infused with chameleon dye to mimic any background. Unfortunately the helmet with its built in tactical computer and enhanced audio receiver wasn't ready.

"She talk to you?"

"No."

The Major glanced over where the women were picking up their gear. "Ask her when your birthday is."

"Hey, Brando!" Donovan bellowed. "When's my birthday?"

"April 1st, 2043," she shouted back.

"How did you know she would know?" Donovan asked.

"It's my job to know my team. Brando likes orders," the Major explained. "Give her an order, she sticks to it until another comes along. It's a flaw. The Colonel's working on it." Erickson adjusted his pack. "The Colonel ordered us to get to know each other; he didn't specify how. Bick and I talked to you. She scanned your records."

Colonel Jess strolled up, followed by Auvin and Brando. "Good morning! Hope you're well rested. As you know from the briefing yesterday, the Sloani have stolen four more generators and another matcom, and we get to find them and blow them up."

"So much for our milk run," Donovan muttered.

"Priorities," Jess replied.

"Colonel, this smells as bad as the Sloani. How do they keep getting their hands on our technology?" Brando asked, yanking on the straps of her pack. "It's not like they can sneak into New Austin or on one of our ships and blend in! A generator I can understand, but why keep taking matcom units? They can't transport anywhere without the security codes, and even if they had them, where are they transporting to?" she insisted. "They aren't transporting to Human ships or Human settlements, and those are the only places our matcoms go."

"Agreed. Bets are they're not using the equipment; they're trying to copy it. It's being looked into, but that's not our job. Our job is to stop them."

Bick raised a finger. "No. She's right. We need to copy the matcom log before we blow it this time. It might give us a clue about what's going on."

"Only if there's time, Doctor. Oh, and safety tip, roll your feet as you walk. Top brass thinks vibrations from Iverson's footsteps translated from rock through the liquid and that's how the Sloani knew he was there. Let's get to it."

Seven hours later the teammembers of Viper 3 were inside the Sloani stronghold crouched against the wet wall of a tunnel. Donovan glanced down the line of mottled black, green and puke-yellow uniforms. Everyone was breathing through their mouths except Brando. She seemed unaffected by the thick, stale, fishy stench.

Donovan leaned forward and whispered, "Hey, Brando. How can you stand the smell?"

"Genetics." She tapped her nose. "No sense of smell."

"I envy you." Brando broke into a grin. By Human standards the air was breathable; it just smelled like a Bangkok fish market.

"Dr. Bick?" The Colonel shied away from a plant that was getting too friendly with his shoulder. "Any day now."

Donovan noticed Bick frowning at the dimmed screen in his hand, watching for the telltale energy burst from the stolen matcom. Brando and Erickson's backs blocked the screen's green glow. Bick glared at the Colonel. "I have the same desire as you to see the surface again, but I have to wait until they activate it."

"Space me," the Colonel muttered. "Auvin, anything?"

"Nothing, Sir," the young woman whispered. Donovan knew Bick's microsonar picked up the Sloani, but it couldn't interpret their motives. That's where he and Auvin came in. One hand on the wall, the other firmly on the floor, eyes closed, Donovan knew she was concentrating on sensing any sentient energy signatures heading their direction.

Tendrils of Auvin's long white hair had slithered from under her hat, dancing on a nonexistent breeze. They glowed yellow-orange in the diffuse light. Her pearlescent skin would have done the same without the camo paint Donovan had liberally slathered over her.

"Donovan! Get that hair back under her hat. I think it's waving at me. Makes me nervous."

"Sorry, Sir." Donovan pulled off her hat and stuffed the escaped hair back under for the third time that hour. As beautiful as Auvin's hair was it was starting to piss him off. No matter how many clips and binders he used it managed to work its way free. Right now he'd like to take out his knife and chop it off. See how a military buzz cut looked on her.

Erickson glanced over Bick's shoulder at the motionless screen. "Colonel, it's been hours. We should consider the intel faulty."

The Colonel nodded. "We'll give it two more then head back to the surface. I don't think Auvin can guard us much longer."

Donovan wasn't sure the limit of the Numanorian's abilities, but deep inside enemy territory wasn't the time to discover them.

"Three coming at us," Auvin hissed. "We need to move."

The Colonel stood, gripping his weapon. "Back to the last intersection."

Stealthy they made their way the direction they'd come; Auvin trailing her hand along the wall, eyes still closed, Donovan guiding her backward by her belt. When they reached the intersection, Auvin felt each branching tunnel. "These two are clear."

"Doctor?" Colonel Jess's eyes danced from one slimy tunnel to the other.

Bick consulted the three-dimensional representation of their immediate area on the screen. "That one's a dead end," he gestured with his head to the left.

"They're coming!" The team piled into the right hand tunnel. Auvin paused, concentrating. "We're safe. They're in the tunnel, but going the opposite direction. They're not reacting to our presence."

Everyone sat on the floor, backs against the wall. Iverson unwrapped a protein bar and fed it to Auvin as she continued monitoring.

The Sloani stench was all encompassing in the sweltering tunnel. The closeness of the walls made Donovan feel every mile of dirt and stone pushing down on him. He tried to keep his mind off it by checking his weapon over several times. The team carried Mac-30's; the sweet little weapon could fire rounds faster than a tapster on brain juice, or using different targeting methods could help you place one in the sweet spot no matter how horrific the conditions.

When that got tedious, Donovan switched to watching droplets fall from the tendril of a strange purple plant on the ceiling, losing himself in the cadence of the steady pat, pat, pat. Research had gotten back to them and said the moisture in the Sloani's cave system was a mixture of saltwater and other chemicals. He couldn't remember what kind—when scientists started listing long names his brain checked out. Didn't make any difference anyway. Some of the chemicals and minerals were things no one on Earth or Ramos had ever seen so the scientists had a wonderful time creating new names. Something like sulfur you could wrap your brain around and have an idea of its properties. What properties could krivovichevite with a dash of lemmleinite have? Donovan grabbed a swig from his water bottle, swished it around to ease his dry mouth then spit it on the ground. It washed some of the foul taste from his mouth.

He was about to look at his watch for what seemed the hundredth time when Bick gasped. "Got it! Two levels up. Almost right above us."

"'Bout time, Geek." Brando leaped to her feet, while Erickson let out a soulful sigh. They squished their way up the maze of plant-clogged tunnels, dodging wandering Sloani.

Auvin winced and broke contact to rub her temples. Donovan alerted the Colonel.

The Colonel glanced at Bick. "Auvin needs to rejuice. How close?"

"'Bout a hundred yards, but the generators are on several different levels," Bick said.

"Figuring we may not be able to reach them without attracting attention...we better do this now," Colonel Jess said.

"There's a cave ahead, a room of sorts, two exits," Bick said.

The team gave the cavern a cursory examination as they entered. The only things visible to night-vision were twenty pools of the still, dark liquid and a lot more filth on the floor. The pools were small, ten feet in diameter, not like the lake where Iverson had died. Auvin rubbed her temples again. Donovan slung his weapon behind him, ready for the transfer. "Quick as you can, you two," the Colonel ordered as he and Bick took up stations in the doorway.

Brando turned her back on the scene, guarding the tunnel opposite to where they'd entered. Erickson joined her.

"I hate this part," she hissed.

"Simple energy transfer."

"Treating Donovan like her own private cafeteria!"

"We've been over this."

"Sorry, Sir."

Auvin and Donovan were so still they looked like statues frozen during a serious tongue wrestling session. Intellectually she knew tongue to tongue was the preferred method of energy transfer from Human to Numanorian—something about saliva helping conduct the energy. She didn't know the details, and didn't really care, but the thought of some Numanorian sucking energy from her body gave her the crawlies.

Desperate to ignore what was going on behind her, Brando nervously started picking at a wide scab on her wrist. She'd gotten it yesterday in unarmed combat practice. In trying to dodge one of the Major's attacks she'd met the bulkhead instead. Finally she pulled the scab off. As it began to bleed she wiped the wound on her shirt.

So cold. Ice-Cold. Bone Cold. Arctic sheet cold. When he'd first heard about the Auxiliary program Donovan though it would be sexy to French an alien. The reality was more like making out with an ice cube. His blood pressure dropped making him lightheaded, but he trusted Auvin to know when to stop the flow.

Seconds later she did, but not everything stopped. Auvin's tongue moved against his and a flash of light exploded through his brain. As strange as it was, he recognized the feeling. Auvin was kicking off an adrenal high he hadn't felt since the first time he'd kicked back the throttle of his X-43J and hurtled out of Earth's atmosphere. The world shifted under him and his body began ramping up. His senses sharpened. He became uncomfortably aware of Auvin trying to seduce him with her warmth, her scent, her flavor. An activity which could get him stripped of everything he held dear.

With a sharp gasp, Auvin broke contact. Taking in the look of horror on Auvin's face, Donovan turned. The taste of Auvin still lingered in his mind, clouding his thoughts; fortunately his training took over. His brain registered a Sloani climbing out of one of the pools. "Colonel!" he bellowed, bringing his weapon to bear. The horrifying figure reached for a silver disk attached to a belt worn crossways across its chest. Donovan snapped off two rounds, slamming the Sloani backward into the water, but five more rose from the other pools.

With quick efficiency, Colonel Jess took out the new arrivals, but more surfaces were rippling. "Erickson! Brando! The civilians!"

Erickson and Brando laid down cover fire as the Sloani lumbered toward them. Auvin and Bick fled, and after they had passed, Erickson grabbed Donovan. "Follow them!"

Donovan nearly slammed into Bick who had stopped in the tunnel to consult his scanner. "Slow as they move, if we go right, left, and then right again we should be able to lose them and still get to the generators."

"Good. Erickson, Brando and Bick, take out the two generators closest to the matcom. Auvin and Donovan and I will head for the two located deeper inside the stronghold. With Auvin's help we'll be able to avoid detection long enough to set the charges and get back to the matcom safely. Let's move it people," the Colonel said.

Erickson was relieved when Bick led them to the first generator without any issues. The generator sat in the center of the cave with multiple wires leading from it to several pools. Dark and still, the sight of them caused the Major's heart rate to increase, but they were much smaller than the kind the Sloani had come from. He took a deep breath and immediately regretted it as the smell caused his eyes to water.

"What the... Ideas?"

"Perhaps they're watching TV, Major," came Bick's snide answer.

"Not helping!" the Major snapped.

Bick stared in astonishment at Erickson's outburst, then stepped to the nearest pool. He took readings and punched buttons it for a long, tense moment. "Heat. They're heating the pools."

"If you tell me it's a Sloani spa, I'll shoot you and leave you here."

"Fine. There are a lot more pools in this room than in the room we were just in, and they're smaller. Assuredly, too small for the Sloani to fit into."

"I say we drop a few grenades in there and split," Brando suggested.

Erickson sighed. "Do you have a single female bone in your body?"

"Yeah. My pelvic bone."

Bick snorted.

Erickson refrained from speaking the comment that sprang to mind. "There're three more generators. Plant the C-4 and head out. No vibration."

Carefully, they moved to the generator and got to work. Bick took another look at the nearest pool. "There's something glowing down there."

"Phosphorescence?" Erickson asked.

"If I could take a sample of the water..."

"Negative. Vibration!"

Brando set the timer while Bick snapped a few shots with his camera. Then they stealthily made their way out. Erickson checked in with Colonel Jess as they carefully negotiated the tunnels to their next target.

"We're halfway to our first target, Major," the Colonel said. "We'll step it up, but as soon as your last one's set, get to the matcom. Don't wait for us."

"Roger that."

As they entered the second cavern Bick's foot slipped on a pile of Sloani feces. He landed full force on the ground, knocking the breath from him and slamming his night-vision goggles into his nose. Brando hauled Bick to his feet. "Nice one, Grace." Bick sniffed and wiped at the blood trickling from his nose.

Erickson and Brando knelt and attached the C-4 and the timer while Bick noted the position of the Sloani. A bright glow coming from one of the pools caught his attention. Bick slid off his goggles and headed for it.

"Oh, my," Bick whispered. He knelt over the pond, trying to see into its depths.

"What!" Erickson hissed.

"Eggs. These ponds are full of eggs!" Bick's voice rose a notch.

Erickson hit his com unit. "Colonel! The ponds are hatcheries! Repeat! The generators are surrounded by Sloani eggs!"

A drop of blood from Bick's nose hit the surface of the pond. The water began to boil.

Bick leaped to his feet. "They're hatching! They're hatching! They're hatching! We're gonna have company!"

As one, the team hit the tunnel. Much faster than adults, a black wave of hundreds of tiny Sloani swarmed after them.

With no chance to check the scanner Erickson prayed for safe passage as they pelted through turn after turn, plants slapping him leaving purple and orange smears across his face and uniform. Once certain they'd put enough distance between them and the Sloani young to stop their headlong flight, he signaled a halt.

Bick slumped against the wall, wheezing, the scanner hanging loosely in his hand. Erickson snatched it up. Keying it to their location, his face lost all expression.

Bick grabbed it back. Staring at the screen he shouted. "No! No! No! No! No! No! No!"

A hissing black wall of adult Sloani came lumbering out of the cave openings in front of them. A silver disk sliced through plant life, whizzing past Bick's ear and bouncing off the wall.

Erickson and Brando opened fire into the oncoming horde. Several Sloani plucked disks, preparing to throw them. Brando shot two incendiary rounds into the mass. The explosions went off, temporarily blinding them. The rounds melted and collapsed bodies, but more Sloani filled the hole, headless of their dead comrades. Erickson and Brando worked their way backwards, picking off the enemy with precise shots.

"Bick! How's it look behind us?" Erickson yelled. When Bick didn't answer Erickson risked a glance. The same scene played out behind. A hollow-eyed Bick starred at him, a deep gash dripping blood down his cheek. Erickson ducked as several more disks sliced through the air.

"Colonel! We're compromised! Get out of here!" Erickson yelled as Brando lobbed a few more grenades into the seething mass.

Donovan had finished setting the C-4 on the first generator when the Major's frantic call came in. His gut tightened.

"Let's go," the Colonel ordered, swinging his weapon around front.

"What about the other generator?" Auvin asked.

"According to the readout, it's almost a mile further down. There's no way we can reach it now. Taking out three will slow them down. It's more important we report what they're being used for," the Colonel answered.

Donovan tightened his pack sprinting up and through connecting tunnels heading for the Major's position. When their ears caught the sound of gunfire, Auvin stopped. Slapping hand to wall, she concentrated. "They're...The Sloani, they're backing off. Why?"

"Probably had a gut-full of the Major's firepower. Let's go!" the Colonel said.

Auvin frowned, but broke contact. Donovan cocked an eyebrow. She shook her head.

"We're running out of ammo!" came the Major's harsh words over the comm.

"We're almost there!" the Colonel reassured him. "Keep it up!"

Coming around a corner they skidded to a stop. Donovan and the Colonel began snipping at the group of Sloani between them and Erickson's team. Several Sloani turned to confront this new threat. The Colonel and Donovan shot three of them. They died, their bodies blocking the tunnel. Four more Sloani started to climb over the bodies reaching for their disk weapons.

Auvin abruptly stepped in front of Donovan. He dropped his aim to the floor to avoid shooting her. Holding her hands out several disks which were flying at them slowed and dropped to the floor. Dropping her hands she assessed the situation. Again, she held out her hands. Suddenly the remaining Sloani were blown backwards. They lay stunned on the filthy floor.

Erickson's team maneuvered past the prone bodies, placing several rounds in each to make sure they stayed that way. The besieged unit looked as though a threshing machine had attacked: uniforms in tatters, bleeding from slices caused by the disk weapons. "Anyone seriously hurt?" the Colonel asked.

Donovan dug into his pack and started passing out medical supplies.

Hands on knees, head hanging, Brando managed a short, "We kept them busy enough."

Erickson swiped at a trickle of blood headed for one eye. Gasping for breath he shook his head. "Fine."

Auvin held up a hand toward each of them in turn. "Dr. Bick's energy is lowest, but he's not in immediate danger."

Donovan noticed Bick's hair was matted with blood. "You need to duck more, Doctor," he said, pressing a bandage to the nasty bleeder.

Bick panted, pressing shaky fingers over the slice on his cheek. He glanced at the scanner in his other hand. "Something's wrong."

"What?" the Colonel and Erickson asked simultaneously.

"The Sloani are disappearing off my screen," Bick explained.

"Auvin?" the Colonel asked, a note of tension creeping into his voice.

Auvin placed her hand on the wall. "They're...They're..." She gasped, eyes wide with horror. "They're electrifying the tunnels! I can feel it coming!"

"What! Can they do that?" Donovan barked.

Bick slammed his hand against the wet wall. "A liquid conductor and a stolen generator!"

Brando's face registered disbelief. "Won't it kill them too?"

"Apparently not!"

"Matcom!" the Colonel bellowed. "Go!"

The tunnels they pelted through were deserted. "We're not going to make it," Donovan whispered as his brain calculated the speed of electricity. Even with plant matter to slow it down, they were still too far from the matcom. So much for surviving his first mission.

Auvin grabbed Donovan by his neck. His mouth dropped open in surprise at her strength, then she was on him, her tongue touching his. Before he could prepare himself, the transfer began and his brain checked out.

Donovan's legs buckled and his eyes rolled up as Auvin ripped energy from him. "Grab him."

Brando grunted as she took Donovan's weight, managing to keep him from hitting the floor.

Auvin closed her eyes as the blue static charge raced around the corner. Suddenly, they were floating in the center of the tunnel. The electrical charge sparked and flared, but didn't touch them. It flashed past, leaving them unharmed.

They dropped to the floor.

Auvin staggered to the wall, laying her hand on it. "I don't. I don't feel another."

"Single static burst. Pray they overloaded the generator, but didn't fry the matcom," Bick advised as he started running.

Erickson swept Auvin into his arms as her knees gave way, cradling her. Her head rolled limply to land on the Major's shoulder. The Colonel grabbed the other side of Donovan following Bick as quickly as possible.

The matcom stood at the end of the tunnel, an oasis of advanced technology in a Stone Age world. As they got inside, Donovan groaned and blinked. The Colonel pinned him against the wall with his shoulder while punching in the codes to transport them aboard the Nova. Erickson scooted Auvin as far under a console as he could, then he joined Brando, dropping to one knee to fire as the Sloani reappeared. Brando quickly reloaded. "That charge didn't slow them down at all," she fumed.

Dr. Bick began frantically digging into his backpack. "We need to copy the log!" he reminded the Colonel. "We need to know where they're going! Or who's coming!"

"Screw it! Pull the log crystal!"

"Then we risk frying it!" With a shower of sparks a silver disk buried itself into the wall of the unit. Bick swore. "Strike that." He dropped to the floor and ripped off the access panel.

The Colonel continued punching coordinates into the interface, sparks dropping onto his hands. He flinched and swore, but kept going.

"Anytime now, Big Guy," Erickson prayed as the matcom powered up.

"What if the circuits are fried, Colonel?" Brando asked.

"I end up in your body, and you end up in mine."

"Please! At best, we all end up as a gory pile of mismatched body parts," Bick answered.

"I wish I hadn't heard that," Auvin whispered, pale eyes flickering open.

The Colonel slapped the explosive he'd pulled from his pack to the main panel of the unit and set fifteen seconds on the timer as Bick held up a blue crystalline square. "We're go!"

Erickson and Brando backed into the unit. The five of them barely fit. The Colonel caught Brando's eye. "Now!" Brando pushed the button on the timer at the same time the Colonel keyed the unit. Light bars came up across the entrance and the interior filled with a blue glow. When the light dimmed, the contents of the unit were gone.

Donovan awoke in the hospital ward to a kiss on his forehead. Blinking, he gave Auvin a stern look. "You're not supposed to be doing things like that, Ma'am."

"It's just a kiss, Lieutenant. I was worried about you."

"There's no need for you to worry about me, Ma'am. I'm fine."

She smiled coyly. "We're alone, Michael. You can call me Auvin." She wrapped her fingers gently around his.

She was stunning; her pearlescent skin glowed in the dim light of the infirmary, but her hair wasn't moving so she wasn't a hundred percent. The incident in the cave when she had started to seduce him flitted through his mind. Donovan swallowed and disentangled his hand before the other half of his brain could convince him to leave it. "No, Ma'am, I can't call you Auvin. And you will address me as Lieutenant Donovan. I like my job; therefore, we will be keeping our relationship strictly professional."

Her smile faded and tears sprang to her eyes. "All right... Lieutenant. I just wanted to... Well, I'm glad you're okay." She ran from the ward.

"Welcome to Viper 3, Donovan. God help you," he whispered to himself.

Foliage
by
F.R. Jameson

F. R. Jameson lives, works, and writes in London, England. His first novel "The Wannabes" will be published in 2008. His contribution to Beacons, "Foliage," is a dark, post-apocalyptic tale in which the enemy is inside us all, just waiting for a chance to burst forth.

McGrigor filled his backpack with bottle after bottle of whisky. He watched the others gather food, whatever they could find in refrigerators and pantries—cheese, biscuits, canned goods. Edibles that weren't going to rot too soon. McGrigor just brought bottles of Scotch; all the way up that hill he rattled with the sound of clinking glass.

The Preacher gave him long looks of disapproval, making it clear he'd feel righteously indignant when McGrigor asked for food. Except McGrigor never did. Whenever they stopped, he just raised a bottle and poured back another mouthful of brown liquid.

They walked for hours that day, hitting the higher ground. The Preacher led them, and when he spotted the cottage he spun back excitedly and pointed. The Preacher wore a big smile, but a smile no longer suited his face—whenever he attempted one he just looked like a harbinger of death. His appearance was now so tired and careworn that deep grooves replaced the lines on his face.

There were only four of them walking. McGrigor took the rear; it suited him to keep the others up front. The Kid staggered on in front of him in perpetual shock, his emotions as if pressed hard to a cheese grater. He barely spoke, just followed and stared on with confused moon eyes. He'd seen some terrible things. But they all had.

The Woman walked in front of the Kid. She wasn't that much older than the boy and was holding it together only slightly better than him.

A sob or a tearful murmur accompanied every step; a hand constantly wiped her eyes, her nose, her dribbling mouth. Her constant gasps made her forever breathless.

The Preacher—the guy in charge, the guy who so obviously cared—took the lead. He had that do-gooder Preacher quality, always leading, absolutely convinced salvation awaited them and that they'd somehow be saved. Forever wittering about right and wrong—as if that mattered anymore.

The cabin was isolated on the rocky terrain, but it was shelter, a place to go. The Preacher smiled that dreadful smile, which whilst sincere was as far away from hope as any smile could be.

"Look!" The Preacher was breathless. "I told you I'd find somewhere safe!"

The Woman cheered at the Preacher's announcement, a thin struggling sound, like an asthmatic pleased to have finished a race. The Kid just stopped and stared. McGrigor didn't know if a smile or any other emotion crossed his dazed face.

McGrigor pulled the bag off his shoulder and removed a half drunk bottle. He raised it to his mouth and poured back a long gulp. The Preacher's disapproving glare made him lower the bottle. A stiff drink evidentially wasn't the reaction the Preacher wanted to his news. He wanted joy, rapture, an acknowledgement that he—The goddamn Preacher!—had led them to sanctuary.

In response, McGrigor just took another drink. Why had he even followed the Preacher? He knew it was because he was scared, like a four-year-old who had lost his mother. For some reason McGrigor had believed the Preacher when he started his tales about a better place, somewhere everything was still okay.

McGrigor had believed even though part of him screamed he was being stupid. And now he had woken up, realised there were no sanctuaries, that they were doomed just like everybody else. It was real nice of the Preacher to find somewhere for the night, a place to keep the cold off, but he wasn't going to fall to his knees and proclaim "Hallelujah!" for it.

It took them three hours to get there—the rocky terrain, the treacherous path, the fact they were all so tired. For a long time, the cabin remained rooted on the horizon. McGrigor wondered if it was just an illusion, a mirage, a trick played by their wearying minds to give them a false sense of hope.

The Kid and the Woman took turns at stumbling, their hands reaching out to stop their faces from smashing into the hillside. Whenever it happened they looked up quickly, in the direction of the cabin, as if trying to make sure it was still there, that it hadn't vanished in that instant of distraction.

They reached it just before nightfall, a wood and stone cottage with a couple of rooms—rustic and rural. Once upon a time it was no doubt home to some rosy-cheeked labourer and his plump and fruity wife. Now it stood deserted, now it seemed lost, as if it had wandered away from its hamlet and stranded itself high up in the hills.

McGrigor took a breath—his chest aching, his legs swollen, his brow strained with furrowing. He wasn't drunk; he'd drunk too much for that in recent weeks. The booze kept him going.

In the spirit of charity he should probably have given the Kid some alcohol, remove that dreadful puss from his face. Maybe the Woman would have appreciated it, to stop her crying, maybe make her really cry so she could flush it all from her system. And the Preacher—let him go crazy, let him indulge, get him paralytic so he wouldn't be so ridiculously insufferable.

Problem was, McGrigor didn't want to share. He had a limited supply and didn't have the strength to stagger back to get more. If only he hadn't listened to the Preacher; if only he'd stayed in the city and hadn't been convinced by fairy tales. There was plenty to drink in the city, enough to keep him going—and he'd been stupid enough to walk away.

The Preacher's smile—tombstone teeth in a dead face—tried to force optimism on them all. He waited for them to catch up; he waited for the Woman. She staggered towards him on unsteady and bruised legs. The Preacher took her arm to support her, to give her little choice but to fall into him. This was no righteous Preacher.

With her waist in his clasp, he turned and walked to the cabin. He didn't wait for the Kid; he didn't even look at McGrigor. He just led the Woman, dragged her, to the aged safe-house. If he'd had the strength he'd have carried her over the threshold.

"Here we are!" said the Preacher. "Here we are. This should look after our needs for a while."

It was dank inside. There were three rooms—a front room, what once had been a kitchen and what once had been a bedroom—each with cold stone walls and wooden beams. There was no furniture anymore; the cabin had clearly been abandoned a long time and now mainly functioned as a lavatory for wild animals. The windows were secure, the doors were heavy with big locks, and once inside they'd supposedly feel safe.

The Preacher led the Woman on a tour, like it was their first home, a grin on his face, a sparkle in his eyes—all so distant from the reality of the situation. The Woman snivelled beside him, wanting to sit down, desperate to collapse but too weak to separate herself from him.

The Kid did collapse. He slid down against the wall, his clear blue eyes staring out with no hint of life behind them. McGrigor took another drink, silently toasting what he knew would be his last ever home.

The Preacher let go of the Woman and she fell away from him. An almost faint, her body just remembering it had to bend its legs and drop its behind to sit down. The Preacher looked around at his companions.

"Giles!" he said to the Kid. "How are you, Giles? Are you alright? We're here now. We're away from it."

The Kid didn't even look at him.

"I know you're scared, I know you're frightened, I know you've seen terrible things—but really, we're in the best place now. Trust me."

Again, nothing from the Kid.

"That's it." said the Preacher. "You just rest now." He looked at McGrigor. "You. Are you enjoying that drink?"

"Yeah. Thank you."

"Do you think there are more constructive things for you to do than drink yourself to death?"

"You really would think so, wouldn't you? But to be honest I think I'll just keep on drinking and let death take its chances."

The Preacher glared at him, and McGrigor took a triumphant sip, careful not to spill a drop.

They each settled into a corner for the night. The Preacher would clearly have loved to slip his arm around the Woman, hold her through the night, soothe her, warm her with the heat from his body—but she whimpered when he came near. He whistled it off, a brief tune of disappointment, and then he settled opposite her, his eyes nowhere but on her. The Kid stayed where he'd collapsed, and McGrigor crouched by the door, bottle in hand.

Night fell and McGrigor tried to get comfortable on the cold stone floor. He drank and calculated how long he could keep drinking from the ten bottles he still had. Seven days, maybe more. He'd lost track of how much he'd already drunk; it was like asking someone how many particles of breath they'd used. He figured about a week and then he'd have to decide what to do, whether he could still get some more.

When dawn came the Kid shivered at the cold and clutched his hands around him, the Woman brought her shoulders together, and the Preacher, after a moment of stiffness—after a moment of nervous shaking where he gave away a fraction of what he really felt—grabbed onto the cold as if it were bracing, as if it were something that would do them good.

"What to do?" he asked. "What to do?"

Of course, there was nothing to do—not really, not that would make the slightest difference. There was a chance they were the last four people alive, the soggy cigarette butt of humanity. There was nothing they could do, no decisions they could take, no changes they could make—nothing. They could just wait and stare or wait and sob or wait and drink.

The Preacher didn't agree. He'd clearly been one of those people who enjoyed having every moment of his time occupied. The type who revelled in daybreak starts and enjoyed long hikes to some pointless wherever, who once at that pointless nowhere clung to a grim determination to make the best of it.

The Preacher wandered through the cottage, and McGrigor watched him from the corner of his eye, careful not to stare, avoiding eye-contact. The Preacher had an eagerness about him, a desperation to please and be pleased. And even though McGrigor knew it was coming, even though McGrigor saw its arrival, he still greeted the Preacher's clap of hands with a shudder. It was an unpleasant sound, a burst of thunder when you're lost in a valley with nowhere to hide.

"Right!" said the Preacher. "We really shouldn't spend all day idle. There are things to do. I think we're going to be here awhile, aren't we? Yes we are. And since we're going to be here awhile, we have to make what they call the best of it."

Only the Woman looked at him, and even she seemed baffled.

"I don't know about you people, but I was cold last night," said the Preacher. "Actually, I do know about you people. I saw you shivering there, Giles, there's no need to pretend to be hardy now. And Linda my dear, I nearly put my arms around you last night to keep your teeth from chattering. And you... Well, how could you possibly get cold with all *that* inside you?"

McGrigor smiled at the stone floor.

"So, what I suggest is that we get some firewood, some kindling for tonight. There are those trees outside and I think we can take off the loose branches quite easily."

"Are they trees?" asked McGrigor, still not looking up.

"They're trees!" said the Preacher. "Do you think I don't know what trees are? Do you really think I'd lead you elsewhere?"

He waited for McGrigor to meet his eye, then realised it wasn't going to happen this lifetime.

"So what I suggest, Giles, is that you go out and get whatever loose branches you can. Either those that have snapped and fallen to the ground, or those you can break off yourself. That way we can make a base for our fire. And—you'll be pleased to hear—I've already taken a look around, and behind this cottage is an axe. It's old and it's rusty, but I think I have the smarts about me to sharpen it up. So what do you say, Giles? You get the easy wood, and I'll come behind and get the solid fuel. Does that sound like a plan? Does it?"

The Kid said nothing, and the Preacher took that as assent.

"Now then, Linda," he said, leaning over her, his mouth a few inches above the top of her head. "Now then—what are you going to do? Well, it occurs to me that we have plenty of canned food—and of course our friend there has supplies if we should ever want to throw a party—but it strikes me it would be silliness to come all this way and then die of scurvy. So what I suggest is: there are a number of bushes out beyond this cottage—and they *are* bushes—and what you could do is take a look if there is anything edible on them. Just go out and pick a berry from each—remembering which you took each berry from—and bring them back here. Don't eat them, whatever you do, just bring them back and show them to me. I'm not a horticulturist, but I have been on enough nature rambles to have a good idea what's sweet and what's not. Can you do that for me? Can you, my dear? Can you?"

"Yes," she said, with a nod that could easily have been a shiver.

"Good." He stroked his hand across her hair, resisting the urge to reward her with a kiss.

"And you," said the Preacher. "What are you going to do?"

McGrigor took a swig from his bottle.

"That's not very helpful!"

"On the contrary," said McGrigor. "It's helping me no end."

"Staggering about like a drunken bum is helping, is it?"

"Maybe if you play nice I'll let you try some and see if it helps you, too." He took another gulp.

"Are you going to do nothing, is that it?" asked the Preacher. His face turned an odd shade of puce, and McGrigor noticed how weary the Preacher looked. "Are you just going to sit there and drink and obliterate yourself? Is that all you're going to do? Is that all you're capable of doing? Is it? Is it? I'm trying to help here, I'm trying to make things easier for all of us, and that task would be a great deal simpler if you would get up off your drunken backside and lend some kind of support."

"What's the point?" asked McGrigor. "How long do you think you're going to live? A day? Two days? Do you think our brief time in this old shack will be improved by you managing to hang curtains? What does it matter? Berries? Do you think we have enough time to die of scurvy? Do you really think—all things considered—that the illness we have to worry about is the common cold, the flu, hypothermia?"

The Preacher's face reddened and his lips pouted; he looked like a child about to throw a tantrum. "Don't say that! Do not say that! You don't know how long we can live for up here. We're away from the city now; we're away from that-that... that illness. It's a different air up here; it's a different feel. You don't know how long we can live for. We could get better, we can make a new start. If we have some heat, if we have some fresh food—you never know what might happen."

"We won't get better," said McGrigor.

"You don't know that!" screamed the Preacher.

"We might get better," the Woman sobbed.

"Don't listen to him," said McGrigor. "It's inside us, in our bones. It's not about to go away because we've started eating berries. Do you understand me? This is it, this is over, this is where we die."

"Don't say that!" said the Preacher, taking an angry step towards him.

"Do you think no one lived on a hill? Do you think no one lived on a mountain? Of course they did—they lived there with all the fire and berries they could possibly want—and it got them too. People went to the goddamn hills when this started, they got in their cars and just zoomed. We haven't heard from them since, have we? Not one of them sent a message back saying its all fine up there, that the human race can be saved with just a switch to higher ground. They haven't done that; they haven't made a peep…. And do you know why? It's not because they're trying to keep all the berries and fire for themselves. It's because it's not safe there either."

Despite the rage popping out in sweat bubbles on his forehead, the Preacher stood a good half a foot shorter than McGrigor, and his eyes darted to the bottle in the bigger man's hand. He took a wary step back, spluttering and clenching his fists but keeping a comfortable distance.

"So, what exactly are you going to do?" asked the Preacher.

McGrigor shrugged.

"That's hardly fair," said the Preacher. "If we're out there toiling, it's unreasonable for you to stay in here and just inebriate yourself."

"Listen Preacher," said McGrigor. It was the first time he'd actually called him that, and surprised confusion crossed the Preacher's face. "I won't eat any of your berries, I'll keep a respectful distance from your fire, and I won't take the benefit of any of your labours. You just leave me be, and I'll let you enjoy your toil."

"What are you going to do when that whisky runs out?" asked the Preacher.

"That's the big question, isn't it? But tell you what, you can let me worry about it."

"Couldn't you just help us a little bit?" asked the Woman, her tearful blue eyes meeting his. It was the first time he'd looked into a pair of eyes for what felt like an aeon. He'd kind of lost his taste for them. "There's a lot to do, and you're the strongest of us."

McGrigor looked away. "You'll manage. If the Preacher is right, this mountain air is so bracing you'll have all the strength and energy you'll want in no time."

"Come on, my dear," said the Preacher. He wound his arm around her shoulders and pulled her to her feet. "Come on, my dear; let's leave him now."

The Woman continued to stare at McGrigor, and he continued to stare away.

With one arm holding the Woman, the Preacher leant down and cupped his hand around the Kid's jaw. The Kid just stared ahead, seemingly unaware of anything around him.

"Come on then, young man," said the Preacher. "You can still be helpful. Yes you can. Let's go outside now, get us some firewood. Don't worry, Giles, I know how dreadful it's been for you, I know how awful it's been for all of us. But it's going to get better from now. I promise."

The Kid staggered up, and McGrigor felt sorry for him—the poor bastard was little more than a zombie.

As the low sun blessed them all, the noise of work began. McGrigor heard the Preacher give his instructions again, and then there was a silent interlude before the sound of lovely hard work beginning. McGrigor guessed the Preacher was sharpening the axe—using stones and swinging the blade back and fore against them. He even heard the Preacher whistling and knew it was entirely for effect; the idiot just wanted to show what a good worker he was, how enjoyable the whole business of labour could be.

McGrigor wondered if anyone else could hear him, and then wondered how far behind the cottage those bushes were. Maybe the Woman was just out of his sight and the Preacher was once again pretending it was just the two of them in a countryside idyll.

Eventually McGrigor straightened his limbs and made it out of the cottage, sitting on the doorstep with the sun's rays upon him. Of course, in his right hand was a sensible daytime draw of whisky.

He squinted at the view. He hadn't realised how far up they'd come, how far they'd removed themselves from the city. It was a grey, amorphous mass in the distance. The Preacher had promised to take them away from it.

It wasn't going to save them, though.

The Preacher had managed to snap the Kid into something resembling work. He slowly bent down and picked up dry twigs and branches and made a neat little pile. He still stared vaguely though, he still looked like he had no comprehension of the world around him. McGrigor heard the Preacher, still sharpening the axe, the repeated sound of metal against rock. The Woman came round the corner. She held the frayed hem of her T-shirt in front of her—a tray for her collected berries—and she hesitated when she saw McGrigor. She stumbled a little, bit her lip, and then perched down next to him.

"Hi," she said. "Are these berries edible?"

He looked at them, a collection of reds, oranges and greens. "I've no idea. I'm not what you'd call a berry man."

"Oh," she said.

"Don't worry, the Preacher will know."

"Is he a preacher?"

McGrigor shrugged and smiled.

The scream was revolting. They'd heard similar screams, but somehow up here it was much worse. They'd got used to that sound in the city—from friends, loved ones, strangers at the distance—but up here it echoed, up here it was only the scream and a void.

The Kid convulsed in agony. Blood spurted from his eyes and mouth, and he screamed as if his tongue were being ripped loose. His arms and hands writhed at his side, and blood dripped down from his fingernails.

The feet were first to go. The feet were always first to go. He screamed as his toes and heels broke through his skin and attached themselves to the ground. He staggered as the blood spurted from his soles, but he couldn't fall—he was spiked to the ground by his own skeleton. He tried to pull away, to raise his feet up before they took hold, to snap himself off at the ankles—but he was stuck, caught in agony, and he cried out in desperation.

The bones in his feet took firm hold of the ground beneath him, and then his flesh started to break apart. His shins first, ripping out of the skin and muscle of his legs. The blood sprayed off, both red and green. The shin-bone gleamed in the sunlight, the white of the bone tainted by a plant-like hue. His arms went next, the bones forcing themselves up so that the blood and flesh dropped to the stone below.

The convulsions were extreme, his hips and waist shaking themselves free of flesh—his stomach and colon slipping down as if slurry. They splattered to the ground, rotting almost instantly in the sun. He screamed again, a gargle—as he was now without tongue. What had once been his heart, what had once beat and kept him alive, now burst from his chest. Moments before it had been the centre of a human being, now it looked like long forgotten carrion.

Only the head remained, the final hint of humanity on a twisted skeleton. The skin and tendons and veins and muscles were all torn away at the neck, the face showered and smothered in blood. But despite the tortured expression of terror and pain, the Kid was still recognisable. His eyes still wide.

His head spasmed. *Its* head spasmed. It rocked back and fore, jerked violently, tried to free itself from the encumbrance of flesh. The rigid skeleton stood transfixed; in a strong wind it would only bend slightly. The head contorted, blood and flesh flew from it, red and green globules thrown through the air, removing the last taint of man.

It only took a moment, but it seemed so much longer because of the sound. Somewhere in that husk of a head was still a larynx, and the Kid screamed—hoping for someone to save him, for the pain to end.

It didn't last long. Every sinew fell away, and all that was left was a distorted skeleton, a dark artist's terrible representation of a bare human being, a green twisted sketch of a man rooted to the ground, the eyeballs hanging in their sockets as two shiny flowers.

"No!" screamed the Preacher. He charged forward, the axe above his head, the blade glinting in the sunlight.

The Woman got up, spilling her berries, eager to help. McGrigor grabbed her arm and threw her back, flung her through the doorway to the cottage. She gave a scream and a thud as she hit the floor.

The Preacher made it to what had been the Kid and almost slipped on his blood. He steadied himself—his look of anguish visible from the cottage—and took a swing.

The skeleton was tough; you couldn't just break it with a swing of an axe. You could pierce it maybe, but you weren't going to fracture the bone. It shook a little at the blow, but didn't really move. The flower eyes swung from side to side, staring at the Preacher with cold accusation.

The Preacher tried again, swinging at the leg. This time the handle of the old, neglected, damp axe snapped, and the blade spun away. The skeleton stood, while the Preacher fell to his face on the blood and flesh splattered rock.

McGrigor stepped inside the cottage and looked at the Woman. He shut the door behind them, bolting it as securely as he could.

It had started six weeks earlier—people just began to change. A few changed, and then all in their vicinity changed, and soon it was clear that everyone was sick. While there was still a media—when there were still enough people alive to run newspapers and television and the internet—various theories were put forward. Pundits said it was a virus from outer space, that it was a chemical weapon leaked from one of the world's more aggressive regimes, that it was a sudden step in evolution.

It didn't really matter, all that mattered was that millions of people were dying, sprouting into these terrible plants.

The Preacher raised himself on slippery fingers, wailing skywards at the horror of it all. He looked at the cottage, and his wail stopped, his righteous fury as to what was happening in the world choked by his immediate fury. He staggered forward, getting his balance, his shirt smothered by what had once been the Kid.

McGrigor grabbed one of the empty bottles and rammed it into the wall—breaking it. He heard the Preacher yelling at him, yelling at them—some garbled rant as he charged towards the cottage.

"What are you doing?" asked the Woman.

"It's in all of us," said McGrigor, his eyes not leaving the Preacher. "It's already there inside us; it's just a question of when. But if you go near one of those things, if you break it—say with an axe—then it gives off a spray, an invisible scent that speeds up your own change. If you roll around in that thing's blood, that also accelerates your transformation. That bastard Preacher is so stupid he's managed to do both. He'll be gone by morning, and I'm not having him in here when he does."

The Preacher raced towards them.

"What are you doing?" he yelled. "What are you doing to me? You can't leave me out here! I brought you here. I made this place. I gave it to you. You filthy drunk! What the hell are you doing? How can you do this to me? My dear, don't listen to him, don't listen to what he's telling you. Let me in there please, you have to let me in. Don't listen to what he's saying, just let me in—just bloody let me in!"

He reached the door and started to shake it. McGrigor stood the other side with broken bottle in hand, just in case the Preacher was more powerful than he looked. The Preacher grabbed at the door, rattled it, but got little give.

The Preacher went to the window and McGrigor went with him, holding up the jagged weapon. The Preacher shuddered, unwilling to break his hand through just to have that forced into him. He vanished from sight and McGrigor went to the next window and the window afterwards, and each time found the Preacher on the other side pushing his fingers to the glass.

"Let me in!" screamed the Preacher. "Please let me in. You have to let me in, you just have to!"

"You have to let him in!" yelled the Woman, still on the floor. "Please, you have to let him in!"

"How long do you want to live for?" snarled McGrigor. "Do you want it to be a day or do you want it to be an hour? If it's the latter, then I'll unbolt that door right now. Why not? If you want to give yourself up so easily then why don't we do that? But I figure if you marched all this way, then you're not that keen on a quick death. And if that's the case, then shut up and let me do this!"

"Let me in!" said the Preacher, weeping now. "For God's heart, let me in!"

"Let him in," cried the Woman, "Let him in."

"Shut up!" barked McGrigor.

They made it round every window in the cottage, the Preacher's face becoming more anguished as McGrigor's became more determined. They did a second loop, dancing together through the stone wall. It was as if the Preacher thought he'd get to a window McGrigor had forgotten, as if he thought McGrigor would keel over drunk. They went round a third time—McGrigor more animated with the bottle, bored of the game, annoyed that the Preacher wasn't taking the hint.

Evening fell and the Preacher drifted away—he wasn't at any of the windows, he wasn't in sight. McGrigor peered out but couldn't glimpse him. He guessed he was hiding, waiting. McGrigor kept the broken bottle at his side, just hoping his own stock of strength lasted longer than the Preacher's.

He unscrewed the top of a full bottle and took several gulps. The Woman continued to stare at him, fear in every inch of her.

"I'm sorry," he said. "I've just got very used to looking after myself. That isn't about to change now, and you should feel thankful I've saved you too."

The night time gloom came on them fast. McGrigor kept vigil, trying to penetrate the dark—but there was no Preacher, no movement. That insufferable bastard couldn't have changed yet; they'd have heard it. They always screamed, every single one of them screamed.

The Woman brought her knees up in front of her and started to rock backwards and forwards. There were tears on her cheeks, but they didn't look fresh, they looked like they'd been wept months ago and had stained the skin permanently. She didn't look at McGrigor; she just looked at that solid stone floor on which—you'd imagine—it would be impossible for any plant to grow. McGrigor paced in front of her, a full bottle in one hand, the broken one ready in the other.

The first rock shattered the glass just as full darkness came. It burst through the front window and landed beside the Woman's legs. She screamed but seemed unhurt. McGrigor held his weapon up and moved cautiously to the broken frame, he couldn't see anything.

There was another smash, in the kitchen this time, another rock hurled through the glass. McGrigor ran, ready to confront the Preacher if he came through. Again he peered out and there was nothing. There was no movement, no glimpse of man—only a third smash, this time in the bedroom. The Woman screamed as McGrigor raced past her. Again there was nobody trying to crawl through, no smug face of the Preacher.

The other window in the front room exploded—this time a shard of glass flew by and cut the Woman's ankle. She screamed and then stopped, clutching it with a pained expression that showed more stoicism than McGrigor had credited her with. Again there was no Preacher, but McGrigor knew what was next and made it to the kitchen before the rock took out that other window, and to the bedroom before the stone removed the remaining pane. He even jabbed at it with his trusty weapon—but there was no hand reaching through, there was no Preacher.

He stood and listened. There were no windows anymore. There was no sound. He wouldn't have said the Preacher was the kind of man to crawl through broken windows. He certainly wouldn't crawl through to have a bottle forced into his face. It was all down to waiting again, it was all down to who lasted the longest—him or the Preacher. He took another swig of whisky.

He patrolled the inside of the cottage. It was darker inside than out, but McGrigor soon found a path and even knew when to raise his feet to climb over the Woman's legs. She was quiet, maybe listening in the dark, maybe dozing.

He talked the whole time, letting the Preacher know he was awake. He invited him in, told him what would happen if he tried to get in. He called him a bad preacher, a worthless preacher, a lecherous preacher, a lonely preacher, a preacher without a flock.

There were no sounds outside; when he stopped his monologue he couldn't hear a thing. Sometimes he thought the Preacher was near—that he was crouching down just below one of the windows, waiting for his opportunity. He could almost smell the Preacher's sweat, that disgusting mix of salt water and pollen they always produced at the end. He stayed vigilant, stayed awake, stayed ready. His hands trembled, he knew too well what would happen if the Preacher got in, if he was allowed to change within four close walls. He and the Woman would be gone by afternoon, and he intended to live longer than that—even if he was the last man on Earth.

The Preacher was furtive, the Preacher was quick, the Preacher was sneaky. McGrigor looked out at the darkness and wished it was light, wished there was something to see. His legs ached, his chest was filled with fluid—weighing him down, drowning him.

His throat hurt but he continued to speak: "You alright there, Preacher? How you doing, Preacher? I don't recommend coming in, Preacher, I really don't!" He wanted to sit down, he wanted to rest, he wanted to close his eyes for a moment. How could the Preacher have more energy than him? How could he possibly have more stamina? He was sicker, older, wandering around on rough terrain as opposed to the flat floor of the cottage. It wasn't right he could do that. It was wrong he had so much fortitude.

Then it happened. McGrigor was prowling the front room while the Woman shivered in silence. They heard the scream; it came from the direction of the kitchen. Both swallowed with familiar dread. McGrigor slammed the kitchen door, bolting it so nothing in there could get out. The scream burst in at them—dreadful, high pitched and accelerating. It seemed to go beyond the range of a human voice box, as if every muscle, tendon and bone was being forced through a grinder to create this scream.

The Woman scrambled to her knees and clutched McGrigor's legs. The scream got higher—they could hear bones tear through flesh, the limbs of the plant ripping apart the limbs of the man. There was the splat of blood and the slide of flesh and the scream stopped. Somewhere in the dark was another of those plants. The Preacher's eyes staring out, a sad flower.

McGrigor shook the Woman's grasp from him and collapsed to the floor, leaning back against the wall and taking another sanctuary bolt of alcohol.

He should never have left the city, but they were everywhere in the city. You'd find them on street corners, in supermarkets; the doors of second floor apartments were broken down and there it was in front of the TV. People cut them—they used knives, they used machetes, they charged at them with their cars.

But it didn't matter. It was soon clear that if you broke one, something was released that sped up your own illness—so before long you'd replaced it. That was the reason they couldn't research it properly. No matter how many layers of protective clothing the scientists wore as they wielded their scalpels, it always got through, it always took them. Soon there was no one left to research it, and even the thinnest slice of hope was given up. It got into you, got into your bones, twisted their DNA, made you something that wasn't you. As soon as it was strong enough, it discarded the flesh and the heart and the brain and stood on its own in the world. It destroyed what was you and then replaced you.

Edgar Speller was the first—he was a nobody, a farmer, a man who'd never done anything interesting in his life. Two weeks later the President of the United States was on television announcing his plans to save the world; in two more weeks there was no President of the United States. Not long after that a band of survivors came together and made a bid for the higher ground. One of them took on the mantle of authority and told them things would be better up there.

McGrigor was sitting in a doorway when they found him. They'd jumped on him, hugged him, held him as a friend. He hadn't really believed the Preacher, but he had no better idea and nowhere else to go. There'd been seven of them originally, but they'd lost three on the way—one before they even left the city—and now there were only two. Possibly the last man and woman on Earth, Adam and Eve in reverse, soon to leave this planet with nothing but animals and plants.

As dawn came they sat on opposite sides of the front room. McGrigor had let the broken bottle fall, but kept a firm grip on the whisky-laden one. The Woman looked as if she was in a trance, her eyes open but nothing there.

McGrigor stood slowly and took a swig of booze. He glanced at the Woman, and then cautiously opened the kitchen door.

There it was, right outside the broken windows, a green/white twisted version of a human skeleton. He stared at it, examining the skull, trying to make out something of the Preacher, a sign it had once been a man. It was clearly based on man, but distorted. The agonies of death had stretched and bent and elongated the skull, so it was now impossible to place a human face on top of it—even if you knew what that face had looked like.

The only humanity was the eyes, the same eyes that had been there when it wore an overcoat of flesh. Now they shone in pain and agony, in astonishment at what had happened, even though they knew it was coming. They were the Preacher's eyes, but they weren't. No one's eyes really look like that except in the throes of torture. Before long the whites would turn green, and then other similar flowers would grow across the bones—green and blue, green and brown, green and green—the fruit of this unusual plant.

McGrigor bolted the kitchen door and sat opposite the Woman—Linda. They stared at each other across the cold floor.

"Do you want a drink?" he asked.

She shook her head.

"You sure?"

Her shake was more of a tremble this time, but still adamant.

"You should," he said. "It's good for you."

He watched her, her hand still clutching her injured leg, her eyes still weepy. He'd never seen them anything other than tearful. When he first saw her, she already looked like she couldn't walk from sobbing.

"What have you lost?" she asked.

"What have I lost?" he said. "The usual, a few people, a few things—what would basically constitute my life. How about you?"

"My parents," she said.

"Yeah, I lost my parents too. At least I think I did. They live a long way from here and one day they didn't pick up the phone. By that point it was just too far to travel, so I had to assume I'd lost them. In a way that's more comforting, as there's always that small chance they might still be there."

"I lost my brother," she said.

"I think I lost my sister. She lived near my parents. Did you see yours?"

She nodded.

"Sorry."

"I lost all my friends."

"I lost both of mine." He smiled. She didn't acknowledge it.

"Did you lose a partner?" she asked.

"I lost my girlfriend. We were in the process of breaking up. It had all got very unpleasant and then this happened. Kind of put what went before into context. I don't regret what I said to her. A lot of it she deserved. I just wish we'd both had that time to move on. You know, that period where you try to meet someone else and the break up doesn't look so bad anymore. How about you? Did you lose a boyfriend, husband, some dashing fiancé?"

She shook her head.

He took another bolt of whisky.

"We're going to die, aren't we?" she said.

"We were always going to die," he said. "We just weren't going to die like this."

"It's so horrible," she sniffed. "I'm going to die alone."

He laughed. "We're both going to die alone."

"I just feel so ill," she sobbed. "I feel so sick and tired. I feel thirsty."

"Do you want that drink?"

"Yes please."

She raised her hand from her ankle and the wound was red and green. He stared at it.

"Sorry," he said. "It's too late."

He shot across the floor, grabbed her arm and yanked her up. She offered no resistance. He opened the bedroom door and hurled her in. She screamed as she landed, looking at him with hurt and confused eyes. Eyes like flowers. He shut the door and bolted it tight.

She was infected—they were both infected—but she wasn't far off, and he didn't want to sit with her as she turned. She used up her last dregs of strength throwing her weight against the door. She screamed, she begged, she pleaded—and then she stopped, the only sound he heard was soft weeping.

There were the windows, of course. They were all broken, but she'd seen him with the bottle and he didn't reckon she was any more foolhardy than the Preacher. He guessed she'd stay where she was, and he'd stay where he was.

He took another drink. Back in the city he'd noticed how the alcoholics were more resilient to this infection. The drunks in the bars and the winos on the street corners all seemed to be the last to go. There must be something in alcohol that suppressed it, kept it under control. It was only when they ran out of booze that it happened.

He had nine bottles left. Maybe seven days drinking. What was he going to do when he ran out? He knew he'd made a mistake following the Preacher—but despite his cynicism, part of him had believed the Preacher's sermon, had hoped there'd be a new lease of life higher up. He now knew how wrong he was. His future lay back in the city, near a bar, a pub; maybe with some like-minded dipsos who'd also figured it out.

But what was he going to find if he went back? Would he be the only one, would he wander familiar streets alone, staring at green eyes to try and find old friends? Maybe it was better to accept his fate up here, maybe it would be simpler to find the highest point and throw himself off. He didn't know what to do—drink himself alive or drink himself to death. He had nine bottles left. He took another swig and thought he'd decide in a day or two.

Deconstructing Fireflies
by
Kristi Petersen & Nathan Schoonover

Kristi Petersen's short fiction has been featured in The Adirondack Review, Barbaric Yawp, Chick Flicks, Afternoon, *and a host of other publications. She is pursuing her MFA in Creative Writing at Goddard College in Vermont. Nathan Schoonover has been a paranormal investigator for fifteen years. He is the co-host of* The Ghostman & Demon Hunter Show, *a Certified Paranormal Investigator with the New Jersey Ghost Hunters Society, and a Field Reporter for the Ghostly Talk Internet Radio Show. Petersen and Schoonover are currently in search of a publisher for their novel* Linewalkers. *Their contribution to Beacons, "Deconstructing Fireflies," is a classic loss-of-innocence tale is a unique, near-future setting.*

My son likes to take things apart, and perhaps before The Shortage mothers would have written this off as the typical penchant of boys. But mothers before The Shortage did not live on farms populated by Barn Boys who camp out in the old cement milk house, doing dickens with the whiskey. Mothers before The Shortage did not have to listen to the Barn Boys howling at night as they re-wire the chickens and make bets on how fast they can get them to lay eggs before the birds' hard ruby eyes roll back in their heads and their feather-coverings catch fire in a rain of sparks. Mothers before The Shortage did not have to worry about husbands with byrotechnic degrees who teach their sons that harming the animals is okay—not only do we just breed more in the laboratory, but the metal they're made from prevents them from feeling pain.

Despite the influence they've had on little Nate, Jigger, Hap, and Lair are not the worst my husband could've found for Barn Boys. They spend their days doing useful things: oiling the pigs' joints when the mud seeps through their skin; feeding the cows and fine-tuning the chickens' groins so there's enough eggs down the market shelves, which keeps us out of trouble with the Government. They fix the tractors and keep the plumbing running smooth. They till the fields every day without having to be told, and they know which chemicals enhance the growth rate of which plants. All of that's good: there's little time for policing. We're responsible for feeding all of Cleghern. Have been ever since Collier farm over in Newton burned to the ground last year. Collier had such lazy Barn Boys, you see, that the man himself had to waste his afternoons baling hay and shearing the meat off the cow frames.

He could only keep up with his lab production late in the p.m., and one November midnight he passed out from exhaustion and knocked into the AutoWeld. When it tipped over, the whole place went up.

Still, it's at night I really worry about what goes on by the single burning lamp behind the milk house's shoddy window. If I have to ensure my husband stored my Grandmother's oak-frame bed or Spode china out of harm's way, I go down in daylight. I wouldn't want to be around the Boys at dusk, because that's when the booze comes out. You see, gargantuan Jigger, hat-headed Hap and hairy Lair, since they don't have dental insurance or go to the doctor much, attribute their rock-solid teeth and robust health to the unique blend of ingredients brewing in the homemade still.

Despite what I do, little Nate is always down there at that hour. He is fascinated that Jigger doesn't use the message pad to summon the cows: he calls them in to pen by just cupping his hands on either side of his smeary mouth and making a noise through the neat hole above his upper lip—a hole, he claims, put there by his Daddy's stubbing out a cigarette when he was my son's age. At least, that's what he told Nate, who believed it with all his heart and came running to tell me. Nate's very bright, but he's impressionable, and after that he'd asked Jayce, "Could you make a cigarette hole in my upper lip?" Of course, that was out of the question, so the only unsavory habit he's been allowed to pick up from Jigger is taking things apart.

Little Nate is obsessed with the workings of the farm— not how things are done, but how things are un-done. How the milk gets drained from the cow's udder; how the big hay rolls get cubed down into bales; how the thin layers of skin over the cow frames are shorn free and become steaks next to his father's six-egg breakfast in the morning; how Hap dissects a distributor cap. He'll watch the Boys clean their stunners, and then come inside and seize something—my mixer, my blender, or the kerosene lantern, for example—and take it apart. He doesn't hang around to watch anything go back together, which is why I spend my afternoons, when I'm not choring, reassembling. But Sunday morning, he took apart his bedroom lamp and shrieked while I scrambled like a short-circuited cockroach and barely pulled it together before the dark fell. Now that he's torn apart that lamp four mornings in a row, I'll have to curtail his time with the Barn Boys.

Saturday was Sporting Day, and Jigger, Hap and Lair went hunting. Jayce had created a couple of eighteen-point bucks, as I recall, and that's what they were after, but they've got an endless amount of time to hunt since there doesn't need to be a deer season anymore—people like my husband just keep filling the woods. I think, honestly, Jayce spends too much time breeding herds just so he can keep his good Barn Boys around and sharp. That day, though, they didn't get that eighteen-pointer. They brought home a dozen bucks, all between four and twelve points. We're supposed to refurbish the deer frames, heads and all, to use them for next year's herd. So when they carted them all in on the back of the flat-bed truck, singing like they were young men who had just experienced sex for the first time, little Nate ran out to see.

The Boys spread the carcasses out on the lawn and dragged them down to the butchering slab to disassemble them: shear off the skin and meat, tear out their wires, and chop off their heads. I looked out the kitchen window and saw Nate standing there, far enough away so he wouldn't be showered with guts, watching. And it was the way he was watching, unmoving, the early summer breeze twitching small pieces of his blond hair, that made me stop peeling the onions.

The Boys hurled the heads into a pile on the side, and from a distance, it looked like caramel raisin pudding. I shuddered. There was something sad in those eyes—even if they were just diamonds underneath the coal-colored LiquiGel Jayce uses. I wondered what the last image their eyes registered could've been. A field of sunflowers? A white moth? Did it hurt when the bullet ripped through their flesh coverings?

Jayce swears it doesn't, but I know better because he makes them with nerves. They feel something, I'm sure.

Jigger crouched down, pointed to the pile and spread his hands wide, shaking his head, and I wondered if little Nate asked him if he was gonna take the heads apart. I expected the Boys would soak them in solvent; that's what you do to clean the skulls before refurbishment, you just let them soak until the brains, eyes and sinews turn to mush and only the metal frames are left. But they didn't. They piled the heads onto a large tarp and dragged them over to the cold cellar, a stone structure built into the hill next to the house. Hap climbed up and Lair gripped the heads in his stubby-fingered hands as Jigger lit up a corn silk cigarette. They lined up the heads in a row on the roof. They were going to let those heads rot and fester and smell in the sun for three weeks and let nature and the maggots take care of most of it.

Little Nate came bounding inside and dashed up to his room. It overlooks the cold cellar, which meant he was going to see those heads in the morning when he woke up and at night before he went to sleep. At bedtime, I tried to settle down with Jayce, but instead of seeing his wiry gray hairs bend in my breath, I saw those vacant, soulless eyes staring at little Nate, clutching his toy screwdriver as he slept.

I decided I didn't want those things eyeing him, so I crept into his room, carefully avoiding the litter of rusty farm tools and pieces of old cars Hap lets him have, and flicked on the lamp. I squinted my eyes to try to see the deer on top of the cellar, and thankfully, the room's reflection on the glass had curtained them for the moment.

On Sunday, the dawning of God's day, the lamp incident happened. It has happened every morning since.

I figure it'll pass, but it doesn't. Every morning Nate awakens, takes the lamp apart, and forgets about it until before dusk. Then he cries that the lamp must be back together before nightfall: "They'll come in, Mommy! But they'll stay!" While he screams, I scramble to get the lamp reassembled before Jayce returns and starts yelling about how things that cost him good credits are being treated around this house. Usually, I haven't even put the lamp back together entirely correctly: the harp is bent, the shade's akilter, the socket's crooked on the base, and the wires are exposed so it might even spark in the night and set the peeling wallpaper ablaze—then I tuck little Nate into bed, but he can't fall asleep with the light on. However, I suspect if he wakes in the middle of the night to a dark room, he'll start shrieking when he gets a look at those heads. So after he's asleep, I creep back into the room and switch on the lamp.

Supper is late tonight because I thwarted another lamp incident before finishing the venison. I set Jayce's plate down in front of him and rummage in the drawer of the old metal cabinet—one that's outlived its usefulness in the lab—for a knife and fork.

"That was quite a lot of nice venison we got on Saturday," I broach the subject.

"Yeah." Jayce lifts his utensils. "This looks good. New formula's an improvement over last year. Lots of stew, loaf, and pie."

I hate the way he speaks of the meals that include meat. It makes them sound about as appetizing as motor oil.

"I think you should get used to that." Outside, I hear the Barn Boys yowling, and I wonder if they've started their dickens early tonight. "After what the Boys brought in on Saturday, we're going to be eating it into next summer."

He sets down his knife and considers me with a solid gray eye. "What's the matter, babe. You having problems with them killing things again? I can tell them to do any more slicing and dicing down at the slab past the corn field so you don't have to see it."

I hate the way he brings that up all the time, too. While it's true that since the abortion I haven't exactly been keen on watching them slaughter animals, it has nothing to do with the fact that I understand that this is what we do with our lives. We create or slaughter, we donate or eat.

"No, I don't have a problem with that," I say. "What I have a problem with is the heads on the roof of the cold cellar and the stink. Why can't they just soak the damn things in Postmort?" I sit in the rickety chair across from Jayce and pick up my fork. The handle is slowly twisting off it. I reach for the cloth napkin and unfold it across my lap.

"That's not the way Jigger likes to do things, Ilse." He shoves in a mouthful of creamed chipped venison. It'd looked delicious when I'd set it on the table, but the thought of the deer's brains and the white film of maggots in them has repulsed me. "They like to do things natural."

I get up from the table and take my plate to the porcelain sink, which is due up for its monthly bleach and re-bugging. "There is very little that's natural anymore."

He shrugs. "Natural won't work. Cloning the whole animal takes too long." He sips his tea. "These were older models anyway. I'm not even going to refurbish them this time around. I'm coming up with a faster, sleeker design. Just let them have their fun."

"It's sick and unnecessary."

"Ilse, I told Jigger the Boys could keep these as trophies."

The bugs in the sink stretch their elasticized arms and grip pieces of venison from my plate. It's always bothered me that although they're metal, they never seem to lose their appetite; when they hear the clank of the plates against the porcelain, they emerge like feisty snakes and snatch their meals. But that's why Jayce traded for them: they're expedient models that leave no trace, and the fines for wasting food these days are pretty high.

I'm sick of the metal beasts. "And where are they going to put these ghastly things?"

"Probably on top of the milk house," he says.

I shiver. "When people come in the driveway, that's the first thing they're gonna see."

"I know. But they're proud of 'em. These are trophies, honey. And good trophies means they'll stay around longer."

"I don't like little Nate staring at those things. Do they have to be across from his room? Could they set them elsewhere?"

"It's really the best place. The sun shines intense and hot there. There's no shade." He lifts his glass of orange juice; for the first time, I notice he's got a gut. A small one, but it's there. I should cut the sugar out of his diet, but it probably wouldn't do any good since I know he has a few nips of bourbon in the lab. I don't care that he drinks, as long as I keeps the production up and doesn't take the habit out on us.

"Well, Sunday while you were in town doing the goat thing he took apart his lamp and couldn't get it back together. Which was fine, until the sun started to pull down and he was screaming and crying," I say.

Jayce sets down the glass and burps. "His light's been on every night. He's afraid of the dark, that's why he's throwin' a fit."

"No." I turn on the water to rinse off the now picked-clean dish. "I've been putting his light on. If the light's on, he can't see the deer heads. He can only see his own reflection."

"Well, stop doing that. You're probably freaking him out. He's thinking there's ghosts in here, or God knows what." Jayce is gentle; although I imagine in his mind he is muttering, *Foolish woman, your silly ideas,* he won't say it. He just frowns, squeezes a piece of over-done toast in his fingers, slaloms it through the gravy, and pops it in his mouth. A dollop of juice dribbles over the gold band on his fourth finger. "Kid might not cut it as a byrotechnic. Not the way he's going." He takes another mouthful of his venison. A chunk drops from his chin to the plate. "Maybe I should start having him spend time with me in the lab."

That thought doesn't appeal to me, either. So he'll grow up like Jayce, putting things together with no sensitivity? I cast my eyes to the sink. The bugs have retreated to the drain now, but their pointed appendages have left gray scratches in the porcelain that'll have to be buffed away before next inspection. "I never should have let him watch them disassemble those deer."

"I told you, it's a good thing for him to get used to seeing. If he doesn't make byrotechnics, he'll be a great Barn Boy. He'll always have work."

I look out the window. The Boys aren't in the milk house yet: Lair's sitting on a log, brushing his long hair with what looks like a couple of tines of old pitchfork, shortened and re-formed; Hap's knelt down on the old well cover, blocking his hat with a brick; Jigger spits. "That's what I'm afraid of."

He pushes his plate away and stands up, comes over to me, sets his hands on my hips and kisses the back of my neck. He smells like ammonia, burning hair and a faint something else, his characteristic musk that makes me think of the seven ferrets, his first projects, that we kept in the upstairs room before little Nate was born. I feel him sigh against my back. "Do you have plans tomorrow?"

I think. Just the usual chores, maybe some shopping. "Not really."

"Why don't you take him to the zoo for the day?"

The zoo, where Jayce gets the DNA. The zoo is the last bastion of live animals. Well, live totally organic animals. The ones that aren't extinct. Each state has one zoo—there aren't enough natural creatures to fill more than that—well, except for Wyoming. Not as many things died there, I guess.

Jayce toys with a curl of my hair, which has sprouted a few grays. In the mirror, when I see them, they remind me of spring dandelions in the field. "It'll reinforce that the things we slaughter here aren't real beasts, not really, and that'll make him feel better. Maybe it'll even inspire him to come and watch me assemble things."

I don't see how this will make little Nate feel better, because he'll just go and see the deer and then come home and see those empty, haunted, soul-less eyes staring at him in the night. But I concede.

We're naturally up early around here, so I load little Nate, a couple of sandwiches, thirty credits and the Farmers' Card and start the long drive across the state.

The zoo is expansive, as open and wide as the photos I've seen of a place called Africa. We stroll through the aviary. The rocks are spattered with bird waste, and I reach out to touch it. There are still germs, but I don't let that stop me. I haven't seen bird crap since I was a little girl, and looking at it makes my eyes hurt because it is good and real, the kind of good that oatmeal would be after not having tasted it in a dozen years. The Inca terns, their feet bright as poppy petals, move so differently. Warm, squirming, lighter than the ones Jayce makes, and their sounds are notes that make songs, not pre-programmed tunes with clicks at their conclusions.

The bellies of the Siberian Tigers sway when they pad across the grass and plunge into their man-made pond, swatting at fish with their paws. To watch them eat, the twist of their heads in one, smooth motion, makes me long for a cat. Not the cat Jayce made me, pretty and white and puffy and perfect Katrina, but a cat. One that still knows when it's hungry because its stomach tells it, not because the timer in its brain has gone off.

In the reptile house there are Mata Mata turtles, their flattened heads maneuvering like leaves at the bottom of the spring where we draw the water, and little Nate laughs, because, he says, "the leaves have eyes!" He presses his hands flat against the glass.

"Mommy, will their eye coverings come off? Do they have diamonds or cobalts or emeralds or rubies?"

"Those," I say, crouching down, "are real eyes. Like ours. When the animal dies, they will rot clean through and there will be nothing left."

A keeper in khaki goes to the right of the diorama all decked out with fake giant fronds and dirt. He opens the door, and there's a musk-wet-mold smell like carpet in a flooded basement, and that, too, brings me back to that time when there were turtles. Real turtles you could keep in a terrarium. I had a little snapping turtle. Pappy. Pappy the snapping turtle. When The Shortage came, we had to eat him.

I buy little Nate an ice cream at the stand disguised as a giant butterfly. Within a few minutes, vanilla ice cream and strawberry sauce coat his chin. He points to the camouflage-netted dome that rises like a giant egg behind a tangled gateway of branches. *Insect World*, the sign announces. "Can we see the bugs?"

"Haven't you ever seen the real ones on the farm?" The outside insects are the only creatures not manufactured; there are special farmers who just breed live bugs. Plant life has become so important, and there have been few successes in imitating pollination.

There are also not many decent parts to eat on most insects.

He shrugs and bites off the point of the cone, sets it on his mouth, and sucks. The ice cream drains like a lowering lake. "Yeah, but I can't catch up with 'em to touch 'em."

So we wander through the magical door, and there's a floral rush of scents, wild geraniums and blue flag irises, blueberries and black-eyed Susans, Mexican sunflowers and mint. Butterflies are in avid flutter, like small colorful confetti. "Welcome to the Butterfly Garden," says the lady in the turquoise uniform. "Don't pick the flowers and don't touch the butterflies."

Which is, of course, exactly what Nate does. He crouches by a patch of daisies and waits for a harmless Comma or Red Admiral to come by; when one settles on a nearby nettle, it doesn't move when he pinches his fingers together and picks it up. I glance around to be certain no one's looking and then grab his sweaty hand. "We don't want to do that, Punkin. We can't afford the fines. But over here there's a pond. Would you like to see that?"

I know that he wouldn't. He camps by a thistle to wait for a Painted Lady, and after that it's a long afternoon of watching him touch each unfortunate Mourning Cloak, Checkered Skipper, and White Peacock as though he were tinkering with a clock; he pokes their thoraxes and brushes their wings with his pinky.

I sit on a bench to rest as Nate wanders over to look at a glass room where there are pupae hanging from branches, looking like tiny pieces of rice.

It reminds me of the maggots that must have been in those deer heads.

I see him slip on a pair of headphones, and he stands completely still, that same kind of completely still he was the day he'd watched them bring the deer heads home. His pale green shorts have a smear of dirt up the back, and I remind myself to instruct him not to wear his dress clothes when he's out watching the Boys mess with filthy things.

He trudges back to me, his eyes bright with curiosity. "Does the sun carry the spirits like my lamp?"

"Like your lamp?"

"Yeah. The deers come into my lamp at night and light it up, and in the morning, I take it apart to let them all out so Daddy can use them again. Is that what the sun does? Like when I help Daddy? It sucks up the old spirits of the dead things and then puts them back into the butterflies when they're sleeping in the hanging bags?"

I chuckle, not only because it's cute, but because I hear Jayce's voice in my head: Foolish woman! He thinks the souls are turning on the lamp! My actions have created a regular quagmire in his child brain, and it was so obvious! Next to us, a father is hoisting his strawberry-haired tot with flushed cheeks up onto his shoulder, and I hear snatches of soft words, farmers and bugs and real, and I decide I will stop this lamp business, once and for all. "They don't go into your lamp, honey. That's me. Mommy turns on your light for you so you won't be afraid if you wake up."

He blinks at me, pooching his lower lip out and furrowing his brow so that I can see the miniscule lines that will one day become wrinkles, perhaps when I'm no longer around. Then he looks up through the dome netting, maybe at the veins of canvas that plunge his face into serpentine shadow patterns. "The sun doesn't take souls?"

"No. The sun is—it's gas. It's hot gasses that warm the earth and make the plants grow, and it nourishes the butterflies, but it doesn't carry their souls."

Silence again. He reaches up to slip his sticky hand into mine. We walk further down the path, to the display of butterflies that are just beginning to emerge from their pupae. Now they look like long-grain rice, that nutty dark stuff that used to be plentiful in organic stores when I was a child but is now nearly impossible to get.

"Mommy?"

"Yes, dear?"

"So then, where do they go?"

"Where does who go?"

"The souls of the deer. If Daddy doesn't use them and the sun doesn't take them, where do they go? Are they waiting to hurt me?"

There really isn't a concept of Heaven anymore. The churches now teach very basic Reincarnation, perhaps to help people accept the fact that their food is no longer organic and to encourage the byrotecnic farmers to recycle their metals. "You don't have to be afraid of the souls. They go—up into the night sky, where—where all the twinkling lights are. And they're very, very happy. There's no more pain, and no more sadness—"

"Daddy says they don't hurt. The animals."

"Sometimes, honey, they do. Like—like when you have a sunburn. When they twinkle in the night sky, they're twinkling because they don't have to be hurt anymore. They're twinkling with happiness, just like when Daddy winks at you."

He seems to accept this, and I want to be out of the heat. "Come on."

The Firefly Cave is welcome relief from the sun's watery eye and we descend into black lights and cool smells of green earth and moss. He leaps to grab the fireflies, and I just can't stop him. "We need to go." I finally say. "The zoo is closing in an hour."

"No."

"Yes, Nate."

"No."

"We can see these at home. You know the big tree that glows at night? The big evergreen? We can go see them there. Every night for the rest of the summer."

It's too dark for me to see him thrust out his lower lip, but I know he's doing it. Then he slips his hand in mine and leads me to the gift shop, where he plunges his hands into a barrel of colorful projects that he can assemble and take apart, assemble and take apart: insect gliders crafted of metal with moving parts. "Please?" he begs. "I'm not going to take my lamp apart anymore. I understand, now."

I smile, thinking I will have to buy him a new lamp anyway—it's been through the wringer so many times it sits on his bedstand looking bashed up. "Okay." I buy him ten credits' worth of metal spiders, butterflies, bumblebees, fireflies and ants. We sit on the park benches and he's eager for me to open one of the packets and put it together. I tear open the red wax paper and empty a small body, black plastic head the size of a large blueberry, two curvy sprig-like antennae, and a set of wings. Slot A goes into Slot B goes into Slot C—much like the gliders I'd played with when I was a child, except a little more complicated and with batteries—and the butterfly is done. "Look, Punkin," I say, but he has not shown any interest in my putting it together. He takes the butterfly in his sticky hands, pulls wings from body from head from antennae, and thrusts it back in my lap.

"I could show you how to put it together," I say.

He shakes his head. "Can you do another one?"

So packet after packet I open: the indigo of the Red-spotted Purple, the blood red of the ladybug, the chocolate of the brown recluse, the fuzzy blinding yellow of the bumble bee, the putrescent green of the firefly. As I do each he takes it apart, and when he's done deconstructing every insect I've lovingly set up, I pile him in the truck for the long ride back across the state's waving grains and lavender sunsets.

"Mommy, can we put the bugs back together again when we get home?"

I want to answer that I think we've had enough of that for one day, but it's the first time he's shown an interest in actually putting something together on his own—shown an interest in putting something back together rather than taking it apart, and I take this as a sign maybe he's growing out of his phase. At least I know he'll no longer be taking apart his lamp. "We'll see."

"I want you to show me how to put them together."

I smile and pat his pajama bottoms. "You want me to show you how to put them together?"

"Yeah." He peers back out the window, and I wonder if he sees things moving in the woods in the whorling dust; the wolves, maybe. The wolves that Jayce wished they hadn't forced him to make.

Nate falls quiet, and a few bumpy miles down the road, where it begins to turn to dirt and get to our farm, he is asleep.

The night is close and even sleeping without the sheet is like being cloistered in a warm bath; Jayce snores but it isn't the noise that keeps me awake. I roll over and look out the window, past the sheer black curtains that flutter despite the lack of breeze, and there's the faint, green aura from the firefly tree a half-mile from the house. When we'd first bought the farm, back before Jayce had driven himself gray and little Nate was still a star in the sky, the tree had been by itself, standing, watching over us on summer nights; now, it's shrouded behind a decade or so of woods the Boys had planted.

I rise from bed and sneak into Nate's room, click on the lamp, and sidle up to him. "Punkin."

He opens his eyes, closes them, opens them again. "Mommy?"

"Come on. I want to show you something, something special." I set aside his yellow plastic screwdriver. "Put your boots on, and we have to be quiet. We don't want to wake your Daddy."

He nods, folding back the pale green sheet and sitting up, letting his legs dangle over the floor. He studies the boards for a moment, then reaches out and turns off the lamp.

We creep down the hall like Jayce and I do on Yule Day at four a.m. when we're drunk and setting out the last of our sons' gifts: toe by toe, hunch your back, avoid the third board from the wall on the right because it makes a pop-splinter sound. When we get to the bottom of the stairs, I unhitch the thick metal bolt on the door and set a hand on his back to usher him outside.

The lawn is quiet, and the corn rustles and everything is moving, alive, and breathing, and again I wonder why that could be when there's no breeze. The milk house light burns low, meaning the fire's last flames are licking themselves apart and the Boys, I imagine, are passed out, Jigger's fleshy leg propped up on an old milk can.

"There." I point. "See the glow?"

"We're going to the firefly tree!"

"Yes."

"Really?" He tightens his grip on my hand.

"Yes, really. Now stick close to me." I step barefoot onto the pile of sand below the front step of the paint-hungry porch. I wonder if I should have consulted Jayce before doing this: we had decided that the day he was old enough to understand, we would take him to the tree to explain what had happened there. Neither of us had planned on tackling the subject without the other.

"I can't see, Mommy. Turn on the flashlight."

"Just give your eyes a minute to adjust. We don't want to frighten them." I crush blades of grass under my feet, and they prickle like pins. In the barn, the owl Jayce built for me last Valentine's Day hoots his awareness of something moving in the dark that shouldn't be. There is a distant clank of metal on metal, and I imagine Jigger knocking over his foot rest.

The tree looms larger with every step, and then we are at the edge of the woods and I reach up to part the low-hanging branches of a pair of elms that guard the clearing. We step through, and I hear little Nate gasp and he's that topiary-still again. His face is illumined, a small pale-green moon, and he reaches to the tree to touch a branch.

The fireflies shimmy and part and spiral up and away into another section of the tree, and he runs in pursuit. I want to chase him, but am stopped when my toe stubs the bottle.

I bend down to pick it up; the label is still legible: *To Ilse. Tenth Anniversary Dandelion Wine. Jayce.* He'd vinted this himself, working on it for at least a year before the date; I probably hadn't noticed the collection of jugs, tubes, orange peels and lemons in the back corner of the lab because I'd been busy cooking up my own surprises: garlic cheese, pear preserves, ground wheat wafers.

Nate giggles and runs around the tree, tripping and getting caught in the tall weeds that have sprung up over the years; he falls and gets dirty, leaps into the air and swats the fireflies.

"Come here," I call. I set the bottle next to me and sit on the grass. He crawls into my lap and his breaths are quick and loud. "I just want you to look at them all. Don't touch. Just look."

His hair tickles my chin.

"Why are they all here, Mommy?"

"Because this place is—natural. This place, this is where your soul came down from the sky." I can't tell him about that unusually warm first of May. The Boys had been, for once, whooping it up somewhere else on account of the Spring Festival, and we'd come down to the tree, the two of us with our much-too-rich gifts to share. The fireflies hadn't been out yet, but we hadn't needed them, and when we'd finished— the last of the wine drained, the cheese gone, sticky dots of the pear preserves at the corners of our mouths—we'd set the bottle at the base of the tree in hopes it would bring good fortune. I wonder, now, if I were to put the empty bottle to my ear, would I hear the echoes of that night, the little wishes that had scaled the tree boughs to the Heavens. "This," I say, rubbing his cheek, "this is where you were given to us."

"What does that mean?"

"Created. Made."

"Like Daddy does with the deers?"

"No, not like the deer. Daddy and Mommy made you together."

He squints. "Is that where I came from?"

"Yes. Your soul came down, and you went inside me, and I kept you safe and warm."

"Did you see what my soul looked like?"

"No. You can't really see a soul."

He is quiet for a long time and the crickets fill in the hole between us. Then he climbs off my lap and stands up, stuffs his little-man hands into the pockets of his near-threadbare peejays, and heaves a sigh. "Can we come back tomorrow?"

"We'll see, honey. Mommy has lots of chores."

"But Mommy, you said 'every night for the rest of the summer'."

"We'll see."

I climb to my feet and take his hand to lead him back through the thicket and across the lawn to the house. He rushes a few steps ahead of me, his head down, and for the first time I look at him and realize that he may very well, indeed, grow up to be just like Jayce.

August is ebbing when the Boys finally take those ghastly heads from the roof of the cold cellar; the days have pleasantly trundled by in a tumble of little Nate's deconstructing and assembling the animatronic bugs in his room. He doesn't follow Jigger out to call the cows in; he doesn't watch Hap dissecting car parts; he hasn't taken apart the new lamp I had Lair make for him. I'm overjoyed about all of these changes— I'm even happy to provide him with scissors and all the empty mason jars he wants "to keep the parts in", he says. However, he has been tired— the kind of tired where trying to rouse him from bed in the morning for breakfast or chores is a thirty-five minute affair. When I mention my concern to Jayce, of course he just answers "Probably a growth spurt or something. He's eating, right?" in between his gulps of orange juice.

Sporting Day again, and the Boys have killed off the last of Jayce's herd. They roar in on the truck and scream about eighteen-pointers and how these are gonna be beauties, and I resign to turn away from the scene and go right back to that apple pie I've been working on. I pick up the corer and set to work, thrusting the round instrument and listening to the blades cut through the flesh of each green fruit with a corporeal, wholesome *ffft*.

Nate comes down and runs to the decrepit window. He presses his fingers on the sill, resting his chin on the wrinkles of his joints. I hear the Boys whooping and the clang clang of metal legs and arms clattering against each other as they're all chucked onto the tarp.

"Would you like some apple?" I take three slices and put them in a bowl.

He turns from the window and walks to me and I see that his pale yellow shirt has some black smears on it. "Mommy, can you put my bugs back together?"

"You know how to put them back together." I pluck the seeds from the core and drop them into an aluminum pouch to save for the Boys to plant. "You've been doing just fine the last few weeks. Eat your apple." I motion to the bowl. "There's even some cinnamon on there."

"No," he says, his blue eyes hot with defiance. He frowns and folds his arms in front of his chest.

"Don't tell me no." I finish peeling another apple; the peel falls into a spiral. "I'm sure you can do it. Why don't you get your tweezers and your jars and show me?" I wipe my floured hands on my jeans and turn on the sink, and I hear him tromping into his room, the boards beneath his feet whining like the shutters in a strong wind, that sound that I sometimes hear at night when I know no one's awake and the shadows of the leaves on the trees splatter the walls in camouflage. Then there's silence.

I turn off the water.

A clunk, like a bag of beer bottles, and a *swoosh*. Silence. *Swoosh*. Silence. *Swoosh*.

I dry my hands on a towel and step to the base of the narrow, crooked stairs.

There is a sudden rush of hot air through the open window, and I hear Lair's laughter and Jigger's command to cut that shit out let's go down the milk house. Then I see little Nate at the top of the stairs, hauling with all his might a paper bag from a long-defunct department store. The bag slams against every step, foreshadowing disaster, and I think maybe I have been wrong, maybe he's been out in the milk house and the Boys have convinced him to drink! Maybe that's why he's been so tired!

"See?" He gets to the bottom step, and the bag tips over and a few of my mason jars spill out, rolling like marbles across the warped floorboards.

I pick one up and peer inside. There's one of his father's razor blades and a pair of tweezers, and a pile of something that's like the wood dust at the bottoms of fireplaces in summers: black bodies shredded like mouse feces, wings splintered into fine gray powder, miniscule antennae crushed and cock-eyed. Fireflies. He's been going to the tree and getting real fireflies.

"I took the bugs apart like Daddy. I took them all apart and now they don't work anymore!" He pooches his lip out, like he's going to cry. "Where did they go?"

"Where did who go?"

"The souls! I couldn't find the souls! If you put the bugs back together they'll come back, right?"

I don't know what to say.

I look out the window and a river of light flows from the milk house down the drive. I hear Jigger and Hap and Lair, howling with laughter, louder than they've been in awhile. I'm not sure what it is when I first hear the bang and the glass in the window shatters like so much rock candy. Then I see the gold sparks and the feathers, and I know the inside walls of the structure are tarred in downy flesh from the Boys overheating another chicken.

Editor's Note

For those unfamiliar with the inner workings of this project, the Beacons anthologies utilize a novel approach to selecting and preparing stories. Works are selected from two sources: direct submissions to Tyrannosaurus Press and its associated ezine, *The Illuminata*; or entries in the Illuminations Speculative Fiction Writing Contest, which precedes each anthology. Contest entries are scored by a panel of judges on a variety of factors, including style, readability, and originality. All stories scoring 70% or more of possible points are offered a chance at inclusion; any stories scoring over 90% of possible points are guaranteed inclusion.

After the initial story selection is complete, the same panel of judges reviews each story, offering suggestions and identifying flaws. These items are compiled by the editor and submitted to the authors for consideration. The workshopping process is not just intended to improve the individual story, but to help each author develop his overall writing style. Discussion between author and editor is encouraged, and the process is complete only when both parties are satisfied with the work or both agree to disagree and part company.

In my role as editor, it is this workshopping process that is the most rewarding aspect of the Beacons anthologies. By helping other authors identify issues in style, continuity and plot, I am constantly forced to reexamine my own writing style and motivations. I believe that my writing has improved as a result, and I can only hope the contributors to this anthology found it to be as rewarding an experience.

It was an honor and a pleasure to work with each contributor in this anthology. You have my thanks for your patience, and my congratulations for a job well done.

Bret Funk

Printed in the United States
120731LV00003B/7-18/P